# STARRY SKIES OVER THE CHOCOLATE POT CAFÉ

A FEW MINUTES OF COURAGE MIGHT CHANGE
YOUR LIFE

JESSICA REDLAND

Boldwood

First published in Great Britain in 2020 by Boldwood Books Ltd.

Copyright © Jessica Redland, 2020

Cover Design by Debbie Clement Design

Cover Photography: Shutterstock

Every effort has been made to obtain the necessary permissions with reference to copyright material, both illustrative and quoted. We apologise for any omissions in this respect and will be pleased to make the appropriate acknowledgements in any future edition.

A CIP catalogue record for this book is available from the British Library.

Paperback ISBN 978-1-83889-138-1

Large Print ISBN 978-1-83889-788-8

Ebook ISBN 978-1-83889-140-4

Kindle ISBN 978-1-83889-139-8

Audio CD ISBN 978-1-83889-236-4

MP3 CD ISBN 978-1-83889-785-7

Digital audio download ISBN 978-1-83889-137-4

Boldwood Books Ltd
23 Bowerdean Street
London SW6 3TN
www.boldwoodbooks.com

*To Liz*
*Pen pal, beta reader, fabulous friend xx*

*To see a person – to really see them – is to notice all of their magic.*

*To love a person – to really love them – is to remind them of their magic when they've forgotten it's there.*

# 1

A rattling of metal stirred me from my sleep. Rolling onto my back, I lay still for a minute or two, steadily transitioning from the world of dreams into the world of reality.

The rattling started again and I smiled. 'I can hear you, Hercules. I'm on my way.'

My two-year-old Flemish Giant house rabbit was more effective than any alarm clock I'd ever owned. At 6 a.m. every morning, without fail, he nudged the door of the huge dog crate where he slept at night and kept rattling it until I got up and let him out.

Peeling back the duvet, I paused for a moment and my stomach sank as I registered what day it was: Christmas Eve. Great. Sighing, I pulled on my slippers and a fleecy top, then made my way to the crate.

Hercules wiggled his scut as soon as he spotted me, just like a dog wagging its tail. I swear he identified as dog rather than rabbit. The moment I opened the door, he bounded out of his crate for cuddles, then followed me into the bathroom, eager for more attention. It wouldn't surprise me if, one morning, he rolled onto his back so I could tickle his belly.

After I'd put some fresh food and water out for him, I took a shower, the powerful flow helping to ease the tension in my shoulders. It was nearly over. There was just today to get through, then tomorrow, then Christmas was done for another year. Of course, I wasn't out of the woods at that point. There was still New Year's Eve to face – the worst day of all – but one step at a time. One *difficult* step at a time.

Christmas Eve used to be my favourite day of the year. Even as a child, I preferred it to Christmas Day. My dad pulled out all the stops to make Christmas Eve exciting and magical. In the morning, our house would be filled with the tantalising aroma of gingerbread as the pair of us mixed the dough then rolled out the shapes needed for our construction project. When the gingerbread was ready, we'd build and ice a house and Mum would help me decorate it with sweets. Sometimes she only had the energy to manage a few minutes up at the table but even the smallest amount of time meant the world to me.

Dad and I would spend the rest of the day making Christmas crafts while seasonal music played. When dusk fell, we'd wrap up warmly and wander up and down the local streets, looking for the best-decorated house. I'd take a notepad and felt-tip pen with me and we'd award scores out of ten for how pretty they were. The winner was treated to a home-made congratulations card and a bar of chocolate through their letterbox 'from Santa's Elves for the prettiest house ever'.

As bedtime approached, Dad and I would go outside and bang a wooden 'Santa stop here' sign into the middle of the front lawn – or into the flowerbed if there'd been a heavy frost – while Mum made hot chocolate with marshmallows.

We'd each open a Christmas box containing a book, new PJs, a pair of slippers and, in my box, a teddy bear. Wearing our new gifts, we'd finally watch a family Christmas film – just the three of us plus my new teddy – snuggled on the sofa together. Perfect.

'So, my little Pollyanna,' Dad would say as we prepared drinks and snacks for Santa and the reindeer after the film, 'do you think Father Christmas will remember to visit this year?'

I always giggled when he called me Pollyanna, after the main character in the children's book of the same name. 'My name's not Pollyanna. It's Tamara.'

'But you're just like Pollyanna, aren't you? A little ray of sunshine and positivity in our lives.'

Then he'd hug me tightly and tell me how much he and Mum loved me and how lucky they were to have me, especially when 'the black cloak' wrapped itself round Mum and she struggled to see the sunshine through the darkness.

'Promise me you'll always be like Pollyanna,' he'd say.

'I promise.'

And it wasn't hard back then, despite Mum's situation. An eternal optimist, just like Pollyanna, I could find the good in anyone and any situation, no matter how dire. I believed in the Tooth Fairy and Father Christmas. I believed that friends and family were people who loved you unconditionally and would never hurt you. I believed that people were good and told the truth.

As the years passed and my life changed beyond all recognition, I still tried to be Pollyanna every day. I tried so hard to keep my promise to Dad. I believed that 'the black cloak' would lift from Mum like it had done on The Best Day Ever. I believed that I'd leave foster care one day and be reunited with Mum again. And I believed that all my foster families genuinely cared about me and had my best interests at heart, especially my foster sister Leanne.

But it turns out that not all people are good, they don't tell the truth, and they don't care who they hurt or how they do it.

I stared at the array of bright-coloured polo shirts – my work uniform – hanging in my wardrobe like a rainbow.

'I suppose I should show willing and go for the festive red today, shouldn't I?' I said to Hercules. 'One nose twitch for no, two for yes.'

Bending down, I gave his soft ears a stroke, then pulled on my jeans and red polo shirt before making my way down two flights of stairs and through the internal door at the back of The Chocolate Pot, a café I'd set up in the summer, thirteen years ago when I was twenty-two.

Switching on the lights, I paused and smiled as I looked round. My café. My home. Every time I stepped through the door, I couldn't help feeling a swell of pride at what I'd achieved.

An eclectic mix of mismatched wooden tables of varying sizes were flanked by wooden chairs, padded benches or high-backed leather armchairs. The combination of wood, colour and lighting created a warm and inviting ambience. The soft cream walls were a sea of colour courtesy of a large collection of vintage metal signs. Some signs advertised cakes, coffee and milkshakes, and others represented the seaside: boats, beach huts and, my personal favourite, a red-and-white striped lighthouse just like the one down in Whitsborough Bay harbour. Just like the ones Mum used to paint.

As I passed each pillar on my way towards the serving counter and the kitchen, I flicked on the red and white fairy lights wrapped round them. It was nowhere near opening time but there was no harm in making the place look pretty already. Despite dreading Christmas Eve and Christmas Day, I still loved the lights and decorations, and thrived on the buzz of excitement that surrounded Christmas. Plus, of course, it was a hugely profitable time of year with fraught shoppers keen for sustenance. The tips were generous too and my team worked hard so they definitely deserved them.

I switched on the multi-coloured lights draped round the slim-line tree in the corner between the counter and the window and paused to turn a couple of the decorations which were facing the wrong way. I'd gone for a nautical theme this year with sailing boats made from driftwood with material sails, glittery seashells and starfish, clear glass baubles filled with sand and shells, and brightly coloured fabric and felt beach huts. Every year, we received compliments galore about the unique Christmas decorations in The Chocolate Pot. I'd casually thank the customers and tell them that everything was made in North Yorkshire and available from 'The Cobbly Crafter' on Etsy. It was the truth. After all, they *were* available from Etsy if anyone wanted to buy them – I just failed to mention that 'The Cobbly Crafter' was me. There was no need for anyone – staff or customers – to know that crafting was a huge passion of mine. There was no need for anyone to know *anything* about me outside of work. I let them see what I wanted them to see: a successful entrepreneur, an excellent chef, and a fair boss who stood for no nonsense. When you let people in – fully in – they have a habit of letting you down, so it's easier to keep them at arm's length. That way, they won't break your heart. I'd learned that lesson the hard way.

Behind the counter, I switched the coffee machine on, then headed into the kitchen to start baking. As a child, Dad had ignited a spark of passion in me for baking that had never burned out, no matter what life had thrown at me. Although the gingerbread house had been his Christmas Eve speciality, his skills in the kitchen hadn't ended there. His grandparents had owned a bakery and he'd loved spending his weekends helping out. I tried not to think about how different things could have been if they hadn't retired and sold the bakery while he was still at school, sending him down a completely different career path; one that took him away from me.

Dad and I baked something together most weekends and he always turned it into an adventure, talking in hushed tones about 'secret recipes' and 'magical ingredients'. I relished the ninety minutes or so of peace and solitude each morning when I had the kitchen all to myself and often imagined Dad by my side, a finger pressed to his lips as he glanced furtively towards the door before adding something 'special' into the mixture.

With a name like The Chocolate Pot, it probably isn't a surprise that our speciality is anything chocolate-related. As well as a good range of teas and coffees, we serve a variety of hot chocolates, changing flavours with the season and trends. There's always a speciality chocolate cake of the day, a flavoured chocolate brownie, a regular brownie, and various other baked goods, all freshly made on the premises. Vegan? Gluten-free? We have something to suit everyone.

Monday to Saturday, the café opened at half eight to catch the pre-work takeaway trade. On a Sunday, like today, we opened at ten.

I didn't normally work on Sundays other than to bake first thing but, with Christmas Eve being one of our busiest days of the year, there was no way I was going to stay upstairs when my team would be rushed off their feet.

Maria, my assistant manager, arrived at about 9.20 a.m., just as I was taking the brownies out the oven.

'Morning, Tara! Do I smell cinnamon?' she asked, sniffing the air as she stepped into the kitchen. 'Or is it gingerbread?'

'Both. Cinnamon and gingerbread brownies.' I placed the tray-bake down on top of the oven. 'I made some gingerbread reindeers and snowmen last night which I've iced this morning, and there's a sticky ginger cake baking.'

'I'm salivating,' Maria said. 'I'll dump my stuff upstairs, then give you a hand.'

The first floor acted as an overspill café on busy days and had the potential to be used as a function room. There were additional toilets upstairs and a small staffroom.

Listening to Maria running up the stairs moments later, I took a deep breath. It was hard to believe that this was going to be my twenty-seventh Christmas without my parents, and my fourteenth completely on my own. Where did the years go?

The buzzer on the oven signalled that the sticky ginger cake was ready, providing a welcome refocus away from reminiscing. I'd be fine. The day was going to whizz by, especially if the nonstop craziness of yesterday was anything to go by. After that, I could retreat to the flat where Hercules and I would pretend it was just a regular weekend.

\* \* \*

Maria's best friend, Callie, appeared around mid-afternoon with a buggy, a toddler, and Maria's five-year-old daughter, Sofia, who immediately leapt into my arms for a hug.

'Hi, Tara,' Callie said, looking frazzled as she blew her fringe out of her eyes. 'Any chance of a table?'

'You're in luck,' I said, smiling as Sofia pressed her soft, cold cheek against mine. 'It's barely stopped all day but that table opposite has just come free. Would you like that one, Sofia?'

'Can I have the pink chair?'

'You certainly can. Let me put you down so I can clear the plates.'

Sofia immediately clambered onto her chosen chair. As I cleared and wiped the table, I watched Callie with admiration as she simultaneously parked the buggy containing her sleeping baby son, Tyler, and removed a coat from her two-year-old Esme.

'Are you excited about Santa coming tonight?' I asked Sofia.

She nodded. 'And it's my birthday on Friday. I'll be six.'

'I know. That's two lots of presents to open. What have you asked Santa for?'

Sofia looked up at me, eyes wide, face solemn. 'For Mummy and Marc to get married so George can be my brother. And George has asked for the same so Santa will make it happen, won't he? I want a proper family.'

'I'm sure he'll do his best,' I said, swallowing hard on the lump in my throat. A family? As a youngster, how many times had I been asked what I wanted for Christmas and been unable to give an honest answer? I'd politely asked for some art or craft supplies when all I really wanted was the one thing Santa could never bring me – my parents.

A queue for tables had formed again and I reassured the customers that there wouldn't be a long wait. Nobody seemed to mind and it filled me with joy to hear them saying the amazing food and great service was definitely worth it.

All day, The Chocolate Pot was filled with excited chatter and laughter – exactly how I loved it. Judging by the piles of bags everyone seemed to be carrying, it looked like they'd all left their Christmas shopping until last minute.

I gazed wistfully at a group of women exchanging gifts. I hadn't purchased a Christmas present for anyone or received a gift in return for well over a decade. In fact, I hadn't received a gift of any kind in all that time. I insisted the team didn't buy me anything for Christmas and nobody in Whitsborough Bay knew when my birthday was because, like Christmas and New Year, it was no cause for celebration. After what happened on the weekend of my twenty-second birthday, the day meant nothing to me. Just like the people who'd ruined it.

When Sofia appeared at the counter to pick which gingerbread snowman she wanted, my thoughts turned to her Christmas wish for a family. How long had Maria and Marc been seeing each other? It had to be at least two years. Maria had been damaged by a very toxic relationship with Sofia's father, Tony, and Marc's wife had left him for another man when George was a baby so neither of them had been looking for love. Sofia and George had other ideas. Best buddies at the same nursery school, they kept nagging for play-dates. Eventually Maria caved and arranged to meet Marc and George at The Chocolate Pot one Saturday. I recalled looking across at the four of them chatting and laughing and marvelling at how Maria and Marc had only just met yet they already looked like the perfect family. I therefore wasn't surprised when the playdates turned into proper dates. I also remembered thinking how lucky Maria was. Tony had treated her so badly yet she'd managed to push the hurt aside and move on; something I'd never been able to do.

'I hope Santa brings you and George everything you've asked

for,' I said to Sofia, placing her snowman on a pink plate and handing it to her. 'I'll wish for it too, should I?'

'Ooh, yes please,' she gushed, giving me the biggest smile ever.

I watched her returning to the table with her snowman in one hand and the plate in the other. Yes, I'd wish for a happy ever after for Maria and Marc. And try not to think about how I would never have mine.

## 3

Hercules didn't need to rattle the bars on his crate on Christmas Day morning because I was already awake and had been for the past two hours. It was the same every Christmas Day. I always seemed to open my eyes at about four and, that was it – wide awake.

Christmas Day was the one day of the year when I tried not to think. About anything. Hercules and I liked to sit on the sofa and watch back-to-back episodes of *Friends*. Well, I say Hercules liked it and I often imagined that his favourite 'friend' was Chandler, but I really had no idea whether he was entertained by *Friends* or not. What I did know was that he enjoyed snuggles on the sofa in front of the log burner.

My *Friends* binge-watch was one of only two Christmas traditions I had. I'd done it with Hercules's predecessor, Titch, and her predecessor, Dinks. We even had a special way of selecting which season to watch. I'd take one suit from a pack of cards and spread the ace through to the ten in a circle, then place the bunny in the middle. Whichever card they touched first would dictate our viewing and we'd see how far we could get before bedtime, sometimes dipping into the next season. Some families played board games or charades on Christmas Day. This was my game with my family.

At 5 a.m., the central heating clicked on and I listened as the pipes in the old building filled, gurgling intermittently. I lay there gazing round my flat, thinking for the thousandth time how much I loved it. Not all the shops and cafés on Castle Street have flats above them and those that have are often rented out. Some of the traders hate the idea of living above their business, believing you could never escape from work if you live there too. When my business *is* my life, why would I want to escape?

Castle Street itself is a cobbled street off the main shopping precinct in the North Yorkshire seaside town of Whitsborough Bay and contains a good mix of independent shops and businesses. When I moved in, the building was already used as a café and I knew exactly how I wanted to refurbish it but I'd struggled to see a vision for the flat. I remember panic welling inside me a few days after completing on the purchase, wondering if I'd just made the second biggest mistake of my life. What had I been thinking of, taking on a rabbit warren of tiny storage rooms, a dilapidated bathroom with no running water, and a damp problem from a hole in the roof which the previous owner had obviously got a builder mate to temporarily 'fix' so I wouldn't notice it until it was too late? There was something about it, though, that made me believe it could be incredible.

Fortunately, I found a builder with vision. After the café opened for business, Owen stood on the cobbles and spent ages staring up at the top floor then went round the back and did the same, before going inside and bashing intermittently into the plasterboard ceiling and walls with a hammer, shining a torch through the holes. A week later, he came back with some drawings and I couldn't quite believe it was the same building I was looking at. It turned out the plasterboard hid ceiling beams and thick wooden pillars.

'I'm not sure how you feel about open-plan,' Owen said, 'but this space is fantastic. It's double-height so I'm thinking loft-style living with a mezzanine floor at the back and a roof terrace above your first floor. It's not going to be cheap but, if you're planning to make this your long-term home, it'll be worth it.'

And it had been. It took about a year to get the building works finished while I rented a flat above a shop on the other side of the street. A few years ago, I found the missing piece to truly make it my haven – hygge. I'd actually never come across hygge (pronounced hoo-ga) until I overheard a couple of women talking about it before my Pilates class. As soon as I got home, I went online and knew that I'd found my style. A Danish concept for creating a feeling of cosiness, comfort and well-being through simple things, hygge is about candles, blankets, oversized sweaters, hot chocolate in front of a roaring fire, a cup of tea and a good book. The only part I hadn't embraced was 'togetherness'. Although, if one woman and a giant rabbit could constitute togetherness, then perhaps I'd actually embraced the concept fully.

I turned over in bed, looked towards Hercules's crate, and sighed. 'Happy Christmas,' I muttered, peeling back the duvet.

After feeding us both, then showering, I changed into fresh snuggly clothes – very hygge.

'Which *Friends* season are we going for today?' I asked Hercules, placing him on the floor with the shuffled playing cards in a circle round him. He moved towards the eight of clubs then changed his mind and headed in the other direction.

'Season one?' I asked when Hercules hopped onto the ace. 'We're going back to the start, are we?'

And that was our Christmas Day. Just me, my rabbit, season one of *Friends*, a spot of crafting and the occasional break to eat some leftovers from the café.

As bedtime approached, it was time for my second Christmas

tradition. I made my way to the large dresser in the dining area, paused, then reached for the handle on the middle drawer and slowly pulled it open. Lifting out a bright yellow photo album, I placed it on the dining table, then took out a snow globe and gently shook it. Miniature white flakes swirled and danced before settling at the hooves of a pair of carousel horses.

As long as I live, I'll never forget that amazing day in Herne Bay on the south coast. I was only seven at the time yet I clearly remember riding on one of the cream and gold horses on the carousel on the pier. I'd chosen a horse called Emma because of her violet and pink saddle – my favourite colours at the time. Dad sat behind me, holding me tightly round the waist, while Mum sat beside us on a horse with a bright red saddle and bridle which matched her coat. I was laughing, Dad was laughing and, best of all, Mum was too. And not pretend laughter, trying to assure me everything was fine. This was proper, genuine belly laughing. Her long, reddish-brown curly hair flew behind her and her red coat billowed as the horses gained momentum, galloping and leaping over imaginary fields and hedges. Still giggling, we ate ice-creams on the pier, then chased each other along the sand and shingle beach.

If I could go back to one day in my past and relive it over and over again, that would be the day. Because, for whatever reason, Mum was free that day. The black cloak that smothered her was at home in a locked box and I got to see my beautiful mum live her life and love her life. We christened it The Best Day Ever and bought the snow globe to forever capture the memories.

Afterwards, Mum would often shake the snow globe, a smile playing on her lips, no doubt remembering how elated she'd felt. Then she'd sigh and put it down again, her shoulders slumping. I always imagined her echoing my thoughts: Why couldn't all days be like The Best Day Ever?

In my flat, I shook the snow globe again before setting it back down on the table, then suddenly shivered. I padded into the lounge area and added another log to the burner, watching the flames licking the edges of it. As I made my way back towards the dining table, I became aware of the changing light in the flat. I turned to face the giant arched window and gasped. Fat white flakes of snow were tumbling towards the cobbles. Dashing to the dining table, I picked up the snow globe, then returned to the window where I shook it again. Holding my arm outstretched, I was mesmerised by the miniature flakes tumbling against the backdrop of larger ones. Magical. Completely magical.

Hercules nudging against my legs drew me out of my trance. I carefully placed the snow globe on the dresser then picked him up for a hug. 'Fancy looking at some photos with me?' I asked.

Sitting down, I placed Hercules on the table next to the album and stroked his back and ears.

'This is me as a baby,' I said, opening the first page. 'And this is my mum. Wasn't she beautiful? And my dad. Handsome, wasn't he? Do you think I look like them? I've got Mum's hair. Mum used to say I have Dad's hazel eyes, but I can't tell from these photos.' I turned the pages gently, giving Hercules a running commentary. But each image was a little more blurred than the last, and my voice a little wobblier with each explanation, until I couldn't speak anymore. Hot tears rolled down my cheeks and splashed onto the plastic film. Reaching the end of my childhood photos, I closed the album. 'Happy Christmas, Mum and Dad,' I whispered. 'I miss you.'

Putting Hercules to bed for the night, I brushed my teeth, put a fresh pair of PJs on, then curled up under my duvet with Waffles, the bear who'd arrived in the last ever Christmas Eve box. The one before my family fell apart.

# 4

The door to The Chocolate Pot opened just before our 5 p.m. closing time the day after Boxing Day. I got ready to make my polite but firm 'takeaways only' speech, but it was only Carly, the owner of the shop next door – Carly's Cupcakes.

'Is it a bad time?' she asked, coming over to the counter.

'Terrible,' I deadpanned. 'Absolutely rushed off our feet.' The café was completely empty and had been for the last twenty minutes or so.

She laughed. 'It's been dead next door for about half an hour so I've rebelled and closed a whole five minutes early.'

'Living life on the edge,' I joked.

'I need to get cleaned up next door but are you free for a cuppa when we're both organised?' she asked.

I nodded. 'Half five?'

'Perfect.'

'And let me guess... salted caramel hot chocolate?'

'Gosh, yes please. Heaven in a mug. See you shortly.'

I walked her to the door, locked it, turned the closed sign round, then made my way to the till to run off the sales report and cash up.

With everything cleaned by quarter past, I let Cody and Lana, two of my student part-timers, go early, then quickly ran upstairs to check on Hercules. Unless the café was heaving, I usually took a short break around mid-morning and another one mid-afternoon to give him some attention, so he was never more than a few hours without company. None of my team knew about him.

Returning downstairs, I set to work making the hot chocolates. I'd only just placed the finished drinks on the counter when Carly knocked on the door. She thrust a bouquet of flowers at me when I opened it.

'What are these for?' It had started raining again so I quickly ushered her inside. The Christmas Day snowfall had been short-lived with overnight rain removing all evidence of a white Christmas and there'd been showers on and off ever since.

Carly smiled. 'For helping me find the courage to tell Liam how I felt about him.'

'All I did was give you a little nudge.' Shortly before Christmas, Carly had finally told her lifelong best friend, Liam, that she'd been in love with him for years. Thankfully, the feeling had been mutual.

'And it was exactly what I needed so thank you.' She smiled gently. 'And the flowers are because I know that Christmas is tough for you.'

I shook my head vigorously. 'Christmas isn't tough. Why would you think that?'

She looked at me with sympathy. 'I won't push. But if you ever want to talk about it...'

For a moment, I felt quite choked up. Nobody had ever invited me to talk about it before. Nobody had bought me flowers either. Ever. Well, other than Garth, but the less said about that, the better.

'I love daisies,' I eventually managed. 'Thank you.'

'It's a pleasure. Sarah said they were your favourites. Are you okay? Have I upset you?'

Was I about to cry? Good grief. I turned away from Carly. 'Of course not. I'll pop these in some water. Your drink's in the purple mug.'

Filling the sink behind the counter with water, I took a few deep breaths. It was ridiculous that a small demonstration of kindness like that could reduce me to tears but her offer to talk showed that Carly genuinely cared and it was such a long time since anyone had shown that. As for the flowers, they were the perfect choice. I regularly treated myself to a bunch – usually daisies – from Sarah, who ran Seaside Blooms at the other end of Castle Street. Daisies had been Mum's favourite and she'd often included them in her lighthouse paintings.

I lifted my special sunshine-yellow mug off the counter and led Carly to a pair of high-backed armchairs towards the back of the café where no passing customers could see us.

'So how was your first Christmas as a couple?' I asked.

Her eyes shone. 'It was amazing. Best Christmas ever.' She told me what she'd done and talked about some of the gifts she'd received. Then her smile slipped as she asked in a gentle tone, 'How was yours?'

'Good, thanks. Really busy.' Over the years, I'd learned to be very vague about my plans – or lack of them – but always made out I had lots on.

Carly sipped on her drink, looking at me thoughtfully.

'What?' I self-consciously wiped my mouth. 'Have I got a chocolate moustache?'

She shook her head. 'No. I know I said I wouldn't push but I can't help thinking about you and being on your own over Christmas and—'

I frowned at her. 'Who said I was alone?'

'I came to that conclusion myself. You never mention your family and I know you don't have a boyfriend.'

I picked up my spoon and stirred my drink as butterflies took flight in my stomach. If I was willing to open up about my past, Carly would be the person to whom I'd open up. But was I ready to do that? And which part would I share? It was such an emotional, humiliating mess.

'I'm sorry,' she said. 'I've just done exactly what I promised I wouldn't do. Do you want me to go?'

I shook my head. 'I *do* want to tell you. I think. It's just that...'

It was just that I'd built an impenetrable stone tower round me and I'd lived safely behind it for thirteen and a half years. If I let Carly take down some of those stones, the whole structure might collapse and I'd be vulnerable, exposed and open to being hurt again. But this was Carly and she'd proved herself a good friend over the past four years or so, never pushing for information about my past, never interfering. She was only asking now because I'd recently told her I'd been married. I'd never let anything slip out about my past before. Maybe I'd subconsciously revealed that little snippet because I wanted to talk about what happened.

'Okay,' I said, taking a deep breath to quell the rising panic. 'I'm not ready to talk about Garth yet, but I will tell you about my family.'

'Are you sure?'

'I'm sure. It's not pretty, though.'

Carly nodded. *Poor woman has no idea. Oh well, here goes...* I took another deep breath and stared into my hot chocolate, unable to look Carly in the eye. 'Once upon a time, there was a little girl called Tamara Chadwick...'

# 5

I remembered my early childhood in London as being very happy, despite the challenges my mum faced. She'd often say, 'Sorry, princess, but Mummy's wearing her black cloak today.' On those days, she'd cry a lot and sleep a lot, but my dad was an exceptional man who devoted his weekends to me. We baked together, cooked dinner, kicked a ball round the garden, and climbed trees or played hide and seek in the park. I loved it when he read me stories because he gave all the characters accents. Dad had such a zest for life that he could always make Mum smile, even on her darkest days, albeit briefly.

Whenever I asked Dad what I could do to make Mum happier, he hugged me tightly and insisted that I made her happy every day by being me – their little Pollyanna. *Pollyanna* was one of our favourite books. It told the story of an orphan who had to live with her miserable aunt, Miss Polly, and I loved the grumpy voice Dad used for her. Pollyanna radiated positivity and wouldn't let anything get her down, frequently playing 'the glad game', which her dad had taught her. The game involved finding something to be glad about in any situation, no matter how bad it initially seemed. Mum seemed to like me playing 'the glad game' on her dark days – I was glad she was staying indoors during the winter because it meant she wouldn't catch a cold, or I was glad that she'd had a nap instead of playing with me because that meant she would be awake enough later to watch a film with Dad and me.

But one summer's day, when I was eight, the darkest day ever arrived and there was absolutely nothing to be glad about.

It was the school holidays and Mum brought a blanket downstairs and said she'd nap on the sofa while I played with my dolls. Dad kissed us both goodbye and went to work as usual, telling me that we'd bake an apple pie when he got home. We never baked that pie.

As the afternoon stretched into evening, my stomach started rumbling. Mum was asleep and Dad still hadn't arrived home from work so I made myself a cheese and crisp sandwich. I was about to eat my second quarter when I saw a police car pull up outside. I crept to the side of the window and watched two policemen get out and look up at our house, shaking their heads. Even though I saw them open the gate and walk the few paces across the front yard, I still jumped at the sound of the door knocker. Somehow I knew there was bad news coming and I didn't want to answer the door.

They knocked again and Mum stirred. 'See who that is, Pollyanna,' she murmured. 'There's a good girl.'

'It's two policemen,' I responded.

I noticed her sharp intake of breath, her hand fluttering to her throat and the glance towards the clock on the mantelpiece.

'You'd better let them in,' she said when they knocked once more.

The sad looks and the grave tone of voice when one of them asked if Mum was home confirmed my worst fears. Definitely bad news.

In the lounge, I pressed myself against Mum's side as they

spoke. I didn't understand it all but certain words jumped out at me like accident, fall and hospital. They weren't good words. Then one of the policemen said, 'I'm so sorry.' I can still sometimes hear Mum's agonised scream in my dreams and feel her clinging onto me so tightly that I could scarcely draw breath.

I later discovered that Dad had been a health and safety manager. He'd visited a building site in response to allegations of unsafe working practices. The owners swore they were fully compliant and took him on a tour to prove it but the scaffolding rig they climbed on collapsed and that was that. Not so compliant after all.

Mum couldn't cope without Dad. She pulled her black cloak tightly round her after the policemen left and, even though she tried to remove it, it was far too heavy. I tried to get Mum to play 'the glad game' but she couldn't find any positives and neither could I. He was the best and, without him, we were both lost. No amount of positive thinking or creativity could draw a reason to be glad.

My teacher at school was worried about me. Obviously she knew I'd lost my dad but when I started showing up in dirty clothes, hair unwashed, smelling, she realised things weren't right at home. I'd tried my best to keep it all going but I was still too young to properly look after myself. My teacher arranged for some social workers to visit. They saw the state of the house and the state of Mum and, next thing I knew, I was whisked away for emergency foster care. I'm sure it wasn't that straightforward or quick, but it felt that way to me at the time.

My first foster home was with a lovely widow in her fifties who'd been unable to have children of her own. She told me that she and her husband had provided a home for more than fifty kids over the years, and she'd continued the amazing work on her own after he died. Two months after I moved in, she found a lump in her breast so I couldn't stay. The next couple – Mr and Mrs Ashwell – had also been unable to have children so had adopted two and would foster between four and six at a time. After eight months with them, they had to move to Florida for Mr Ashwell's job and could foster no more.

I longed to return to Mum but my social worker would look at me with sad eyes and say, 'Your mum isn't well enough to look after you, Tamara. I'm really sorry.' Not well enough to look after me but also not well enough to see me. I didn't see her at all while I was on my first foster placement and I only saw her for an hour when I was with the Ashwells; an hour in which all she did was hold me and sob and apologise that the black cloak was getting heavier and heavier. That was the last time I ever saw her.

After the Ashwells, I had a few weeks here and there before they found me another 'long-term opportunity' with the appropriately named Foster family. I liked it there too but it only lasted five months. I can't even remember why I had to leave but I do remember Mrs Foster sobbing so much when she tried to break the news that Mr Foster had to do it instead. I didn't cry. I was so used to that conversation that I'd known it was coming, probably before they had. We played 'the glad game'. Mr Foster said that he would have fond memories of when Pollyanna came to stay because he had two wonderful sons but had always wanted a daughter too. Mrs Foster agreed, through lots of tears and snot, and said that meeting someone who 'sees the rainbows even through the torrential rain' would have a positive impact on her outlook forever.

For me, it was yet another lovely family to walk away from, but there were always positives. I was glad to have met them all.

I was approaching eleven and being constantly on the move and away from my mum had started to dampen my positivity. It wasn't just changing family all the time. It was changing schools. Changing friends. Changing my life constantly. Packing, unpacking,

packing again. Never really belonging. But then I was placed with the Sandersons and, finally, I found my long-term home.

Right from the very start, Kirsten and Tim Sanderson treated me like their own child and their daughter, Leanne, was like the big sister I'd always longed for. I'd struck gold, almost literally. The Sandersons were absolutely loaded. Tim was a director for an investment bank in the city and Kirsten owned Vanilla Pod, a successful chain of bistros across South London. They had an enormous four-storey townhouse called 'The Larches' in Kensington and, on my first day there, they said there were five spare bedrooms and I could choose the one I wanted. Five! I remember staring at them, wide-eyed, wondering if I'd misheard. I'd been used to the box room in all my foster homes and I'd been used to sharing too. When I made my decision, they asked me about my favourite colours and my hobbies, then commissioned a designer to create the bedroom of my dreams. I'd finally had some good luck.

Their daughter, Leanne, was seventeen when I turned up. When she came home from college on my first day, she squealed with excitement, hugged me tightly and told me how thrilled she was to have a baby sister.

I'd only been with the Sandersons for a few months when Kirsten picked me up from school early, her eyes red, her face grim, and I knew the day that I'd always dreaded had arrived. Standing in the church at Mum's funeral a week later, clutching tightly to Kirsten's hand, I played 'the glad game'. I was glad that Mum was no longer strangled by that cloak most days and I was glad she'd been reunited with my dad. I missed them both so much. I clung onto every single memory from too few years together, replaying each one over and over so I'd never forget and never let go.

Mum had intermittently kept diaries over the years which came into my possession after she died. From them I discovered she was bipolar and had battled depression and anxiety since her early teens. Dad was always so supportive and without him, she fell deeper into despair. My Pollyanna approach to life had been a blessing but wasn't enough to pull her out of the darkness. A couple of nights after I left, she'd taken an overdose and only survived because a neighbour found her. It turned out it wasn't her first attempt and Dad had covered up others. Three years and several failed attempts later, on what would have been Dad's birthday, she took a way out that couldn't fail – a tumble off a passenger bridge in front of a speeding train. That damn black cloak of hers had a hell of a lot to answer for and, ever since, I'd tried not to wear black. I needed my world splashed with colour.

* * *

Back in The Chocolate Pot, I looked up at Carly with tears clouding my eyes. 'So at age eleven, I was an orphan. Losing Mum was painful but I'd really lost her the day Dad died and I'd grieved for them both then. Despite such pain, I focused on my promise to Dad to always be his positive Pollyanna. I believed I was the luckiest girl on the planet with so much to be glad about when I was placed with the Sandersons. I'd been given a second chance to be a permanent part of a loving family and, as well as two wonderful parents, I had this amazing big sister to look up to. And Leanne wasn't just a sister. She was a role model and a friend. Or so I thought.' I shook my head. 'What Leanne did... What she put me through...' I paused as my heart raced and I felt quite nauseous. I couldn't do it. After all these years, I still wasn't ready to talk about it. Guilt? Shame? Both?

'Are you okay?' Carly asked, her voice and expression full of concern.

I hadn't talked about my parents or my time in foster care to anyone and I felt peculiar, as though I was on a precipice somewhere between laughing hysterically and sobbing uncontrollably. It genuinely could go either way.

'I'm sorry,' I said, wearily, 'but I can't tell you the rest. Not tonight.'

Carly reached across the table and squeezed my hand. 'You look exhausted. Do you want me to go?'

I nodded slowly.

'I'm so sorry about everything.'

We stood up and I picked up both mugs. 'You understand why I haven't talked about them before?'

'Yes, and I'm sorry for quizzing you. I shouldn't have asked.' Carly looked genuinely mortified.

'I like that you care enough to ask. And, if I hadn't wanted to tell you, I wouldn't have. I'd have remained an enigma.' I gave her a half-smile, hoping it was enough to convey that I wasn't upset with her.

'I absolutely promise I won't push you about Garth or what happened with your foster sister,' she said as we headed towards the front door. 'But I'm here when and if you're ready.'

I thanked her as she stepped out into the rain, but I wasn't sure if I'd ever be ready. Talking about my parents and time in foster care had been hard enough, but talking about Garth and Leanne was on another level.

## 6

I cut off the thread, placed my needle safely in my pin cushion, turned the miniature bobble hat the right way round and added it to the basket of colourful hats and scarves I'd spent the day knitting. Christmas might be over for one year but it was never too early to start making decorations for the next one.

'Sorry, Hercules, but I'm going to have to move you.' He was partially draped across my knee, doing a great impression of a hot water bottle. Reluctantly, I lifted him up and placed him back on the armchair, stroking his ears. 'I'll get changed, then I'm going downstairs to relieve the team. I won't be long, though.'

Pulling off my snuggly clothes, I changed into my jeans and a purple T-shirt, pulled my long, curly hair back into a knot, then made my way down to the ground floor. At the bottom of the stairs, I paused and listened at the door. Loud music signalled to me that all the customers had gone and the team were cleaning, which wasn't really a surprise considering it was New Year's Eve.

Unlocking the door, I stepped into the café and smiled. The chairs were stacked on the tables and two of my other student part-timers, Nathan and Molly, were diligently mopping the floor. I loved that standards never slipped when I wasn't working and I had Maria to thank for that. Like me, she ran a tight ship.

I greeted Molly and Nathan and asked them to put their mops down and follow me to the front of the café by the serving counter. Maria was busy cashing up, counting a bundle of notes from the till. She smiled at me and indicated with a raise of her finger that she was nearly done.

'Can you grab Sheila and Brandon from the kitchen?' I asked Molly.

She nodded and made her way behind the counter and past Maria.

Sheila had been with me for a little over a year. Now in her late fifties, she had run her own café in Hull before semi-retiring to Whitsborough Bay. A gifted chef, she was content to spend most of her time in the kitchen and I was more than happy to use her talents that way. Brandon was another of my part-time students.

Maria lifted the tray out of the till and placed it on the counter with the printed sales report for the day. 'You're going to be dead chuffed when you look at the figures for today.'

'It's been busy, then?'

'Busy? Oh my goodness, it's barely stopped all day. Then, poof, they all disappeared. Anyone would think they had somewhere better to be. The last half hour was dead so we're nearly cleaned up already, the cakes and leftovers are packaged up ready for The Hope Centre, and there's a plate of quiche and salad for your dinner tonight.'

'Thank you so much. Super-efficient as always.'

A few minutes later, Molly emerged from the kitchen, followed by Sheila and Brandon. 'Gather round,' I said. 'Firstly, thanks for today. Maria tells me you've been busy.'

There were murmurs about it being 'packed', 'heaving' and 'never-ending' but it was all good-natured. They weren't scared of hard work and I knew they all preferred to be kept busy as it made the shift go faster.

'And thank you for everything you've done this year,' I continued. 'I'm very proud of you all.' I looked round the smiling group. 'It's New Year's Eve and I'm sure you have somewhere else you'd rather be right now so you're welcome to head home and I'll finish off.'

Chattering excitedly, they headed upstairs to retrieve their belongings from the staff room.

'Have I told you lately that you're the best boss ever?' Maria said.

'Get away with you. It's New Year's Eve. Anyone would do the same.'

She shook her head, smiling. 'You're sure you won't change your mind about seeing in the New Year with us?'

I grimaced. 'Thanks but I prefer to stay in for New Year. Have a good time, though.'

'We'll try. What are your plans, then?'

'I'll drop off the food at The Hope Centre and then, as far as I'm concerned, it's no different from any other Sunday night. I'll have my tea, watch TV or read, then go to bed.'

'You will stay up past midnight to see the New Year in?'

I shrugged. 'Probably. Too many fireworks going off round town to make it worth trying to sleep.'

'I've got your stuff.' Sheila handed Maria her bag, coat, and scarf. 'Thanks for the early finish, Tara.'

'Happy New Year, everyone,' I said, opening the door to let them out. 'Have a great evening, whatever you're doing, and I'll see you next year.'

Wishing me all the best, they bundled out of The Chocolate Pot and set off in different directions along the cobbles of Castle Street. I stepped outside, watching them for a moment, before looking up at the fairy lights strung between the shops and cafés like a ribbon of stars connecting the buildings. Another week and they'd stop being illuminated at night. Another week or so after that and they'd be gone for another year. It was always a sad day when the cherry picker appeared and the lights were taken down. I might not celebrate on Christmas Day but even I felt like there was something magical about Christmas on Castle Street. Each business took pride in creating enticing window displays and the whole street looked and felt so warm and inviting.

I pulled the door closed behind me and moved towards the middle of the cobbles. Standing under the white lights, I gazed up to the starry sky as I often did on an evening, wondering if my parents were up there somewhere looking down on me. Were they proud of me? Had I turned out how they'd hoped, despite everything? Glancing up and down the street at the fairy lights in the various shop windows, I felt alive and, for a brief moment, I was Pollyanna again, believing in everyone and everything.

A very brief moment.

'That's enough of that,' I muttered to myself. Stepping back into the café, I locked the door, then made my way to the counter and reached for my yellow mug. Hot chocolate time.

While my gingerbread hot chocolate cooled, I put the till tray away in the safe, finished mopping the floor, and emptied the buckets. Switching off all the lights except those at the very back of the café, I took my mug and the sales report to one of the high-backed leather armchairs. Glancing down the sales figures, I smiled. Maria was right – very impressive. They must have worked their socks off.

A knock on the door made me jump.

'It's only me,' shouted a woman through the letterbox.

I smiled as I recognised Carly's voice.

'Have you been busy?' she asked when I let her in.

'Maria said they never stopped. What about you?'

'Same. It's all good, though.'

'Do you want a drink?' I hoped she'd say no. The sooner I could get to The Hope Centre – a local charity for the homeless and vulnerable – the sooner I could be back upstairs with Hercules, shutting out the world and ignoring the fact that it was New Year's Eve. Christmas Day was bad but New Year's Eve was even worse. It held too many memories and too many regrets.

'I've just had one, thanks,' Carly said. 'I came to do you a favour. Liam's loading some cupcakes into my car for The Hope Centre. We wondered if we could take your donations and save you the trip.'

'Really? That would be brilliant. Thank you.' Relief flowed through me. I'd never have been able to drop-and-run. They'd have insisted on inviting me in and making me a drink and I'd be asked how I was seeing the New Year in, followed by the curious expressions when I revealed I'd be doing nothing.

'Do you need a hand with anything?' Carly asked.

'No. It's all bagged up ready to go. Give me two minutes and I'll be out.'

\* \* \*

'I'm freezing,' Liam said after we'd loaded up the car. 'I'm going upstairs to grab a hoodie.' He disappeared into Carly's shop.

'Are you sure you won't join us tonight?' Carly asked, closing the boot.

Why did people keep asking me that? I shook my head. 'I haven't celebrated New Year's Eve since my wed—' I stopped but I was too late. I'd already said half the word.

'You got married on New Year's Eve.' Carly looked at me with big, sad eyes. 'That's why you don't celebrate it.'

What was going on? Why did I keep revealing information?

'I met Garth on New Year's Eve,' I muttered. 'He proposed the same day two years later and we married exactly a year after that.

I'll regret the day I met him forever so, thanks to him, I hate New Year's Eve with a passion.'

'I'm sorry,' Carly said. 'I'm not pushing, either. I'd never have mentioned it if you hadn't nearly said "wedding". The offer's still on the table. I'm here if and when you're ready for the next part of your story.'

Liam stepped out of Carly's Cupcakes, pulling a hoodie over his head. 'That's better. Are we all set?'

Thanking them both for taking the food to The Hope Centre, I wished them a Happy New Year, then headed back into The Chocolate Pot, shoulders drooped. So Carly knew a bit more. That tower was going to keep crumbling, wasn't it? I should never have let my guard down with her. I should have kept it strictly about business but it had got harder and harder to keep Carly at arm's length. She was so warm and friendly and she made me laugh. I missed having a friend in my life who could do that. Although the last person who'd done that had been Leanne and look how that turned out. Better to keep a distance. Safer.

* * *

'Hercules?' I called, returning to the flat. I placed my plate of tea in the fridge and the sales report on the worktop. 'Where's that gorgeous bunny rabbit?'

Hercules came bounding towards me, his nose twitching. Bending down, I scooped him up into my arms, kissed his head, and stroked his ears. When I'd researched how to care for house rabbits, I'd read that they didn't particularly like being handled and that had been true for Titch and Dinks. Not Hercules, though. He was the most adorable, affectionate, snuggly bunny in the world. Animals. Better than humans any day. Always there for you with unconditional love and hugs.

'Let's get you some food,' I said, putting him back down. Obedient as always, he followed me to his feeding station in the kitchen where I put some fresh water in his bowl, topped up his food pellets and added a handful of chopped cabbage and kale into his third bowl.

While he munched, I filled myself a glass of water, headed over to the sofa, and sat for a moment, looking round. I wondered what my team – or anyone else who knew me, for that matter – would say if they could see me in my home environment. They'd probably be surprised. The only people who'd ever seen the inside of my flat were the trades. Even Carly had never been in. I'd always engineered it so that I went to her flat or we stayed downstairs in the café. With comfy seats, cosy lighting and plenty of refreshments to hand, there'd never been a reason for her to venture upstairs.

I doubted anyone would guess I had a house rabbit, and they'd be stunned to discover that I was a closet crafter. Everyone knew I did Pilates and that I sometimes went swimming, although I let them assume I meant a few lengths in the warmth of the leisure centre pool rather than a bracing dip in the North Sea. Dad had been a keen swimmer and had taught me, taking me to the local indoor pool regularly from when I was a baby. Kirsten and Tim had loved it too and had introduced me to open water swimming in the River Thames. It was so much more exhilarating than a chlorine-filled swimming pool and I was immediately hooked. Leanne detested swimming and Garth had never learned so it was something that just belonged to the three of us. The first time I'd donned my wetsuit and ducked beneath the waves of the North Sea, about two weeks after moving to Whitsborough Bay, I'd known it was a little part of my old life I was going to cling on to – something untouched by Leanne and Garth, something that somehow kept that tiny connection with Kirsten and Tim as well as to my dad.

I set the log burner going and lit the scented candles on the hearth. With warm-white fairy lights on, the ambiance was exactly how I liked it. It normally relaxed me immediately, yet I couldn't seem to settle.

And I knew exactly why – sodding New Year's Eve and memories of Garth.

He didn't deserve even a minute of my precious time yet I knew I could easily waste the whole evening on him if I didn't pull myself together. Sighing, I picked up the sales report from the kitchen worktop and took the stairs up to the mezzanine level – my office and crafting studio – where I entered the figures on my account's spreadsheet. Calculating the percentage increase in sales from the same date the previous year made me smile although it wasn't about the money. For me, it was about running a successful business. It was about me making decisions that affected my life instead of someone else making them for me. It was about me being in control instead of being controlled.

Picking up an A4 pad, a clipboard and some pens, I returned to the lounge area and started a wish list and planner for The Chocolate Pot for the year ahead. There were going to be a few staff changes. One of my full-timers, Niamh, would be going on maternity leave in March and wasn't planning to return, and two of my students, Lana and Cody, were going to university in September. Lana was staying in the area so wanted to keep her part-time job but Cody was going... actually, I wasn't sure where he was going, but it wasn't local so he needed replacing. I also had a hankering to do something else in the community, but what? I'd always supported The Hope Centre with leftovers. Could I do something more for them? Workshops about food preparation on a tight budget, perhaps? Or maybe I could work with colleges in the area, providing guidance to students interested in running their own businesses and mentoring anyone who decided to make a go of it?

Either of those options would be perfect for getting out and about a bit more. I spent far too much time in the flat, thinking, regretting.

The next couple of hours passed quickly while I scribbled down more ideas. When my stomach rumbled, I took it as a cue to stop working, retrieved my quiche and salad from the fridge, and settled myself at the table with a magazine.

As soon as I stopped focusing on the business, Garth was in my head again. Perhaps I should have accepted Maria's or Carly's invite to spend the evening with them instead of moping round the flat, stewing about the past. Maria and Marc were hosting a party at Marc's house but it sounded like it was all couples and their kids. Not for me. It was hard enough being on my own, thinking about what Garth had done to me, but being surrounded by happy couples and children, knowing that he'd made me into a person who could never have that, was a million times worse.

Keen to empty my head of all Garth-related memories, I thought again about Sofia and George's adorable request to Santa for them to unite as a proper family. I was exceptionally cynical about romance in my own life but couldn't seem to stop being a romantic Pollyanna when it came to other people in love. My Christmas wish for Carly and Liam to get together had come true. I hoped my wish for Maria and Marc would come true too. Despite what happened with Garth, I still believed true love existed; just not for me. How could I not believe in love after I'd seen my parents together? Even on her darkest days, Mum had always looked at Dad with such adoration, and everything he said and did showed how much she meant to him. Kirsten and Tim, my foster parents, had clearly been very much in love too. Despite demanding careers, they always made time to be together and they used to write affectionate messages to each other on Post-it notes and leave them round the house. Whenever I thought about them, I pictured them laughing or dancing. Yes, I certainly knew what true love looked like.

'You're the only fella for me, aren't you, Hercules?' I said, picking him up. 'How about you and I see the New Year in with a film-fest?'

Curling up on the sofa with Hercules, we immersed ourselves in a couple of action movies. Car chases, guns, explosions – exactly what I needed to distract me from my fourteenth New Year's Eve in a row, all alone, thinking about how different things could have been if I'd never met Garth Tewkesbury. If I'd never been fostered by the Sandersons. Or if my wonderful dad hadn't died, leaving my mum unable to cope with me, or with life.

## 7

I was piping chocolate ganache onto the top of a chocolate and raspberry gateau on Wednesday morning when Maria burst through the kitchen door, grinning. We'd opened for business again on the second but Maria had booked it as holiday so this was her first working day.

'Happy New Year!' she declared brightly.

'And the same to you.' I put the piping bag down and picked up a dish of plump raspberries. 'How was the party?'

'Amazing.' She removed her gloves and thrust her left hand towards me. 'Guess who got engaged on New Year's Eve?'

'Oh Maria, that's amazing news. Congratulations.' I put the raspberries down and admired her ring. 'Vintage? It's gorgeous.'

'It was Marc's grandmother's and I love it. Couldn't be more perfect.'

'Why don't you dump your stuff upstairs and make us some coffees while I finish up here, then you can tell me all about it?'

* * *

Five minutes later, we sat at one of the tables at the back of The Chocolate Pot with a couple of lattes.

'So how did he propose?' I asked.

'Oh, Tara, it was so lovely. It was about an hour before any of our guests arrived and Marc had made me a cup of tea so I was relaxing on the sofa while he and the kids were drawing at the table. They announced that they'd all drawn some family pictures – Marc included – and they wanted to show me them. They lined up in front of me and the kids turned their pictures round one at a time, revealing the words "will you marry me?" and, when Marc turned his round, there was a ribbon taped to the back with the ring dangling from it.'

'That is so gorgeous,' I said, a warm and fuzzy feeling in my stomach.

'Isn't it? I absolutely love that he involved the kids. They were so excited. As soon as I said yes, Sofia asked if she could call Marc Daddy and George asked if he could call me Mummy. My heart melted.'

'I'm not surprised. I'm so happy for you.'

'I can't believe how lucky I am,' she gushed. 'After how Tony treated me, I genuinely didn't believe there were any good men out there. I certainly didn't believe in love or marriage.'

'And then you met Marc?'

She nodded, her eyes sparkling. 'He completely swept me off my feet. The first time he kissed me, it was as though he flicked a switch inside me and suddenly I believed in love again. I believed in magic. And I knew that he was the one for me forever.'

I smiled, not trusting myself to speak. Love. Magic. Forever. Yes, I'd felt that too the first time Garth kissed me.

Maria continued to enthuse about how happy Marc made her and how thrilled Sofia and George were that they were going to become a family. I smiled and nodded and said, 'aww,' occasionally, but I wasn't really in The Chocolate Pot with her. I was an eighteen-year-old again on the private roof terrace off my foster parents' bedroom with Garth Tewkesbury, longing for midnight to arrive so that I could kiss that gorgeous man.

'Five... four... three... two... one...' The countdown drifted to us from the revellers downstairs at the New Year's Eve party at The Larches.

'Happy New Year,' Garth whispered, cupping my face in his hand and slowly lowering his lips to mine. Fireworks exploded above us and fireworks exploded inside me. I had never experienced a kiss like it – gentle, yet somehow passionate too. I fell for him right then and there. It didn't matter that, at forty, he was more than twice my age. It didn't matter that we'd only met that evening. It didn't matter that I knew very little about him except his name, occupation and that he was Leanne's estranged cousin. He made me laugh and that's what I'd always dreamed of – someone to make the dark days brighter, just like my dad had done for my mum. Leanne had said we'd be perfect for each other and I trusted her. I trusted her implicitly. What a mistake that turned out to be.

Closing my eyes for a moment, my heart racing, I could still feel his lips against mine, his hands in my hair, his body pressed against me. And I hated that I could still feel that sense of desire and longing for a man who had hurt me so badly. I shuddered and tuned back into what Maria was saying.

'... so I think I've got champagne flowing through my veins right now.'

I smiled. 'I'm not surprised. Any plans for the big day or is it too early to say?'

'Yes, we have plans, but it might be a bit out there.' She wrinkled her nose.

'Saying "I do" while dangling from the air sea rescue helicopter?' I ventured.

'Not quite *that* out there.' She sipped her latte. 'We'd like it to be this year. We both love Christmas and so do the kids, of course, so we're thinking a Monday in late November or early December.'

'A Monday? Oh. That's different. Why a Monday?'

'A Saturday or even a Friday wouldn't work for the venue we want because they're too busy. A Monday, on the other hand, is their quietest day.'

'Where is it?'

She wrinkled her nose again. 'Marc and I would love to get married and hold our reception right here in The Chocolate Pot.' She released a nervous-sounding giggle. 'I told you it was a bit out there.'

I stared at her open-mouthed. A bit out there? She wasn't wrong.

\* \* \*

'Promise me you'll think about it,' Maria said as I walked her to the door after we'd cleared up that evening.

'I'll definitely think about it and please tell Marc that it's certainly not a no. It was just a bit unexpected. I've never considered The Chocolate Pot as a wedding venue.'

'Look at it,' she said, sweeping her arm round the room, taking in the lights twinkling on the pillars, the tree in the corner and the bespoke decorations. 'It's so magical at Christmas. And it's where we met so this place is extra special to us both. We don't want a huge wedding and we don't want a traditional top table or anything like that. It's not us. We want our wedding day to be relaxed and informal with a buffet, music, laughter... and The Chocolate Pot's Christmas magic.'

Her enthusiasm was infectious and I couldn't help smiling. 'If you ever leave this job, which I hope you never do, you'd do great in a sales role.'

She grinned. 'I promise I won't pressure you, but I've done some research online about how to get licenced for weddings, so I'll email you the links tonight and then leave it with you. Whenever you're ready. No pressure at all to say yes. None. You won't break anyone's heart if you say no.'

Laughing, I opened the door. 'Get yourself home, email me your research and we'll see.'

Closing and locking the door behind her, I leaned against it and swept my eyes round the ground floor. She was right about the place feeling magical. Customers often commented on it at Christmas – probably half the reason we had to practically shove some of them out the door at closing time. A wedding, though. Hmm. Assuming we could get a licence, it wasn't beyond the realms of possibility. The first floor was bright and spacious, having been deliberately created as an overspill café/function room. We could hire in folding chairs and create a ceremony space upstairs, move the guests downstairs for a buffet while we cleared the chairs, then have a disco upstairs if that was what they wanted, or simply put the tables and chairs out again and have two floors available for mingling and chatting.

But it wasn't the logistics that concerned me. It went much deeper than that.

\* \* \*

'Hercules?' I called, returning to the flat a little later with my plate of dinner. 'Where are you?'

He bounded across the wooden floor, nose twitching, ready for cuddles.

I picked him up. 'Guess what? Marc proposed to Maria on New

Year's Eve and they want the wedding in The Chocolate Pot. Do you think we can pull that off?' I smiled as Hercules twitched his nose as though in agreement. 'I think you might be right. A Christmas wedding. Might be nice to do something different. It's just that...' I shook my head.

After sorting out some food for Hercules, I heated up my slab of lasagne in the microwave, added a leafy salad, then took it over to the table with a crafting magazine. But, once again, I was distracted. Weddings. And, more specifically, my wedding.

I hadn't wanted to get married. It wasn't that I didn't believe in marriage because I absolutely did. After all, my parents had been great role models for what a successful marriage looked like, even when one half fought a tough battle with their mental health every day. For me, the objection was to the ceremony itself. Kirsten and Tim had been wonderful foster parents and they couldn't have done more to make me feel like a part of their family rather than the foster kid who never left, yet there was this nagging feeling of being disloyal towards Mum and Dad. Dad, rather than Tim, should have been there to give me away, patting my arm proudly. Mum, rather than Kirsten, should have been fussing with my dress and telling me I might be all grown up and getting married but I'd always be her little Pollyanna. Yet they weren't there and hadn't been for a long time. I'd worried that I'd find their absence too overwhelming and would cry throughout the wedding, which surely wasn't a good omen for a happy marriage.

Garth understood – or at least he said he did – yet he somehow got exactly what he wanted. He was oddly old-fashioned, declaring no living together and no sex before marriage so, if I wanted to have a proper relationship with him, I didn't really have a choice about getting married.

I suggested eloping as a compromise but Garth didn't agree with 'sloping off' as he put it. Why wouldn't I want to show the

world we loved each other? Was I embarrassed by the age difference? Why would I hurt the Sandersons and Leanne by cutting
them out of such an important day?

Although I didn't think of it as 'winning' at the time, Garth won.
As always. The tiniest of compromises was his agreement to a small
wedding – church (also at Garth's insistence) followed by a reception in the Chelsea branch of Vanilla Pod rather than a grand hotel
or country estate.

Kirsten invited me for a walk through the park one Sunday
afternoon in early October, three months from the wedding. We
huddled together on a bench for warmth as we watched children
tossing bread to the ducks on the pond.

'Are you having doubts about Garth?' she asked.

'Gosh, no! Why do you ask?'

'You seem sad whenever your wedding is mentioned.'

I shook my head. 'It's not Garth. Definitely no doubts about
marrying him. It's the wedding itself. It's just that...' I tailed off. I
didn't want to lie but how could I tell the truth without hurting her?

She took my hand and squeezed it gently. 'It's just that you wish
your mum and dad could be there to see it,' she suggested.

'Yes. I'm sorry.'

'There's no need to apologise to me. I completely understand
and I'm sure I'd feel the same if I was you. But you know that Tim
and I are making no assumptions, don't you? Tim can walk you
down the aisle, I can, we both can, or neither of us can. It's your day
– not ours – so make it what you want it to be. All we want is for you
to be happy.'

I lay in bed that night and, as I often did, I imagined what Mum
and Dad would think of the situation and realised that they probably wouldn't have understood why I was making such a fuss, especially when the Sandersons had been my foster parents for longer
than my real parents had been in my life. I wasn't being fair to

them. They loved me and I loved them and I had to stop feeling guilty about them doing anything that, in a fair and just world, Mum and Dad would have done.

Despite my reservations that it was the wedding Garth wanted rather than what I wanted, it turned out to be a wonderful day. Kirsten played mother of the bride to perfection, making me feel as special as if I'd been her own flesh and blood while also acknowledging how proud Mum and Dad would have been. Leanne was a beautiful bridesmaid in a simple floor-length dusky lilac dress. As Tim walked me down the aisle, beaming at me, I felt quite overwhelmed with emotion. I wasn't related by blood but, as far as my foster parents were concerned, I was as much their daughter as Leanne was. I had to admit that Garth had been right about making it a day that my second family could share. I resolved to stop feeling guilty for loving my new family as much as I'd loved Mum and Dad and accept that there was space in my heart for everyone.

When I stood at that altar, joining hands with Garth to say our vows, I started trembling when the vicar talked about 'in sickness and in health'. What if something happened to Garth? What if he fell ill and was taken from me? With the twenty-two-year age gap, it struck me that there'd come a point, albeit several decades away, when I might lose him. The thought of him not being in my life made me gasp for breath, causing the vicar to pause to ask if I was okay. Of course I was okay. I was marrying the most perfect man in the world; it was just that the strength of my feelings for him was a little overwhelming at times.

If only he *had* been perfect.

If only his vows *had* meant something.

If only …

## 8

I tensed as I heard Maria's key turn in the lock the following morning. I still hadn't decided about hosting the wedding. She'd emailed me the information about obtaining a wedding licence and it didn't sound too challenging. She'd already pre-empted the biggest objection by proposing a Monday so the main barrier – the one that had kept me tossing and turning all night – was me and my past. Getting engaged at New Year? Celebrating their wedding with a small gathering in the café where the bride was assistant manager? It had so many echoes of my own wedding. The thought of reliving that day again, albeit vicariously, filled me with dread.

'Morning,' Maria called. 'I smell brownies. Maple syrup?'

'Good guess.'

Opening the oven, I removed a couple of traybakes – salted maple brownies and black forest gateau brownies. I popped a chocolate sponge onto the shelf, closed the oven door again and set the buzzer. In the second oven, croissants and pains au chocolat were almost ready for any customers wanting a takeaway.

'Anything I can do for you?' Maria asked, poking her head round the door.

'No, I'm fine thanks.'

She hovered for a moment, grinning, as though hoping I'd give her some good news. I couldn't. Her smile slipped and she cleared her throat. 'I'll put my stuff upstairs.'

I could hear her footsteps slow and heavy on the stairs. Closing my eyes, I breathed in and out, in and out, slowly, steadily. Maria had given me six and a half years of loyalty. She'd shared ideas to develop the business, she was great with customers, she was a good cook, she was reliable. She'd never asked anything from me, yet she'd given me everything. I was going to have to say yes and hope that I could get my act together before the wedding. It wasn't like we were talking next month. It was nearly a year away. I could sort myself out in a year. I nearly laughed out loud at that thought – hadn't managed it in nearly fourteen years so why would another eleven months make any difference?

Maria returned to the kitchen. 'Do you want a drink?'

Her eyes were red. Oh, no. I'd made her cry. I was a horrible, horrible person and it was all *his* fault.

'A black coffee would be great, but there's something I need to say first.'

'It's fine. I understand. It was a big ask.'

I shook my head. 'It wasn't a big ask. It was just that... forget it. But I've made a decision and, if you're serious about a Monday working for you, then you can have your wedding in The Chocolate Pot.' I tried to sound positive and enthusiastic but, when she looked at me doubtfully, I knew I'd failed.

'It's okay. We'll find somewhere else. I don't want it to become an issue.' Her voice trembled as she spoke and I hated myself for still being so influenced by my past. Why couldn't I move on?

'I *want* you to have your wedding here,' I said, my voice strong and enthusiastic. 'It will be amazing and I'm honoured you think so much of The Chocolate Pot that you want to get married here.'

Maria clapped her hand over her mouth, eyes sparkling. 'You *really* mean that?'

I nodded, smiling. 'I really mean it. As long as I can get the licence, I'm on board.'

She squealed and grabbed me in a hug. 'Oh my God, Tara. Thank you so much. This means so much to us. Do you mind if I ring Marc and tell him?'

'Go for it.'

The buzzer sounded shortly after Maria left the kitchen, signalling that the pastries were ready. While I was loading them onto cooling racks, one of our regulars, Colin, appeared for his usual order – pain au chocolat and a white hot chocolate for breakfast, and a plain brownie for his morning break in the shop where he worked.

While I mixed Colin's drink, I had the strangest sensation of being watched and turned towards the window. A blond-haired man was bending forward, hands cupped either side of his face as he peered into the café. There was something familiar about him, but I couldn't quite place him.

'You're sure I can't tempt you with a special brownie, Colin?' I asked. 'We've got salted maple and black forest gateau flavours today, fresh from the oven.'

'Thanks, Tara, but you know me. Creature of habit. They sound good, though.'

I smiled as I poured his drink into the flask he brought in each day. Creature of habit? I could certainly relate to that. Nearly fourteen years on my own and I was definitely one of those.

Still aware of being watched, I frowned when I saw that the man hadn't moved from the window, his nose pressed against my clean glass. Who was he? As though realising I'd clocked him, he dropped his hands and backed away.

I nipped into the kitchen to get Colin's pain au chocolat and brownie. When I returned, the man was gone. It was only when Colin left that it struck me who it had been. Jed Ferguson. The man who'd sold me the building. The man who'd ripped me off to the tune of nearly twenty grand. I hated Jed Ferguson nearly as much as I hated Garth Tewkesbury and I'd have been happy to live out my life never seeing either of them again. What the hell was he doing back in Whitsborough Bay? He was meant to be in Australia. And, more importantly, what was he doing with his greasy nose pressed against my window?

# 9

When I discovered the truth about Garth and why he'd married me, I knew that my charmed life in London was over. Thanks to him, I lost my second family, my home and my job in one fell swoop. Kirsten and Tim hadn't done anything wrong but I never, ever wanted to see Leanne again. As far as I was concerned, she was dead to me. I was certain my foster parents would be disgusted with her if they learned the truth, but blood is thicker than water. She was Kirsten and Tim's only child and, if it came down to a choice, they'd have to choose her. And I understood that, but I couldn't stick around to watch it happen and face rejection yet again. Plus I was ashamed. How could I have been so naïve? How had I not seen what she was doing?

With only a car full of hastily packed possessions to my name, I sat in a petrol station parking space with a map and a pen. I had absolutely no idea where to go so fate was going to make that life-changing decision for me. I closed my eyes and moved my hand round the map of the UK before bringing the pen down onto the page and drawing a small line. Opening my eyes, I laughed at my new home – The North Sea. Hmm. A boat? A drilling platform? Perhaps not. I followed a straight line west until I hit the coast. Whitsborough Bay. I had a vague idea that it was a popular seaside resort but that was the extent of my knowledge. Holidays with the Sandersons had been abroad rather than in the UK so North Yorkshire was completely unfamiliar to me. Tossing the map onto the passenger seat, I pulled out of the petrol station and drove north towards my new home and new life.

There was never any doubt about what I was going to do when I settled in Whitsborough Bay, or elsewhere if the town was unsuitable. I was going to continue with the passion my dad had ignited in me and what I'd trained for over the past eight years. I'd worked in Kirsten's chain of bistros, Vanilla Pod, since I was fourteen and had lapped up knowledge from some amazing chefs and baristas as well as learning all about exceptional, efficient service from the front-of-house staff. Garth and Leanne might have taken my family, my job and my dignity, but they couldn't take my knowledge, skills and experience away from me. I'd find an empty premises and I'd open my own café. I had no doubts about my ability to run a successful café as, despite Leanne being manager of the Chelsea branch of Vanilla Pod, I'd been the one running it. The only unknown entity was Whitsborough Bay. Would I discover a town over-run with cafés and no space for mine? I didn't envisage replicating a sophisticated bistro like Vanilla Pod, but I certainly wasn't looking to open a 'greasy spoon' café either. Would my vision of somewhere in-between fit?

I like to think that my parents were watching out for me when the pen chose Whitsborough Bay because it couldn't have been more ideal. I fell in love with the town from my very first glimpse of the sea. It was mid-afternoon on Monday 10th May – the first day of the rest of my life. The sun had come out to welcome me and it kissed the sea which twinkled like a million stars.

Whitsborough Bay Castle came into view, standing high on a cliff overlooking the sea. I couldn't take my eyes off it and had to stop and get out the car so I could take it all in. An overwhelming feeling that fate had found somewhere to call home took my breath away and I had to lean against the car, gulping in deep breaths of fresh air.

When I'd calmed down, a man walking his dog smiled at me and made a comment about the lovely weather. Moments later, a couple walking on the other side of the road smiled and said 'hello'. Both times I had to check round me to make sure they weren't speaking to anyone else, but there was nobody else there. They'd spoken to *me*. They'd welcomed *me*.

Back in the car, I followed brown signs for 'hotels' and found myself on a road called Sea Cliff which, true to its name, was a cliff overlooking the North Sea with large hotels and apartment blocks on one side and a wide promenade, parkland and trees on the other.

I checked into the first decent-looking hotel advertising vacancies. The drive had drained me and I couldn't face traipsing from one hotel to the next. Finances weren't too much of an issue. My parents had owned our house and property prices had rocketed in London over the years. The sale proceeds plus compensation and a life assurance payout for Dad's accident meant a substantial inheritance, although I'd have happily traded every penny to have them both back. Kirsten and Tim had been adamant that I wasn't to touch any of my money. They continued to support me and insisted that I save my inheritance to invest in property or a business in later years when I was ready. I bet they hadn't expected me to be doing it so soon and so far away from them. I hadn't expected to be doing that either.

After showering and dining in the hotel restaurant, I felt refreshed enough to explore. It would be dark within the hour but I could certainly wander along the cliff path opposite the hotel and see where it took me. The earlier warmth had long gone and I was glad I'd grabbed a coat. Dark clouds scudded across the sky, threatening to burst at any moment. They weren't going to force me back to my room, though. After everything I'd been through, a drenching was nothing.

Crossing the road, I hastened past some tall trees. The path widened then split around a grassy area where a colourful wooden rowing boat sat in a flowerbed. I took the right-hand path, closest to the sea, then stopped. Wow! Those trees had been hiding the most incredible view. If it was that good in an approaching storm, I couldn't wait to see it on a bright day or perhaps at sunrise or sunset. South Bay curved round in front of me, lined with pretty white, coloured, and brick buildings. There was a sandy beach to the left and Whitsborough Bay Castle on the cliff in front of me. Below that, a river led into a harbour where... oh my goodness... there was a red-and-white striped lighthouse. What were the odds? Mum and Dad had definitely drawn me to Whitsborough Bay. Mum had a thing about lighthouses, particularly striped ones. A gifted artist, she'd often drawn or painted lighthouses, although always at night-time and always with a beam of light breaking through the darkness. She'd say that, whenever she felt lost or lonely, she'd look for Dad – her very own bright, shining lighthouse, guiding the way to safety.

Dad would often tell me a bedtime story about a little girl called Pollyanna who lived in a striped lighthouse who needed to remain positive at all times or the light wouldn't shine to keep the sailors safe. He'd sing a song to the tune of 'Twinkle, Twinkle, Little Star':

> *Pollyanna, little light*
> *Shining bright on stormy nights*

*Keeping boats away from shore*
*Saving lives, that's what you're for*
*Pollyanna, little light*
*Shining bright on stormy nights*

As I stood on that clifftop looking down towards Whitsborough Bay's lighthouse, I could hear his voice so clearly in my head, feel him holding my hand, stroking my hair, kissing my forehead, and telling me he'd always be our lighthouse, keeping us safe and guiding us to happiness. Tears tumbled down my cheeks and I gripped the back of the bench in front of me, gulping in the air, as the wind swept my hair across my face, and the cloud burst, battering me with rain.

'I'm lost and lonely, Dad,' I whispered into the wind and rain. 'I need you to be my lighthouse.'

And, at that moment, a beam of light swept across the sea and I knew he was there with me. They both were.

The next few days were spent exploring my potential new home. There were a couple of cafés on North Bay but otherwise the area was fairly undeveloped. It's got a hotel, apartments, shops and several lovely cafés now, but the two cafés back then were very much about bacon baps and a coffee served through a hatch and, if you wanted to sit down, you could chance the battered plastic seating on the wasteland next to the building. They definitely weren't what I envisaged for my business, not that either of them was for sale.

South Bay is the more commercial side of Whitsborough Bay with chip shops, ice-cream parlours, pubs and amusement arcades.

There were a couple of businesses for sale along the seafront but they were completely unsuitable, one being too cramped and the other in a poor position, tucked away at the far end.

On the Thursday, I explored the town and came to Castle Street. The moment I walked down the cobbled street, a feeling of peace and calm flowed through me. My step slowed as I gazed into each shop window. There appeared to be a good variety of retailers – a florist, a bookshop, a specialist teddy bear shop, a jeweller's, a stationery store – and none of them were high-street chains. Then about halfway down on the left-hand side, I spotted a bright orange 'for sale' sign and my heart started to race. My pace quickened as I approached the shop and I gasped when I realised that, not only was there a property for sale, it was already a café. Bonus.

I stood at the other side of the street and surveyed Ferguson's. The sign had seen better days, with the 'g' hanging at a peculiar angle and the apostrophe missing. There were three sets of windows, suggesting three storeys, and the top floor had significant height. I wondered whether it was all café or whether there was a flat above the retail space. I hoped there was accommodation as I ideally wanted to live above my café.

Most of the businesses on Castle Street were painted in pretty pastel shades but Ferguson's was not pastel and was definitely not pretty. It was some sort of putrid-looking mustard-green colour and the whole building was desperately in need of a fresh lick of paint in a completely different shade. A ripped and faded green and yellow canopy was suspended above the ground floor door and windows and a couple of grubby-looking plastic tables and chairs were positioned outside, although nobody was seated in them.

It wasn't the greatest first impression but most of the other properties on the street were immaculate so I could see exactly how it could look. The poor state of disrepair suggested to me that it would be priced well or that a good deal could be made.

I crossed the street, opened the door to Ferguson's and took a deep breath, which I very much regretted. The smell of greasy ovens, eggs, and chip pans in need of a change of oil hit me. A sullen young woman momentarily looked up from the till but she didn't smile or offer a friendly greeting. I made my way to a table towards the back from where I could take it all in.

Ferguson's definitely fell into the 'greasy spoon' café category – Formica tables, lino floor, all-day full English breakfast on the menu. To be fair to the owners, it was clean – which I hadn't expected from the outside – but it was soulless.

Looking at the menu, I realised I'd need to order at the counter so I made my way back there and ordered a coffee and cheese toastie. Despite attempting to engage the woman in conversation, I didn't manage to raise even a smile.

Returning to my table, I studied the three customers. It was nearly noon so I'd have expected the café to be quite a bit busier. An elderly man was reading *Bay News* – presumably the local newspaper – while drinking tea for one. A middle-aged man was tucking into a fry-up and reading a tabloid newspaper, and a woman in her early twenties was eating a sandwich and reading a gossip magazine. When she finished, she took the plate behind the counter, so clearly she worked there too, which only made two real customers and me.

The building was fairly wide but it was also very deep meaning there was lots of space and the potential to use it far more effectively. In fact, the whole place was full of potential. I could visualise ripping out everything and starting over, creating a warm and inviting place to eat, relax and chat with friends and family.

When it arrived, my coffee and toastie were tasty enough, but the service was slow and uncaring. I was served by the young woman who'd been eating her lunch and I tried to engage her in conversation too, keen to get a feel for how successful the café was, but she clearly hadn't a clue and seemed anxious to return to the serving counter to do very little except stare out the window.

\* \* \*

I found the estate agency representing the sale on a side street. The agent I spoke to – Ian – seemed far more willing to have a chat and eagerly handed me a copy of the sale particulars. He confirmed that there were only three storeys but the top floor was double-height as I'd suspected and, while not used as accommodation now, previously had been. He also told me that the owner was desperate to sell because his family were emigrating to Australia in August. There'd been a couple of viewings when it had gone on the market at the start of the year, but nothing since and definitely no offers.

Clutching the particulars, I wandered up and down Castle Street a few more times, my heart racing and my head spinning with ideas. I felt almost dizzy with excitement and had to sit down in a small park at the end of the street to calm myself down. This was it! I'd found my café. I'd found my home.

\* \* \*

Ian arranged for me to meet the owner, Jed Ferguson, for a full tour the following day. I arrived just before the café closed. Jed was in his mid-to-late twenties, with thick blond hair and green eyes shielded by ridiculously long lashes. Let's face it, he was gorgeous... and boy did he know it. As he shook my hand, he looked me up and down – hate that – and said, 'You're younger than I expected.'

A feeling of instant dislike powered through me and I gave him my hardest stare. 'What's age got to do with anything? Are you going to show me round or should I ask the estate agent?'

The shocked expression on his face was priceless. I suspected nobody had ever put him in his place like that before. Ha! If he'd hoped to go on a charm offensive, he'd picked the wrong woman. No man was *ever* going to charm me again.

With a shrug, he reached past me, turned the shabby cardboard sign round to 'closed' and locked the door.

'Welcome to Ferguson's.' He indicated that I should sit down. 'I'll give you a bit of background then take you for a tour, if that's okay with you.'

Nodding, I sat down opposite him.

'It's a family business. It was originally a carpet shop but my parents bought the building and re-opened it as a café in the eighties. They ran it together and I had a part-time job here throughout school and college. When they retired, I somehow ended up working here full-time, although that was never the intention.'

He paused and looked at me expectantly but I wasn't going to ask him to expand. I was here to fact-find and make another enormous life-changing decision – not to listen to his life story.

'Anyway,' he continued, 'My wife, Ingrid, is a sun-worshipper and can't stand the English weather. She's been keen to emigrate to Australia for ages and I'm running out of excuses to say no. Our daughters are aged two and four so, if we go now, there's loads of time to get settled before they're ready to start school. It'll be weird, though. I've only ever lived in Whitsborough Bay. Are you from—?'

I scraped the chair back and rose to my feet. 'How about that tour?' I knew where that question was heading and I wasn't about to share that information with anyone.

'Oh. Okay.' He stood up too. 'Kitchen first?'

I followed him behind the serving counter into a cramped but clean kitchen. From the dimensions on the particulars, I knew it was a good size but it was so badly organised, I felt sorry for anyone who worked in there. Some of the equipment looked as though it might have been there since Jed's parents started the café.

I followed him up the wooden staircase to the first floor.

'The top two floors aren't connected,' he said. 'You access the top floor from a private staircase at the back of the café and this is the only access to this floor, although both floors have an external fire escape, of course.'

The first floor was a large but cluttered space. Broken tables and chairs were piled up by the windows along with an old rusting fridge. Who in their right mind would haul a fridge up all those stairs instead of taking it outside and disposing of it properly?

Jed's cheeks coloured as he clocked my stunned expression. At least he had the decency to look embarrassed.

'Erm, it's...' He shuffled on the spot. 'I've kept meaning to clear it out.' He cleared his throat. 'There are toilets up here but most customers use the disabled one on the ground floor. As you can see, it's a good space. It would provide plenty of extra seating if you needed it.'

Clearly they'd never needed it at Ferguson's, or at least not over the past few years, which would make it easier for me to put my offer to him. It was obvious that he was running a failing – or should that be failed – business and there was no way I was prepared to pay for a business that had no decent assets and no goodwill. With the dilapidated exterior and tired interior, Ferguson's didn't exactly scream, 'Amazing business opportunity' but I could see through it. There was massive potential but I'd be starting completely from scratch and therefore I only wanted to buy the premises, not the business.

'How many covers do you have?' I asked.

He frowned. 'Covers?'

'How many people can you serve at once?'

He shrugged. 'There are twelve tables downstairs. There used to be thirteen but...'

I opened the door to check out the two unisex toilets while he rabbited on about removing a table because a member of staff was superstitious about having thirteen. I still wanted to know how many covers they could do but he obviously didn't have a clue. The footprint was similar to one of the branches of Vanilla Pod so I could make a good guess myself.

'What are the business rates?' I asked as we made our way back downstairs.

'I'm not sure.'

'Turnover?'

'Erm...'

'Utility costs?'

'I think Ian has those details,' Jed said, heading towards a door at the back of the ground floor.

Perhaps it was mean of me to quiz him, especially when the rates and utilities *were* on the particulars, but a good business owner should have details like that at their fingertips so, for me, it was more evidence of a failed business.

As we walked up the two flights to the top floor, Jed started wittering on about his move to Australia again. 'Have you ever been there?'

'No.'

'Neither have we. Is it crazy to up sticks and move to somewhere you've never visited?'

Not crazy at all. I'd just done it myself. But I wasn't going to share that with him. 'Depends on the circumstances.'

'The thing I'm most worried about is taking my girls away from both sets of grandparents. It's not right, is it? Would you move away from your family like that?'

Family. I stopped dead on the stairs, trying to steady my racing heart. I'd tried so hard not to think of them all week but now my foster parents were so vivid in my mind that I could almost smell Kirsten's perfume. They'd be back from their holidays and would hopefully have found my letter. What would they have made of it? Had they been upset? Angry? What lies would Leanne and Garth have told them? I'd done the right thing by leaving but, at that very moment, I missed them so much, I could barely catch my breath.

'Are you okay?' Jed asked, turning round.

I clung onto the handrail. *Act normal.* 'Yes, erm... dust in my eye.' I swiped at the ready tears and took a deep breath. *Focus.* 'Ian tells me it used to be a flat upstairs?'

'It was but that was a long time ago. The previous owner turned it into a load of small storage rooms and we never got round to changing it. My parents didn't want to live at work and neither did Ingrid.' He unlocked the door and flicked on a light. 'Are you thinking of living here?'

I didn't get a chance to answer because I stepped into the 'flat' and gasped. Oh. Definitely not what I was expecting. But he hadn't lied. He'd said it was a load of small storage rooms and that was exactly what it was. It looked like somebody had been handed a pallet of wood, some plasterboard, a nail gun and been issued with the challenge to fit in as many stud walls as was humanly possible.

'It's big,' Jed said. 'I know it might not look it but you could probably convert it into a two-bedroom flat.'

'It's like a storage unit,' I muttered, wandering down the first of several narrow corridors and looking into the door-less entrances to each room. Some rooms contained crates of paperwork and others stored old furniture but the ones furthest from the stairs were empty.

'There's a bathroom,' Jed called to me, his voice muted by the mass of plasterboard. 'And there's the fittings for a kitchen although I can't remember where. I never come up here.'

I placed my hands on my hips and took a few deep breaths. Downstairs was good. I could work with downstairs. But the flat? It would need completely gutting and it would need a heck of a good builder with major vision because seeing a way of converting this shambolic storage unit into a home was a stretch too far for my imagination. Although it did give me another bargaining chip.

'I didn't come across a bathroom,' I said, returning to Jed.

He pointed. 'You have to go round that way to get to it. It's in the corner.'

I followed another narrow corridor to a room in the far back corner and nearly laughed out loud. There was an avocado-coloured toilet, a matching sink hanging off the wall, and ancient-looking pipework where a bath had once been.

'Seen enough?' Jed asked when I made my way back to him again.

'Plenty. I can see why you and your parents never got round to doing anything up here. That's a hell of a project for someone.'

His face fell. 'But not you?'

'I didn't say that.'

'So you *are* interested?' His eyes twinkled and he gave me what I'm sure he thought was a charming smile but it just wound me up.

'I need to do some number-crunching. If I did make you an offer, it won't be anywhere near the asking price because of the amount of work needed.' I opened the door and started to make my way downstairs.

Jed was hot on my heels. 'I'll admit it needs work up here but there's nothing wrong with downstairs.'

I paused on the first-floor landing, turned and raised an eyebrow, but I managed to stop myself from verbalising my thoughts. The business probably meant a lot to his family and I wasn't going to insult him but if he thought there was nothing wrong with the café part, then he clearly had blinkers on and that probably explained why the business had failed.

Stepping through the door and into the café, a flutter of excitement made me smile. This was definitely the place. I could feel it. I wiped the smile from my face before I turned to face Jed, adopting a strong, confident business-like tone. 'I'll do some thinking tonight and get in touch with the estate agent tomorrow either way.'

'Can you give me any indication?' he asked, sheepishly.

I sighed. 'I've already given you it. If I offer, it won't be at asking price.'

'Why not? It's a good price.'

'It isn't.'

'It is.'

'No it isn't,' I snapped.

His expression hardened. 'What would you know about the price of businesses round here? You're obviously not local with that accent and you look like you're barely out of college so—'

'You can stop right there.' I fixed him with a hard stare and injected every bit of strength and maturity I could find into my voice. 'I may be young but I was brought up in a family business running a chain of bistros so I know what this business is worth. It's basically a greasy spoon café that's barely ticking over so, if I do decide buy, I'll be buying the premises only.'

'You can't do that,' he cried. 'It's the business that's for sale.'

'And I'm really sorry but it's not a viable business.'

Suddenly, he could quote facts and figures, trying to convince me it was a good going concern.

I cut him off again. 'I have to go. You need to sell and I'm looking for premises but If I make an offer, it will be for the premises only and nothing will sway me otherwise. It will be up to you whether you accept that or not but bear in mind that I'm a cash buyer ready to go immediately. Would you risk walking away from that when you're emigrating in about three months' time? I certainly wouldn't in your position. But, it's your choice. I'll see myself out.'

'It's the business that's for sale, not the premises,' he called. 'The business.'

'And the premises are the only thing of value,' I snapped back. It took every ounce of self-control to stop me from slamming the door behind me. I stormed down to the park at the end of the street and flung myself onto one of the benches overlooking the sea, muttering under my breath. Viable business, my arse. But as the sea breeze cooled my flaming cheeks and I felt the anger ebb away, I wondered if I'd been rude. Yes, I probably had been but he'd pushed me. He was trying to pull a swift one by selling a duff business and he'd tried that on the wrong person. No man was ever going to dupe me again. Ever.

I spent the evening in my room at the B&B scribbling sketches of how the downstairs of Ferguson's could look when I got my hands on it. I didn't need to do any number-crunching. I already knew what I'd offer.

Ian didn't flinch when I called into the estate agency the following morning and presented my decision.

'I think that's a fair offer considering the state of the premises,' he said. 'If you want to take a seat, I'll ring Mr Ferguson and put it to him right now.' He headed for a desk at the far end of the open plan office.

I couldn't stop fidgeting as I sat in the leather tub chair in the reception area, watching Ian's facial expressions and trying to work out whether they meant good or bad news. Jed *had* to accept. He'd be an idiot not to and, as Ian said, it *was* a fair offer considering the work required.

'He hasn't accepted but he hasn't said no,' Ian said after an excruciating five minutes. 'He needs to talk to his family. He wanted me to push you for more but I made it clear that it was a best and final offer, like you said.'

There was nothing I could do except wait it out. And wait I did. Not very patiently. I explored all the other streets in Whitsborough Bay, the surrounding villages and the nearby towns but nothing compared to Castle Street and what Ferguson's could become. I found an empty one-bed flat to rent above a newsagent's a few doors down on the other side of Castle Street and took out a six-month lease. It was a cheaper and more practical option than staying in a B&B and, even though I wanted to move into the flat above the café, I'd have to prioritise the retail side over accommodation so it could be quite some time before I'd be able to live onsite. Assuming Jed saw sense and accepted my offer.

Finally, a week after my tour, Ian phoned. My heart leapt seeing his name on my screen, then sank when I was told that Jed couldn't accept. I could picture Ian cringing as he made a feeble attempt at further negotiation. By then, I'd done masses more research, sourcing a builder and equipment. I knew roughly how much it was going to cost to convert the café and I wasn't willing to raise my price so I left the offer on the table, hoping Jed would snap before I did.

He did. It took him nearly a fortnight to finally accept but on Thursday 3rd June, halfway through the late half-term holiday, Ian called to say that Jed had reluctantly accepted my offer and hoped I appreciated what a bargain I'd secured.

'What made him change his mind?' I asked.

'He says it was the arrival of June taking them that step closer to emigrating.'

I could hear the doubt in Ian's voice. 'And why do you *really* think he changed his mind?'

'Strictly off the record, I think half-term has done it. The town has been heaving but the café has been quiet and I think it was a wake-up call that you were right about the business failing. It's too big a risk for them not to have it sold and sorted before they go so, congratulations, you'll soon be the new owner of Ferguson's.'

Things moved quickly after that. A 'sold' sign appeared outside the café the following day and Ferguson's officially ceased trading on the Saturday. I hadn't expected him to close quite so soon but, if Ian was right about the poor half-term sales, there was no point in prolonging things, especially when the café was probably trading at a loss each day.

Via Ian, we agreed that I'd take over on Thursday 1st July to allow time for Jed to clear the café and for our solicitors to do their thing. From my vantage point in my rented flat down the street, I watched as a skip was delivered outside Ferguson's on the Monday after they closed. Jed met a couple of builders there shortly afterwards and, over the next two days, the three of them steadily emptied the café of all the furnishings and equipment into the skip or a lorry. Every load took me closer to my dream and I was chomping at the bit to get inside.

On Wednesday morning, before any of the shops opened for the day, I made my way over to the café and peered through the windows. I couldn't see into the kitchen but everything else had been stripped out including the serving counter and shelving. Had that been a conscious decision that I probably wouldn't want to keep anything or had it been a case of sticking two fingers up to me, making sure I couldn't have anything I hadn't paid for. Either way, Jed had done me a favour, saving me the cost of having it all ripped out myself.

'Imagining how it's going to look?'

I jumped at his voice and banged my head on the window.

'Sorry,' he said. 'I didn't mean to startle you.'

I rubbed my head. 'It's fine. No permanent damage.'

We both stared at each other for a moment. What could I say? *I'm sorry your business failed.* I did feel a fleeting moment of sympathy but, ultimately, I'd done him a favour. He'd sold up and had plenty of time to get his affairs in order before starting a new life on the other side of the world.

'We've cleared everything out,' he said. 'It's in the hands of the solicitors now.'

'Thank you.'

'Soon be yours. Are you excited?'

I frowned, surprised at his friendly tone. 'Very. I can't wait to get in there. I've already got a builder lined up and a rapidly-filling storage unit.'

'If you want to get started, I have no objections. It's empty. I'm only here today to take the final meter readings because I forgot to do it yesterday. I won't be back again.'

I frowned at him. 'What's the catch?'

He shook his head, smiling. 'There's no catch. The place is empty so, if you're ready to get going, you might as well make a three-week headstart and be open in time to catch the summer trade.'

'So what's in it for you?'

He laughed gently. 'Are you always this suspicious of people? Why does there have to be a catch or something in it for me?'

'Because I generally find that people only do nice things to serve their own purpose.'

He put his hands up in surrender. 'I'm the one taking the risk here. I'd be handing over the keys before you've paid me. But it's up to you. The offer's there. I can drop the keys off with Ian when I'm done here or you can wait another three weeks and get started then.'

I looked into his eyes and he seemed genuine enough. Not that I was a good judge of character after what Leanne and Garth did. I couldn't think how he could benefit, though. He was right; I'd be the one accessing the building before I'd paid him a penny and I was the one who'd be able to open in time for the lucrative summer trade.

'Thank you. You're on.' I held out my hand and we shook on it and, for the first time, I gave him a genuine smile. Maybe not all people were bad.

Turns out I should have trusted my first instinct. Jed was no different to Leanne or Garth. He used, he manipulated and he lied. Two weeks later – a week before the official completion – my builder, Owen, and his team had made massive progress. They'd skimmed the walls, sanded and varnished the stairs, laid new floors, and re-fitted the kitchen. The biggest difference was outside, though. With the ripped canopy gone and the whole exterior repaired and painted in a warm peach, it now looked classy instead of tired. It was taking shape very nicely and I was on an absolute high. Another two to three weeks and we'd be open for business.

Then Ian phoned. There was another offer on the table of ten grand more and I could up my offer or lose the business.

'He can't do that,' I yelled down the phone. 'I've spent a fortune on work already.'

'You're not the official owner yet,' he replied sharply. 'You should *never* have done anything before contracts were exchanged. I'm sorry, but I don't see that you have a choice.'

'Then give me Jed's number and I'll have it out with him.' I was actually shaking with rage.

'You know I can't do that.'

'This is so unfair. I can't talk about it right now. I'll have to call you back when I'm not so mad.' I hung up on him.

I nearly wore a hole in the carpet pacing up and down in the flat and stamping my feet. It was so typical of how people worked. Ian was right; I had no leg to stand on. I *should* have insisted on an early exchange of contracts. I *should* have had something in writing but, once again, I'd been naïve and I'd let a man dupe me. Jed was probably rolling around laughing that he'd managed to screw me over like that. Would I ever learn?

When I'd finally calmed down, I had to accept that I had no choice because I was far too financially and emotionally committed already. I called Ian back and reluctantly increased my offer in response to Jed's blackmail. Ian didn't appreciate the use of that word. He could package it up however he wanted but we both knew I'd been conned and I was livid with myself for allowing it to happen.

The following Monday, contracts were exchanged ahead of Thursday's completion but I arrived at the café to find more bad news.

'Did you get a full structural survey?' asked Owen.

I shook my head. 'Just a valuation.' My stomach sank. 'Dare I ask why?'

'Come with me.'

I followed him up the internal stairs to the flat. 'I know we're not doing anything with the flat yet but after that torrential downpour last night, I thought I'd check there'd been no leaks.'

He pushed open the door and I followed him to the far corner and into the poor excuse for a bathroom. Chunks of soggy plasterboard lay on the floor and there were dirty marks where water had trickled down the walls.

'A standard valuation should have picked this up,' Owen said. 'But someone has bodge-repaired it recently. These plasterboards are new.'

'I wonder who'd do something devious like that,' I said flatly, my fists clenching.

'We'll need to let it dry out but then repairing it is going to have to be a priority to avoid further damage.'

I clenched my teeth as he gave me a rough estimate which cemented my absolute contempt for Jed because, on top of the offer increase, it meant I'd been ripped off to the tune of about twenty grand. And the real rub was that it was my fault again for not commissioning a full structural survey. Another valuable lesson learned the hard way. Don't trust anyone. Ever.

My first shift in The Chocolate Pot after taking down the Christmas decorations always felt flat. With the fairy lights, decorations and tree packed away until November, we were back to everyday normality. The excitement was gone, the anticipation was gone and somehow the magic was gone. And, despite how emotionally draining I found the festive period each year, I missed it. Talk about a contradiction, desperate for it all to go away, then feeling sad when it did.

It was mid-morning on a dull but dry Monday. The upstairs was closed and the downstairs was about half-full, mainly with elderly shoppers meeting friends for coffee and cake. I slowly ran a damp cloth over the counter. It didn't need cleaning but it gave me something to do.

'Penny for them,' Sheila said, emerging from the kitchen, wiping her hands on a tea towel.

'I'm not sure they're worth a penny, Sheila. I was just thinking about how different the place looks with all the decorations gone.'

Sheila nodded. 'I said the exact same thing to my Eric when we took ours down at home. Shame we can't have that Christmas magic all year round. Mind you, I think this place has its own magic all the time. There's always been something special about The Chocolate Pot.'

She grabbed a mug and filled it with hot water. 'Do you want a drink?'

'No thanks. I've just had one. You really think it's magical in here?' Compliments about the café always made me feel warm inside.

'My Eric says I'm soft in the head when I say stuff like this but I've always had this unshakeable feeling that someone's watching over The Chocolate Pot, making it a warm and happy place to be.' She turned to me and smiled, her eyebrows raised with an unspoken question.

*Yes. I feel it. Every single day.* But I couldn't tell Sheila that so I shrugged. 'I'm glad you like it here.'

I watched her swirl her teabag then drop it into the bin. 'My Eric says I talk nonsense. He says it's because I love my job, work with some great people and this place is so colourful, but I'm not so sure. There's something about The Chocolate Pot. I can be in a right foul mood then I step through the door and I'm instantly lifted.'

'Definitely the sea of colour.' I hoped my voice sounded light-hearted and my expression didn't betray the emotions swirling inside of me.

'You've created something really special here.' She smiled at me. 'Oh well, best be getting on. Those quiches won't bake themselves.'

I leaned against the counter when she disappeared into the kitchen, my heart racing. Why hadn't I been able to respond properly? All I needed to say was: *Yes, Sheila, I feel it too. I think it's my parents.* Would that really have been so difficult? I sighed and shook my head. Yes, it would.

Rinsing out a cloth, I wiped down the front of the drinks fridges. Why hadn't Sheila directly asked me if I felt the same? The question had been clear in her expression but why hadn't she said it out loud? My shoulders drooped. Of course. Because anytime anyone asked me anything that wasn't about the business, I clammed up. I changed the subject. I went quiet. So they'd stopped asking. They'd stopped trying to get to know me because I'd made it obvious I wasn't willing to share. Somewhere along the way, they'd stopped sharing information with me too. Did I really know any of my team? I knew that Cody and Lana were going to university in September, but did I know what they were studying or their career aspirations? Not a clue. I knew Niamh was going on maternity leave, but I knew nothing about her partner, or even if she had a partner. Why wasn't she coming back after maternity leave? I'd never asked.

\* \* \*

'I'm a bad person,' I said to Hercules when I returned to the flat after work. 'I've shut them all out. They've got families and lives that I've shown no interest in. I've never asked questions and I've closed down conversation-starters. For what? Because I was too scared to let anyone into my life so I've avoided being let into theirs.'

Starting tomorrow, things were going to have to change. I wasn't about to let the world and his wife know about my past, but I could open up about a few things. Why had I never told anyone about Hercules or either of his predecessors? Why didn't I admit I was into hygge? Why didn't I tell them I was The Cobbly Crafter? And why didn't I ask them about their lives? Why was every conversation about work?

Glancing at the clock, I tutted. I needed to get sorted and out to my meeting. I lifted Hercules off my knee and prepared him some fresh vegetables.

'Should I tell the team about you?' I asked him as he tucked into his food.

But doubt set in. How would I suddenly introduce a giant house bunny into a conversation about the day's specialist brownies? Maybe I'd start with asking them questions instead and gradually build up to sharing information. Maybe.

* * *

I felt guilty leaving Hercules on his own for the evening, but it was time for my Bay Trade meeting. They were only held monthly so I didn't like to miss one. Bay Trade was a group of entrepreneurs from in and around Whitsborough Bay. It had been set up by an artist and jewellery-maker called Skye, her partner, Stuart, and their best friend, Nick. The idea was to share business news and ideas, help each other, promote each other and exchange services for 'mates' rates', or even for free where appropriate. They only let one of each type of business join so I was the only café-owner in town which made me feel pretty special and was another reason for keeping up regular attendance.

Many of the Castle Street traders were members including Carly, Jemma who ran the teddy bear shop, Charlee who owned the chocolate shop, and Ginny who owned The Wedding Emporium on the other side of The Chocolate Pot. Sarah, the owner of Seaside Blooms, had married Nick a few years back so she was an active committee member. I classed those people – and many of the other Castle Street traders – as friends yet, like my team, I barely knew any of them. I'd attended monthly meetings, gone on pub crawls and leaving dos with them, and had helped them all out with their businesses at one time or another yet, with the exception of Carly, I only knew superficial details about their lives and they knew nothing about me. I hadn't wanted to let anyone in to hurt me again but I'd gone so much further than that. I'd completely retreated from the world.

Running down the stairs, I rang Carly. 'Hi, it's me. Are you coming to Bay Trade?'

'Oh my goodness, is it tonight? I've completely lost track of what day we are. Hang on.' I listened to a muffled conversation, presumably with Liam. 'Hi, Tara. Yes. Give me five minutes to change my top and I'll be down. Shall I knock for you?'

'Yes please.'

I sat down on one of the chairs by the window but couldn't sit still. My heart was racing and my palms were sweating. I felt like I was on that precipice again, like when I'd talked to Carly about my family but, this time, I wasn't torn between screaming and crying. This time, I wanted to jump, knowing that there was a safety net to catch me. There were people round me who cared. I hadn't let them in, but they genuinely cared. It was time.

\* \* \*

Carly and I walked up to Minty's together – a popular bar at the top of town. The owner was a member of Bay Trade and was happy for us to use the function room upstairs with Monday being a quiet night in the bar.

Our meetings were fairly informal but there was always a slot at the start where the members could share news or flag up any issues with which they wanted support.

'Good evening,' Skye said, 'and a Happy New Year to you all. I hope you had a good Christmas and New Year, business-wise and celebration-wise. I have a few messages from members. Karen and Steff from Bay Fitness are offering a twenty-five per cent discount on the first three months of bootcamps to anyone who signs up this month, but they're making that forty per cent for Bay Trade members which is an exceptional saving. So have a word with Karen and Steff if you're interested, and please spread the word among your customers.'

'We've got some fliers if anyone can put any in their business,' Karen said, waving some fliers in the air. I smiled at her. Karen ran my Pilates class on a Tuesday evening and I was pretty certain she ran a bootcamp right before it. I'd never looked into bootcamp but maybe I'd give it a try at those prices. Like Colin with the same order every day, I had definitely become a creature of habit and I was the only one who could change that.

'Mandy's moving premises,' Skye said. 'Sleek Cut will be in that new row of shops at the top of Ocean Ravine from next week and she's offering discounts to anyone producing one of her fliers.'

Mandy, Bay Trade's hairdresser, also waved a wad of fliers in the air.

'And, speaking of premises,' Skye continued, 'the last bit of news comes from outside the group. We've been approached by someone looking for premises in the town centre, ideally on Castle Street, although they're open to other locations if the premises are big enough. If any of you are thinking of selling up later this year or know of anyone who is, please let one of the committee know.'

'Who is it?' someone shouted.

Skye shrugged and looked at her partner, Stuart, suggesting she wasn't sure.

'The person who approached us has asked to remain anonymous,' Stuart said. 'Sorry, guys.'

'Why anonymous?' I asked. 'Are they planning to set up in competition with one of us?'

It was Stuart's turn to shrug. 'I genuinely don't know what they're planning to do. All I know is that they aren't doing it until late in the year.'

'Anyone else got anything they want to raise?' Skye asked.

I took a deep breath and stood up. 'Yes. Me.' I moved to the front to stand alongside Skye and Stuart. 'I did some thinking over New Year. I've got an idea, and I wondered if anyone would like to join me. Between us, we've got an amazing amount of knowledge and experience in how to run a business and I'm sure we've also got some valuable experience in what not to do.' I paused as I took in the smiles and nods of heads. 'My proposal is to work with local colleges and the university to establish a mentoring programme for any students or even any staff who might be thinking of setting up their own business. It doesn't have to be something big like setting up a shop or café. It could be anything like making cards to sell at craft fairs, offering guitar lessons, tutoring, dog-walking, vlogging. We could provide advice and guidance on their business plan, how to keep their accounts, how to handle marketing and publicity. It may be that students work with one mentor or they work with several of us depending on our areas of expertise. Anyone interested in joining me?'

I had a heart-stopping moment when the room was silent, then hands started shooting in the air and there were murmurs of 'great idea' and 'I'm in'.

'Sounds like you've got lots of interest,' Skye said. 'I'm certainly up for it. How do you want to proceed?'

'I propose that anyone who's interested meets at The Chocolate Pot at half seven next Monday evening and we throw a few ideas around. I might even provide drinks on the house.'

'And brownies?' someone shouted.

I laughed. 'Ooh, now you're pushing it. But, if you want to find out if I do, you'll have to come along, won't you?'

Heart thumping, I retreated to my seat beside Carly. I'd run staff meetings but I'd never stood up and addressed a large group like that in the whole of my life. It had given me quite a buzz, especially when they reacted so positively.

'Go, you!' Carly whispered. 'I'm loving that idea. I'm definitely in.'

'Thank you. I just hope some of them turn up on Monday.'

'They will. I know it.'

Ninety minutes or so later, Carly and I walked back towards Castle Street together.

'Do you need to rush back, or have you got time for a hot chocolate?' I asked as we approached our end of the cobbles.

'There's something on your mind, isn't there?'

I nodded and took a deep breath. 'I want to tell you about Garth.'

## 11

I was extremely grateful for everything that Kirsten and Tim Sanderson did for me financially and I never took it for granted, but I didn't need a private education, holidays abroad and a wardrobe full of designer clothes to make me happy. What I needed was stability and people who genuinely cared about me and I was very fortunate because they also gave me that. And they gave me a big sister.

Leanne was beautiful and, as far as I could see, it was on the inside as well as the outside. She exuded confidence and she taught me to believe in myself. That's the one thing I will always remain glad about because she turned a mouse of a girl into a self-assured woman and that strength of character has always remained with me.

Always immaculately turned-out, Leanne made me her pet project. She taught me how to tame my frizzy curls into sleek waves, how to apply make-up and how to shave/wax/pluck. Over the years, we must have spent a phenomenal number of hours sitting at her dressing table or mine, preening ourselves. She regularly took me shopping, educating me in different designer labels and how to accessorise. I eagerly lapped it all up although it wasn't because I was interested in handbags or shoes – it was because I loved spending time with Leanne and those were the things she seemed to enjoy.

Thankfully our relationship wasn't only about vanity. She occasionally took me to the cinema, the theatre or museums. Considering there was a seven-year age difference and she was therefore in a very different place to me physically and emotionally when I arrived on the scene, Leanne was exceptionally generous with her time.

From the moment I moved in, Leanne had a constant swarm of devoted male followers round her, some of whom she introduced as gay friends, others as hetero friends. She always had a boyfriend in tow too and they were without exception gorgeous and rich, and usually much older than her. As far as I could tell, she never had her heart broken, always being the one to end the relationship.

When I was sixteen, I returned to The Larches after my final school exam, expecting the house to be empty because Tim and Kirsten were at work. I was therefore surprised to find Leanne there, pacing up and down in the lounge. She was still officially living at home but spent most evenings staying over with her boyfriend or friends.

I'd barely removed my school blazer before she told me she had a congratulations-on-finishing-your-exams gift for me, which she knew I was going to love. I remember looking round the room expectantly, but there were no gift bags or boxes.

'It's in your bedroom,' she squealed, grabbing my hand and running upstairs with me.

I had all sorts of thoughts running through my mind. Perhaps she'd had my room redecorated, or she'd bought me some new clothes. Pausing outside my bedroom door, she insisted on blindfolding me with a furry sleeping mask – essential for maximum impact. Then she opened the door, led me to the bed, and told me to put my hands out and touch my gift.

I did as instructed and screamed as I touched something warm. Shoving the mask away from my eyes, I screamed again. There was a man lying on my bed. A very gorgeous but very shirtless man.

'Hi, Tamara,' he said, flashing me a sexy smile. 'I'm Isaac.'

'Hi,' I muttered, backing away. I looked at Leanne, waiting for the punchline on a joke I didn't understand. Why was there a half-naked man lying on my bed?

She walked round to the other side of the bed, kneeled on it and ruffled his hair. 'Isaac's twenty-eight and he works out which I think is pretty obvious. He's an actor and he's just secured an amazing role. Your boyfriend.'

'This is some sort of joke?'

She raised one perfectly drawn eyebrow at me. 'Do you see anyone laughing?'

'Then I don't understand.'

'What's there to understand, baby sister?' she purred. 'There's a half-naked man on your bed and he's going to play the part of your devoted boyfriend and teach you a few things that I can't.'

My heart started racing and I hardly dared ask the question. 'What sort of things?'

'All sorts of amazing, exciting things. But he'll start with the basics. Like how to kiss, because I know you've got no experience in that yet, have you?'

Colour flooded my cheeks. That was private stuff. And it wasn't my fault. I'd been to an all-girls private school and I didn't have any friends. I wasn't bullied, but everyone knew I was a foster child and 'not one of us' so they avoided me and, if I'm honest, I avoided them too. I put my head down and I studied hard. There were occasional social gatherings with a local boys' school, but I gave them a wide berth. When a school full of girls made me feel invisible, why would I want to add a school full of boys into the mix? So, at age sixteen, I'd never even kissed a boy.

My gut reaction was to turn and run but I still couldn't shake the feeling that this was a joke that I didn't understand and that I'd look like an idiot if I fled.

'Excuse us a moment, Isaac.' Leanne ruffled his hair again, then returned to me, put her arm round my shoulders and led me onto the landing, closing my bedroom door behind her.

'I thought you'd like my present,' she said, her tone dripping with hurt. 'Don't you think he's gorgeous?'

'He is, but—'

'But what? You want to get married and have children one day, yes?'

'Yes, hopefully.'

'And you've had how many boyfriends so far?'

'None.'

'And you've kissed how many boys?'

'None.'

'Oh dear,' she said, dragging out the words for emphasis. 'The thing is, kissing is very important in any relationship. If that's not working, the relationship isn't going to work. Imagine you meet the man of your dreams. You go on this amazing date and he leans in to give you a kiss goodnight, but you don't know what you're doing so it ends up being all awkward and slobbery. Do you think he's going to ask you on another date?'

I didn't like her patronising tone but she had a point. 'Probably not.'

'Definitely not. So that gorgeous beast of a man is your temporary boyfriend – or playmate as I like to think of him – and he's going to teach you all about kissing. And perhaps build up to a few other things. But no sex. He knows that's strictly off limits. A little kissing can't do any harm, though, can it?'

I wasn't sure. It was all new to me.

'Can it?' she prompted, poking me in the ribs.

'I suppose not,' I muttered.

'You could sound a bit more grateful.'

'I am. I think. It's just that, when you said you'd got me a gift, this isn't quite what I was expecting.'

'Giving you what you expect would be boring. Life should be full of the unexpected. Life should be full of Isaacs. So are you ready to go back into your bedroom and play with your gift?'

My cheeks flushed again. 'I'll speak to him.'

'You'll do more than that.'

'Maybe one kiss?'

She rolled her eyes at me then smiled and pulled me into a hug. 'You'll love it. I promise. Just relax and consider it the next part of your education. Your exams are finished and now you're learning a far more important lesson. You're learning about life.'

Opening my bedroom door, I looked towards Isaac lying propped up on his arm, a gentle smile on his lips. An hour or so being taught how to kiss by a man who looked like he'd stepped out of a Hugo Boss advert was not going to be a great hardship. I looked up at Leanne. 'Can he put his shirt back on?'

'Of course he can.' She clicked her fingers at him, making me wince. 'Shirt. Now.'

He did as he was told.

'Would you mind sitting on the edge of the bed instead of lying on it?' I asked him.

Obediently, Isaac adjusted position and gave me a dazzling smile.

Butterflies going crazy in my stomach, I swallowed hard, licked my dry lips and shuffled towards the bed, absolutely terrified.

'Tell you what,' Isaac said, standing up. 'How about we pretend we've just been on a date? We've been to see a romantic film and

I've walked you home. It's been a brilliant evening and I'm about to kiss you goodnight.'

'Okay.'

I looked up into his dark eyes. 'Close your eyes,' he whispered, 'and tilt your head back slightly. Relax your mouth.'

Then, for the first time ever, I felt a man's lips touch against mine.

'That was just a gentle peck on the lips,' Isaac said, 'but now I'm going to kiss you properly. I want you to try and copy what I'm doing.'

'Are you going to put your tongue in my mouth?' I'd seen that on films and overheard girls at school talking about it. The very idea of someone else's tongue in my mouth was repulsive.

'Not this time,' he said. 'We'll build up to that.'

Clearly satisfied that I was taking my education seriously, Leanne left us to it before we kissed again. I definitely relaxed more, knowing we weren't being watched. It never entered my head that she was filming me. Why would it? I trusted Leanne and never in a million years would I have expected her to be so manipulative and devious. Maybe if I'd not been the invisible foster kid at school, I'd have known that having a 'playmate' wasn't normal, but I had no idea. No idea at all.

\* \* \*

After the initial awkwardness and discomfort, I started to enjoy my congratulations-on-finishing-your-exams gift. I started to enjoy it very, very much. Over the next six months or so, my 'education' with Isaac continued. We never went out together and he never came round when Kirsten and Tim were home. Roughly fortnightly, when The Larches was empty, Leanne would arrive with Isaac and brief us both on the 'objectives' for the lesson.

I liked Isaac, but I didn't fall for him. I suppose it's hard to fall for someone when you know nothing about them. I'd always imagined the man I fell in love with would make me laugh, make me feel safe and be there for me no matter what, like Dad had been there for Mum. I imagined he'd be my lighthouse. While I could appreciate Isaac's model good looks and his toned physique, I wasn't shallow enough to be sucked in by appearance. For me, it absolutely was all about the personality and I had no idea who the real Isaac was. Leanne had been very clear that chit-chat was an unnecessary distraction from our objectives.

The practical side of me knew that Isaac didn't love me either but I liked the way he acted like he did. If he really was an actor, he was a good one. Every touch was so tender and he was so attentive to my needs. I once asked him what was in it for him, especially when there was no sex. He laughed and said, 'If someone offered to pay you to do this every fortnight, wouldn't you? Beats waiting tables or pulling pints.' Of course. Money. If it wasn't about sex, it had to be about money. If Leanne was paying him, I suspected she was paying him well.

In the New Year, Leanne announced that Isaac wouldn't be returning and introduced me to Dominic – yet another mature, toned, gorgeous man. My relationship with Isaac had been strictly clothes-on, or at least on my part. He'd taken his shirt off several times and I had to admit that it did feel good running my hand over his chest or down his bare back. Leanne made it clear that Dominic was going to take me to the next level but, again, no sex. My 'objective' was to learn how my body responded and reacted.

I was in my second term at catering college by then and working several evenings in Vanilla Pod so I didn't see Dominic as often as I'd seen Isaac. He was my 'playmate' for well over a year before I received my eighteenth birthday present – Mattia. My 'objective' for my time with Mattia was to learn what I needed to do to please a man.

Leanne continued to educate me in her own way. She'd often remind me that my 'playmates' were our little secret and I must never let her parents know. Alarm bells probably should have sounded but they didn't. Having a secret with my big sister made me feel really special. She'd eagerly lap up all the details about progress in my lessons and paint this beautiful image of the future where I'd meet the man of my dreams and have such a perfect life with him because I knew how to please him and knew how he could please me. I idolised my big sister so much that I never questioned any part of it. Since becoming part of her family, everything Leanne had done with me or for me had seemed to be in my best interests so there was no reason to believe that my 'playmates' weren't a continuation of that care and attention.

Turns out it was all about preparing me for Garth. Everything had been about him, from Leanne teaching me how to look and dress to everything my 'playmates' taught me to the rosy picture of how my happy future could look. Everything. I hadn't a clue that my big sister was grooming me. Perhaps not in the true sense of the word but my 'education' was for one purpose and one purpose only – to prepare me for becoming Garth's wife.

Leanne always emphasised that my 'playmates' weren't proper boyfriends so I should never romanticise them like that. They were teachers and I was to embrace the lessons, but if she or they got the slightest inkling that I'd developed romantic inclinations, they'd be replaced. I'd be lying if I said I wasn't attracted to all three of them and I'd be lying even more if I said I didn't enjoy my lessons because I did. If school had been that much fun, I'd have achieved top grades in every subject. With hindsight, I suppose the pleasure element was another reason why I never questioned the set-up. Nobody was getting hurt, I was learning, I was enjoying learning, and there were plans in place to protect me if I got too involved. What was there to complain about?

\* \* \*

At Christmas, Leanne bought me the most stunning deep-blue evening dress. It had a fitted bodice with dropped straps resting above the elbows and a full-length flowing skirt with a split to the top of the left leg. Accompanying it were high strappy blue sandals and a matching clutch bag. Kirsten and Tim insisted I try it on and they hugged each other when I appeared at the top of the grand staircase. Kirsten shook her head, her eyes sparkling. 'Our little girl is a grown woman now,' she said. 'You are an absolute vision in that.'

I was a little shocked when I saw myself in the mirror. I'd never worn anything quite so grown up. My classmates had likely worn gowns like it at the graduation ball but I hadn't attended, so an evening dress like that was a first for me.

'When will I wear it?' I asked.

Leanne smiled at me. 'Mum and Dad are letting us host a party here on New Year's Eve while they're away. The dress code is black tie and all eyes are going to be on you in that dress, my beautiful baby sister.'

When we had some time alone later that evening, Leanne sidled up to me on the sofa. 'If you love the dress, you'll be beside yourself when you see your main present on New Year's Eve.'

'A new "playmate"?' I whispered, already feeling excited at the prospect.

'A million times better than that,' she said, squeezing my hand. 'You're going to love me forever.'

\* \* \*

After Christmas, Tim whisked Kirsten away to Jamaica. Although Leanne had moved out by this point and was living with her boyfriend, Darryl, she moved back in to keep an eye on me and to prepare for the party. I'd once asked her if Darryl knew about my playmates but she swore he didn't and I had no reason not to believe her.

On the morning of New Year's Eve, Leanne burst into my bedroom and plonked herself down on the edge of my bed. 'Good morning, sleepyhead. Tonight's the night,' she gushed.

I rubbed my eyes. 'For the party?'

'And for your gift. You can't have it until tonight but do you want to know what it is?'

I wriggled into a seated position. 'Yes, please.'

'It's a *real* boyfriend. One you can tell people about. One you can go out on real dates with.'

'You've picked me a boyfriend?' I tried to keep my voice steady, not sure whether to be grateful or insulted that she'd not consulted me. Between long hours at work, family time, and my 'playmates', I'd never had any free time to properly date and I'd have liked the chance to pick my own boyfriend.

'Thank you, Leanne,' she snapped. 'That's so good of you, Leanne.'

'Please don't be like that,' I said. 'It was just a surprise. I assumed you and I would maybe go out to a bar together and I'd meet someone that way.'

'Aw, Tamara, you are so sweet and innocent,' she said, gently pushing a curl away from my eyes. 'It doesn't work like that. Men who pick up girls in bars are only after one thing and we have not spent the last two and a half years investing in your education only to have you jump into bed with the first man who buys you a drink.' She stood up and wandered over to my window, sweeping open the curtains. 'The man you're going to meet tonight has been hand-picked for you by me and I know you're going to fall in love with him instantly because he's everything you've told me you've always dreamed of.'

She returned to the bed and sat down again.

'What's his name?' I asked, my interest definitely piqued.

'His name's Garth Tewkesbury. He's a detective in the Met and on his way to his next big promotion.'

'Wow! So how old is he?'

'Forty.'

My eyes widened. 'Forty? That's more than twice my age.'

'So? Why would you waste time with a boy when you can have a man? Believe me, boys are stupid and pointless. Think about the staff at Vanilla Pod in their early twenties. They're all idiots who spend their time out of work being loud and drunk, aren't they? And the ones in their late twenties. And probably the ones in their thirties too.'

She was right. I'd overheard so many conversations at the end of the shift about drunk nights out or their latest conquests and it all sounded so unappealing.

'Tell me more about Garth,' I said, settling back against my pillow.

\* \* \*

I was so nervous getting ready for the party that my hands were actually shaking. Leanne had to take over and do my make-up for me. All day she'd extolled Garth's virtues and her enthusiasm for him was infectious. Back then, I was the eternal optimist. For me, if my big sister said she'd picked out the man of my dreams, then she'd done exactly that.

Although I'd been quickly reassured that the age difference

wasn't a problem for me, it struck me that it could be for someone else.

'Do you think your parents will mind the age gap?' I asked Leanne as she styled my hair.

'If it was a random forty-year-old, perhaps. But Garth is family.'

I twisted round to face her. 'He's what?' Garth Tewkesbury? The name didn't ring any bells and I thought I'd met everyone in the Sanderson family over the years.

'Turn back round so I can finish your hair.'

Doing as instructed, I waited eagerly for her explanation.

'You know my Uncle Rick?'

'Yes.' He was Tim's much older brother but they weren't particularly close. He lived in the USA and I'd only met him once at a family wedding.

'Uncle Rick is Garth's dad. Garth's parents split up when he was a toddler and it was a nasty divorce. His mum moved away from London taking Garth with her. She completely cut off our side of the family and changed their names so nobody could find them. Garth and I have known each other for years but obviously the name meant nothing to me. It was only when I was telling him about you that we started talking more about families and then discovered we were related.'

'Oh my God! Small world! Do your parents know about him yet?'

'Not yet.' She shrugged. 'I toyed with telling them but I didn't want some big family reunion to get in the way of you meeting him. I'm so convinced he's the one for you that, right here and now, I'll say I reckon the two of you will get married.'

'You really think so?' Even though I'd been a little miffed that Leanne hadn't consulted me, my 'playmates' had been good matches. Could she have nailed it for a future husband? The idea excited, thrilled and terrified me in equal measures.

'I'm certain of it. So I've made a happy ever after for you and Garth my priority. Mum and Dad will understand.'

She beamed at me in the mirror and excitable butterflies swarmed in my stomach. It was going to be the best New Year's Eve ever.

\* \* \*

'He's here,' Leanne whispered, slipping her hand into mine later that evening. The party was in full swing, the music barely audible above the volume of chatter, laughter, and the clink of glasses. Waiting staff circulated the ground floor of The Larches with silver trays of champagne and canapés and, for the past ten minutes, I'd managed to calm my nerves by watching the bar acrobatics of a pair of mixologists making cocktails. But now the nerves were back.

Leanne squeezed my hand. 'Stay calm. Deep breaths.'

'Where is he?'

'He's speaking to Darryl near the door. You'll need to turn round but do it slowly, casually.'

I did as instructed, heart thumping, searching for Leanne's boyfriend and my first glimpse of the man who my sister was convinced I would marry. Oh. My. God.

'What do you think?' she whispered. 'Did I pick well or did I pick well?'

She'd picked well. Garth Tewkesbury was everything I'd ever dreamed of and so much more. Six feet four with an athletic-build, dark hair and chiselled cheekbones, he was a better-looking blend of my three 'playmates', maturity adding to the appeal.

'Gorgeous,' I whispered back.

At that moment, he turned towards us and gave me such a warm and tender smile that my heart melted. I'd half-expected a knowing grin fuelled by an assumption that he'd already won me over but, instead, he looked genuinely thrilled to see me and that smile absolutely did it for me.

He said something to Darryl who nodded, then they both made their way towards Leanne and me.

'Be cool,' she whispered, giving my hand another squeeze before releasing it. 'Remember everything I've taught you.'

As he came closer, I was mesmerised by his piercing blue eyes. He reminded me a lot of a young Mel Gibson. But looks to die for weren't everything and there was no way I'd fall for him unless he had a personality to die for too, no matter how strongly my body was reacting to him.

He kissed Leanne on each cheek and complimented her on her gown before turning to face me.

'This is my sister, Tamara,' she announced proudly. 'Beautiful, isn't she?'

He seemed to drink me in and I realised I was holding my breath, desperate to hear his verdict. Close up, Garth was by far the most attractive man I'd ever seen in real life. Which had to mean that there was a mistake somewhere. Leanne might be right about him being the man of *my* dreams, but there was no way I could be the woman of *his* dreams when he could surely have his pick of stunning women.

'She certainly is,' he said, raising my hand to his mouth and gently kissing it, while his eyes never left mine. 'I can't tell you how much I've been looking forward to meeting you, Tamara.'

Nobody had ever kissed my hand before. I felt like a heroine in an Austen novel, being wooed by an English gent. I had to fight hard not to ruin it all by giggling childishly, fluttering my eyelashes and saying something stupid.

I took a deep breath and turned on what I hoped was a confident and self-assured smile. 'It's a pleasure to meet you, Garth.'

Leanne and Darryl made their excuses and moved away, leaving us alone. Garth selected two flutes of champagne from a passing waitress.

'To the New Year and to new beginnings,' he suggested, clinking his glass against mine.

I repeated the toast and took a dainty sip, even though I really wanted to gulp it down for courage.

'Leanne tells me you have a talent for baking and that your brownies are the best she's ever tasted.'

'Brownies were one of my dad's specialities,' I said. 'We often made them together when I was little and we loved to experiment with flavours, although not always with great success such as...' I tailed off, hearing Leanne's voice in my head telling me not to witter if I got nervous.

Garth didn't seem to mind. He steered me towards a couple of high-backed chairs that had just become free. 'What was your biggest disaster?'

'Banana and custard.'

He laughed. 'I love banana and custard and I love brownies but together...?'

'Exactly. Never try it.'

He leaned in closer, his leg resting against mine, his eyes twinkling. 'Tell me more about your dad...'

It seemed he had a personality to die for too. For the next hour, he remained completely focused on me, asking me about my real parents and sharing the challenges he'd had being brought up by a mother who hated his father so much that she told Garth he was dead.

He made me feel as though I was the only person in the room, as though everything I said was the most interesting or funniest thing he'd ever heard. People kept passing us and saying hello and he'd smile politely but never lose focus from our conversation. Best of all, he made me laugh. Not flirty showing-off laughter, but proper belly laughter.

He apologised that he was going to have to circulate for a while but would join me again before midnight. As he moved round the room, laughing and chatting, he repeatedly caught my eye and smiled, making my heart flutter. It was hard to remain focused on my conversations with any of the other guests when all I could think about was midnight and being with Garth once more.

At 11.30 p.m., he returned to me and asked if there was somewhere quiet we could go. 'This party is superb but it's loud and chaotic. If it's okay with you, I'd really like to kiss you at midnight and I'd like that moment to be as special and beautiful as the person I'd be kissing.'

And that's how we ended up on the roof terrace outside Kirsten and Tim's bedroom with fireworks exploding round us and inside me as Garth gave me that life-changing heart-melting wonderful first kiss.

And that's the evening I fell head over heels in love with the man my sister had hand-picked for me who seemed to be a match for me in every possible way. The man who asked me about my past and cared about my memories. The man who encouraged me to talk about my passion for baking and crafting. The man who made me laugh. Of course, I realised later that he knew exactly how to make me laugh and he knew exactly how to make me fall in love with him because Leanne had told him everything there was to know about me. She'd told him which emotional buttons to press. Just like my 'playmates', everything Garth said and did that night – and beyond – was an act.

* * *

We started dating. Proper old-fashioned dates where he'd turn up in a suit and I'd wear a pretty dress. We both had work and our hours clashed so we only had Tuesday evenings and Sunday afternoons together. He'd take me out for a meal or to the theatre on the Tuesday, with Sundays being a walk, a museum or a boat trip. He was as attentive as ever and always a perfect gentleman.

Kirsten and Tim were stunned to discover that I was dating their nephew. They insisted on having him over for dinner as soon as possible, eager to be reacquainted. They weren't keen on the age gap, but he was part of their family, Leanne vouched for him and, perhaps unsurprisingly, he charmed the pants off them and allayed any worries.

Every date with Garth felt like a first date, wondering when he would hold my hand and, even better, when I'd be able to melt into one of those incredible kisses again. It really was the dream relationship, the only downside being that I'd have liked to have seen him a lot more often than I did.

He whisked me away to Paris for New Year two years after we met and proposed to me on New Year's Eve at the top of the Eiffel Tower. I was twenty and he was forty-two. We immediately set the date for New Year's Eve the following year and I couldn't wait to become Garth's wife.

\* \* \*

Slumping back in my chair at the back of The Chocolate Pot, I looked at Carly and shook my head. 'I should have realised that nothing and nobody is that perfect. I should have realised that real relationships aren't packed with back-to-back movie-perfect moments. But I didn't. I was so naïve.'

'It wasn't your fault,' Carly said. 'I don't think any relationship is perfect all the time but there are plenty that are pretty close so I don't think it's unreasonable for you to have believed everything he said and did.'

'You're not just saying that?'

She shook her head. 'You said the marriage didn't last long...?'

'Just over four months and then...' I started shaking. 'And then I discovered it had all been a lie.'

'You weren't really married?'

'No. I was properly, legally married but that was about the only real thing about it. I found out that Leanne and Garth...'

I closed my eyes and tried to find the strength to go on. My palms were sweating and my head was thumping.

'You don't look so good,' Carly said. 'Do you want some water?'

I opened my eyes and slowly shook my head. 'I'm sorry to do this again. I thought I could tell you the rest but I'm going to have to stop there for now.'

'You look drained.'

'I feel it. It was hard re-living it. I know you probably have a million questions but—'

'It's your story to tell in your own time,' she reassured me. 'I can tell how painful it is.' She stood up and hugged me tightly. 'I think you're amazing, for what you've been through and for facing up to it now.'

'I don't feel very amazing. I feel like an idiot for letting them manipulate me and lie to me.'

'Was he seeing Leanne too?' she asked, pulling her coat on. 'Is that what happened?'

I sighed and nodded. 'Something like that.'

As I let Carly out, I shuddered. Something like that? If only it had been that simple.

## 12

Tears rained down my cheeks and my legs shook as I slowly made my way back upstairs to the flat after Carly left. Telling someone for the first time ever about my 'playmates' had been mortifying but that embarrassing revelation wasn't a patch on what happened next.

I sat down heavily on one of the stairs as a wave of nausea overcame me. I felt clammy and sweaty, my pulse racing, at the thought of putting into words what caused me to flee from London and sever all ties with my former life. Sitting on the cold step for several minutes, I took deep gulps of air until the nausea subsided and I was able to pull myself to my feet.

When I'd made the decision to tell Carly about Garth, I knew it would be difficult but I really thought I'd be able to tell her all of it. Actually saying it out loud for the first time was so much more emotionally and mentally draining than I'd anticipated but I'd made a start. Was saying it aloud enough to help me heal, though? Only time would tell.

As soon as I opened the door to the flat, Hercules bounded over to me and nudged at my legs. Scooping him up, I nuzzled his fur, feeling safe and loved. 'I've missed you, Hercules. I'm sorry I've been out all evening.'

I must have stood there for about ten minutes, holding him close, drawing strength from his warmth.

'It's all out in the open,' I told him, sitting down on the sofa and stroking his back. 'Well, not quite all of it, but I've told Carly the start and she didn't think I was weird and run away. That's a relief, isn't it?'

I lit the log burner and we sat together for half an hour or so as I watched the flames flickering and, with each passing minute, I felt more and more relaxed. I'd needed that. I'd needed to release it.

Carly wouldn't tell anyone. She'd repeatedly assured me of that as she hugged me goodbye, but she hadn't needed to. I knew I could trust her. She'd been such a good listener, letting me get through it in my own time instead of constantly firing questions at me.

'Wait here,' I said to Hercules. Retrieving the yellow photo album from the dresser, I sat back on the sofa and opened it. It was the only time I'd done that outside of Christmas Day since leaving London.

My fingers lightly brushed over the photos of Mum and Dad. When I'd moved into foster care, I only had three photos – one of me with Mum, one of me with Dad, and one of them together. A couple of weeks after Mum's funeral, Kirsten and Tim presented me with some boxes and crates salvaged from my family home. They'd wanted to take me there so that I could collect anything important to me but social services had warned them it would be too upsetting and potentially dangerous for me. Somewhere along the way, Mum had slipped through the system. She'd turned to drink and had become a hoarder. It was so bad that the Sandersons had to employ a team of professionals to clear and deep-clean the house, watching out for anything that could be passed to me. Despite the filth and chaos elsewhere, it turned out that my bedroom had been kept pristine, like a shrine. There were books, games, dolls, teddies, clothes – everything you'd expect an eight-year-old to have. And, as though she'd known what lay ahead, Mum had placed a plastic crate in there containing all the family photos, her jewellery box, newspaper clippings about Dad's death, her diaries and a few keepsakes including the snow globe bought on The Best Day Ever.

I asked about the lighthouse paintings. Kirsten had instructed the cleaners to look for them but they'd reported back that they'd all been daubed in black paint and slashed. It made sense. Her real lighthouse had left her floundering in the darkness so she'd blacked out the beams in her paintings for good.

Kirsten and Tim sat at the enormous dining table with me as we gradually went through each item. Some things were familiar, yet others held no memory for me and they were the ones that upset me the most – how could I have forgotten so much when I'd desperately tried to hold onto everything I could about my parents and my childhood?

The photos were wonderful. From the days before digital, they were all in development envelopes. The year had been written on the front of each envelope in marker pen, so we were able to look at them in chronological order. My absolute favourites were from The Best Day Ever.

Years later, I gathered the best of the photos and compiled them into the yellow album – Mum's favourite colour, representing rare moments of sunshine and happiness before being engulfed back into darkness and hopelessness. When I looked through the album each Christmas, I normally closed it after the last photo from my childhood home but now I took a deep breath and turned the next page for the first time since fleeing from London.

I'd been at my first foster home for such a short time that I didn't have any photos from then, but there were pictures from being with the Ashwells and the Fosters. I hadn't stayed in touch with either family. In the great scheme of things, I'd spent such a small part of my life with them that staying in contact didn't feel necessary. It was nice to have a few family photos, though, reminding me of the kindness they'd shown me, even if they hadn't been able to provide me with a permanent home.

I took another deep breath then turned to the page to where my life began with the Sandersons. Because I'd been with them for longer than I'd been with my own parents and because we'd been on so many family trips and holidays, I had loads of photos. When I was sixteen, I sat in the dining room one rainy day in the Easter holidays, a mass of images spread across the table. I'd decided to fill the rest of the yellow album with photos of my second family but there were so many that I didn't know where to start. Kirsten joined me and suggested choosing photos that represented my very happiest times. We sat there for hours, laughing as we reminisced. Leanne turned up while we were giggling.

'What's going on?' she demanded.

'We were just remembering that time in Crete when you got an olive stuck up your nose,' Kirsten said.

'I could have died that day,' Leanne snapped. 'I couldn't breathe.'

Kirsten rolled her eyes. 'Don't be so dramatic. It was funny.'

'Hilarious.' Leanne stropped off to her bedroom then left the house shortly afterwards without a word to either of us.

I hadn't thought about that day in years, yet now the memory was so vivid. A few months later, Isaac appeared. Had seeing me giggling with her mum sparked some sort of jealous rage and been the trigger for Leanne to humiliate me with the introduction of my 'playmates'? I knew I'd already been earmarked for Garth by then but was it possible she'd further developed her plan?

I closed the album and leaned on the table with my head in my hands. That little strop about us laughing together hadn't been the only incident. There'd been little signs, little digs, little quips all along and I hadn't noticed any of them at the time. Maybe I hadn't wanted to. Maybe I'd placed Leanne that high on her pedestal that I couldn't acknowledge her flaws.

Kirsten and Tim bought me a stunning watch for my twenty-first birthday and presented it to me over a family meal that evening. The inscription made me cry: *To our beautiful daughter who makes us proud every day xxx.* Kirsten cried too as she hugged me. Next moment, Leanne snatched the watch out of my hand, demanding to know what the fuss was all about and why everyone was blubbing.

'Didn't they have enough space for the word "foster"?' she asked flatly, handing it back to me.

Tim immediately pulled her up on it but Leanne made out that she was joking and of course I was just as much a part of the family as she was. She must have said that through gritted teeth and with her fingers crossed. And she must have hated me so very much to pretend to be my friend yet do what she did.

Stomping round the flat, Hercules bounding along beside me, I recalled more and more occasions when Leanne had let her guard down momentarily and said something snide then back-tracked and made out it was a joke or that I'd misheard. What about the time when I'd badly burned my back on holiday in the Dominican Republic and had to stay indoors for two days? Had Leanne applied her low-factor lotion instead of the high-protection sunscreen I needed for my pale skin? And what about the time I had to miss the family theatre trip because my art project mysteriously got damaged? Had she done that?

As I curled up under my duvet, I stopped thinking about Leanne and started thinking about Kirsten and Tim instead. When I burned my back, Tim missed out on swimming with dolphins to stay in the apartment and keep me company. And Kirsten refused to go to the show, even though she was the one who wanted to see it the most, so that she could help me repair my artwork. They'd always been there for me with a smile, a hug and kind, encouraging words.

A tear slipped down my cheek and I curled up into a ball, clutching onto my duvet. I missed them. I missed them both so much, my heart hurt, but I'd been left with no choice.

The day I found out the truth about Garth and Leanne, Pollyanna died. Two of the people I loved and trusted had lied and deceived me and I needed to get away from them. Far away. But that meant cutting myself off from another two people I loved and trusted who hadn't let me down. There'd never been the slightest doubt in my mind that they knew anything about it and Garth had even confirmed that.

As I made my way down the stairs at The Larches for the last time ever, a hastily packed suitcase in each hand, I tried and failed to ignore the family photos adorning the wall. There were as many photos of me as there were of Leanne. As far as Kirsten and Tim were concerned, I'd been their daughter. They'd meant those words engraved on the watch. And Leanne had known it.

I couldn't do it. I couldn't walk out with no explanation, but I couldn't stay and wait for them to return from their trip to Hong Kong either.

Dumping my cases on the ground floor, I made my way to their home office, sat at Kirsten's desk and took out a pad of paper and a pen.

*Dear Kirsten and Tim*

*I discovered something terrible about Garth this weekend. He's not the man I thought he was and it turns out that our marriage was one borne out of convenience rather than love, or at least on his part. Our marriage is over and can never be repaired.*

*Sadly, this also means that my life in London has to be over. Kirsten, I am so sorry to leave Vanilla Pod without serving notice. It's been a privilege and an inspiration to learn from you and your talented team. Thank you so much for giving me such a valuable opportunity to pursue the career my dad was never able to.*

*I cannot thank you both enough for opening your hearts and your home to a scared, bereaved child, and for always making me feel like I belonged in your family. You have cared for, protected and taught me so much about the world and the type of person I want to be. Unfortunately, you could have done nothing to protect me from the path that others chose for me. I will forever regret my marriage and the events that led up to it, but I will never regret the day I met you both.*

*I don't know where I'm going. Fate will decide that. I know you played no part in what happened but I beg you not to try to find me. I need to cut all ties. I need to lock the past away. If you do find out what happened this weekend, then I'm sure you'll understand why I can't be part of your family anymore.*

*With warmth, love and my eternal gratitude to you both,*

*Tamara xx*

I cried as I read the letter over and over, then placed it in an envelope from one of the drawers. If I left it somewhere visible, there was a strong possibility that Leanne would find it and destroy it. I could just imagine her, playing the innocent: *I have no idea where Tamara is. She upped and left Garth with no explanation at all. Poor man's devastated. Left us in the lurch at work too.*

Walking over to the bookshelves on the opposite wall to the desk, I searched for a particular book, slipped the letter between the pages, and returned it to the shelf. I'd text Kirsten when they were back from their trip and tell her that *Pollyanna* had a letter for her. Then I'd switch off my phone for good. If Leanne did search The Larches for a letter, there was no way she would think to look there.

I couldn't stay at The Larches any longer in case Garth or Leanne appeared. Finding a hotel for the night, I hid there, ignoring the barrage of calls and texts. I wasn't interested in anything either of them had to say.

As I drove north the next morning, leaving London behind, one of the hundreds of thoughts whirring around my mind was: who am I? The orphaned child, Tamara Chadwick, had grown up and found a new family. Although I hadn't accepted Kirsten and Tim's kind offer to adopt me, I had shown I cared by changing my name to Tamara Chadwick-Sanderson. For four months, I'd been Tamara Tewkesbury. But the orphan, the foster child and the wife no longer existed and I had no idea who I was anymore. I was going to have to start over in so many ways, finding myself as well as a new home and business. The starting point had to be a new name. I certainly wasn't going to keep Tewkesbury – every connection to that man had to be firmly stripped from my life – but fear of being found meant I couldn't use Chadwick or Sanderson. I'd simplify my first name to Tara; close enough to Tamara to not seem weird but a change nonetheless. What about my surname? And then it struck me. My new surname would be Porter, after the author Eleanor H. Porter, creator of *Pollyanna*. Garth and Leanne might have destroyed my Pollyanna-style beliefs but they couldn't erase her from my life entirely. Thanks to them, I couldn't have my foster parents in my life anymore but I wouldn't let them take my mum and dad away from me too.

With the connections they undoubtedly had, I suspected that Kirsten and Tim would be able to find me, even with the name change, but I knew they were decent people who'd respect my wishes. It didn't surprise me when a card arrived at The Chocolate Pot that first Christmas, delivered via the Birmingham-based solicitor handling my annulment; a location chosen to throw any search for me off the scent. I immediately recognised Kirsten's beautiful calligraphy. Another arrived on my birthday, and so the pattern continued. A stack of cards sat in a box in the corner of my office, filed in date order, all unopened. From the thickness of them, I could tell they all contained a letter too. Much as I missed my foster parents, that part of my life was over. I couldn't let them in because, to do so, would be letting Leanne back in. Garth had hurt me. I'd loved him and trusted him and he'd betrayed me, but he'd only been part of my life for a few years. Leanne had been my sister, my role model, my mentor and my friend for well over a decade. She'd broken my heart and I could never have anything to do with her ever again.

I wiped my eyes and took a deep breath. *Enough. Stop thinking about them. That chapter of your life has closed and that's the way it needs to stay.*

## 13

Carly knocked on the café door the following morning about forty minutes before Maria's start time.

'How are you feeling this morning?' she asked as soon as I opened the door.

I smiled ruefully. 'Different.'

'Good different or bad different?'

'Good, I think. Coffee?'

'I thought you'd never ask.'

'Grab a seat in the kitchen and I'll make them.'

I handed her a cappuccino a few minutes later.

'Did you manage to get any sleep?' she asked as I bent down to check on the raspberry brownies in the oven.

'I didn't think I would.' I straightened up and gave her a weak smile. 'It took me a while to drop off but, when I did, I slept like a log.'

'Were you okay on your own?'

I paused for a moment. *Tell her.* 'I erm... I wasn't actually on my own. I had Hercules.'

'Who?' She raised her eyebrows and I could guess what she was thinking: *A man? Called Hercules?!*

'He's my giant house bunny.' I bit my lip and my pulse raced as I waited for Carly's reaction.

Her eyes widened and her mouth dropped open. 'Your what?' She grinned at me. 'Oh my gosh, Tara. You're full of revelations at the moment.'

While adding the ingredients for a chocolate cake into a mixing bowl, I told Carly all about Hercules and promised I'd introduce them soon.

She stayed for about twenty minutes and we chatted and laughed while I continued working. Although my past wasn't mentioned again, I knew that coming round before work was her way of reminding me she was there for me whenever I wanted to talk about what I'd already revealed or move onto the next part. I'd forgotten how comforting and reassuring it felt to have someone caring and worrying about me, which got me thinking about Kirsten and Tim once more.

As I lightly kneaded the dough for a batch of plain scones after Carly left, I thought about the box of cards again. Cutting them out of my life had definitely been right for me at the time, but had it been right for them? I'd removed myself from their lives because I wasn't their biological daughter, but I hadn't given them any say in whether they wanted me to do that. Would they have had to make a choice between Leanne and me, especially when I'd moved away? Perhaps not. They'd been my parents in all but genes since I was ten and they'd always made it clear that they viewed me as their own daughter, but I'd abandoned them when things got tough. Had that been a mistake?

Tuesdays were usually fairly quiet but we were busy from about ten and even had to open the upstairs shortly after eleven.

By mid-afternoon, we finally had a lull. Niamh, my pregnant

staff member, was busy wiping some sticky fingerprints off the glass cake display unit. I looked at her baby bump and felt disgusted with myself for not having asked her anything about her pregnancy. I'd arranged shifts around her antenatal appointments and I'd regularly checked how she was feeling, but it had been all very formal. What did you ask a pregnant woman, though? What did you ask anyone? Fear of letting anyone in had built that wall between business and personal life and I'd done everything possible to keep that segregation. If I asked about their personal lives, they might want to know about mine.

'How's it going?' I asked Niamh, kicking myself for such a weak opener.

She looked up and smiled. 'Good. It seems to have quietened down. Tables four and six are nearly finished, and I'll check on table eight for more drinks in about five minutes.'

I inwardly cringed. She'd assumed I was asking about work. Time to try again.

'Great. And what about you? How are things with you and the baby?'

'Fine. I don't think I'll need any more time off before I finish.' She lovingly stroked her bump. 'I should be able to organise my check-ups for Mondays.'

I smiled. 'Okay. Don't worry if you can't get them on Mondays. I'm sure we can work round it as long as I've got some notice.'

'Thanks. I appreciate it. Oh. That's table four wanting the bill. Can I give you this?'

I took the cloth from her, grateful that table four needed attention because there was no way I could attempt a third question. Talk about a message coming loud and clear: Tara Porter is all about the business and not the person.

Molly, one of my students, appeared from upstairs. 'It's all clean and closed off up there.'

I decided to try again. 'How's college going?' I asked.

She frowned. 'I don't go to college anymore.'

'You don't?'

'No. I got my A Levels last year.'

'Then you're at university?'

She shook her head and started cleaning the coffee machine. 'Not yet. I'm taking a year out and resitting my Chemistry because I got a B but I really need an A to do my preferred course. That's why I wanted the extra shifts.'

'Oh. I didn't realise. So will you be leaving in September?'

'No, but I will need to go back to just weekends and school holidays again, if that's okay. If I get my A, I'll be going to York University, but I can't afford to live there so I'll be commuting. Plus, I want to be around to help Mum with my brother. It's been tough for her since Dad left.'

'Your brother?'

Molly rinsed the cloth in the sink again. 'Yeah. He's got cystic fibrosis.'

I hadn't even noticed a customer approach the counter so was surprised when Molly said, 'Hi there, what can I get you?'

Watching as she deftly made a couple of lattes, I felt like such a failure. How had I not known that Molly was taking a year out or, even more significant, about the errant dad and the brother with cystic fibrosis? In all honesty, I hadn't even known she had a brother.

'Can I ask you a question?' Molly said when the customer left. 'You're not thinking of selling this place, are you?'

'No. Never. What made you ask that?'

'There was a man upstairs earlier asking questions.'

My jaw tightened. 'What sort of questions?'

'Things like how many customers we serve in a day, whether we're significantly busier at the weekend, whether we do evening events... that sort of thing.'

'Did you tell him anything?'

She shook her head. 'I just said it was a very busy and successful café but I didn't elaborate.'

'That just sounds like a nosy customer. What made you jump from that to me selling this place?'

She giggled. 'Sorry. Missed out the most essential part. He said, "What do you think it would take for your boss to sell up?" I laughed at him and said you'd need to be on your deathbed before you even thought about selling up.'

My jaw clenched. 'What did he look like, this man?'

'Tall, blond and tanned. Probably early forties.'

'Jed,' I muttered. 'Jed Ferguson.'

'Who?'

I shook my head. 'Nobody. But there's nothing to worry about. I'm definitely *not* selling and, if I was, which I'm not, he'd be the last man on earth I'd allow to get his grubby little paws on my business.'

'He seemed nice,' she said. 'Nosy but nice.'

'Well, he isn't. And if he comes in here again, please let me know. Immediately.'

\* \* \*

Closing time couldn't come soon enough for me. I felt shattered as I climbed up the stairs to my flat with my plate of dinner. Hercules was already waiting for me by the door, eager for cuddles. I put my plate down and hugged him.

'That nasty Jed Ferguson was in The Chocolate Pot today,' I told him as I put out some fresh food. 'Or at least I think it was him. The description sounded about right. Well, apart from the part where she said he was nice. I'm certain it was him looking through my window and I'm pretty sure it'll have been him asking the Bay Trade guys about premises.'

What was he doing back from Australia? And what right did he have to question one of my team? My shoulders slumped. At least he bothered to ask them questions. It would appear that I never did. What an eye-opener my conversations with Niamh and Molly had been. I knew I struggled to let people in, but there was a difference between that and completely shutting people out. Things had to change.

* * *

'Namaste,' said Karen at the end of my Pilates class that evening.

'Namaste,' the class repeated.

I breathed in and out deeply a couple more times, then opened my eyes. Back in the flat with Hercules, I'd come so close to ditching Pilates, but I decided that an hour of exercise and relaxation might do me the world of good. And it certainly had.

Until I finished rolling up my mat and heard his voice.

'Of all the Pilates classes in all the towns in all the world, she walks into mine.'

I leapt up, my mat springing open, tension instantly returning to my body as I turned to face him. He looked exactly how I remembered except he now had a deep tan which accentuated his green eyes. The years had been kind to him, with no sign of hair loss and only a few crinkly laughter lines. Yet I still couldn't bear the sight of him.

'Except it's not your Pilates class is it, Jed?' I snapped. 'And it's not your town either. What the hell are you doing back here?'

'Ooh, still feisty after... what is it? Thirteen years?'

'About thirteen and a half. And you haven't answered my question.'

'Taking a Pilates class,' he said. 'It's good for the body and soul.'

Shaking my head, I bent down and rolled up my mat again, muttering under my breath. For some ridiculous reason, I couldn't seem to get the ends to curl under. That *never* happened.

'Do you want a hand?' Jed asked.

I turned my head and narrowed my eyes at him. 'From you? Never.'

Exasperated, I grabbed the mat as it was and tried to drape it over my arm. It didn't want to play.

'Thanks, Karen,' I said, heading for the door, wrestling with the stupid piece of foam.

'Thanks, Tara. See you next week,' she said.

I knew he was behind me as I made my way out the sports hall and down the corridor. He was probably looking me up and down, just like the first time we'd met.

When we made it into the car park, I turned to confront him. 'What? What do you want?'

He looked a little shocked at my raised voice. 'Nothing. There's only one exit from the building so I have to come this way. And my car's parked over there in case you think I'm following you. It's the white one.'

I looked to where he pointed and my stomach sank. It was only parked right next to mine. Sighing, I continued walking.

'And it *is* my town.' He moved into step beside me.

'What?'

'When I said that, admittedly stupid, line, you said it wasn't my town and I'm saying it is. I'm Whitsborough Bay born and bred which is—'

'Yeah, yeah, which is more than can be said for me.'

Jed laughed. 'Wow! Age certainly hasn't mellowed you.'

'And it hasn't improved you,' I snapped.

'Touché! And if you'd have let me finish, I was going to say I'm

Whitsborough Bay born and bred which is why I'm here at the moment. My parents and extended family still live here.'

My voice softened. 'So you're just here for a holiday?'

'Sort of.'

We reached the cars. I unlocked mine, stuffed my misbehaving mat in the boot, then slammed it closed.

'And you're going back to Australia?'

'Yes. Next week.'

'Glad to hear it. Safe trip.' I made my way down the side of my car, thankful that there was a wide space between the two vehicles as it would be just my luck to open my door too far and take a dent out of his car. I wouldn't have cared about damaging his property, but I didn't want to look like even more of an idiot in his presence than I already did.

'And then I'll be back for good in October.'

I stopped dead, one leg in the car, my body crouched ready to sit. 'What?'

'I said I'll be back for good in October and looking for premises for my new business. See you then.' He climbed into his car and slammed the door.

Leaping up, I banged on his window. He wound it down and raised an eyebrow at me.

'You can't have The Chocolate Pot, you know. It's not for sale.'

'Everything's for sale if the price is right.'

'You could offer me ten million pounds and The Chocolate Pot would still *not* be for sale.'

Jed laughed. 'Just as well I'm not looking to regress.'

'Then what were you doing asking one of my staff questions about the business today? Because I know it was you.'

He laughed again. 'Checking out the competition.' Then he wound his window up and floored the accelerator, leaving me with my mouth open and my heart pounding.

I sat in the driver's seat, breathing deeply. 'Checking out the competition?' Did that mean he was going to open a café when he returned in October? I shook my head. So what if he did? His style was 'greasy spoon' and therefore a completely different clientele. Besides, there were currently no affordable, suitably sized premises available for lease or purchase on Castle Street or any of the other side streets and an independent business could not afford the main precinct.

But as I drove back to The Chocolate Pot, my heart wouldn't stop thumping. There might be no suitable premises available now but businesses closed all the time. Owners retired, circumstances changed, customer tastes changed, trends came and went and, for a multitude of reasons, businesses failed. In my thirteen and a half years on Castle Street, I'd lost count of how many I'd seen open and close. October was nine months away and a lot could happen during that time. An awful lot.

## 14

The following Monday, Carly turned up at The Chocolate Pot shortly before 7 p.m. to help me get ready for the extra Bay Trade meeting. I'd had several emails of support about the proposed further education mentoring programme and had six confirmed attendees, including Carly. I was therefore thrilled when eight had turned up by half past.

Carly and I had rearranged the tables on the ground floor to make one long table and I'd borrowed a flipchart and stand from the library so I could write down ideas for everyone to see. When they were all settled with drinks and tucking into brownies, I stood up.

'Good evening everyone and thank you so much to you all for coming out on such a cold night to discuss my proposal. Tonight is just an opportunity to get together and throw a few ideas around. There's no obligation to commit to the project. Although if anyone decides it's not for them, then I'll give you a bill for the drinks and brownies and never speak to you again.'

Ginny from The Wedding Emporium next door quickly

dropped her brownie on her plate and joked about me only being able to charge her for half.

'Seriously, though, I want this to be fun and informal. I want everyone to feel they can share ideas and be involved in a way that works for them. If you decide it's not for you, then I completely understand. We've all got so much to do running our own businesses that it's amazing so many of you are here to explore this.'

I took a deep breath and looked to Carly for encouragement. She smiled and nodded eagerly, knowing what was coming next.

'I'm really keen to hear your suggestions but there's one key decision I've made already and that's the name of the project. I'd like you to chat among yourselves for a couple of minutes. I need to introduce you to someone very important. Back shortly.'

Smiling at the intrigued expressions on the group's faces, I ran upstairs, returning a couple of minutes later with Hercules in my arms. Gasps and squeals of delight came from the group as they spotted him.

'This is Hercules, my Flemish Giant house rabbit. He's two years old and he loves cuddles.'

'Can I hold him?' asked Sarah from Seaside Blooms.

'You certainly can.' I secured Hercules in Sarah's arms and he looked very content as several hands reached out and stroked him.

I returned to the flipchart and addressed the group. 'You might be wondering what a giant house rabbit has to do with anything but I brought him down because he's the inspiration for the name of the project.' I turned over the flipchart cover to reveal a fresh page containing the project name. 'Welcome to Project Hercules. The name means strength and power and the vision for this project is to share our knowledge and experiences with students who might like to set up their own business. Knowledge is power and mentoring will give them strength. How we do this is what we're here to discuss tonight but I hope you all like the name.'

As a round of applause rippled round the room accompanied by cries of, 'Love it', I had to swallow the lump in my throat. I was so relieved. Hercules brought me strength. He and his predecessors had provided me with much-needed company over the years and their unconditional love had given me the strength to keep going and face each day.

* * *

After we closed The Chocolate Pot for the day on Tuesday, I said I had something to show the team and dashed upstairs. The look of astonishment on their faces when I appeared with a giant house bunny would stay with me forever.

Word spread and I had to bring him down on Wednesday too to introduce him to those who hadn't been working on Tuesday. And again on Thursday.

Watching them coo and stroke him, it seemed quite ridiculous that I'd ever kept him secret. After all, he had no connection to my past whatsoever. Nobody was going to look at him and suddenly guess everything that I'd kept so well hidden.

## 15

We decided to initially focus on Whitsborough Bay TEC for Project Hercules as the courses at that college were vocational and therefore the more likely source for budding entrepreneurs. If it went well there, we could extend it to the sixth form college and university.

The TEC Principal, Malcolm Dring, was very receptive to the project and invited me to his staff meeting at the end of January to pitch the idea. In February, we were invited into various lessons to promote our services and we took a table at the careers fair that month which generated a lot of interest.

By early March, we were up and running with our first students, a couple of staff members and a few evening classes attendees – an audience we hadn't previously considered. It was all fairly informal with students being allocated to the Bay Trader who had the most appropriate expertise but, after a conversation with one of my students, it struck me that there was something we could do that was so much wider than business mentoring.

Olivia was a final-year catering student with a dream of running her own business from a converted horse box that she'd take to festivals and events.

'I've got the horse box already,' she told me. 'My grandparents run a farm and they've given me a disused one. My dad's a joiner so he's going to help me convert it and my mum's happy to do the driving until I'm old enough for the right licences.'

She had reams of information to show me about the venues she'd visit, the finances, and the food she'd sell. She'd even drawn a sketch of what the finished horse box would look like.

'This is all very impressive,' I said. 'You've clearly done stacks of research and you know exactly what you're doing. So how can I help?'

'I've got no confidence,' Olivia said.

I flashed her a warm smile. 'You have just spent twenty minutes talking animatedly to a complete stranger about your well-researched plans. What would make you think you have no confidence?'

'I know I can cook and I believe in my business idea but I'm really scared of confrontation. What if there's a queue and someone pushes to the front? What if someone complains about my food and demands their money back? What if another retailer has a go at me for being parked too close to their pitch? I'd die.'

She certainly wouldn't die but it raised an important need. Whether they were going to set up their own business or seek employment, there was a demand among the students for life skills. The following day, I found myself in Malcolm Dring's office once more, pitching another idea and, by the time the students returned from the Easter holidays, Project Hercules had extended to include a series of short workshops around self-belief, making a positive first impression and being assertive when facing conflict or negativity.

Partway through my first session on creating positive first

impressions, I asked if there were any questions. Glancing round the room, I took in the flushed cheeks and averted gazes and kicked myself. All the students were there because they lacked self-confidence so asking a question out loud in front of their peers was not something they were going to relish.

'I'm going to hand you some Post-it notes each and I want you to take a few moments to scribble down any questions you might have or observations you want to share about first impressions. When you've done that, come up and stick them on the whiteboard and we'll spend some time going through them. And don't worry, I won't ask who wrote what. This is just to get a discussion going based on what you want to know so I can tailor this session for you.'

It took a moment but then one student bent her head and started writing, quickly followed by another. Soon the board was full of colourful Post-it notes. I addressed the first couple then flinched as I removed the third.

'My first impression of you is that you are naturally confident. There's no way I'll ever be like you. Do you have any *real* idea what it's like to be shy and scared?' I read out loud, emphasising the word "real" which had been capitalised and underlined.

I perched against the desk and looked round twelve pairs of curious eyes. 'It's a great question and the answer is yes. I know exactly what it's like. I never used to be like this. You see, my parents died when I was young and I moved from one foster home to the next feeling scared and vulnerable...'

* * *

I sat in my car for about ten minutes after that workshop, thinking about what I'd shared and the impact – the positive impact – it had on those young people. I'd been very selective with my information, of course, but the story of a shy young girl moving from home to home then moving away from everything and everyone she knew to set up her own business from scratch really drew them in. They started to ask questions. They wanted to know how I'd done it. How had I overcome my fears? How had I found the strength to change?

The more I opened up, the more they shared about their own inhibitions and, for the first time ever, I realised that my past had the power to do good. Instead of hiding from it, I could harness it and help others face their future.

Since the launch of Project Hercules and the subsequent introduction of my rabbit to my team, I'd continued to ask the team questions and had noticed that they seemed genuinely touched when I enquired after a family member's health, a night out or an exam result. In return, I shared some snippets about my personal life. It felt uncomfortable at first and quite exposing but I took baby steps and, before I knew it, conversations became natural. I was still guarded, only talking about 'safe' everyday subjects like Hercules, Pilates, films I'd watched or books I'd read, preferring to keep the focus on getting to know my team rather than sharing too much about me. They didn't know anything about my parents or foster families even though I now knew all about their families. I hadn't told Carly the final part of the story either. I still couldn't bring myself to say it out loud. She remained under the belief that Leanne and Garth had been seeing each other and I hadn't let her think any differently. It was easier that way.

But as I drove back to The Chocolate Pot after my workshop at the TEC, it struck me that I'd shared something significant about my past with a group of strangers that I hadn't shared with my team. It was only fair that I let them in a bit more, starting with Maria.

* * *

It was raining heavily by the time I got back to The Chocolate Pot. The combination of the bad weather and it being late afternoon meant there were only a handful of customers. Most of the cleaning had already been done and Molly was busy giving the menus a wipe. I asked Sheila and Molly to hold the fort while I went upstairs for a word with Maria.

'Don't look so worried,' I said as she sat opposite me with her hands tightly gripped round a mug of tea. 'I want to tell you something but it doesn't affect this place or the wedding so please don't panic.'

She let out a sigh of relief. 'I thought you were going to tell me they'd made a mistake and revoked the wedding licence.'

'Nothing like that. It's about me. You might have wondered why I never talk about my family and there's a very good reason...'

Maria only needed the highlights – not the (almost) full story I'd given to Carly. I told her about losing my parents and going into foster care. I told her I got married when I was twenty-one but it turned out to be a big mistake and the marriage ended quickly and badly leaving me with serious trust issues so I avoided relationships. As for Kirsten and Tim, I went for something vague: *They were wonderful people but their daughter resented sharing them and turned against me. I thought it would be better to sever contact than cause a family rift.*

'I don't like to talk about it,' I said, 'but it cropped up today when I told the students I hadn't always been confident. It's a small town and someone here is bound to have some sort of friend-of-a-friend connection to one of them so I'd rather you and the rest of the team heard it from me.'

'You're going to tell the others?'

I nodded. 'I don't want to make a big thing of it but I'll try to slip it into conversations over the next couple of weeks.'

She nodded. 'I won't say anything.'

We both stood up and pushed our chairs in but Maria didn't move away from the table.

'I get why you didn't say anything before,' she said. 'It can be hard to talk about the past, particularly if it's a difficult one.' She picked up her mug and walked towards the stairs then turned and smiled gently. 'Don't let your past define you, Tara. You're stronger than that. And don't feel you have to tell people about it. You choose what to share and you choose when and, if you really want to share, then find the truth that works for you. People don't have to know your deepest secrets to know you. I never knew anything about your past until now but I think I know you pretty well. You don't work with someone as long as I've worked with you and not get a real sense of exactly who they are.'

She smiled again and skipped down the stairs, leaving me with my mouth open. I certainly hadn't seen that coming.

## 16

On Friday 4<sup>th</sup> May, I turned thirty-six. I was awake before Hercules again and lay staring at the ceiling, very aware of an approaching anniversary. On my birthday fourteen years ago, I was blissfully happy, very much in the honeymoon-phase of my marriage, I loved my job at Vanilla Pod and counted my blessings for being part of a caring loving family. Little did I know that my entire world was about to collapse a few days later. Tuesday would signal fourteen years since I discovered my husband wasn't the person I thought he was. Wednesday would be the anniversary of finding out the truth and Thursday would mark fourteen years since I fled from my old life and let fate decide my future.

Was it time to finally tell Carly the truth about Leanne and Garth? It was May Day Bank Holiday weekend so we'd both be exceptionally busy but it would be Bay Trade again the following Monday and, like me, Carly didn't like to miss a meeting. Maybe she'd be free to join me afterwards for the final part of my life story.

I didn't tell my team that it was my birthday because it still didn't feel like it was cause for celebration. Maybe I'd celebrate it next year. Or the year after.

The usual card arrived via the solicitor from Kirsten and Tim, which I whisked away and placed on the internal stairs before anyone saw it. I'd add it to the back of the box, unopened, after work.

* * *

'I'm getting bored of the gym,' Nathan said, looking up from mopping the floor in front of the counter after we'd closed for the day. 'I'm thinking about taking up swimming again.'

I pressed a button on the till to print off the sales report. 'Sounds like a good plan. I've never gelled with the gym but I love swimming.'

'What's the new pool like?'

I paused before I answered him, carefully picking my words. 'It looks nice.'

'Is it busy on an evening?'

'I don't know. I don't use it on an evening.'

He looked surprised. 'You go before you start baking? I didn't think it opened that early.'

'It doesn't.' I sighed. It was time to release a bit more information. What harm could it do? 'I don't swim at the pool. I swim in the sea.'

He leaned on the mop and stared at me for a moment, mouth agape.

'Open water swimming is so much more invigorating than a pool,' I said. 'If you ever want to give it a go, I'm happy to accompany you but it's weather and tide dependent and it's a very early start. And, of course, you'll need a good wetsuit.'

'I'd love to try it. Thank you.' He smiled then continued mopping.

I ripped the sales report off the till and smiled too. *There now. That wasn't difficult, was it?*

So now they knew about open water swimming but I kept back the information about the hygge and the crafting. I couldn't do it. I couldn't put every part of me on show; I had to keep something back. Maria was right. It was up to me what I shared and when I did it and I still couldn't fully let anyone in. I couldn't let that tower be fully destroyed because, if it was, there was nothing left to protect me. No lighthouse. Nothing.

Back in my flat that evening, I made my way up to the mezzanine level with my birthday card and pulled out the box containing its predecessors. I sat on the floor and stared at the pale blue envelope with the solicitor's address crossed out and a redirection label stuck over it. Kirsten always addressed envelopes using calligraphy. She used to laugh and say that most people probably didn't even notice it, but it made her feel like she'd given their card or letter that bit of extra special care and attention. That was Kirsten all over.

I placed it at the back of the box and my fingers brushed over the other colourful envelopes. Should I...? No. I hastily shoved the lid back on the box and pushed it into the corner. I wasn't ready. I needed to tell Carly the final part of my story first. Lifting my phone out of my pocket, I texted her to ask if she'd be free after Bay Trade the following week and, after a speedy reply to say she would be, I picked up my needle-felting basket and made my way to the dining table with it. I concentrated on stabbing a barbed needle into the wool; watching it gradually emerging into the shape of a Santa was the perfect task for keeping my mind occupied and ignoring my birthday for another year.

# 17

Having started my education on what goes on behind closed doors at the age of sixteen, it seemed ridiculous that it was five and a half years later that I actually lost my virginity. As I lay in Garth's arms on my wedding night, I had to concede that he'd been right again. He'd been right about a church wedding and our families being involved, and he'd been right about waiting until our wedding night before we fully consummated our love. It was a beautiful moment for both of us, made all the more special for having waited for three years.

I knew I wasn't Garth's first. He was, after all, forty-three by then. He told me that he'd been a bit of a lad in his teens and early twenties but hit his mid-thirties and realised that all his mates were married or in long-term relationships and he felt like he'd become a bit of a joke – the eternal bachelor, scared of commitment. He resolved to stop screwing around and find a meaningful relationship but it wasn't easy. He kept meeting women who had too much baggage or who had the same 'use and abuse' approach he'd grown tired of.

He'd met Leanne a few years earlier through a mutual friend

and they found they moved in the same circles and kept bumping into each other. They started meeting up but just as friends. He confided in her about his relationship situation and she told him that she had a younger foster sister who'd be perfect for him. And it went from there.

I'd been married for a little over four months when I turned twenty-two and I felt like I was in a cosy love bubble where nobody could touch us. The thing about bubbles is that they tend to burst. My birthday fell on a Tuesday so Garth took me out for a meal that night and showered me with gifts. One of them was a weekend for two in a luxury spa in Surrey for the coming weekend.

'For me and you?' I asked, raising my brow in doubt; definitely *not* his sort of thing.

He grimaced. 'It was meant to be for you and Leanne but something's cropped up and she can't come. You're going with Krystal.'

My stomach sank. 'Krystal? But I barely know her.' She was a friend of Garth's and Leanne's and I'd never really gelled with her, finding her as false as her nails.

'Then this will be the perfect chance to get to know her,' he said, tension in his tone. 'I know it's not ideal but can't you make it work? I can't change the dates.'

I didn't have much choice. Kirsten was in Hong Kong with Tim and there was nobody else I was close to. It was Krystal or go alone. 'Okay. Thank you. It's a great gift.'

As he kissed me and pulled me back to bed, I couldn't stay annoyed with him. So Krystal wasn't my favourite person but it was only one weekend and we'd spend most of the time having treatments. It would be fine.

I wasn't working on the Friday. Garth had arranged for someone to swap shifts with me so that I could have a relaxing day to get packed and organised before Krystal picked me up later that afternoon. I'm not sure how long he thought it took to throw a few swimming costumes and a couple of evening outfits into a bag but, by 9 a.m., I was packed and wondering what on earth I'd do for the next seven hours. Then a thought popped into my head. What if I went early and had a day of peace on my own without Krystal rabbiting in my ear about handbags and shoes – things I still had very little interest in, despite Leanne's lessons? If I did that, I could also avoid being trapped in a car with her for the journey each way.

Not wanting anyone to try to talk me out of it, I set off and decided to text Garth and Krystal when I arrived because, by then, it would be too late for them to change my plans. It had to be the first devious thing I'd ever done in my life and, as I drove to the spa, I realised that, outside of work, it was pretty much the only decision I'd made for myself in years and it felt quite liberating. I was still on cloud nine with Garth and, at that point, I still believed the sun shone out of Leanne's backside, but I realised that, between them, they controlled my life and I'd let them. Things were going to change when I got back and my first change would be to insist that Garth either sorted out the refurbishment at his apartment so I could move in properly or I sorted it out myself. It was ridiculous that, after four months of marriage, it was still very much a clinical-looking bachelor pad while most of my belongings remained in my old bedroom at The Larches.

Garth rang as soon as I'd checked into my room and didn't sound too happy with me for taking off without Krystal. I told him that I'd looked at the spa's website and loved his choice so much that I wanted to spend an extra day there, taking advantage of all the treatments. The flattery worked and he reminded me not to rush back on Sunday because he'd be working all weekend on a big case so I'd be alone in the apartment with nothing to do.

My alone-time at the spa was so good. I went swimming, had lunch, had a pedicure, read a book and thoroughly enjoyed myself. With each passing hour, I felt more and more relaxed but also more and more focused about what I wanted from my marriage and my career.

Then Krystal arrived and ruined it. She never shut up. She had a childish whine to her voice and, despite her being about fifteen years my senior, her outlook on life was so immature. She'd never worked, thanks to a wealthy husband, and seemed to find it hilarious that I also had a wealthy husband yet I was still 'just a poxy waitress'. I couldn't be bothered to point out that I was management in the family business and, even if I had been waiting-on staff, there was nothing wrong with that.

By the Saturday evening, I'd had more than enough. My head was pounding from Krystal's constant yapping. Even when we were having a massage and the masseuse advised silence for better relaxation, she never let up. We dined at seven after which she suggested an evening in the bar but I genuinely couldn't bear another minute in her company. I told her I had a headache, which was true, and was going to have to abandon her for an early night.

Back in the tranquillity of my room, I sat on my bed for ten minutes. I really couldn't face another day in Krystal's company as she was making me feel stressed rather than relaxed. I had to get out of there.

I hastily packed and snuck out the back way. I didn't want to officially check out in case Krystal somehow found out I'd left.

As soon as I pulled out of the grounds, I felt the tension ebb from my body. There was no point driving back to the apartment because, as Garth had said, I'd be on my own with nothing to do. It made more sense to stay in my old bedroom at The Larches. I'd still be on my own but at least I'd have my belongings with me and could spend Sunday crafting or curled up on their soft corner sofa with a book instead of perched on Garth's uncomfortable leather couch.

I'd only driven a few miles when my eyelids started drooping.

The mixture of relaxing activities but tense company had exhausted me. Checking into a hotel might be a better idea. Or, better still, I could drive to The Manor. I pulled over and checked my map. I was maybe seven or eight miles away. I put the map down and started driving again with the windows down to help me stay alert. Garth had inherited The Manor – an old mansion house set in extensive grounds and woodland – from an eccentric uncle. We'd stayed there a few times. It was ostentatious and cold but it had potential. I could imagine, with a lot of work and vision, it would make a wonderful family home. He employed a couple from the nearby village to keep an eye on it, clean it and maintain the grounds. Hopefully they wouldn't mind me turning up unannounced to ask for the key. At least I could get a good night's sleep there then text Krystal in the morning and apologise that I'd gone home feeling poorly. I'd probably spend Sunday there too, having a mooch round the grounds and thinking more about what I wanted my future to look like – much easier without Krystal wittering in my ear.

I drove past The Manor on my way to the village and glanced right, then slammed on the brakes. There were cars parked all along the driveway. My first instinct was that it had been broken into or that the caretakers were holding wild parties there when they knew we weren't expected. Enraged, I abandoned the car by the entrance wall and stormed up the drive but, as I neared the house, I stopped dead. That was Garth's car right outside. Next to Leanne's.

Squeals of laughter hit me, mixed with the deep bass thump-thump-thump of music. A man and woman staggered down the steps, laughing, a bottle of champagne dangling from his hand. He was shirtless and she was dressed only in a basque and stockings. What the heck?

My heart raced as I hesitated by the front door, unsure as to whether I should go inside or run. Somehow I found the strength to take those few more steps and my mouth dropped open in shock.

There were people everywhere. Some wore lingerie, some wore costumes, some wore rubber and chains, and some wore nothing. There were couples kissing and couples groping and, as I made my way through the building, I saw things that made me gasp and wince. It wasn't just couples and there was a hell of a lot more going on than kissing and touching. The Manor was clearly the venue for a very adult party and my husband was the host.

A woman dressed in a black PVC catsuit and red killer heels ran her long fingernails gently down my arm. 'I haven't seen you here before,' she purred. 'You look lost. Would you like me to show you the way?'

'Erm...' I cleared my throat. 'I'm looking for Garth. Do you know where he is?'

She licked her red lips and smiled seductively. 'Garth's where he always is. In the dungeon.'

The dungeon? I shuddered. 'And Leanne?' I whispered, the words sticking in my dry throat.

'With him.' She ran her fingernails down my arm again, a little harder this time. 'But there's always an open invitation to anyone who wants to join them. Would you like me to accompany you?'

Feeling as though I could be sick at any moment, I ran back to my car and rested my hands on the bonnet, gulping the fresh evening air. What the hell had I just seen? Who were these people? Who was my husband? Who was my sister?

I slumped into the driver's seat, head in my hands, trying to work out what had just happened. From what catsuit-woman said, this wasn't a one-off, so Garth and Leanne clearly had some sort of X-rated double life. So much for him working all weekend on a case. As for Leanne having other plans meaning she couldn't come to the spa with me, that hadn't been a lie. Garth had just failed to mention that her other plans had been to play dungeon-master with him. Oh God, were they...?

Starting the engine, I slowly drove back to the spa, grateful I hadn't checked out. I lay on my bed, my head spinning. Was Krystal in on it? Was a luxury spa break her payment for keeping me away from them and their perverted party?

* * *

When the dawn light seeped through my blinds, I was still lying on top of the duvet, fully clothed and wide awake. A couple of hours later, there was a knock on my door.

I reluctantly rolled off the bed and inched it open.

'Wow! You look like shit!' Krystal said, curling her lip up and stepping away from the door.

'I'm not feeling well. Sorry. Can you have breakfast without me?'

'Thanks a lot,' she snapped. 'You know I hate eating on my own.' Then she turned and stomped down the corridor.

Closing the door, I sighed. Typical self-centred Krystal reaction, not bothering to express sympathy for me or ask if I needed anything. If she was in on it, then she'd done her duty by making sure I was still at the spa. Little did she know where I'd been last night.

I stayed in my room until lunchtime then phoned Krystal, leaving a voicemail to say I was feeling better but not well enough for lunch and was going to stay in my room for the rest of the afternoon before driving home. I didn't want her alerting Garth to me leaving early.

Then I drove back to The Manor, needing answers.

The cars were all gone but I felt too ashamed to drive to the caretakers' house to ask for the key. What if they knew? What if they cleared up after the parties? What if they'd been party guests?

There was no alarm system and the glass was single-glazed so I knew I could break-in easily. I drove round the back to double check there were definitely no vehicles parked there. Confident that there was nobody around, I hurled a stone through a pane of glass in the kitchen door, turned the key and let myself in.

The house was pristine. The caretakers – or someone else – had obviously been in and cleaned, all evidence of a party completely gone.

My mission was to find 'the dungeon'. I imagined it to be a cellar but I couldn't find any doors that could possibly lead to one. Wondering if it was upstairs instead, I tried the doors along the corridor but each opened into a bedroom or bathroom. They all looked familiar from the tour Garth had given me the first time we stayed and nothing about any of the rooms looked unusual.

The last door I came to was the only one with a lock on the outside. I remembered Garth saying he had no idea where the key was but wasn't interested enough to know what was inside to search for it or break the door down. Could that be 'the dungeon'? I reached for the doorknob and was surprised when it turned. Gulping, I pushed the door open, steeling myself ready to see manacles on the wall and other horrors. I certainly wasn't expecting a cinema room. Reclining leather seats faced a large screen and there were shelves packed full of DVDs. Normal. Or was it? Slowly moving towards the shelves, the images from last night's party burning in my mind, I had a feeling the films wouldn't be those I'd expect to view in a mainstream cinema. I sighed. No. Definitely not mainstream. And so many of them. There had to be hundreds, if not thousands.

On the lower shelves there were what looked to be photo albums. Crouching down, I lifted one out and flicked through a few pages, my stomach churning. I slammed it closed, not needing to see any more.

As I pushed the album back into its space on the bottom shelf, something caught my eye on the spine of one of the DVDs on the shelf above: TAMARA (10). What? It was hardly a common name. I grabbed the box and flicked it over but there were no clues on the plain cover.

Rushing over to the DVD player, I shoved the disc into the slot and, moments later, the image appeared on the screen. My already racing heard thudded even faster as I recognised my bedroom. And me. And Mattia. Somebody had been recording us. Or, more specifically, Leanne had been recording us. Dashing back to the shelves, I found an entire section: TAMARA (1), TAMARA (2) through to TAMARA (12) with just that (10) out of place.

Anger surging through me, I swept them all onto the floor then threw myself down next to them and ripped open the boxes, snapping each disc in half. Back on my feet, I yanked the one from the DVD player and did the same before grabbing the DVD player itself and hurling it towards the wall.

Returning to the shelves, I swept row after row of porn films to the floor, shaking with rage. Glass paperweights interspersed between the DVDs joined the carnage, some landing on the growing pile of films, their fall cushioned, while others shattered on the wooden floor, shards of colourful glass flying in every direction.

Panting, I stared at a final paperweight that had somehow survived on the end of a shelf. I grabbed at it. It moved yet remained secured to the shelf, my hand still clenched round it. At that moment, the entire bookcase moved, revealing a stone staircase, just like in old horror films. Oh my word. I'd just found the entrance to 'the dungeon'.

I hesitated at the top of the steps, terrified as to what I might find down there yet knowing that I had to see it for myself. I needed to know who I'd married.

Legs shaking, head pounding, I slowly made my way down. The

basement of The Manor must have been the same size as the ground floor. A stone-flagged corridor ran down the middle with rooms either side.

The first door on my right had a sign nailed to it stating 'The White Room'. I opened it and flicked on the light. There were white walls, white marble floors and a sturdy-looking wooden structure in the middle with chains and shackles dangling from it. Whips and chains hung from hooks on one of the walls. Taking a deep breath, I closed the door and moved into the next room: 'The Red Room'. This one was decorated in red and black and had a very similar structure to the one in the previous room but as part of a four-poster bed.

Continuing my tour of the basement, I found racks, knives, masks, ropes, cages and candles. Some rooms were beautifully decorated in soft colours, silk and satin, the only suggestion of something a little 'different' being the enormous glass cabinets full of sex aids. Others looked more like torture chambers from the medieval times. And there was pretty much everything in-between.

I tried to be open-minded. I knew that there were people who were into different things and I wasn't going to judge them for it, but this was my husband and my sister living a lifestyle I knew nothing about. My head was bursting with questions. How many people had crowded into that cinema watching my 'playmates' educate me? What had they been doing while they were watching? Had they then descended into 'the dungeon' thinking about me? And where did I fit into all this? Were Leanne and Garth planning to introduce me to their world and, if so, when? If not, where did I come in? Why the marriage? Absolutely nothing made sense.

I hadn't opened all the doors but I'd certainly seen enough and I needed air. I sat in my car with the door open for an hour or so, trying to decide how to play it. Then I texted Garth:

✉ Was on my way home and spotted I was near The
Manor. Decided to take a detour and wander round
the grounds. Looks like there's been a break-in.

He phoned me immediately but I didn't answer. Next minute a
text came through:

✉ Are you OK? Don't call the police and don't go
inside. I'll be there within the hour. Promise
me you won't go inside.

I texted back:

✉ Too late. Already inside. The intruders have
gone but there seems to be some damage. Are you
sure you don't want me to call the police?

\* \* \*

Heart thumping, nausea welled inside me as I waited in the cinema
room. Over and over, I practised what I wanted to say. Would I be
able to find the courage to confront him or would I crumble? I
looked round the room, drawing strength from the destruction
surrounding me and the opening to the secret passageway which
remained exposed.

My heart raced even faster as I heard his car screech to a halt on
the gravel outside. He shouted my name as he ran up the stairs and
I could hear the panic in his voice. His footsteps grew louder as he
ran along the corridor, then he stopped in the doorway.

'Looks like this is the only room that got damaged,' I said.

His eyes flicked from the mountain on the floor, to the passageway, back to the mountain, then to me.

'You've been down the stairs.' But it was more of a statement than a question.

I fought hard to keep my voice strong and steady. 'I have. I'm not sure I'd recommend your interior designer. It seems to be quite a mish-mash of styles down there.'

'Tamara, I—'

I raised my hand to silence him. 'Don't lie to me. Don't try to explain it away, saying it was your uncle's or some other pathetic attempt to cover it up. I was here last night. I met some of your friends. I know about your lifestyle. What I don't know is where I come in.'

He looked at me, all wide, innocent eyes, and then his expression changed as though he couldn't be bothered to keep up an act any longer. 'I needed a wife,' he said, flatly.

'You needed a wife. What the hell does that mean?'

He stepped through the carnage and walked over to the window, then turned to face me. 'There were rumours at work. Rumours that I was a swinger. Rumours that I was into an "alternative lifestyle". My bosses made it clear that I wouldn't progress any further if I didn't do something to squash those rumours, like get myself a respectable wife.' He shrugged. 'I could do that. Leanne and I had moved in similar circles for a few years. I told her my predicament and she said she knew a few women who might play the dutiful wife. I met them, we dated, but the chemistry wasn't there. She asked me what turned me on. I said lots of things as she was very well aware but, for the perfect wife, I liked the idea of young, innocent and vulnerable.' He paused and flashed me his most dazzling smile and I knew what was coming next. 'She said that sounded just like her baby sister.'

'How old was I then?'

'Fifteen. She showed me photos, then arranged for me to observe you while you were out shopping. I liked what I saw. Who wouldn't? I knew I needed to wait until you were eighteen so I found a few respectable girlfriends in the meantime to keep my bosses happy.'

'What about Isaac, Dominic and Mattia? Was that all part of the sordid little plan?'

He nodded. 'It was Leanne's idea. She said you were completely innocent, as I wanted, but she thought I'd enjoy you more if you came to me with a certain level of experience, so we chose the boys and asked them to get you ready for your wedding night.'

'And you videoed it without my consent.'

He glanced across at the wreckage and smiled. 'Shame you destroyed them.' He looked me up and down and added in a seductive low voice, 'They were my favourites.'

I tightened my fists, willing myself to stay calm rather than shout and scream and hurl things at him. I wanted to do that so much, but my need for answers was stronger. 'What made you so certain I'd fall for you and agree to marry you?'

He laughed, as though I'd just asked the most ridiculous question. 'Because Leanne knew you so well, of course. She knew your ultimate fantasy was a true gent who made you laugh and made you feel safe. I'm used to playing different roles and I'm *very* good at it. I'll admit that the caring English gent was a new one for me, but I was happy to give it a go and I have to admit that, for a vanilla, you were pretty damn good.'

A vanilla? I had no idea what that meant and I didn't want to. The lack of remorse in his voice was like a slap across my face. 'Did you ever love me?' I asked. 'Even a little bit? Or was it all a role play for you?'

Silence.

I gulped, forcing back the tears. 'Did Leanne ever tell you why she set you up with me?'

'She might have done.'

'And...?'

'And isn't it obvious? She was sick of sharing her home and her parents with a string of... how did she put it? I think the phrase was "pathetic snivelling orphans". She didn't get why she wasn't enough for her parents so it was her way of getting revenge. Can't say I blame her.'

I ran my hands through my hair, trying to make sense of it. If she'd hated me that much and wanted rid of me, there were so many other things she could have done. Why this? Especially when it had meant having to spend so much time in my company.

'I'm not buying the revenge thing. There had to be something else in it for her.'

'There was. She got the run of this place, any time she wanted, with anyone she wanted.' He paused dramatically. 'Including me.'

I'd suspected it but it still hurt hearing it.

'What about Darryl? I thought they were happy together.'

'They are but they're not exclusive. It's the lifestyle that binds them. Leanne's an insatiable woman with varying tastes like myself and, as you've seen, The Manor is all about satisfying everyone's needs.'

The smug look on this face. The confident arrogance in his tone. Hate flowed through my veins. I wanted to hurl myself at him and claw at his eyes. I wanted to push him through the window. But why should I risk getting into trouble?

'If you needed a wife that badly, why couldn't you have married Leanne? Why drag me into it?'

He grinned as he rolled his eyes at me. 'I like innocence and Leanne is hardly innocent.'

My stomach was churning. I had to get out of there but there was something I needed to do first.

'You might have underestimated my innocence.' I leaned

against the doorframe and beckoned him towards me, willing my voice to come over as seductive. 'I have needs too.'

Garth smiled as he sauntered towards me. 'Anything I can help with?'

'Definitely.'

He came closer still. 'Well, I never. You saw something downstairs that interested you, didn't you?'

'It all interested me.'

He was right in front of me and I fought hard against the rising bile in my throat as he reached out and cupped my face with his hand.

'And I think it will interest my solicitor,' I said as I brought my knee up between his legs. 'Especially all the photos I took.'

'You bitch,' he gasped, bending over in what I hoped was absolute agony.

'Me? I think you might be confusing me with Leanne.' I gave him a shove, sending him to his knees. 'My solicitor will be in touch.'

\* \* \*

When Carly left The Chocolate Pot after hearing the final part of my story, I slowly made my way upstairs. Even though it had been painful to reveal the rest, I didn't feel sick or shaky like I had last time. I hadn't broken down in tears either. Was it because the story ended on a high? I'd walked away from Garth and Leanne. I'd refused to be controlled by them and had started again.

'But I didn't walk away from everything, did I?' I said to Hercules. 'What they did is still controlling how I behave. I still don't trust people. I've made progress but I'm still guarded. And I'm still hiding from Kirsten and Tim.'

I stood up and Hercules followed me over to the arched

windows. Wrapping my hands round my mug of tea, I gazed up and down the street. Although Castle Street was a hive of activity during the day, it was peaceful at night. There were no bars, pubs or restaurants on the street so the only passers-by either lived above one of the businesses or were cutting through.

Ten minutes ticked past and I didn't see a single soul. Absolutely nobody. I turned and looked round my empty flat, then back to the deserted street and, at that moment, I felt completely and utterly alone. Shuddering, I turned away from the window. I'd never felt like that before. Or had I? Had I always been alone but, until now, had refused to put a label on it?

Abandoning my mug on the table, I ran up to the mezzanine and quickly composed an email to Jim, the manager at The Hope Centre, asking if he'd be interested in me helping their users prepare nutritional meals on a tight budget. If he said yes – and I had no doubt he would – then it would give me another reason to be surrounded by people instead of hiding in my flat, broken.

## 18

Dressed in my wetsuit with a towel draped round my shoulders, I sat cross-legged on the sand at South Bay on the morning of Sunday 1st July, watching the sun rise behind the silhouetted lighthouse. It was the fourteen-year anniversary of The Chocolate Pot officially becoming mine. Two more weeks and it would be fourteen years since opening for business. The team didn't know. It wasn't that I'd specifically kept it hidden; more that I'd never made a fuss about it. None of the original team still worked there so it was easy to let the anniversary slip by.

As I'd glided through the gentle waves earlier, with the sky above me gradually lightening, I'd come to a decision. I was so proud of The Chocolate Pot and everyone who worked there that we deserved to celebrate so, when The Chocolate Pot turned fifteen next summer, we would. I tried to convince myself that the wait until the café turned fifteen was because it was a more rounded number than fourteen, being halfway between two decades, but I knew it was because I still wasn't ready. It didn't feel right celebrating my business – and therefore my new life in Whitsborough Bay – while I continued to battle with my past.

The steadily rising sun lit the lighthouse, the red-and-white stripes emerging from the blackness. That's what I needed to do – step out of the shadows and into the light.

'I'll make you a promise, Mum and Dad,' I whispered. 'By this time next year, I'll either have dealt with the past and finally moved on or I'll have locked it in a box and buried it for good because you both know and I know that I can't continue like this.' A gentle breeze kissed my cheeks and I smiled. 'This isn't living. This is existing. Yet I have so much to live for. So very much.'

* * *

The summer months flew past and I continued to take baby steps. I kept talking to my team, finding out about their lives outside of work, and steadily revealing elements of my past – the parts I wanted to reveal as Maria had suggested. I often talked about my dad and his love of baking and even admitted to Sheila that I agreed with her about someone watching over the café and that I believed it to be my parents. I felt closer to the team and I noticed them laughing more with me, with each other and with our customers. The Chocolate Pot had always been a warm and friendly place but somehow that had lifted a notch.

Before we knew it, the first couple of months back at school had whizzed by and the October half-term holidays arrived. October turned into November on the Thursday of that week.

'What's so interesting?' Maria asked, joining me by the window on 1st November and looking out onto Castle Street.

'Over the road. The gallery's sold.' My stomach felt like it was on a spin cycle as I watched a workman hold a ladder against the building so a colleague could attach a SOLD sign at a jaunty angle across the 'for sale' board.

'Jed?' Maria suggested.

'Bound to be.'

'You really think he'll open another café?'

'It's what he knows. It's what his family knows. And he called this place "the competition" so I doubt he's about to open up a tanning salon.'

'But right opposite us?' Maria shook her head. 'That's not on, is it?'

'No, but that's how arrogant gits like him operate. Oh, God. The thought of seeing his smug face every single day...' I shuddered.

'I think someone needs a hot chocolate,' Maria said, moving away from the window.

'Got anything stronger back there?' I tore my gaze away and smiled as I saw Maria rummaging in the cubbyholes for my favourite yellow mug. She knew exactly how to cheer me up.

'I'm afraid not,' she said. 'What flavour?'

'Baileys.'

Maria laughed. 'And what flavour would you like from the range we *do* stock?'

'Chocolate orange. Thank you.'

Grabbing a cloth from the sink, I returned to the window and wiped some marks from the inside, shaking my head. I suppose it had been inevitable.

Galley's Gallery was one of those businesses that was always destined to fail. The owners had spent a small fortune restoring the crumbling façade and refurbishing the dilapidated former clothing store but spent nothing on market research. If they'd tested the market, they'd have discovered that Galley's distinctive style was not right for the area. Galley painted cityscapes and cartoon cats and dogs in an industrial setting. Perhaps if they'd stocked local artists alongside Galley's work, they might have stood a chance, but there was no coherence between Galley's paintings and our local area.

Where were the seascapes? The hills? The sheep? I didn't get it and I clearly wasn't alone.

The manager, Anastasia, became one of my takeaway regulars from late January. She told me that sales hadn't been too bad in the run-up to Christmas last year, but they'd dipped off to virtually non-existent from the New Year. Apparently the owners weren't too worried, anticipating the summer season would make up for the bad start to the year. It didn't. When Anastasia announced in late September that they were closing with immediate effect, I wasn't surprised.

Starting at the SOLD sign outside the gallery now, my stomach churned.

'We've got nothing to worry about,' Maria assured me, placing my drink on the counter. 'The Chocolate Pot is established, the customers love it and it runs like clockwork. If Jed's setting up in competition with us, he's the one who should be worried.'

I smiled. 'You're right. He can't hurt us.' I hoped I sounded more convincing than I felt. Customers could be fickle and even the most loyal could find a new favourite place. Whitsborough Bay teemed with cafés but we somehow all had our own place and speciality. All I could do was hope that Jed was going for something niche or that his ability to run a business hadn't improved over the years.

'We should be glad that we won't have an empty premises opposite. That *never* looks good.' She picked up a tray of drinks and headed towards the back of the café.

I smiled to myself. Maria had just played 'the glad game' and she was right about empty premises looking bad.

'Good to see you smiling,' Maria said, returning with the empty tray.

'I've got a lot to be glad about.'

## 19

Calm seas were forecast for Sunday morning so I arranged to pick up Nathan and go for an early morning swim. We'd done that quite often since I'd first invited him to join me and I had to admit I enjoyed the company.

'Are you okay?' I asked him as I drove towards Lighthouse Cove. 'You seem very fidgety this morning.'

'I want your advice on something, but it's a bit embarrassing.'

'Fire away.' I gave him a reassuring smile. Whatever was on his mind, it couldn't be as embarrassing as telling Carly about my 'playmates' or my husband's 'dungeon'.

'It's Molly,' he said eventually.

'Our Molly at The Chocolate Pot?'

He nodded. 'I've always liked her but she had a bit of an on-off thing with Cody so I backed off.'

'Did she? When?'

'Last year. He's at uni in Edinburgh now. I don't think they stay in touch and, well...'

'If you like her, just ask her out,' I said when he tailed off. 'What's the worst that could happen?'

'She could say no.'

'And the best that could happen?'

He smiled. 'She could say yes.'

'And you'll never find out which it is if you don't ask. If it's a no, then you've still got a friend. It might be slightly awkward when you're on shift together at first, but that'll pass. But I don't think it'll be a no.'

'You don't?'

'No, I don't. And I think you should ask her after your shift today. You're not on again together until Thursday so that's plenty of time to lick your wounds if it's a no which, as I say, I don't think it will be.'

'Thanks, Tara. You're the best.'

'It's true. I can't deny it.'

Out of my peripheral vision, I could see he was grinning. It warmed my heart, not just thinking of two lovely young people getting together, but that Nathan had come to me for advice. That would never have happened before. And I'd never have noticed Molly gazing at him fondly across the café before, quickly averting her eyes if he looked up. I'd always thought that I had everything I wanted at work but getting to know the team had given me something I never even knew was missing. It made me feel valued. It made me feel wanted. And I hadn't felt that way in such a long time.

I parked the car and we pulled on our wetsuits then crossed the road. Leaning against the sea wall, we both paused to take in the view. There was nothing like seeing a dark expanse of ocean stretched before us, brightening as the sun steadily rose.

'Race you to the sea,' I called, sprinting down the steps.

\* \* \*

Back in the flat after dropping Nathan home, I showered then sat down ready for a busy day of crafting. The Christmas decorations would be going up in The Chocolate Pot the following week. I always decorated on my own because it was more practical to do it when we were closed. The thought of trying to work round customers and staff members carrying trays of hot drinks was too much like an accident waiting to happen.

Needle felting had quickly become my new favourite craft. I'd made a few decorations that way over the past five or six years, but it had become a bit addictive for me this year and I'd produced more than expected which was something I had to be thankful to Jed for. After our encounter outside the gym in January, I'd been so angry that I'd wanted to punch something – or someone – which was not exactly the state of mind I was usually in after an hour of Pilates. Back home, I dug out a needle felt penguin I'd previously abandoned and there was something about stabbing a barbed needle into the wool that did wonders for my mood. What a tension-releaser.

I was super proud of the needle felting decorations I'd made over the past year and was dying to hear what the team thought of them next week. It would be the perfect opportunity to reveal my secret identity as The Cobbly Crafter but I wasn't sure I was ready. I'd already revealed so much.

As closing time at 4 p.m. approached, I stretched, cleared my crafts away, changed out of my snuggly clothes then made my way downstairs to check how the day had gone. I opened the door then screamed at the cries of 'Surprise!' Party poppers exploded and streamers were unfurled in my direction.

My heart thumped as, mouth agape, I looked round the sea of faces. In among my team – including all those who hadn't been on shift that day – were friends from Bay Trade and some regular customers. Carly was there with Liam and her sister, Bethany. I spotted Marc with George and Sofia, and Maria's best friend Callie and her kids. So many people and they were all smiling at me.

'I don't understand,' I said, completely flummoxed as to what was going on.

'You wouldn't let us make a fuss on your actual birthday,' Maria said, 'so we decided to celebrate your half-birthday.'

'My what?'

'You are exactly thirty-six and a half years old today,' Carly said. 'So happy half-birthday to you.'

I pressed my fingers to my mouth and blinked back the tears, feeling quite emotional. 'Oh my God! I can't believe you've done all this.'

There were hugs and gifts. So many gifts. Having had no birthday presents since my twenty-second birthday, it was a shock to see so many brightly coloured gift bags and packages, knowing they were all for me.

By half four, several more Castle Street traders joined us after their own businesses closed. I'd never seen The Chocolate Pot so full and it gave me a valuable insight into what it might look like at Maria and Marc's wedding later this month and how we could use the two floors.

I felt like I was in a dream. Everywhere I looked, there were people smiling, chatting, laughing and they'd all gathered for me. I'd set myself up for an isolated existence yet somehow I'd managed exactly the opposite. For the first time since primary school, I had friends. Real friends. Swallowing hard on the ever-present lump in my throat, I blinked back tears once more.

I spotted Maria and Carly craning their necks then whispering to each other and nodding. Carly disappeared upstairs and, moments later, the guests from up there traipsed down to the ground floor.

Maria and Carly stood together four stairs from the bottom and asked everyone to gather round.

'I think we're all here now,' Maria announced to the hushed gathering. 'A huge thank you for joining us today as Tara reaches that highly celebrated milestone of thirty-six and a half years.' She paused for laughter. 'For anyone who doesn't know me, I'm Maria, and I'm the assistant manager at The Chocolate Pot, I've worked here for seven years now and this is my way of thanking Tara for taking a chance on me and for being the best boss ever.'

She looked at Carly who smiled. 'Hi, everyone. I'm Carly from Carly's Cupcakes next door. I opened my business five years ago and, when Maria asked if I'd like to help her organise a half-birthday event for Tara, I jumped at it. From the very start, Tara's always been there for me with advice, guidance and a helping hand. I'm very proud to call her my friend.'

My bottom lip started to wobble as they both smiled warmly at me. I hoped the speech was nearly over because I was already close to losing it and any more nice words would tip me right over the edge.

'You can probably tell that we both think the world of Tara,' Maria continued, 'but we know we're not the only ones. Tara, you're going to hate this, but tough. We distributed some pieces of coloured card to as many guests as we could and asked them to either write down what they like most about you or a funny anecdote involving you.'

I put my hands to my burning cheeks. 'You didn't.'

'We really did,' Carly said. 'We've compiled a scrapbook that we'll give to you later, but we wanted to share a small selection.'

'The first one's from Sarah from Seaside Blooms,' Maria said. 'Where are you Sarah?'

Sarah raised her hand. 'Here.'

Maria held up a piece of card. 'Sarah says, "On the day I took over Seaside Blooms, I started the morning with a drink and a croissant from The Chocolate Pot. It was also the start of a new friendship. Tara, you're a brilliant chef, an inspiring entrepreneur, a gifted mentor and an amazing friend. Happy half-birthday".'

Everyone clapped as I made my way to Sarah and hugged her.

Maria and Carly took turns to read out a few more lovely comments then announced it was time to cut a cake that Carly had made.

'Sheila, do you want to bring out the cake?' Maria called.

Carly put her arm round me and whispered in my ear. 'I made something that's special to you but nobody knows why and they won't hear it from me.'

The lights dimmed and a decidedly off-key chorus of 'Happy half-birthday' began as Sheila emerged from the kitchen holding a large cake covered in candles.

As she got closer and I could see the theme, I gasped. A carousel. A bright yellow and red canopy protected the cream horses. One of them was ridden by a woman in a flowing red coat, and another by a child and a man. Carly had remembered every bit of detail.

My eyes met Carly's and she gave me a gentle smile as I fought to hold back the tears.

'Thank you,' I said. 'It's perfect. Today is perfect.'

'The Best Day Ever,' she whispered.

I took a deep breath, battling to control my emotions, then leaned forward, readying myself to blow out the candles. What to wish for? The obvious thing was to wish for Jed to leave me alone and to leave Whitsborough Bay, but I caught sight of Nathan standing nearby, and pictured his earnest expression on the seafront earlier as he'd talked about Molly. Taking a deep breath, I blew. *I wish for Nathan and Molly to find love together.*

With great reluctance, I cut into the masterpiece that Carly had created.

'Why a carousel?' Lana asked, gazing at the intricate horses.

'Because I've never made one before and it seemed very summery and seasidey,' Carly responded. 'I know it's not summer anymore but we are at the seaside.'

I loved that she'd anticipated an answer to questions about the cake. Although I'd opened up about losing my parents, I hadn't talked about Mum's mental health challenges and subsequent suicide. As Maria had said, they didn't need to know everything.

I couldn't quite believe the effort and attention to detail that everyone had gone to. If I'd ever had any doubts about Whitsborough Bay being home and these people being my family, they evaporated that day. And at that point, I couldn't keep the tears at bay any longer and spent the next hour or so blotting my cheeks and blowing my nose.

\* \* \*

Back in my flat that evening, exhausted but happy, I curled up on the sofa with Hercules and read through the entries in my scrapbook. It was a revelation seeing myself through the eyes of others. I wondered whether they'd have said the same things a year previously but so what if they wouldn't have done. The person they saw now was the person I really was.

Making my way over to the huge pile of gifts spread across the dining table, I slowly opened each one, savouring the sensation of peeling back the tape or peeking into a gift bag. I'd been well and truly spoilt. As I stood back and surveyed the generosity of my guests, it struck me how 'me' all the gifts were – the cosy me that I kept hidden. Perhaps I hadn't kept it that hidden after all. Perhaps, despite my protective tower, they all really did know me. That feeling of being alone nudged at me again. I pictured all the couples and families from my party earlier and wondered for the first time whether I'd made a huge mistake in refusing to have a romantic relationship ever again. I could spend my evenings at Pilates, at Bay Trade, at The Hope Centre or mentoring but I would always come home to an empty flat and go to bed alone. Did I really want to do that forever?

## 20

'Namaste,' said Karen on Tuesday night, a couple of days after my half-birthday.

'Namaste,' the class repeated. I was already on my feet, though, and rolling up my mat.

Why? Why did he have to come to my Pilates class? Karen wasn't the only instructor in Whitsborough Bay, so why couldn't he go to someone else's class and torment their customers instead?

'Thanks, Karen,' I muttered, dashing out the room.

But, of course, that idiot was hot on my heels.

'Here was me thinking you'd be putting out the red carpet to welcome me back,' Jed said, striding beside me.

'Perhaps I would have done if you'd actually been welcome.'

'Aw, that's mean.' He gently patted my arm with his mat. 'And it's no way to treat your newest neighbour.'

I stopped and turned to face him. 'So the rumours are true – it *is* you who's bought the gallery?' I'd had a steady stream of Castle Street traders in over the past couple of days, some asking what I knew, and others clearly knowing more than I did. And none of them were happy.

'I might have done,' Jed said.

'Oh grow up, Jed. It's a simple question. Did you or didn't you?'

'Yes, I did, if you must know. I'll be able to wave to you every day.'

'And I'll be able to give you the finger every day.' I turned and walked away.

Jed laughed loudly as he ran after me. 'Who's being childish now?'

'You started it.'

'And you continued it.'

I stopped and turned to face him. 'What did you expect? There are three cafés on Castle Street already. *Three.* Do we really need a fourth? What are you trying to do to us all? To the street?'

He looked taken aback for a moment but then shook his head, scowling. 'It's a free market. I can run whatever business I want and you can't stop me. Scared of a bit of healthy competition?' He sounded like a petulant schoolkid and I half-expected him to add 'so ner'.

I shook my head and continued striding across the car park. He kept pace beside me.

'There's competition and there's being an idiot,' I declared. 'Castle Street is the best street in town and you know it, but what makes it the best is the diversity. The street would have benefited from something new and different to attract even more customers, not a fourth bloody café. The rest of the traders aren't impressed so don't expect the red-carpet treatment from any of them either.'

'So you've been bad-mouthing me to everyone, have you?'

We reached the cars and I unlocked my door. 'Get over yourself. Not everything's about you. And this isn't about me either. In an ideal world, I don't want the competition. Who would? But I've got a great business and a great team so I'm not worried about you damaging that. What I don't like is the impact the lack of variation will have on the street. And I didn't need to start rumours about that. The others worked it out for themselves. Good luck.' I jumped into the car, slammed the door and started the engine.

Jed looked a little shell-shocked but I didn't care. The man was clearly just as clueless about business now as he'd been fourteen years ago when I bought the premises from him. He'd obviously not thought about the impact of too many of the same type of businesses on Castle Street or how the traders would react to that. If he wanted a war, then he'd got one and I already had the strongest army.

\* \* \*

I was so riled when I got back to the flat that I headed straight for my needle felting. That poor robin was certainly created from hate rather than love, although he still looked pretty damn good when I'd finished him.

Taking my laptop down to the dining table, Hercules sat on the padded seat beside me while I checked for any Etsy enquiries. I tended to find an increase in questions and orders after Bonfire Night – which had been last night – as though that was the key date after which the countdown to Christmas started.

My mobile beeped with a text from Nathan while I was mid-message.

✉ I took your advice and asked Molly out at your party. We went out for a meal tonight and we're going out again after work on Thursday. Thank you

'And that makes three wishes and three success stories,' I said to Hercules. 'I wonder if I should take a trip to Hearnshaw Park and throw a coin in the wishing well to get Jed banished. What do you think?'

Thinking about Jed made me angry again and I couldn't concentrate on my work. I couldn't seem to relax either so it was pointless trying to watch TV or a film. If I felt this tense from a five-minute encounter with him, what was it going to be like having him opposite, no doubt trying his hardest to put me out of business?

## 21

I spent Wednesday evening decorating The Chocolate Pot and revelled in the excited reactions from staff and customers when they arrived on Thursday and saw the lights and decorations. The compliments came in thick and fast about The Cobbly Crafter's latest designs, yet I remained tight-lipped about my alter-ego.

'Two flat whites and two pieces of millionaire's shortbread to take out, please.'

My ears pricked up as I recognised the voice of Anastasia from the gallery around mid-morning. I stepped out of the kitchen as Ellen, one of my full-timers, started making the drinks. 'Hi, Anastasia. How's it going?'

She shrugged. 'It's weird not working every day. I don't have it in me to be a lady who lunches so I confess I'm a bit bored at the moment.'

I picked up a paper bag and slid the two pieces of shortbread into it, placing them on the counter. 'I see the gallery's sold.'

'Yes. I'm heading over there now to take the final meter readings and to do a handover with the new owner.'

My jaw clenched. 'Lucky you.'

Her eyebrows raised. 'Ooh, tell me how you really feel about him.'

'Let's just say we have history and leave it there.'

'You were involved?'

'God, no! He was the previous owner of this place and the purchase wasn't the smoothest. I certainly wasn't seeing him. Urgh.' I shuddered at the thought.

Anastasia laughed. 'I can't believe you'd say "urgh" about him. I know that beauty is in the eye of the beholder – as those damn awful cats and dogs in Galley's paintings prove – but Jed Ferguson is sex on legs.'

'Are you sure we're talking about the same person?'

'Unless there's another Jed Ferguson. Tall, blond, tanned, yummy Australian accent?'

I shook my head. 'Sorry. Not seeing it.'

She laughed again. 'Then you might need glasses.'

A few minutes after Anastasia left, Ellen was wiping down a table by the window. 'Tara, is that the Jed you were both talking about?'

'Where?' I joined her by the window and looked out. Jed was in the middle of the cobbles talking to someone I didn't recognise, and laughing. 'Yes, that's him. Before I created The Chocolate Pot, this was his family's café.'

'And you really think he's opening a café over the road?'

'Certainly seems that way.'

'He's brave. There's no way he can compete with The Chocolate Pot. Anastasia's right about him, though. He *is* lush.'

I narrowed my eyes, but I couldn't see it. Although I had to concede that he wasn't altogether unpleasant-looking when he was laughing – proper laughter rather than nasty vindictive laughter directed at me. But looks weren't everything and I knew that, on the inside, he was a very ugly man. And, yes, I suppose I had thought he was attractive when I'd first seen him, but I'd thought the same of Garth. I rest my case.

* * *

Ellen poked her head round the kitchen door later that afternoon. 'Joyce and Peter wondered if you had five minutes to spare.'

'For them, always. I'll be two minutes.'

Joyce and Peter were a couple in their mid-seventies who came into town every Thursday afternoon for a mooch round the shops, no matter what the weather, then stopped by for afternoon tea and a chat with the staff. Everyone loved them, and not just because they were good tippers. Peter was usually fairly quiet, but Joyce was the sort of woman who you warmed to instantly. She always had something positive to say about the food, the décor, or compliments about a team member's hairstyle or make-up.

'Good afternoon, you two,' I said, making my way over to their favourite table and sitting down – something I wouldn't normally dream of doing, but they'd always insisted on me joining them if I had time. 'How was your afternoon tea?'

'Delicious, as always,' Peter said.

'We loved the Malteser cake,' Joyce gushed. 'Although Peter stole a Malteser off mine.'

'I did not. You had two on your piece and one happened to fall onto my plate.'

'Rubbish,' Joyce said. 'You stole it. Anyway, Tara, we wanted to speak to you about your Christmas decorations. They are so beautiful.'

'Thank you.'

'We were looking at those penguins and snowmen on the tree and we'd love to get some for our grandchildren. Would you do me a huge favour? If I give you the money, do you think you could order me five penguins and five snowmen from the person who makes them?'

'I can do you one better than that,' I said. 'I ordered too many. I'm pretty certain I've got at least five of each upstairs if you want them now. It would save you on postage.'

'That would be wonderful, if you don't mind. Actually, if you have six of each, I wouldn't mind one of each for my own tree.'

'Haven't we got enough decorations already?' Peter protested.

'You can never have enough decorations,' she said, shutting him up.

I checked she was happy with the price, throwing in a little discount for a bulk purchase, then told Ellen where I was going before running upstairs. I wouldn't have done it for everyone, but they were such good customers. As I packed the decorations into a small gift box, though, I wondered if I'd done the right thing. What if word got round and other people started asking me for them? I don't know why I was so reluctant to let people know that I was The Cobbly Crafter, especially after all the progress I'd made in letting people in, but I still couldn't bring myself to do the reveal. Despite everything positive that had happened since I'd started opening up, I still couldn't fully smash down that wall. I'd have to emphasise again to Joyce that they were surplus and nip it in the bud immediately.

'Here you go.' I handed over the box when I returned to their table. 'You were in luck because that was exactly the number I had left. This is the business card from the woman I buy them from, in case you or anyone else want to check out her other items.' The cards only included a Cobbly Crafter email address and my Etsy site – no phone number – so had zero link back to me.

'Thank you.' Joyce popped the card into her purse. 'I really appreciate this. I'd better let you get on.'

I was about to move away when Joyce said, 'Oh, by the way, I see you have a new neighbour.'

My shoulders slumped, but I tried my best to sound cheerful. 'It looks like it. It was a shame about the gallery. It's always sad when a business fails.'

'It was hardly surprising, though,' Peter said. 'Those cityscapes were depressing and the poor animals looked like they needed a good feed.'

I laughed. 'To be fair, they probably weren't to everyone's taste.'

'At least Jed has better taste,' Joyce said.

'You know him?' I drew out a chair and sat down again.

'Oh yes. We're good friends with his parents. They live in Great Sandby, round the corner from us. Such a shame what happened to him in Australia.'

'Oh yeah...?'

'Joyce! I don't think it's up to us to—'

'Janice and Richie didn't say it was confidential.' Joyce flashed him a look that clearly said, 'butt out'. She leaned in conspiratorially. 'It was his wife. Nasty piece of work, she was.'

Despite my loathing of gossip, I found myself moving closer, intrigued. 'What did she do?'

'What didn't she do? Going to Australia was Ingrid's idea. Jed never wanted to go, but she went on and on at him about emigrating. The café wasn't doing too well so Jed finally agreed as long as they did it well before their little ones started school. Turns out the real reason she wanted to emigrate was that her ex-boyfriend was in Australia and they'd been emailing each other a lot. As soon as she got out there, they started an affair and then she—'

'Enough,' Peter interjected. 'If Jed wants everyone to know his business, he'll tell them. I insist this stops now.'

I'd never heard him speak so sternly and wondered whether Joyce would ignore him and continue, but she nodded. 'You're right.

Anyway, Tara, his parents are thrilled to have him back with his two girls, but it's such a shame that—'

'Sorry to interrupt,' Ellen said, lightly touching my arm. 'But Malcolm Dring's on the phone and I know you wanted to speak to him.'

'Oh, yes, I do. Can you ask him to hang on for a couple of minutes?' I turned back to Joyce. 'Sorry. What were you saying?'

I noticed Peter giving her a hard stare, clearly trying to silence her again.

'Nothing. I was just going to say that it's such a shame that bad things happen to good people. Jed's such a nice young man and that woman knew it and took advantage.' Joyce sighed. 'You'd better get to your call. Thanks for sorting out these.' She pointed to the box of tree decorations.

'No problem. See you next week.'

I took my call from Malcolm from Whitsborough Bay TEC but, afterwards, all I could think about was Joyce's tale, or the part of it that Peter had allowed her to tell. I couldn't stand the man, but nobody deserved to be dragged to the other side of the world so their wife could have an affair with her ex, away from friends and family and the natural support group that would rally round at times like that. I knew how hard it could be with nobody to turn to. Still didn't make him a nice bloke, though, no matter how much Joyce gushed about him.

## 22

A loud bang on the door shortly before 7.30 a.m. on Saturday morning made me jump and drop my spatula on the floor, splattering buttercream everywhere.

I opened the door to Carly who was wearing the biggest smile I'd ever seen. 'Liam proposed last night,' she squealed.

'Oh my goodness. Congratulations.' I hugged her tightly. 'I'm so thrilled for you both.'

'Let's see the ring, then,' I said when we pulled apart.

Carly held her hand out and I smiled at the platinum band with a large diamond and two smaller ones set either side of it.

'It's gorgeous. The boy has taste, but I already knew that because he picked you.'

'Aw, thank you. I'm so excited.' I could tell. She could barely stand still and it gave me a warm and fuzzy feeling inside.

'Have you got time for a celebratory hot chocolate?'

'Only if I'm not disturbing you.'

'If you don't mind drinking it in the kitchen while I do some baking...'

She made her way into the kitchen while I made us both drinks.

'I didn't see it coming,' she said, taking her drink from me. 'Obviously, I knew he was going to ask me at some point, but I thought he might do it at Christmas or New Year. He knew that's what I'd be expecting and he wanted it to be a surprise so that's why he went for last night.'

'How did he propose?' I asked as I sieved flour into a mixing bowl.

'We'd been invited for dinner at his parents' house and it was such a mild evening that he suggested we go early and have a walk. His parents, like mine, still live in the houses we were both brought up in and, as kids, we used to spend hours wandering round the streets and across the fields, chatting about anything and everything. Neither of us have been on a walk round there since leaving home so it was a lovely trip down memory lane. We passed Farmer Duggan's field. Do you remember me telling you that we made snow angels in there when we were fifteen and it was then that I realised I saw him as more than a friend?'

'I remember. Aw, was that where he proposed?'

She nodded. 'The field was boggy so we didn't go in and obviously it's not the time of year for snow angels but we leaned on the wall just past the stile and reminisced about that day and how it was the moment we both fell in love. We turned to walk back towards his parents' house and he said, "What's that on the stile?" I could see something catching the streetlight and, when I stepped closer, it was the ring. He'd planted it there as we passed and I turned round to see him on bended knee. When we got back to his parents' house, it turned out they were all in on it. My parents were there too with Bethany and Joshua and they had champagne, balloons and happy engagement banners. It was a special moment.'

'When do you think you'll get married? Next year?'

She shook her head. 'The year after. We're a couple of weeks into the shop's busiest season so I don't have time to look round venues at the moment. We'll look at the start of next year ready for the following year. We're thinking maybe September. But, because we're waiting for a couple of years, we would like to celebrate getting engaged. I know you have Maria's wedding on Monday, but I wondered how you'd feel about an engagement party here two weeks tonight.'

The buzzer went on the oven so I bent down to retrieve a tray of caramel and banana blondies. Placing the tray on a cooling rack, I turned back to Carly. 'Sorry about that. Two weeks tonight, you say? So that would be...?'

'The twenty-fourth. It's the Saturday between the Best of The Bay Awards and the Christmas tree lights switch-on. Liam and I would sort out the decorations and we can help with the catering, but we understand if it's too much happening at once. We were only thinking of that date because Liam's sister and her family are coming up from Exeter that weekend. She'll be up again at some point next year, though.'

I smiled. 'No, it's all good. Yes, you can book The Chocolate Pot for that night.'

Carly squealed. 'Yes! Thank you so much.'

'Pleasure. I'm so excited for you both.'

'Me too. I can't believe I'm finally marrying my best friend after lusting after him for so many years.'

'The best things come to those who wait,' I said.

'They certainly do.'

I put a tray of sticky toffee brownies into the oven. 'Do you think I should start promoting The Chocolate Pot for functions from next year? Assuming Jed doesn't beat me to it and nab the business.'

'Have you seen any more of him?'

'No. There were workmen in yesterday, as you'll have seen, but I didn't spot him. You know Joyce and Peter? They told me why he's back from Australia.' I cringed. 'If I tell you, I'll sound like I'm gossiping.'

'Not if you *only* tell me because I won't tell anyone else, so it's not like we're spreading it.'

Reassured, I told her about my conversation with Joyce.

'Is it making you see him in a different light?' Carly asked.

'I'll admit that there's a teeny-weeny fragment of sympathy for him, but Joyce seems to think the sun shines out of his arse, whereas I just think he *is* an arse. Therefore, I can't help wondering if there's more to it than Joyce said.'

'You think he was up to no good too?'

'I don't know. Maybe. When I met Jed, he looked me up and down and acted all flirty. What's to say he wasn't a saint?'

Carly shrugged. 'I've never met him so I can't comment. I usually find there are two sides to every story and, somewhere in the midst of it, is the truth.' She gulped down the last of her hot chocolate. 'I'd better go. I need to put the finishing touches to a birthday cake for collection at nine. You're sure about the party, though?'

'I'm very sure. Why don't you both come round after we close tomorrow and we can do some planning?'

'That would be perfect. Thank you again. And yes to you running functions next year, by the way. You'd do brilliantly.'

I saw Carly to the door, then stood in the fresh air for a couple of minutes.

'You can stare at it as much as you like, but it's not going to go away.'

I turned to face my nemesis. 'For your information, Jed, I wasn't even looking at your stupid café. I was thinking.'

'About me?'

I wrinkled my nose and frowned at him. 'As if. Get over yourself.' I stepped inside and moved to close the door, but Jed put his foot out to stop it.

'Any chance of a coffee?'

'None whatsoever.'

'But I'm thirsty and I haven't got a kettle yet.'

'Have you got a tap?'

'Yes.'

'Then have some water.'

'I haven't got any mugs or glasses either. And I'd really like a coffee. Please.'

'Oh, for God's sake. Wait here.' I strode across to the counter and grabbed one of our paper takeaway cups then strode back and thrust it at him.

'What's this?'

'A cup. So you can have some water. Don't forget to recycle it. Goodbye.' With a shove, I closed and locked the door then returned to the kitchen where I released a deep breath. That had been mean of me. I was never mean. Why did he make me behave like a little kid?

Moments later, a key turned in the door and I heard Maria's voice saying, 'No, it's not a problem. We're not officially open for another ten minutes, but I'm sure I can sort you out a coffee. The machine will be on already.'

'Thank you. Very kind of you.'

I poked my head out of the kitchen and Jed gave me a satisfied smirk. Horrible man. I wasn't sorry I'd been mean to him after all.

## 23

On Monday morning, I placed the final collection of balloons in the corner of the first floor then stepped back and smiled at Sheila. 'What do you think?'

'It looks beautiful,' she said. 'I knew it would look good, but this is something else.'

'It's pretty impressive, isn't it?' I dug my phone out my pocket. 'I need to take some photos while it all looks immaculate.'

Maria and Marc had chosen a grey, pink and ivory colour scheme for their wedding. I'd hired in some silver chairs with ivory seat pads and ivory voile bows fastened to the backs. Sarah from Seaside Blooms had already been in with the flowers. She'd made large pink and white arrangements on plinths for upstairs and downstairs, a table arrangement for the register signing table upstairs, a matching one for the café counter downstairs, a collection of small arrangements in sparkly silver vases for the tables, and some swathes of ivy and gypsophila for the staircase and round the windows.

'Anything else need doing?' Sheila asked when I'd finished taking photos.

Whipping my list out of my pocket, I scanned down it. 'No. I think that's all done so get yourself home and changed and I'll see you back here at one.'

The 2 p.m. ceremony would be attended by a small, select gathering of roughly twenty guests. More guests were invited from 4 p.m. including several of the Castle Street traders, although they'd mainly be joining us from six onwards once they'd closed for the day and had the opportunity to freshen up and change.

Back downstairs, I let Sheila out then checked on Nathan and Molly in the kitchen who'd both skipped lectures for the day.

'We need about another half an hour in here,' Molly said, while Nathan removed a couple of quiches from the oven.

'Okay. I'm going to get changed so can you make sure the door is on the latch when you leave?'

'Will do,' Molly said. 'I can't wait to see Maria in her dress. I bet she looks stunning.'

'I bet she does too. See you both later and thanks for this morning. You've been amazing.'

'We've enjoyed it,' Nathan said, smiling. I was pretty certain that part of the enjoyment came from working together. They were such a cute couple, yet they made sure that their relationship remained professional at work.

All the staff were invited to the ceremony and had been told that partners were welcome to join them afterwards. Maria wanted it to be informal and for everyone to enjoy themselves. There was still work to be done, though, so I decided to pay everyone a bonus on the assumption that they would enjoy themselves and be guests, but they would all help out where needed, stocking up the food, preparing more hot food during the evening, clearing away plates and glasses. We weren't licensed so Maria and Marc had provided several bottles of wine, cans of lager, and soft drinks.

I was showered, changed and back downstairs at 12.30 p.m.,

wearing a dress. When I lived in London, I wore dresses all the time, but couldn't actually remember the last time I'd worn one in Whitsborough Bay. I'd chosen a dark blue wrap-around dress with a large floral print. It fell to just under knee-length at the front but was shaped to almost floor-length at the back. The style seemed to fit with the informal wedding vibe that Maria was keen to have – smart and classy without being too formal. I wasn't convinced I'd make it through the entire evening in the strappy blue heels so I placed a pair of ballet pumps at the bottom of the internal stairs just in case.

My phone rang.

'Hi, Tara,' Carly said. 'Just checking whether now's a good time to bring the cake over.'

'Perfect timing. I'm downstairs.'

'Bethany and I will be there in two minutes.'

I was opening a packet of silver serviettes when there was a knock on the door. Pulling it wide, I expected to see Carly and Bethany.

'Oh. It's you,' I snapped, instantly feeling on edge. 'What do you want?'

'Do you greet all your customers like this?' Jed looked and sounded amused which only wound me up more.

'No. But you're not a customer. You're a...' I stopped myself just in time. He really wasn't worth it and I resented how much he'd occupied my thoughts over the past few weeks.

'I'm a what?'

'It doesn't matter.'

'It clearly does or you wouldn't have started to say it. Go on. Spit it out. I'm not a customer. I'm a...'

'You're just the former owner of this building and an arrogant con artist.' There! I'd said it. And, my goodness, did it feel good to finally tell him what I thought of him after all these years.

But Jed looked shell-shocked. 'I'm a what?'

I planted my hands on my hips and narrowed my eyes at him, determined not to feel guilty for calling him on his deception. I wasn't the one in the wrong. 'You heard me.'

'And what am I supposed to have done to be labelled "an arrogant con artist"?'

'Oh, don't play the innocent with me. You ripped me off when I bought this place.'

'How?'

'Wanting ten grand more or you'd sell to a mystery new buyer. You knew I'd have no choice but to cough up because we'd already started on the refurb. I can't believe I fell for that no-catch-nothing-in-it-for-me bollocks. Then there was the leaky roof that you'd had temporarily patched. Cheers for that. It cost me nearly ten grand extra to sort that out too. And all because you threw a strop that I only wanted to buy the building and not your failing café.'

He stared at me for a moment, mouth open. Ha! There wasn't much he could say to that, was there?

'Coming through with a cake,' Carly called.

Jed stepped aside to allow Bethany and Carly to shuffle into the café, holding the cake between them.

'There's a round table for it over there.' I pointed then turned my attention back to Jed. 'Did you knock on the door for a reason?'

'Yes, but it doesn't matter. I can see you're busy. I'll leave you to it.'

'Good.'

'I...' He shook his head. 'Forget it. It doesn't matter.' He turned away and I closed and locked the door. Idiot.

'Sorry about that,' I said to Carly and Bethany.

'Who was that?' Bethany asked. 'He's dreamy.'

I frowned. 'Really? Why does everyone keep saying that?'

'Because he is,' Carly said, 'and even you admitted the other day that he was good-looking. It's only because you can't stand him that you refuse to admit he's gorgeous.'

'But who is he?' Bethany persisted.

'It's Jed. Our new neighbour,' I said.

'From the gallery?' she asked. 'Is it true that he's opening a café?' I nodded.

'We don't know that for certain,' Carly said. 'He's not categorically said he's opening a café, has he? And nobody else seems to know for definite. Right now, it's speculation because of what he used to do.'

'What else would he do, though?'

Carly smiled. 'Tara! He's been living in Australia for fourteen years. He could have retrained several times over and got a stack of new skills. Just because he had a café before doesn't mean he's going to open another one.'

'Maybe not. But he could have made it clear from the outset if that wasn't the case.'

'Maybe he wants to keep what he's doing confidential, just in case anyone else beats him to it,' Bethany suggested.

'Okay. I admit defeat. There is a *slim* possibility he might not be setting up a café. But I don't want to talk about him anymore. Let's see this cake.'

Carly carefully lifted off the tall cardboard box that had been covering it.

'Aw, it's gorgeous.'

'Thank you,' Carly said. 'It's simple but effective.'

It was a three-tier sponge cake and I knew that Maria and the kids had chosen a different flavour per layer. George had gone for chocolate cake, Sofia had chosen vanilla and Maria had picked toffee sponge. Each tier was decorated with sugar ruffles, starting in deep grey, graduating into light grey then steadily becoming ivory as they reached the top layer. Ruffled pale pink roses adorned the various layers and a cute penguin bride and groom wedding topper – chosen by George and Sofia – stood among the roses on the top layer.

'Do you want to look round before everyone gets here?' I asked Carly. 'It might help you visualise how you can use the space for your engagement party.'

'Yes, please.'

'I've got a few bits to sort out so help yourself.'

The pair of them headed towards the back of the café then disappeared upstairs. Five minutes later, they reappeared.

'It looks amazing,' Carly said. 'Even better than I imagined.'

'She's right,' Bethany added. 'I love it.'

'I'd better go and get changed,' Carly said. 'See you in a bit.' She went over to the round table and adjusted the angle of the cake stand then grabbed the cardboard box and I let them both out.

I was about to shut the door when I spotted Jed marching towards me across the cobbles.

'What now?' I snapped.

Solemn-faced, he handed me an envelope, then turned to leave.

'What's this?'

He turned round again with a sigh. 'I'm sorry,' he said, a tenderness in his voice I hadn't heard before. 'I honestly didn't know. It explains a lot.' Without waiting for a response, he turned and headed back to his shop.

Weird. I was about to tear the envelope open when Nathan and Molly arrived back, with Sheila and Brandon just behind them. Nathan put some music on, a few more of the team arrived, and soon The Chocolate Pot was a hive of noise and activity. I shoved the envelope against the coffee machine, out of sight, out of mind.

## 24

Marc and Maria's wedding was lovely. The celebrant had a great sense of humour and she involved Sofia and George in the ceremony.

George was Marc's best man, wearing grey trousers and a waistcoat with a matching bow tie. Sofia was a bridesmaid along with Callie's daughter, Esme, in silvery-grey dresses with sparkly bodices and big net skirts. Maria wore a simple but exquisite dress with silver detailing on the back and round the waist and Marc wore a grey three-piece suit with a pale pink cravat and pocket handkerchief.

The whole thing made me feel a little dreamy about doing it all again, one day, but with someone who actually loved me. Then I quickly forced that thought out of my mind. Never going to happen.

There weren't any formal speeches. When we moved downstairs for a glass of bubbly, Marc and Maria each proposed a toast, then George and Sofia got in on the act and proposed their own. The two children were so adorable that I started imagining how it might be to have kids of my own. It was overpowering and I had to take a few minutes in the kitchen to get my act together. Marriage?

Kids? Neither of those things were ever going to happen. I had some great friends who I'd finally (almost fully) let in, but I was never going to look for love again. Been there, done that, got the broken heart, bruised ego and emotional scars for life. Yes, I sometimes felt very alone but that's how it had to be.

* * *

The party had pretty much wound up by 11 p.m. What was left of the cleaning could wait until the morning.

I locked up after the last person left and leaned against the door, smiling. What a great success. Maria and Marc said it had been everything they'd dreamed of, and I'd had compliments galore from the guests about the food and the venue. There was definitely scope for expanding the business into functions next year.

Even though I felt absolutely shattered, I needed some time to wind down. I'd have quite liked to sit in the café, taking it all in, but I was conscious that Hercules had been on his own for far longer than usual and would be desperate for some attention. I'd nipped up to give him fresh food, but hadn't felt I could stay away from the wedding for long.

I removed my sandals and gratefully slipped my feet into my ballet pumps, then carried my sandals and one of the floral arrangements that Maria had insisted I have up the two flights. I placed them outside my flat door, then came back down for a hot chocolate. As I was making it, my eyes fell on the envelope Jed had handed me earlier. I'd completely forgotten about that. Sighing, I reached for it, finished making my drink, then locked up fully and switched off the lights.

'Hercules?' I called, unlocking the door to my flat. 'Where's my gorgeous boy?' He must have heard me coming up the stairs as he was already by the door, scut wagging. 'Let me put everything down, then I'll give you some attention.'

I slipped into some snuggly clothes, then picked up my drink and the envelope, settling on the sofa with Hercules. 'Let's see what that idiot has to say.' I ripped open the envelope and took out a piece of A4 paper, folded into three. As I opened it out, a smaller piece of paper fell onto my lap. I picked that up and gasped. It was a cheque for £25,000. What?

*Tara*

*If I looked shocked when you explained why you believe me to be "an arrogant con artist", that's because I was. We agreed a price for the sale of the premises 14 years ago and, as far as I knew, that was the price you'd paid. I was stunned by what you said and thought there had to be some mistake, but I've made some calls and discovered the truth.*

*Please find enclosed a cheque for £25k to reimburse you for the over-payment on the premises, taking into account the loss of interest and the inconvenience. I hope you find this sufficient.*

*I apologise for any anxiety or financial hardship you may have experienced.*

*Best wishes,*

*Jed*

*PS I hope the wedding went well. From what I could see, The Chocolate Pot looked amazing.*

Shaking my head, I read the note over and over again. What? *What?* He didn't know? How could he not know? It made no sense. It was *his* business. *He'd* signed all the paperwork agreeing the final sum. Hadn't he? Putting my mug, the cheque and the letter down on the coffee table, I ran up the stairs to the mezzanine and located the box file from the sale of the property. Resting it on my desk, I flicked through the papers until I found the sale documents. Yes, there it was – J Ferguson. I squinted at the signature. Actually, that looked more like an 'I' than a 'J'. I flicked back a page. Oh my word. Owner: Jed Ferguson. Owner and Financial Director: Ingrid Ferguson. His wife had been the one behind the finances.

I slumped onto my desk chair staring at the paperwork. All of these years, I'd hated that man for ripping me off and he'd known nothing about it. I pictured his face when I'd hurled the accusation at him earlier. He'd genuinely looked stunned but I'd assumed it was shock at my outburst or perhaps surprise that I'd clearly held a grudge for so many years. I hadn't for one second imagined the shock was because he hadn't known what I was talking about.

Abandoning the paperwork on the desk, I returned to Hercules. 'What am I going to do? There's no way I can keep the cheque. I'll have to return it tomorrow. Oh my God, Hercules. I can't believe it. I've hated that man for over fourteen years and I've hated the wrong person. I'm going to have to give him one hell of an apology.' I pulled Hercules to my side, stroking his ears. 'He's still arrogant, though. And smug.' But my words faltered. Was he? Or had I just assumed that because I'd been so full of contempt for him because of what I thought he'd done?

## 25

The former gallery was a hive of activity all week, but there was no sign of Jed. I'd crossed the cobbles on several occasions during Tuesday, cheque in hand, and spoken to a different tradesperson each time, yet none of them seemed to know whether Jed was expected on site or not. After turning up twice at my Pilates class when I really didn't want to see him, he didn't show up on Tuesday night. Typical.

After traipsing back and forth across the cobbles several times on Wednesday, I left a message with one of the builders to say that, if he appeared, could he come over to The Chocolate Pot. I wasn't convinced it would get to him, but I didn't have time to keep seeking him out. I was desperate to get the cheque back to him but returning it with an apology note seemed woefully inadequate. I definitely needed to speak to him in person and clear the air.

\* \* \*

It was mid-afternoon on Thursday when Carly burst through the door, clutching an iPad. 'Have you seen them?' she cried, dashing to the counter.

My heart thumped. 'Is it the shortlist?' Several weeks ago, it had been confirmed that The Chocolate Pot was nominated for Best Café or Bistro in the Best of The Bay Awards, but the nominations had then progressed through a judging panel with the shortlists due to be announced today.

'Here.' She thrust the iPad at me.

I cast my eye down the shortlist and squealed.

'I'm so proud of you,' Carly gave me a huge hug. 'I've got to get back, but I wanted to check you'd seen them.'

Grinning, I went into the kitchen. 'We've been shortlisted,' I announced, jumping up and down.

'As if there was any doubt,' Sheila said, beaming. 'Congratulations, my dear.'

'It's all of us,' I insisted. 'I'm not The Chocolate Pot. *We* are.'

Returning to the counter, I caught the attention of Ellen and Brandon, to give them the news, then texted everyone else.

The rest of the afternoon seemed to pass in a blur of text messages and people dropping in to congratulate me. It was only as I turned the sign round to 'closed' that I realised that Joyce and Peter hadn't been in for their afternoon tea which was unusual. I hoped that neither of them was ill as it was very rare they missed a Thursday. Damn! I'd hoped to pump Joyce for information about Jed's ex-wife and her part in running Ferguson's.

* * *

Saturday – the day of the Best of The Bay Awards – dawned cold and crisp. I stood in the open doorway to The Chocolate Pot at 6.30 a.m., sipping on a latte, drinking in the peace and quiet before Castle Street and Whitsborough Bay came alive.

Beneath the soft glow of the streetlights, frost glistened on the cobbles like tiny crystals. With an hour still to go until sunrise, the sky was inky black above the shops and cafés. A half-moon rested among a blanket of stars. I gazed up towards the sky for several minutes. 'You'll be there tonight, won't you? Please say you will.'

'At the Awards?'

I snapped my head round. Jed. He was standing a couple of feet away, a bemused expression on his face.

'Erm, I—' I glanced up at the sky again then back to Jed. How could I say I wasn't talking to him without sounding snappy? And I could hardly tell him I was talking to my parents, could I?

'Congratulations on making the shortlist, by the way,' he said. 'I hope you win.'

'Yeah, right.'

'I'm serious.' He inclined his head towards The Chocolate Pot. 'You've transformed that place and if all your food is as good as that millionaire's shortbread Anastasia gave me, then you've transformed the food too.'

I stared at him, waiting for the insult, but none came. And, for some reason, words evaded me too.

'Yes, well, I came in early for a reason,' he said. 'Good luck for tonight.' Then he turned and strode across the cobbles, letting himself into the gallery without a backwards glance.

Taking a final deep breath of fresh air, I stepped back inside, closed and locked the door, then ventured into the kitchen to start on the baking for the day. What just happened? Had he actually been nice to me? And had I just been horrible again? Oh no! The cheque! I never mentioned the cheque. All week I'd been hoping to catch him to return it and apologise. First opportunity to do so and all I'd done was stare at him and accuse him of not wanting The Chocolate Pot to win an award. What was wrong with me? I'd never been nasty to anyone in my whole life. Until

Jed. Was this how it felt to walk in Leanne's shoes? I didn't like it one little bit.

As I lightly kneaded the cheese scones, my thoughts drifted from Jed to the awards ceremony itself. The Best of The Bay Awards were all about celebrating independent businesses in Whitsborough Bay and the surrounding villages and had been set up a few years ago by the Mayor. Each year new categories were added and this was the first time there'd been a specific category for cafés and bistros. We'd been nominated for best business each year but, with so much competition, we'd never made the shortlist, so this year was particularly exciting.

There was going to be a glitzy awards ceremony in a venue called The Bay Pavilion at the far end of South Bay. Businesses could only have tickets for a maximum of eight attendees, taking a full table. With twenty staff, I hated that I couldn't take everyone. It was only right that Maria attended as assistant manager. For the remaining six spaces, I checked who was free and wanted to attend, then got them to each draw paper straws. What else could I do?

I was a little surprised to see Joyce and Peter taking a seat mid-afternoon. 'We missed you on Thursday,' I said, going over to their table once they'd settled.

'Sick grandchild crisis,' Joyce said. 'My daughter was on a training course in York so she couldn't get home to collect her from school.'

'We thought we'd brave a Saturday,' Peter said. 'Bit too busy in town for my liking, though.'

'Especially approaching Christmas,' I said. 'Is it the usual?'

'Yes, please,' they chorused.

'I'll put your order through, then do you mind if I come back and ask you something?'

With their permission, I returned to their table a few minutes later and sat down. 'It's about your friends, the Fergusons, and this place,' I said. 'This was originally their business, wasn't it?'

Joyce nodded. 'Yes. They took it on in the early eighties, I think.'

'And they passed it to Jed when they retired?'

'No,' Peter said. 'Ingrid's parents bought them out.'

'Oh. I didn't realise that.'

'They'd have loved to give it to him,' Joyce said, 'but they needed to sell up so they could pay off their mortgage and retire early. Ingrid begged her parents to buy it for her and, what Ingrid wants, Ingrid gets.'

'Joyce!' Peter warned.

'I'm not being nasty. It's the truth. She pestered them until they agreed. They transferred it into Ingrid and Jed's names although Ingrid had the biggest share. I don't know why she did it, Tara, because she was a nurse. She had no plans to give up nursing and Jed never wanted to run it. Poor lad was left with no choice. His heart was never in it, though.'

Lana appeared with their pots of tea.

'I'll leave you in peace,' I said, standing up. 'Thanks for that, though. It's good to know.'

'Good luck for tonight,' Peter said.

'Thank you. I really appreciate it.'

'You'll walk it,' Joyce said. 'I'm sure of it.'

I'd been hearing that from customers all day and I really wanted to believe it, but I didn't dare. The Pollyanna still lurking inside me was glad to have been shortlisted – an amazing achievement in a town bursting with cafés and bistros – yet being shortlisted wasn't enough. I wanted to win. So very much.

## 26

'You look amazing,' Maria said when I met her in the entrance of The Bay Pavilion that evening ready for the Best of The Bay Awards. 'That's one serious award-winning dress.'

I gave her a twirl. 'It's not too much?'

'It's stunning.'

I'd chosen a deep purple dress with a fitted sleeveless bodice embellished with silver glitter, and layers of tulle on the skirts covered with smaller sprinkles of glitter like stars. I actually felt incredible in the dress and strappy silver sandals, but had been worried it was too dressy. Seeing other guests in floor-length gowns, though, my worries dissipated.

'Wow!' I said, stepping into the function room when the rest of the team had arrived. 'They've certainly pulled out all the stops.'

Two enormous Christmas trees – must have been about twelve feet each – flanked a stage on which there was a microphone podium. Behind that, a large screen displayed rolling images of the nominated businesses in the various categories. Silver, lilac and purple baubles and ornaments hung from the tree branches among purple and white fairy lights. Garlands in matching colours were strung across the walls and wrapped around pillars. The round tables carried the same colour scheme, with deep purple cloths, silver runners and centrepieces created from church candles, pinecones, ivy, and silver and purple baubles.

'I match the colour scheme,' I said to Maria.

'Must be a good omen,' she replied.

Several tables were already full and the excited chatter almost blocked out the Christmas music. We sat down, the team insisting that I took the chair with the best access to the stage ready for collecting the award.

The meal was delicious but I struggled with more than a few mouthfuls of each course. It felt like there was a plane in my stomach doing constant loop-the-loops, making me quite nauseous. I couldn't remember ever feeling so nervous about anything in my life. Why was this getting to me so much? I'd never had a competitive personality. Yes, I'd wanted The Chocolate Pot to succeed and do well, but that was about me being personally driven for success, not about being in competition with others. So why did I so desperately want to win this award?

As the ceremony started, I looked round at the seven eager faces and that plane swooped again. That's when it struck me why I was so nervous and why this was so important – I wanted to win for them more than I wanted it for me. They deserved it. I had such a strong, reliable, committed team and I wanted them to get the recognition they deserved.

'The next award is a new category for this year,' announced the compere, Drew Silvers, one of the DJs from Bay Radio. 'It's for the best café or bistro in and around Whitsborough Bay. The nominations in alphabetical order are, The Chocolate Pot, Evie's, Number 23 and Snackies.' Drew paused as he opened a silver envelope. I could feel everyone watching me as I stared into my coffee and scrunched my napkin on my lap. *Please let us win. Please.*

'And the winner is...'

Swoop went the plane.

'...The Chocolate Pot.'

My heart was beating so fast, I felt as though it could leap out of my chest at any moment. Hand clamped across my mouth, I looked round the table. My team had all leapt to their feet, cheering and clapping, and I felt such a burst of pride. We'd done it. The team had done it. Pushing back my chair, I made my way towards the stage.

The Lady Mayor was waiting at the top of the steps. She shook my hand, kissed me on both cheeks, then led me to the podium where Drew did the same before handing me an envelope and a large glass star on a silver plinth.

'If you want to say a few words...?' He indicated the microphone.

I looked round the room at the sea of faces, all smiling at me, then paused as I spotted Jed on one of the front tables to the right. His smile brightened as I caught his eye and he did look genuinely pleased for me. How strange. Focus, though. I needed to focus.

Leaning into the microphone, unable to stop smiling, I said, 'From the bottom of my heart, a huge thank you to everyone who voted for The Chocolate Pot. My name's Tara and I'm the owner and manager. I'm thrilled to be holding this tonight, but this award isn't for me. This is for my dream team without whom The Chocolate Pot wouldn't be nominated for an award, let alone be receiving one. I'm so lucky to have been blessed with a wonderful assistant manager, Maria, and a fabulous team. It doesn't matter whether they work full- or part-time, they're all enthusiastic, passionate and committed to working hard and delivering exceptional service.' I held the star in the air and looked directly at table six. 'This is for all of you and those who couldn't be here tonight. You made this happen. Not me. You.'

I moved away from the microphone as the audience applauded again. A photographer stepped onto the stage and took several photos, then I was free to return to the team, a big lump in my throat but a huge grin on my face. I deliberately placed the star right in the middle of the table. 'For all of you,' I said. 'Thank you.'

I couldn't wait for the awards to finish so I could get a round of drinks in and celebrate properly. I was so incredibly proud of everything we'd achieved. The Chocolate Pot meant so much to me and to have that recognised in this way was such an honour. My parents and my foster parents would have been so proud of me. If only they were here to see it.

A few swigs of my wine were definitely needed to calm my nerves. I discreetly opened the envelope which contained a congratulations card, a certificate and a cheque for £500. Very nice. I'd divide that among the team in addition to their usual Christmas bonus.

It took another four awards before the shaking finally subsided and my heart was beating at a normal pace. Huge respect to anyone nominated for a BAFTA, Grammy or Oscar. How they managed to look so calm and composed with millions watching was beyond me. It was such a thrilling, exciting, amazing moment.

'And for the final award of the night,' said Drew. 'This is also a new award this year. You may have noticed that we haven't revealed a shortlist for this one and that's because there was one very clear winner as far as the judging panel were concerned. And, when you've watched this video, you'll understand why.'

The stage lights dimmed and a video began playing on the large screen. I recognised an image of The Hope Centre, then the manager, Jim. He briefly explained what they did over footage of their various activities. Had The Hope Centre received an award too? I hoped so. They did such valuable work. I'd spotted Jim and a few of his colleagues at the other end of the function room and made a mental note to catch up with them later.

'Tara got in touch shortly after we opened to ask if she could help with food,' Jim said on the film.

That plane did a loop-the-loop in my stomach again. Had he just mentioned my name?

'She has a café in town, you see – The Chocolate Pot – and they pride themselves on their freshly made home-cooked food.'

My heart began thumping again and I glanced round the table. Most of them were focused on the film, but Maria turned to face me and winked before turning her attention back to the screen.

The film showed Castle Street and The Hope Centre's van parked outside The Chocolate Pot. I could be seen handing over a couple of boxes and laughing with Jim.

'There's sometimes a whole quiche or cake in the boxes,' Jim said. 'She pretends they're spare, but I know she's made them especially for us. Thing is, it isn't just Tara now. She persuaded other businesses on Castle Street to contribute, and then extended it throughout the town. We're so grateful to everyone, but extra grateful to Tara for being the one who started it all. And, as if that wasn't enough, she now runs workshops on cooking with a budget too. She's amazing.'

My heart continued to race as various users of The Hope Centre added in their thanks and explained what the food contributions meant to them and their families. I'd known I was helping, but to see and hear from those who had so little and relied on donations was humbling. Yet that wasn't why I'd come up with the idea. I felt sick. If only they knew.

The image changed to Whitsborough Bay TEC and the Principal, Malcolm Dring, being interviewed outside the entrance.

'Tara approached me at the start of this year,' Malcolm said. 'She said she wanted to give something back to the community and would I consider her and some of the other business owners running a mentoring programme for students interested in running their own businesses. Would I ever? Such a great idea. I never dreamed that Project Hercules would take off in the way it has and become so much more for so many of our students.'

Students I'd helped over the past eight months appeared on the screen, talking about how I'd supported them in setting up a small business, or learning about finances, or in building their confidence.

Members of Bay Trade talked about how I'd helped them. Carly talked about how supportive I'd been when she set up Carly's Cupcakes. The traders talked about me giving out free drinks at the traders' Christmas tree lights switch-on, not expecting anything in return. A few charity leaders talked about how I regularly supported their causes with donations of afternoon tea for two. Then, finally, the filming moved into The Chocolate Pot and a few team members talked about what I was like as a boss. I turned and looked round the table again, astonished. They were all in on it. They knew and nobody had breathed a single word.

But did they know I was a fraud?

The film ended with flashing images of all the participants saying thank you.

'I'm pretty sure there's one person in the room who is in shock right now,' Drew said. 'And that's the person who that film was all about. She's already picked up an award for her business tonight and made it very clear that it was for the team and not her. Well, this award is very much for her. The very first award for Outstanding Contribution to the Community goes to Tara Porter from The Chocolate Pot. Welcome to the stage again, Tara.'

Everyone in the room was on their feet, clapping and cheering, as I made my way to the front, heart thumping, stomach churning. Handshakes and kisses were given, then I found myself in front of the podium for the second time in the space of half an hour only this time I didn't feel proud. I didn't feel elation. I felt sick. I took a deep breath.

'Thank you everybody for such a warm reception.' My voice was shaking. What the hell was I supposed to say? 'Drew wasn't exaggerating when he said that I'd be in shock right now. Oh my goodness. I would never in a million years have predicted this.' I shook my head and took another deep breath. 'It was the weirdest thing just now watching that film and having this realisation that it was me they were talking about because all those lovely things those people said about me... well, I don't think of myself like that. Those people on the film, they're the real stars. Jim and the team at The Hope Centre quite literally give hope to those who need it. I just donate some food. And those students at the TEC? They had it in themselves and only needed a little encouragement and direction. I'm so proud of each and every one of those people in the video and I'm privileged that they've let me be part of their journey to success.' I paused for a moment and looked across at Carly who was wiping tears away. Raising the star in the air, I added, 'This one's for everyone in that video...' I took a deep breath and fought hard to keep my voice steady. 'And it's for my parents and my foster parents who taught me everything I know. I wish they could have been around to see this.' My voice broke and I only just managed to whisper, 'Thank you again.'

I stepped away from the podium, blinking in the bright lights. What had I said? Had I just mentioned my parents and foster parents? What had made me do that?

'Just a few photos,' Drew said, directing me to face the photographer.

I tried my hardest to smile, but it was all too overwhelming and all I wanted to do was escape from the lights and the camera flash and release the scream I could feel building up inside me. I half expected someone to tap me on the shoulder and ask me to hand back the award because they'd made a mistake and discovered that my initial motivation for all those things had been a selfish one – to keep myself occupied so I wouldn't have to face up to how lonely I was. A chat to Jim each evening when he picked up the donations for The Hope Centre, one evening a month at Bay Trade, and several evenings with the students at the TEC had saved me from the routine of returning to my flat after work, all alone, and not speaking to another soul until the following morning. I'd tried to take my loneliness and bury it in a chest in the sand, but there was no use denying it. Watching that video, everyone would have seen Tara the philanthropist. What I saw was Tara-No-Mates. Tara who had nobody. Like someone gaining weight and refusing to acknowledge it by avoiding full-length mirrors, I'd avoided acknowledging the truth about my situation, but that film had been a mirror held up to me and I didn't like what it really showed.

There was no denying it. I had to accept that I really had made a huge mistake in shutting myself off from relationships and setting myself up for a lonely love-less existence because of one failed marriage. All round me were happy couples at exciting stages of their relationship – Maria and Marc starting married life, Carly and Liam getting engaged, and new love blossoming between Nathan and Molly. And I had nobody. I knew it was my fault. I knew I'd sworn off men because of Garth, but more and more often recently...

I was swamped with hugs from the team as I returned to the table. The Lady Mayor was making some closing comments and I knew that, if I didn't get out now, there'd be a parade of people wanting to congratulate me. Grabbing my pashmina from the back of my chair, I whispered to Maria, 'I'm having a hot flush. Just getting some air.' I pressed my purse into her hand. 'Will you get everyone a drink on me?' Before she could answer, I dashed out of the room.

The cool air hit me as I approached the entrance. Shaking out my pashmina, I pulled it round my shoulders. It wasn't going to be much protection against the cold November evening but I had to escape.

The Bay Pavilion overlooked the far end of South Bay. It was an impressive Victorian building consisting of a theatre, concert hall, restaurant, bars and several function rooms all nestled round a huge courtyard and bandstand, the latter being used for summer weddings and outdoor concerts. Out the front and to the right was a stone covered walkway with pillars framing the sea, embedded into a low wall that was occasionally interrupted by steps down to the sand. Lanterns strung between the pillars dimly lit the path. Gulping in the sea air, I ran down The Bay Pavilion steps and along to the far end of the walkway, tears pouring down my cheeks. I could feel the cries of anguish bubbling inside me and threatening to erupt like a volcano. 'Argh!' I cried, beating my fist against the final stone column. 'Argh!'

For a moment, I thought I was going to be sick, but the nausea passed and I slumped onto the wall, leaning against the column and pulling my pashmina tightly round me. Breathe in... breathe out... breathe in...

Eventually, my breathing slowed in time to the waves lapping against the wall. Wow! Where had that come from? It had felt almost primeval, this desperate need to release my anguish.

'Tara? Are you okay?'

I looked up to see Jed standing a few feet away. How much had he seen and heard? I prayed it hadn't been the screaming. The standard response at times like this was, 'I'm fine,' but it was pretty obvious I wasn't.

Swallowing hard, I took another deep breath. 'It was a bit over-whelming and emotional,' I said, wiping at my cheeks.

'May I...?' He indicated the wall beside me.

I nodded.

'It seems you've made quite an impact on this town.'

'It's all lies,' I quipped. 'It cost me a small fortune to get them to say all that.'

He smiled gently. 'Looked pretty genuine to me.'

What response could I give? *Yeah, but I'm a big, fat fraud.* The best response was to remain silent.

Only Jed remained silent too.

'I'm sorry about this morning,' I said when I couldn't stand the silence anymore. Better to change the subject.

'Why? What happened this morning?'

'I was rude to you, as usual.'

'Were you? Here was me thinking it was a massive improvement on the recent low of "arrogant con artist".'

I shook my head. 'I'm so sorry. I shouldn't have said that.'

'Considering what you thought I'd done; it was actually quite tame.'

'You should have heard what I called you at the time,' I said.

'I can imagine.'

Silence.

'I got your cheque,' I said.

'It was the least I could do.'

'I tried to return it all week, but you weren't there. You know I can't accept it.'

Jed frowned. 'Of course you can. It's your money.'

'Which your wife took from me. You can't pay me back from your own money for something she did. It's not right.'

'What Ingrid did wasn't right. If I'd known—'

I shook my head. 'But you didn't know. I really appreciate the gesture, but I *will* return it.'

'You won't.'

'I will. I really am sorry for what I said. I wasn't in a good place when I met you. I think you might have got the brunt of my anger at someone else and I'm ashamed to say I've held onto that anger for a very, very long time.'

Silence fell again and we both turned to face the sea. The sky was cloudless and speckled with millions of stars. The glow from the moon on the water looked like a silvery ribbon pointing to the shore. It was quite mesmerising watching it rippling, as though part of a rhythmic gymnastics' routine.

'I'm sorry about your parents,' Jed said. 'When I saw you looking up to the sky this morning, were you talking to them?'

The emotions started bubbling once more and a sob escaped from me.

'Oh, Tara. I'm sorry. I didn't mean to—'

'It's fine.' I wiped my tears again. 'As I said, it's been an emotional evening. Believe it or not, I'm not one for tears, but everything seems to have set me off this past year. I burned some flapjacks last week and I sobbed for half an hour solid. How ridiculous is that?'

'Not ridiculous at all. Nobody can stay strong all of the time.'

I looked into his eyes and smiled gently. Something about his tone suggested to me that he understood.

'I'm so pleased you won those awards tonight,' he said. 'You've transformed that café. I hardly recognise it as the same place.'

'Thank you.'

'I was wondering about the name. It's quite unusual.'

Another thing I'd never told anyone. I'd been asked about the name before and I always gave my pre-prepared answer: *I wanted to specialise in chocolate and threw around a few ideas. The Chocolate Pot was my favourite one.* I wasn't sure Jed would buy it and, after the way I'd treated him, I didn't feel right about fobbing him off.

'My mum wasn't well. She battled every day with her mental health and, because I was young and wouldn't have understood depression, we used to call it her black cloak. She was never well enough to work so we didn't have enough money for holidays. Dad had one of those Terramundi pots. You know what I mean? Those pots that you fill with coins and smash when they're full? I can still picture it so clearly. It was brown but had white at the top with gold speckles on it. I always said it reminded me of a mug of hot chocolate – a family favourite – so it became known as "The Chocolate Pot". If we managed to lift the black cloak only a little, Dad put a pound coin into The Chocolate Pot. If Mum had a good day, Dad would put in as many coins as he could find. One Saturday when I was seven, Mum woke up feeling great and suggested we all go to the seaside. Dad bundled us into the car and we had the most amazing day in Herne Bay, riding on a carousel and running along the beach. We called it The Best Day Ever because, quite simply, it was. We funded it from The Chocolate Pot although, of course, we had to smash the pot to get the money out.' My throat tightened and I blinked away the tears again. 'When customers come into my café, I want them to feel warm, happy and loved, just like I felt on The Best Day Ever. The Chocolate Pot made that day happen so I couldn't imagine a more perfect name.'

Jed stared at me, his expression soft. 'What a beautiful memory to be able to hold onto.'

I nodded, swiping at a couple more tears trickling down my cheeks. A sudden gust of wind whipped up the net on my dress and made me shiver.

'I should probably get back inside.' I stood up.

In an instant, Jed slipped off his tuxedo jacket. 'I should have done this earlier,' he said, leaning round me to drape it across my shoulders but he must have got a button snagged in my hair because my head suddenly snapped back.

'Crap. I'm so sorry,' he said. 'Hang on.'

As he untangled my hair, I found myself pressed against his chest, breathing in a fresh citrus scent.

'Sorry,' he said again. 'Nearly there.'

I wobbled on my heels and instinctively put my arms round his waist to steady myself. Balance restored, I knew I should let go, yet somehow I couldn't seem to. He felt warm and solid and... oh my goodness, I hadn't held a man for fourteen and a half long years. Every nerve in my body seemed to awaken and spark, my heart thudded, and I felt quite light-headed.

'All free,' Jed whispered, but he didn't take his hands away from my hair and I didn't move away from his chest. I felt his heart thudding and heard his breathing quicken.

'We should get back in,' I whispered.

'We should.'

Swallowing hard, I reluctantly stepped back from his chest, my arms slipping down by my sides. I looked up at him and my heart raced even faster.

'Thanks for the jacket.'

'You've got a mark on your cheek. May I?'

Swallowing again, I nodded slowly. As he gently ran his thumb across my right cheek, a little sigh escaped from my lips.

He cupped my face in his hand, his eyes searching mine. Was he going to kiss me? I wanted him to. I had no idea why, but something had shifted between us. He was definitely going to...

'Tara? Is that you?'

I stepped away from Jed and forced myself to smile at Maria. 'Yes. It's me.'

'Oh, thank God. We were getting worried.'

'I had a moment. It was all a bit much. I'm coming in now, though.' I turned to Jed. 'Are you coming back inside?'

He shook his head. 'I have to go. I need to pick up my daughter from a friend's house. She can't drive yet. It's in a village. So, erm... yeah. I have to go.'

'Oh, okay.' I shrugged his jacket off and handed it back to him. 'You'll be needing this then.'

As he took it from me, our hands connected and my heart raced once more at his touch. Oh no. This wasn't good. I couldn't go falling for the competition. I couldn't go falling for anyone.

'Congratulations again,' Jed said. 'Enjoy the rest of your night.'

'Thanks.'

He didn't follow us but I could sense him watching me as I walked beside Maria.

'Sorry, I didn't realise you were with someone,' she said. 'Are you two friends now?'

'No. But I don't think we're enemies anymore, either.'

I turned back and looked along the walkway. Jed was now leaning against one of the pillars, looking out towards the sea. It took all my concentration not to run back to him and steal that kiss. No, we definitely weren't enemies anymore. But could we be something more? Could anybody? I wasn't sure if I was strong enough to try, but I needed to do something. Despite the progress I'd made this year, I was still existing, not living.

## 27

The sound of Hercules rattling on his cage awoke me as usual the following morning. Ooh, my head hurt. My head hurt a lot. How much wine?

Shoving my feet into my slippers, I padded across the flat, released Hercules from his crate and gave him a stroke before heading to the kitchen and downing a pint of cold water.

After we returned to our table at the awards ceremony, I'd been swamped with people offering congratulations. Some I knew well, others I recognised, and others were new contacts. And every single one seemed to think I was some sort of selfless hero. I smiled politely and drank wine. Lots of it.

'Never again,' I said to Hercules as I swallowed a couple of painkillers with some more water. 'I need a coffee.'

I usually went downstairs to make a proper coffee but I wasn't sure I had the energy for the two flights of stairs. Instant would have to do for now.

A combination of paracetamol, coffee, and a shower had me feeling slightly more human and, by mid-morning, I felt ready to tackle some work.

Logging into my email account for The Cobbly Crafter, I found an email from a company called Yorkshire's Best:

To: The Cobbly Crafter
From: Yorkshire's Best
RE: Stocking your products
Good morning,
Please forgive the unsolicited email. I've been looking at your products on Etsy and I love them. As well as the obvious skill involved in making them, what interests me most is that they're handmade in Yorkshire, which is the reason for the contact.
I'm opening a shop called Yorkshire's Best on 1st December and am seeking unique products that are only made in Yorkshire, ideally in North Yorkshire, as that's where my shop is.
This is therefore an initial enquiry to see whether you might be interested in supplying your products to me. I appreciate you probably have commitments already for this Christmas and may not have the time or capacity to consider this just now, but might you be interested for next year? I'd be very happy to have a telephone conversation, FaceTime or Skype if you'd like to discuss this further.
Thank you in advance.
Yorkshire's Best

'What do you think, Hercules? Could we supply to a shop next year?'

To: Yorkshire's Best
From: The Cobbly Crafter
RE: Stocking your products
Hi there,
Thank you for your email. I'm flattered that you like my products and I

love the sound of a shop stocking only Yorkshire-made products. Great
name, by the way!

I'm pleased that you're looking at next year. Crafting is not my full-time
job so time would be tight to fulfil an order for this Christmas although I
would be happy to have a conversation around whether we could look at
limited samples this year.

My main query would be about pricing. As I'm sure you'll appreciate, the
products you see on Etsy are priced based on what the maker would
want to receive to cover materials and time. There's potential for a little
movement on this for bulk orders but not much. Therefore, a retailer
would need to sell the products at significantly more than I do (too high
for the consumer?) or accept a much smaller mark-up than usual. I'm
sure you've already considered this.

It would be good to have a conversation one evening next week if that
would be convenient. I would prefer telephone.

Best wishes,

The Cobbly Crafter


I spent the rest of the morning and the early part of the afternoon creating additional stock for Etsy, my hangover gradually
subsiding. By mid-afternoon, a reply came through:

To: The Cobbly Crafter

From: Yorkshire's Best

RE: Stocking your products

Great to hear back from you. I'm tied up for the next couple of evenings
but how about a phone call on Wednesday (21st Nov) at 7pm?

You're right to raise a concern about the pricing but please be assured
that I'm not looking to massively knock you down on price. I have a
specific business model in mind that is perhaps a little different from the
norm. I'll explain this to you when we speak.

I'm getting a new phone tomorrow so I'll email you my contact details

then. I'm more than happy to phone you if you prefer, but I appreciate you don't know me and my website and social media aren't up and running yet so I can't direct you to anything. The challenges of setting up from scratch!
Enjoy the rest of your weekend and I'll be in touch soon.

An hour later, it was time to go downstairs to see how the shift had gone.

'Someone's got an admirer,' Maria said when I made my way into the kitchen. 'Those are for you.' She pointed to a gorgeous bouquet of purple and white flowers resting in a bucket in the corner of the kitchen.

'Who are they from?'

'I'm guessing Jed seeing as he's the one who brought them over.'

'Jed?' I felt my cheeks burning. 'Really?'

'I asked him if he wanted to deliver them in person but he wouldn't let me call you down.'

There was a small envelope taped to the front. I ripped it off the cellophane and fished out the card.

*To the most outstanding business owner in the Bay.*
  *Can we start afresh?*
  *Jed x*
  *PTO*

I turned the card over and gasped at the words on the back:

*PS I'm not opening a café*
  *I should probably have made that clear earlier.*

'What is it?' Maria asked.

'Only the best news ever. Jed's not opening a café. He's not going to be competition.'

Maria looked over my shoulder at the card. 'That's great news. Any idea what he's going to do instead?'

'Doesn't say. I'm just relieved it's not another café.'

'The lights are on over the road if you fancy nipping over to thank him and perhaps do a bit of digging at the same time,' Maria suggested.

I looked across the street and nodded. 'I might just do that. Do you need me for anything?'

'No. Off you go. Hope he'll tell you.'

Goose bumps pricked my arms as soon as I stepped outside. A coat might have been a plan. I wouldn't be long, though. I dashed over the cobbles and knocked on Jed's door. The glass on the door and windows had been whitewashed so I couldn't see inside. I banged again but there was no answer. Stepping back, I looked up. There were lights on upstairs too so I suspected he would be up there. After another fruitless knock, I had to admit defeat and run back across to The Chocolate Pot, rubbing my arms to try and warm myself up.

'No answer,' I told Maria.

'Then get yourself back upstairs with those flowers and have a celebratory drink...' She took one look at my shocked expression and laughed. 'No, maybe not more alcohol after last night. A celebratory bath, then.'

'A bath sounds good. Thank you.'

As I lay back in the bubbles half an hour later, I smiled. Jed wasn't opening a café; he'd sent me flowers and he'd put a kiss on his message. Closing my eyes, I pictured us under the stone walkway the evening before, looking into each other's eyes. A shiver of pleasure rippled down my spine and my heart started beating faster.

They'd all been right about him. He really was exceptionally attractive. And if what I'd seen over the past couple of days was true, he wasn't just attractive on the outside. I'd believed Garth to be someone he wasn't. Had I done the same for Jed? Except this time, I'd thought Jed was the bad guy. It was looking as though I might have seriously misjudged him.

## 28

Wednesday signalled exactly a month until the first day of winter but, when I woke up, it felt like winter had prematurely arrived with a vengeance. Even though the central heating had kicked in, there was a definite chill in the air.

Wrapped in my dressing gown with the hood up for extra warmth, I wandered over to the large arched window at the front of the flat and looked outside. It was white-over on the cobbles although I couldn't tell if it was snow or a thick layer of frost.

Opening the front door to The Chocolate Pot half an hour later, after I'd showered and dressed, it became apparent it was a very heavy frost. I couldn't resist stepping out and savouring the crunch beneath my boots. What a delightful sound.

Glancing over the road, I was surprised to see the first floor of Jed's shop lit up. Either he was putting in some very long hours preparing for opening day or he was living there. Although his building was a different style and era to mine, it was a similar size, spread over three floors. Anastasia had told me that the second floor was a basic but clean unfurnished two-bed flat.

Shivering, I stepped back into the café and locked the door.

That was quite enough frost-crunching for one morning. Time to start baking.

The cold didn't keep the customers away. There was a steady flow across the morning, increasing for the usual lunchtime rush. Something about the frost seemed to have brought out the excitement of the festive season because there was lots of laughter and a general buzz of anticipation in the café. I received more enquiries about the Christmas decorations and handed out several business cards for The Cobbly Crafter, telling the team I'd asked her for a box of business cards due to receiving so many enquiries from my customers. I hated lying but nobody seemed to question the plausibility of this.

After my third enquiry of the day, my thoughts turned to my conversation with the manager of Yorkshire's Best scheduled for later that evening. Although I'd received an email with their new phone number, I still didn't know his or her name, but I hadn't given them my name either. Could be an awkward start to the phone conversation: *Hi, is that the owner of Yorkshire's Best? This is The Cobbly Crafter.* Hmm.

'There's something going on at the gallery,' Sue, one of my full-timers, said as she cleared some pots from a window table.

I joined her by the window. A white van was parked outside Jed's shop and a couple of workmen were propping up ladders against the top of the freshly painted shop frontage.

'Looks like they're putting up the sign,' I said. 'I wonder what it'll be.'

'I'd like it to be a nice gift shop,' Sue said, wiping the table as she spoke. 'So many of the shops on Castle Street are specialist. They're great but I'd like somewhere that sells nice things I can buy as presents or as a little payday treat.'

She finished wiping and took the tray of pots into the kitchen, leaving me still staring out the window. A gift shop? Oh my God! Could Jed be the mystery owner of Yorkshire's Best?

I nipped upstairs to the staffroom and dug out my phone, firing off a quick email:

To: Yorkshire's Best
From: The Cobbly Crafter
RE: Quick Questions
Hi
A couple of quick questions before our conversation this evening:
1. Where in North Yorkshire are you based?
2. Did you find me on Etsy or did someone recommend me?
Thanks

A reply came through almost immediately:

To: The Cobbly Crafter
From: Yorkshire's Best
RE: Quick Questions
1. I'm on the Yorkshire Coast. Rather not be more specific. Paranoid about jinxing it!
2. A friend of my mum's bought some xmas decorations from you and she had your business card.
Speak later

My heart thumped. It had to be Jed. It was far too coincidental for it not to be. I'd given a business card to Joyce when I sold her the decorations and she was Jed's mum's friend.

I exited the staffroom and headed for the three arched windows, looking across to the workmen. They were manoeuvring the first half of a shop sign into place. YORKSHI

That plane did a loop-the-loop in my stomach. I couldn't do it. I couldn't tell Jed I was The Cobbly Crafter. Nobody else knew and my former enemy couldn't be the first. I couldn't expose every part of my life to him.

To: Yorkshire's Best
From: The Cobbly Crafter
RE: Quick Questions
Thanks for the speedy reply. I'm really sorry but I'm going to have to cancel our conversation tonight. I've somehow double-booked myself. Wishing you all the best for opening day. I love the Yorkshire Coast. You've chosen well.

## 29

On Saturday night, it was Carly and Liam's engagement party.

'What do you think, Hercules?' I twisted round in front of the mirror in my bedroom, trying to see the dress I'd chosen from all angles. 'I haven't worn a dress in years and now I've worn three in the space of two weeks.' I'd gone for teal this time with a floaty skirt and silver beading round the waist and halter-neck.

Hercules wriggled his nose and buffed my legs, which I suspected meant he couldn't care less about my dress but he'd be very open to some attention. Crouching down, I stroked his ears and back. 'I can't pick you up in case I catch your claws on the fabric. I promise I'm all yours tomorrow, though.'

I looked at my watch. 6.20 p.m. Guests would start arriving at seven but Carly and Liam would arrive shortly for last-minute preparations.

'I'll see you this evening, Hercules,' I said, giving his ears one final stroke. 'Be a good boy.'

\* \* \*

The Chocolate Pot looked fabulous yet completely different to how it had looked for Maria and Marc's wedding. Carly and Liam had gone for a rose-gold and burgundy theme, which I love. Both floors were decorated with balloon bouquets. Sparkly rose-gold jars holding gypsophila, ivy and burgundy roses sat in the centre of each table and I'd filled small glass jars with battery-operated warm white fairy lights and spread them throughout the café.

They'd created a pegboard covered in photos of them together throughout the years. I'd been captivated by it earlier, a big lump in my throat as I took in years of friendship and devotion captured on film. I'd never experienced anything like that and never would, which made that cloak of loneliness wrap round me once more.

The food was going to be fairly simple – wedges, quiches, pies, pastries and salad plus special dietary need options. Carly had dropped off several syrups and trays of fruit to 'pimp your prosecco' and there were bottles of prosecco, lager and wine cooling in tubs of ice in front of the serving counter, as well as The Chocolate Pot's usual range of soft drinks in the fridges, or hot drinks if guests wanted them.

I'd secured four of my students – Brandon, Nathan, Molly and Lexie – to cook, serve food and drinks, and clear up, meaning I could relax and enjoy the evening. Well, try to.

A couple of hours later, the party was in full swing. Carly looked stunning in a burgundy cocktail dress, joking that it was her turn to accessorise with the colour scheme. She'd made a three-tier cake with silhouettes on the side depicting scenes from their relationship: making snow angels, their first kiss in front of the lighthouse, then Liam's proposal on bended knee. Seeing those silhouette images had the same effect on me as the pegboard of photographs, making me all teary. I adored their story; they'd united at school when they were bullied for their looks, becoming the best of friends, and having love creep up on them gradually, both fearing doing anything about it in case they lost their valuable friendship. It had taken a lot of courage and trust for them both to take that step into admitting how they felt. Would I ever have the courage to trust again and let love in?

Carly placed her hand on my shoulder, making me jump and pulling me back to the present. 'Are you okay?' she asked.

I swallowed hard and smiled. 'I was admiring the silhouettes on the cake. You're so talented.'

'I can't take credit. Bethany's the artist. All I did was roll out some icing and cut round what she'd created.'

'You're both very talented, then.'

Carly stared at me for a moment. 'Something's on your mind.'

'No, I'm fine. Miles away, that's all.'

She shook her head. 'I'm not buying it. Something upset you at the awards ceremony last weekend and that or something else is on your mind right now.'

I was about to protest but I'd spent my whole life covering things up and making out that everything was fine and, right now, it wasn't. I'd lost my way and I needed help. I needed a lighthouse.

'Do you have any plans for tomorrow evening?' I asked.

'Yes. Hot chocolate and a heart to heart with you.'

Despite everything, I found myself laughing. 'Yes, please.'

\* \* \*

As I closed the shutters in my flat shortly before midnight, I glanced across the street. The lights on the first floor were on again and I found myself imagining what Jed might be doing. Sanding a floor? Painting a wall? Putting up storage shelves? Was he living there? Were his daughters? I'd absolutely no idea.

I'd dropped a card through his letterbox on Monday thanking him for the flowers and returning his cheque. On Tuesday morning,

I found an envelope on my mat with the cheque inside and a bright orange Post-it note stuck to it:

*Nice try but this money is yours x*

Ripping the cheque up, I'd dropped it through his letterbox again with a note that I wasn't kidding and I couldn't accept it. Two days later, a fresh cheque was waiting on my mat with another Post-it note:

*I could continue doing this all year x*

Closing the shutters fully, I smiled. I could happily keep returning his cheque all year too because every note from him gave me a little thrill inside.

## 30

'That one's yours,' I said, placing a mug of chilli hot chocolate on the counter for Carly the following day, after the Sunday staff had cleaned up and left.

I picked up my vanilla-flavoured one and followed Carly towards the back of The Chocolate Pot. She put her drink down on our usual table, but I walked straight past. 'This way.'

'We're going up to your flat?' There was obvious astonishment in her voice.

'Yes, and I feel weird about it, but it needs to happen.'

In silence, she followed me up the two flights of stairs.

For the first time ever, I was out of breath when I reached the top, damn nerves making my heart race. I paused with my hand on the flat door.

'This is a big thing for me, but if I'm going to tell you what's on my mind, you need to see who I really am.'

'Okay.' She looked bemused.

'Before we go in, what do you imagine my flat will be like?'

Carly shrugged. 'Tidy? Colourful? I haven't really thought about it. I suppose I imagine it to be a bit like The Chocolate Pot décor-wise.'

'It's a little different to downstairs.'

'I'm intrigued.'

'Hercules?' I called as I pushed open the door, but he was already waiting, scut wagging from side to side.

'Hello again,' Carly said. 'You're just as gorgeous as I remember.'

I took her mug from her while she crouched down and gave Hercules a fuss.

'You're not hiding more animals up here, are you? Baby elephant? Alpaca?'

I laughed. 'Just the giant house bunny. And maybe a few décor surprises.'

Carly straightened up and took a couple of steps forward to where the flat opened out. I watched as her head turned from left to right. 'Wow! Oh my word, Tara. I was *not* expecting this. It's amazing.'

'You can have a wander if you want.'

'You don't mind?'

'Still feeling weird,' I admitted, 'but you've seen it now. You might as well explore.'

I took our drinks through to the lounge area, expecting Hercules to follow me, but he surprised me by following Carly instead. Either he was mesmerised by our first ever guest or he was being my guard dog.

The log burner was crackling by the time Carly finished her wander.

'When can I move in?' she asked, eyes wide.

'You like it?'

'Like it? I absolutely love it. I can't believe how much space there is. And it's open plan yet it's somehow really cosy. Is this that Danish thing?'

'Hygge? It is. It's taken me a few years to get it to this point, but I think I've pretty much embraced the concept.'

Carly sat down and took a sip of her drink. 'There's so much to take in. Everywhere I look, I spot something different.'

'Did you go onto the mezzanine?'

'Yes, and I think you have some explaining to do. You don't buy the Christmas decorations in The Chocolate Pot from Etsy, do you? *You* make them all. And the Hallowe'en ones. And the Valentine's Day ones.'

I nodded slowly and shrugged my shoulders apologetically. 'I'm The Cobbly Crafter.' It felt so weird to say it out loud but even more weird that I sounded apologetic. I was sorry that I'd been so secretive but I wasn't sorry about my alter-ego. 'I'll try that again with a bit more positivity, should I?'

Carly smiled. 'That would be good.'

'I *am* The Cobbly Crafter,' I declared in a loud confident voice.

She clapped appreciatively. 'You are unbelievably talented, Tara Porter. I knew you were a great chef, but I'd never have guessed this. I love your work and I love your flat. I might have to kill you and live here myself. No wonder you spend so much time up here.' She pressed her hand against her mouth. 'That sounded rude. I didn't mean it like that.'

'It's okay. And you're right. I do spend all my spare time up here and that's what's on my mind.' I closed my eyes and covered them with my hands. 'Oh, God, this is so hard to say. I feel so pathetic, especially when I brought it on myself.'

'Can I suggest you just blurt it out and we'll take it from there?'

I removed my hands and looked at her. 'Okay. Here goes. I'm lonely.' There! I'd finally said it. I took a deep breath. 'I got upset at the awards because I was watching this video of me doing all this stuff in the community and it made me realise that I have very little in my life except work and work-related things. And I felt like such a fraud because I started doing those things to give me something to do and get me out of the flat. The work with The Hope Centre and the TEC and being part of Bay Trade gives me people to talk to so my life isn't all about being in this building with a giant house rabbit and my bitter memories of my failed marriage.'

Carly was silent for a moment, which was hardly surprising as that had been quite an information dump. 'Okay. Let's take one thing at a time. Let's talk about being lonely. What would *not* being lonely look like to you?'

'I don't know. Going out with friends all the time. Spending time with family.'

'Anything else?'

I hesitated. 'I can't believe I'm going to say this but maybe a boyfriend.'

Carly nodded. 'Let's start with the friends one. Who do you know who goes out with friends *all* the time?'

'Everyone. You. Maria. Pretty much everyone at work.'

'And what makes you think that?'

'They talk about it or they put stuff on Facebook.'

She rolled her eyes. 'Ah! The joys of social media. I had a similar conversation with Bethany just last week. Facebook isn't real, you know.'

'What do you mean?'

'It's all about what people want others to see. I know a few people who use it to have a whinge and moan, but most people I know use it to present the shiny side of life. It's all "look at me, I'm having a great time at the pub with all my wonderful friends" or "look at me, out shopping and eating cake". And because it's accompanied by a fanfare and smiles, we're all fooled into thinking that everyone has a better life than us. What they don't post is the downtime, the bored moments, the mundane stuff we all experience.'

'I get that, I'm not daft, but they're still out doing these things and I'm not.'

'But it's not like you don't do things. You just don't shout about them. And if you want to do more non-work things like trips to the cinema or going out for meals, all you need to do is ask. I'd be up for it. Bethany would. Lots of the traders would. As for your team, Maria and Marc have young kids and they have friends like Callie and Rhys who also have young kids. In my experience, people with little ones tend to do more stuff because they have to keep the kids occupied. And you've got a lot of students working for you. Students go out. That's how it is. Do you *want* to be out partying every night?'

'No, but... I don't know. I feel like I'm missing out on something.'

'Which is why you mentioned having a boyfriend?' Carly shrugged. 'Maybe it *is* time for that to happen, but do you know what I think the real issue is?'

'Enlighten me. Because I haven't got a clue.'

'You mentioned family too and I think you really miss yours and want them back in your life. Why don't you get in touch with Kirsten and Tim?'

I gasped. 'After all this time?'

'It's never too late to reconnect. I know that Leanne and Garth hurt you, but Kirsten and Tim didn't. From what you've told me, they were good people.'

'The best.'

'Then it might be time to let them back in.'

'I don't know. Maybe.'

She narrowed her eyes at me. 'There's something else, isn't there?'

I ran my fingers through my hair and sighed. 'I don't feel like I deserved that award.'

Carly sat forward. 'What? Why would you say that?'

'Because I'm a fraud. The Hope Centre? Bay Trade? Project Hercules? Like I said, my initial motivation for all of those things was because I was lonely. I wasn't just helping others. I was helping myself.'

'I disagree. You were helping others because that's who you are. You couldn't *not* help others. You're a kind person. There might be something in it for you and perhaps some company was your *initial* motivation as you said, but I would argue that there's something in it for everyone who does something for others, even if that's just the way they feel about themselves. Just think of everything you did for me last year. You drove all over town looking for Bethany when she had her meltdown, you stayed up till past midnight decorating cakes when I fell behind, and you gave me the confidence to tell Liam I loved him.'

'That was just helping a friend in need.'

'And that's who you are. You help people. Think about it, Tara. There are loads of other things you could have done to have a bit of company like going to night classes or joining a gym but you chose the things that would help others because that's what comes natural to you. You're not a fraud. You inspire me and you inspire others. And now that I know about your parents and Garth, I'm even more in awe of you than I was before. You've lost your parents, you've been deprived of friendships, and you've been betrayed by the two people you loved and trusted the most. Did you let that get you down? No. You started over and built a new life for yourself, refusing to be a victim. You, Tara Porter, really are Pollyanna. You're a genuinely kind and caring person and I think that's why you've struggled so much to come to terms with what happened in your past. You're a good person and you want to believe that others are too. What Garth and Leanne did to you was so far removed from your values and beliefs that it shocked you to your core and you haven't been able to move on from it because you can't comprehend how people can be that bad. You've been punishing yourself for their behaviour ever since. I think it's time to let go of them and it's time to let your foster parents back in. And I'll be right by your side every step of the way, whatever you want to do and whenever you want to do it.'

'You're such a good friend,' I said, taking her hand in mine and squeezing it as I swallowed the lump constricting my throat. 'It's been a long time since I had one of those. Thank you so much.'

\* \* \*

After she left, I couldn't stop thinking about what Carly said about how she viewed me. She'd echoed everything said by the participants in the Best of the Bay Awards video and it was exactly the sort of person I wanted to be. After I moved into foster care, I was also the outsider at school. At first, it was because I kept moving school and then, when I settled with the Sandersons, it was because I wasn't one of *them*. I navigated the senior school years alone but Kirsten was always there for me at home. I hadn't said a word about my invisibility but it was as though she could sense the pain.

'I hated school too,' she'd said one evening while I did my homework at the dining table. 'I enjoyed the learning but it was the other kids I struggled with.'

I put my pen down. 'Why? Were you bullied?'

Kirsten shook her head. 'No. I just never quite fitted in. I wasn't one of the cool kids but I wasn't one of the geeky kids either. My grades were okay, I was average at sport, I was never in trouble and, as a result, I was off everyone's radar. At parents' evening, I think even the teachers struggled to remember who I was.'

'Did you have friends?'

'Not really. I had some girls I sat next to in different subjects and it was all very polite and civilised, but I wouldn't say we were friends. Acquaintances, perhaps.'

'Were you lonely?'

'Sometimes. It hurt when I was never invited to parties or trips to the cinema, but I suppose at least I wasn't being bullied.'

'You were playing "the glad game",' I said.

Kirsten smiled. 'I suppose I was. I was glad I wasn't the centre of attention because it meant I wasn't being picked on.' She put down her embroidery and patted the sofa beside her.

I eagerly joined her, cuddling into her side.

'The thing to remember, my angel, is that you're at school for such a small portion of your life. Some fit in and others don't. If you're one of the ones who doesn't, then put your head down, study hard, and it'll soon be over. And in that time you have alone, you can discover who you are, who you want to be and what you want to do with your life, knowing you'll never have to see any of those people again.'

'Is that what you did?'

Kirsten ruffled my hair and kissed the top of my head. 'I certainly did. I discovered that I was the sort of person who'd never make anyone else feel insignificant or invisible, that I always wanted to be kind and help others, and that I wanted to be a chef because, much as I loved it, I realised I couldn't make a career out of doing embroidery.'

'And you got to be all of those things,' I said.

'And you'll get to be the things you want to be too. What do you want to be, my little Pollyanna?'

It was an easy one. I looked up at her and smiled. 'I want to be just like you.'

According to Carly, that's exactly what I'd become.

## 31

On Tuesday evening, I went to my Pilates class as usual and couldn't ignore the butterflies fluttering in my stomach at the thought of seeing Jed there. He'd featured in my dreams over the weekend. I'd been on a carousel on a pier, just like on The Best Day Ever, only I was riding a giant rabbit instead of a horse. I'd turned, expecting to see my mum galloping – or hopping – next to me, but it had been Jed and he'd smiled such a warm, tender smile that made me feel the same joy as Mum's laughter that special day. When the ride stopped, the rabbits jumped off the carousel and hopped down the pier. The temperature dropped and snow started to fall before we realised we were in a giant snow globe. Jed took off his coat and draped it round my shoulders. As soon as he touched me, the snow stopped falling and rainbows jumped in front of us like dancing fountains. I made a comment about how beautiful they were, but he shook his head and said I was the one who was beautiful. Cupping my face in his hands, like he'd done outside The Bay Pavilion, he lowered his lips towards mine... then Hercules rattled his crate and woke me up, that promise of a kiss hanging in the air once more.

'Were you looking for someone?' Karen asked as I rolled up my mat after the class.

'No. Actually, yes. Jed? He came to a couple of classes and hasn't been since.'

'He's hoping to be a regular from the New Year,' she said. 'He's too busy getting his shop ready at the moment.'

I hoped my disappointment didn't show in my face. 'Makes sense. Opening day on Saturday.'

'So I hear. Do you know what it's going to be? I've heard rumours and I've seen the sign but Yorkshire's Best doesn't give it away.'

'I think he's trying to keep it a surprise,' I said.

One of the other class attendees wandered over and clearly wanted a word with Karen so I said goodbye and headed out to the car park.

Driving home, I thought about how things had ended on email after my panicked realisation that Jed was the manager of Yorkshire's Best. He'd replied saying he understood and hopefully we could talk next year because he really loved my crafts and was eager to work with me. How guilty did I feel? I'd let him down and he'd responded with kindness. Now that I'd shown Carly my flat and revealed the true identity of The Cobbly Crafter to her, it was time to stop hiding in the shadows. I'd come up with an idea for revealing the news to the team, but it was important to me that Jed knew first.

Back home, after a fuss with Hercules, I typed in an email:

To: Yorkshire's Best
From: The Cobbly Crafter
RE: Huge apology
I hope your final week of prep is going well, ahead of Saturday's grand opening.

You mentioned that your shop's on the Yorkshire Coast. It's in Whitsborough Bay, isn't it?

I know because I live there and have spotted the sign on a building in Castle Street opposite the incredibly successful award-winning café, The Chocolate Pot, run by the most outstanding person in the whole of the Bay.

I appreciate that you'll be busy, but if you do have time for a conversation, perhaps I could visit you at your premises one evening this week? I'm free tomorrow and Friday.

I smiled at the message and toyed with whether to be more cryptic. No. I was sick of secrets. Send.

To: The Cobbly Crafter
From: Yorkshire's Best
RE: Huge apology
I did NOT see that coming!
How about this evening, Tara?
8.30pm
Bring hot chocolate
And some of that millionaire's shortbread if you've got any left x

To: Yorkshire's Best
From: The Cobbly Crafter
RE: Huge apology
You have a deal
And you're in luck with the shortbread x

Kiss, no kiss, kiss? Sod it! Send.

I had fifteen minutes to spare and no way was I going over in my

Pilates gear. What I wanted and needed Jed to see was the real me which didn't mean the me in smart jeans and a tailored top that I presented to the world. I pulled on a pair of soft grey leggings and my favourite Nordic-print oversized knitted jumper. Round the middle was a band of turquoise reindeers so I draped a turquoise shawl round my shoulders before pulling on sloppy tan boots ready to present the hygge me. The real me.

At 8.30 p.m. exactly, I made my way across the cobbles clutching two hot chocolates – chilli and salted caramel, to give Jed a choice – and a bag of millionaire's shortbreads. Slung over my shoulder was a sports bag containing examples of The Cobbly Crafter's work.

Jed opened the door and I swear he did a double take, but he recovered well. It was the hair. I always wore it tied back or pinned up meaning that nobody had any idea that it was waist-length, curly and full of natural red highlights. Kirsten had always commented on how striking my hair was and how lucky I was to have natural curls. Leanne, on the other hand, had tried to convince me to dye it brown and add blonde highlights. I'd refused to change the colour because it was exactly like Mum's, but I had allowed her to straighten it. I'd never straightened it since but I had kept it hidden away so nobody could pass comment on it.

'The Cobbly Crafter, I presume?' Jed smiled, indicating that I should step into the shop.

'The mysterious manager of Yorkshire's Best? We meet at last.' I held out the card tray containing the two drinks. 'Chilli or salted caramel?'

'Which do you want?' he asked.

'I love them both so the choice is yours.'

'I might try chilli, then.'

'It's the one nearest to you.'

He took the drink and laughed when I passed him the bag of millionaire's shortbread. 'I love these and thought I'd tasted the best in Aus, but when Anastasia bought me one of these the other week, the bar raised several notches. You make them yourself?'

'Everything we sell is made on the premises, mostly by me, although some of my team are superb chefs.'

I was dying to turn round and look at the shop.

'It's not finished yet,' Jed said, 'but feel free to take a look.'

I actually felt quite nervous as I turned, not sure what to expect. I felt my mouth and eyes widen as I took it all in.

'Oh my God, Jed. These are amazing.'

It was still a gallery but clearly Jed knew what he was doing when it came to stocking the right sort of art for the area. Whereas Galley's paintings were urban and industrial, these were all rural or coastal. Large round sheep, doe-eyed cows and highland cattle stood in the Yorkshire Dales or on clifftops overlooking the sea. I recognised local landmarks in some of the images including Whitsborough Bay Castle, Whitby Abbey and York Minster.

Ambling round the shop floor, I took in the colourful pictures on the walls, hung on either side of plinths strategically placed round the room, and on display panels in the window. So much warmth and colour exuded from the canvases and prints.

Then I stopped dead, completely captivated, by an image of a lone sheep being buffeted on a windy cliff. Long grass and daisies billowed round its hooves and, above it, dark clouds threatened rain, but the yellow beam from Whitsborough Bay's stripy lighthouse in the distance gave colour and hope. The caption below the canvas read: *If you've lost your way, I will be your lighthouse.*

*Oh my God!* Swallowing on the lump in my throat, and blinking back the tears, I couldn't tear my eyes away. The image and caption could not have been more perfect for me. Oh my goodness. I'd never known a piece of art could be so moving. I reached my hand out towards it and could almost feel the coarseness of the fleece, hear the crashing of the waves, smell the approaching storm.

Suddenly aware of Jed in the room, I stepped away from the painting and focused on spinning a rack of cards, barely taking in the images on them as I tried to compose myself.

Various glass display cabinets were distributed round the room but they were empty, as were several shelving units.

'Who's the artist?' I asked, finally finding my voice.

'Jed Ferguson.'

I gasped. 'These are yours?'

'Hopefully they'll be somebody else's but, yes, they're my work. Mainly pastels but I dabble in paint occasionally.'

'But you were running a café. You're a trained chef.'

He laughed. 'I know. And I hated it. Come upstairs. I've got a couple of chairs up there.'

I followed him up to the first floor and into a light and airy room with a kitchenette at one end, a battered pine table, and a couple of mismatched chairs. A pair of easels stood at the other end of the room near the window, the canvases covered in paint-spattered sheets.

'I've been using this room as a studio,' he said, indicating that I should sit down. 'I'm not sure whether I'll keep it as a studio and move into the flat upstairs, or move the studio upstairs and make this into more sales space. I'll see how the first six months go before I make any expensive decisions.'

'So, chef to artist?'

Jed took the lid off his hot chocolate and took a sip. 'Nice kick. I like it.' He put the cup back down. 'Yeah, chef to artist is probably not the obvious career route. Long story short is that I loved art at school and wanted to go to art college but I stupidly listened to a teacher who told me that there was no chance of making a career out of being an artist.'

'That's a bit harsh.'

He nodded. 'Looking back, he was probably talking from

personal experience and trying to protect me, but someone has to make it and why couldn't it be me? Anyway, I'd worked in my parents' café since I was twelve. If I wasn't going to be an artist, I didn't know what to do, so I trained as a chef. Ingrid, my ex-wife, got a Saturday job in the café when she was seventeen and we got together a couple of years later and married a couple of years after that. She trained as a nurse but still helped out occasionally between shifts. When my parents wanted to retire, her parents bought them out, made Ingrid and me co-owners, and I ended up managing the place. My heart wasn't in it, though. I can cook but I'm not passionate about it. Creating new recipes or thinking of menu ideas doesn't do it for me.'

I smiled. 'I love that part of it.'

'Which is why you're brilliant at what you do and why I was managing a greasy spoon café that was barely ticking over, as I think you called it.'

I cringed. 'Sorry.'

'Don't be. If it had been my decision, we'd never have tried to sell the business because, as you quite rightly pointed out, there wasn't a business to sell, but Ingrid had the majority shareholding and made all the financial decisions. My hands were tied.' He paused to take another sip on his drink. 'She'd talked about selling up and emigrating for ages and I refused, but then I started to see it as my way out of the rut I'd got into. I knew I'd miss my parents, but I was so unhappy at the café. The visas were granted on Ingrid's job so I had flexibility about what I did there. I told her I'd only emigrate if she let me take some time out to work out what I wanted to do with my career.'

'Which was being an artist?'

'Yes, but not at first. That dream had already been destroyed and buried. It was so hard finding a new focus, though. I've lost count of how many jobs I had and none of them were me. Then one weekend, Ingrid was working and I took the kids on a road trip to a town we'd never visited. On the way back to the car, we passed an art supplies shop and the kids asked if they could have some new pencil crayons. They wanted me to spend the afternoon colouring with them so I got myself a couple of canvasses and pastels, set them up in the basement and that was it. I was hooked again and my career was found.'

'How long ago was this?' I asked, keen for him to continue speaking. There was something captivating about his voice, a melodic mixture of North Yorkshire mixed with a sing-song Australian twang. Very nice. Very soothing.

'About eight years back. It took me a couple of years of experimenting, but I found my style and it was thanks to the kids. They loved drawing animals and I noticed that they were always cute and podgy. So I drew kangaroos and possums and koalas and placed them by the ocean or in the bush. Basically it was what you saw downstairs but for Aussie animals. I donated one to the school as a raffle prize. One of the parents ran a gallery and was on the lookout for something new and fresh. She loved the picture and set up an exhibition of my work. It took off so she commissioned more, and eventually I'd sold enough to open my own gallery.'

'That's a lovely story,' I said. 'So did you close the gallery when you moved back here?'

He shook his head. 'It's still there. I've got a manager in with a three-year plan to keep releasing fresh paintings and prints. I'm not sure what we'll do after that, but I don't need to make that decision for some time yet.'

'Are you famous in Australia?' I asked.

He screwed up his nose. 'I wouldn't say famous, but there are a few households with a Jed Ferguson on the wall and there are one or two collectors.'

I made a mental note to Google him later, suspecting he was being modest about his achievements.

'What about you, then?' Jed removed a piece of shortbread from the bag and held it near his mouth. 'Chef and café owner extraordinaire by day and Cobbly Crafter by night...?'

While he devoured two pieces, making appreciative noises, I told him that my mum and foster mum had both enjoyed crafting, that Kirsten had shown me new skills and that I'd developed others when I moved to the coast. Conscious that we'd only just moved out of the enemy-zone and I wasn't sure if he was trustworthy yet, despite the clear heart of gold for capturing those animals so beautifully, I massively glossed over my family history and focused more on setting up as The Cobbly Crafter.

'I never expected it to take off like it did, but I have a strong following on Etsy so I often work long hours. When you're passionate about something you don't really see it as work, do you?'

Jed laughed. 'I once tried to explain that to Ingrid and she never got it. She was an efficient nurse, but she wasn't a very sympathetic one from what I can gather. It's a shame more people don't feel passionate about what they do. I suppose the biggest challenge is finding that one thing. Or those two things in your case.'

'So how does stocking Yorkshire-made products fit with your art?' I asked.

'I know what it's like to be a struggling artist and to be an artist who's had their dreams crushed. If this gallery has even half the success of the one in Australia, the business will be doing well and can afford to support other creative types. I'm looking to stock a range of Yorkshire-made products, bought at a slight discount, and sold for a reasonable price. The creative gets paid what they want, I get what I want by bringing people into the shop who might not have visited if it was only about the art, and the customer gets to choose from a range of gifts at a variety of prices. Everyone's happy.'

'Sounds like—'

Jed's phone rang, cutting me off. He took it out his pocket and frowned. 'Damn. Sorry. I need to get this... Hi Erin. I've completely lost track of time. Can I call you back in ten minutes? Yeah... yeah. No worries. Love you. Bye.'

He put his phone down and grimaced. 'I'm so sorry. Bad dad. That was my eldest, Erin. I was meant to FaceTime her at nine and I completely forgot. She's away at university and she's always busy so—'

But I was already standing up, smiling at him. 'I'll go so you can call her back. I brought a bag of crafts with me to show you the type of things I make. I can probably manage a limited stock of Christmas items if you're interested, but not huge quantities. We can definitely talk about next year, though.'

'Thanks. I'll take a look.'

I headed out the room and down the stairs. 'There's no obligation. If it's not what you want, please say. I didn't have time to print off a price list so I'll email you one later.'

We reached the front door and I swept my eyes round the gallery again, settling on the lighthouse picture. 'I really think these are going to fly out the door,' I said, looking back at Jed.

He smiled. 'Thank you. That means a lot coming from the award-winning most outstanding businessperson in Whitsborough Bay.'

'I'll see you later,' I said, laughing as I stepped out onto the cobbles.

Reaching the door to The Chocolate Pot, I pictured that lone sheep and the lighthouse again. Like that sheep, I'd lost my way but I saw the lighthouse when I arrived in Whitsborough Bay and knew I'd found a safe place to call home. Come Saturday, I'd be first in the queue. I didn't care how much it cost, that painting had to be mine.

## 32

I was up well before Hercules rattled his crate on 1st December. The first Saturday in December was always exceptionally busy, especially in the afternoon. It was the big Christmas tree lights switch-on in town so the café would be packed with shoppers getting warm and grabbing some food and drink before joining the crowds for the build-up outside the main shopping centre. The lights were switched on at 6.30 p.m. by a Z-list 'celebrity' with the team from Bay Radio playing music and running competitions for the preceding hour.

The Chocolate Pot stayed open for an extra half hour until 5.30 p.m. to maximise sales, and it was always quite fraught because, as well as serving the regular customers, we were getting prepared for the special Castle Street traders' event. At the end of Castle Street, overlooking the sea, there was a small park – Castle Park – which was home to another Christmas tree. The Castle Street traders all sponsored it and, in return, the council permitted us to hold a special traders-only event. I supplied hot drinks and Carly supplied cupcakes.

On top of all that, it was Jed's grand opening. I'd told Maria that, as soon as it looked like a queue was forming, I'd be hoofing it across the cobbles because I had my eye on one of the paintings. When I'd emailed Jed my price list, I'd toyed with asking him to reserve me the lighthouse canvas, but chickened out. It was stupid, really, but that image and caption were so personal, so raw, that I couldn't bring myself to let him in. Yet. Not that I had very long to build myself up to it ahead of opening day.

In my email, I asked him if he'd taken on any staff because I could vouch for Anastasia. He replied saying his youngest daughter, Lucy, was going to work there at weekends and during the college holidays but he'd give Anastasia a call. She dropped by The Chocolate Pot on Thursday to thank me for the recommendation because Jed had offered her a job for the opening weekend, telling her he'd work out her hours after that depending on how successful it was.

Yorkshire's Best was due to open at 10 a.m. By half nine, there was quite a crowd outside, no doubt drawn by the wonderful paintings in the window. He'd picked well to showcase his talent, with a variety of settings and animals across the five canvases on display.

'Go on,' Maria said, nodding towards the crowd. 'You know you want to.'

'I can't go when we're this busy.' The downstairs was already full and we were on limited staff until ten. 'I'm sure it'll still be there later.'

But it wasn't. When I managed to nip out shortly before eleven, another canvas hung where the sheep and lighthouse had been. A little shocked at feeling quite so teary about it, I reminded myself that I was glad that I'd seen it and I was glad that somebody else would be able to forever enjoy it. It obviously wasn't meant to belong to me.

I don't think I'd ever seen more than three or four people at a time in Galley's Gallery but there had to be ten times that in Yorkshire's Best. I felt really proud of Jed for following his dream and making it happen, despite the knock-backs. Very inspiring.

Jed looked up from the queue at the till, smiled and winked, which made me go all gooey inside. He pointed to the corner where there was a beautiful Christmas tree made of silver and white twigs. A selection of my needle felted decorations hung from the branches, alongside some driftwood stars and a mix of other items I had left over from previous years. Wicker baskets nestled round the base of the tree contained more of each decoration. I experienced the usual thrill as I overheard some customers talking about how gorgeous they were, and watched with delight as others made their way to the till with their purchases.

Passing by the till, I caught Jed's eye and mouthed, 'Congratulations' then winked at him too. He grinned before focusing his attention back on his customer.

Watching him chatting and laughing, surrounded by his stunning paintings, I couldn't see anything of the man I'd first encountered fourteen and a half years ago. I'd been wrong about him ripping me off, and it seemed I'd also been wrong about him being arrogant. All I saw was a passionate artist who I wanted to get to know better. Whether that would lead to anything other than friendship, I wasn't sure. What I was sure of was that I was open to the possibility of it being more. And that was a massive change for me.

\* \* \*

'Did you manage to get that painting you wanted?' Carly asked as we loaded trays of cupcakes onto the tables in Castle Park ready for the traders' switch-on that evening.

'No. I was too late.'

'Aw, no. Maybe he could paint you something like it?'

I shook my head. 'It wouldn't be the same. Everything about that one spoke to me but it was my fault for not securing it when I saw it. Damn secrecy and privacy. I don't know what I was thinking. It's not like he'd have asked me why I chose that one and demanded to know why I'd lost my way. Valuable lesson learned. If you want something, go for it.'

'Very valuable lesson. And are you going to learn from it?'

'I just have.'

Carly laughed. 'I mean, are you going to action it? I've seen you glancing down Castle Street every couple of minutes.'

I felt my cheeks burn and was glad they were already red from the cold night air. 'No idea what you mean.'

'Yes you do. You have a big fat crush on the delectable Jed Ferguson. You're scared of it, which I completely understand after what you've been through, but I think he's the one you've been looking for.'

'I haven't been looking for anyone.'

'Because you weren't ready until now. This year has been phenomenal for you. The business has reached new heights and you've explored new ground personally. You've opened up, you've let people in and it's all been rewarding. I think you should let him in. And your foster parents.' She nudged me gently. 'And I need to stop telling you what to do, don't I?'

'No. Don't ever stop. You're like the voice of my conscience, pushing me into the things I already know I need to do, but am too scared to.'

'Be brave,' she said. 'A few minutes of courage might change your life.'

I hugged her. 'Thank you for everything this year. You've been nothing short of amazing.'

'Have you seen what Tara made?' Lana asked, approaching Carly after we'd pulled apart. Two needle felted star decorations dangled from her gloved hand. 'We've all got a pair to represent the two star awards we won.'

'They're gorgeous.' Carly raised an eyebrow at me.

'Did you know Tara makes all the decorations in The Chocolate Pot?' Lana asked.

Someone shouted her name so Lana ran off to join her friends and Carly turned to me. 'You've finally told them, then?'

I nodded. 'Thanks to you. You helped me find the courage.'

She clapped her hands together excitedly. 'I'm so thrilled for you. Jed next.'

As 6.30 p.m. approached, there was still no sign of him. I'd emailed him about the traders' event yesterday, realising he might not be aware of it, and he'd replied to say he'd definitely attend. So where was he?

The chatter ceased and the traders turned towards Castle Street, waiting and listening. I loved the moment when cheers and applause could be heard from the top of town as that meant the switch had been flicked, the Christmas tree had been lit, and the rays of light were reaching across town.

Focusing my eyes towards the far end of Castle Street, I smiled as the zigzag of white lights strung between the tops of the buildings lit up, a small section at a time. A figure stepped into the middle of the cobbles and my heart raced. Jed. He glanced up at the lights then ran along Castle Street towards the park, the lights illuminating behind him as he ran, as though they were chasing after him.

He crossed the road as the arch at the end of the street lit up with the words 'Welcome to Castle Street'. I missed the stars on the sign lighting up because I was focusing on Jed, running straight towards me.

'I nearly missed it,' he panted.

'But you're here now. Look at the tree.'

The white star at the top of the tree lit up, followed by all the white lights which flowed up and down the branches, then the red ones, then the green ones. The traders cheered then broke into a chorus of 'We Wish You a Merry Christmas'. With Jed standing by my side, smiling at me as he sang, I wondered if it really could be a merry Christmas for me for the first time since fleeing to Whitsborough Bay.

## 33

The tradition after the lights switch-on was for the traders to go on a pub crawl. We always started in The Old Theatre at the top of town then made our way down the precinct visiting various pubs and bars. A good night was guaranteed as everyone was in high festive spirits.

With Jed in the group, it turned out to be the best pub crawl ever. After the initial hostility towards him when they'd thought he was opening a café, the traders were keen to welcome him to Castle Street. Several of them had popped into Yorkshire's Best and were quite rightly impressed. I could imagine them seeing potential pound-signs for their own businesses with the draw of a successful artist on the street. I'd Googled Jed and suspected many of the other traders had too. It seemed he was quite the celebrity down under and his work had earned him many accolades.

I loved how humble Jed was about his success and how genuinely interested he appeared to be in the other businesses on Castle Street and any plans the traders had for the future. Everyone seemed to want to talk to him and I was thrilled for him that they were so welcoming. The only downside of his popularity was that I couldn't get him to myself, even for a couple of minutes. Every so often, he caught my eye and gave me a gentle smile which set my heart racing and, at one point, he sat beside me on a padded bench, his leg pressed against mine. I held my breath as I relaxed against him and found myself wishing it was just the two of us.

By the fourth pub, the group had dwindled in size and we were down to some of my favourite traders – Carly, Sarah from Seaside Blooms, Jemma from Bear With Me, Ginny from The Wedding Emporium next door, plus father and daughter team Marcus and Lily from Bay Books. My hopes that a smaller group could finally mean an opportunity to commandeer Jed were dashed by Marcus who apparently had friends in Australia and had visited a few times so they got chatting about places they'd both visited.

Pub five was The Lobster Pot, opposite the harbour on South Bay. A busy few weekends, several late nights crafting and too many glasses of wine had taken their toll and I could barely keep my eyes open. There was talk about moving on to The Smuggler's Cavern for karaoke but my bed was calling.

'I'm flagging,' I announced when I finished my glass of wine. Standing up, I pulled on my coat. 'Sorry, guys, but I'm going to have to call it a night. Enjoy karaoke.'

There were protests but I resisted.

'I'll walk you.' Jed quickly gulped down the last of his pint. 'If that's okay with you. I was thinking of calling it a night myself. Been a big day.'

It was more than okay with me. Some alone-time with Jed, finally! Once again, I felt that gooey feeling inside and my heart started to race but I didn't want to look too keen. 'You're not up for a spot of karaoke with the others?'

'Nah. I can't hold a note. I'd look like a right drongo in front of my new mates.'

I laughed at the Aussie phrase. 'We can't have that then.

Carly gave me a hug goodnight and whispered, 'Be brave,' in my ear.

I'd try to be.

An icy blast of air hit us the moment we stepped out of The Lobster Pot. I tightened my scarf and pulled on my gloves. As we set off along the seafront, I stopped and turned to look back at the lighthouse. Spotlights at the base illuminated the tower and I watched for a moment as the searchlight swept from side to side across the harbour.

'Have you forgotten something?' Jed asked.

'Sorry. Habit.' I turned back to him and indicated we should set off walking again. 'I have a thing for lighthouses, particularly red-and-white striped ones. My mum loved painting but she only ever painted lighthouses and always at night with a beam of light shining.'

'Why only lighthouses?'

'She used to say Dad was her lighthouse, bringing her hope and light in the darkness of her depression. I've often wished I had one of her paintings but she destroyed them all before she died. I think it was because, without Dad, the light went out for good.' I wondered whether to mention his painting and how much I'd wanted it, but it didn't seem fair. It was my fault I hadn't spoken up and I didn't want him to feel guilty about something that he couldn't have known.

'That's really sad,' Jed said. 'I'm so sorry. Is that why you settled in Whitsborough Bay? Because of the lighthouse?'

'No. Fate made that decision but, as soon as I saw the light-house, I knew fate had made the right choice.'

'Fate made it? How?'

'I, erm… I needed to get out of London – long and complicated story – and start completely afresh. I sat in a petrol station, opened a map, closed my eyes, and let the pen make the choice.'

'Strewth! You could have ended up in a right dump.'

'I know. Although when I saw the upstairs of the café, "dump" certainly sprang to mind.' I gave him a gentle nudge in the ribs so he knew I was joking.

'I cringe every time I think of showing you round. I'd forgotten how bad it was up there. Even looking at the first floor through your eyes was a shocker. And I'm embarrassed about my behaviour too, trying to convince you the business was viable when it wasn't.'

'You were maybe a smidge pushy but that could have been my fault.'

'It definitely wasn't your fault. I'm nothing like that usually but all I could hear was Ingrid's voice in my head nagging me. She said I had to charm, lie, beg or do whatever it took to make the deal. I was so desperate to get out that I cracked under the pressure. I'm so sorry. No wonder you despised me.'

'Looking me up and down was never going to be a good starting point.'

Jed groaned. 'Did I really do that? No! I'm so sorry.'

'That's okay. It was a long time ago.'

'I know but it's not okay. I promise I wasn't being sleazy and checking you out. At the time, I was happily married, or at least I thought I was. It was the artist in me. The minute you stepped into the café, I had an overwhelming urge to draw you.'

I stopped and looked him in the eye, frowning. 'Why? Why would you want to draw *me*?'

He smiled gently. 'I hadn't thought about drawing anyone for years until that moment but there was something about you. Something completely captivating. You radiated strength and confidence yet there was this cloak of sadness and fear swathed round you. I just wanted to drink you in and capture those emotions on paper or canvas. I hope that doesn't sound creepy.'

I swallowed on the lump in my throat. Not only had he really seen me back then, he still remembered what he saw. 'Did you draw me?'

'I started a sketch as soon as I got home but Ingrid caught me and...'

'And what?' I asked when he tailed off.

He sighed. 'She accused me of eyeing up other women and ripped it up. Anyway, I'm sorry about my behaviour when we first met and also my behaviour when I saw you at the start of this year. All I wanted to do was say hello and see whether that sadness had gone but I went about it completely the wrong way. I don't know who that guy was but it wasn't me.'

'An imposter,' I said, smiling at him. A sudden blast of icy air made me shiver. 'Come on, let's get moving again.'

As we set off walking along the seafront once more, Carly's words rang in my ears. *Be brave.*

I took a deep breath. 'I hope the imposter doesn't return because I like the real Jed Ferguson. A lot.'

Jed didn't say anything but, out the corner of my eye, I could see him smiling.

'How are you finding it back in the Bay?' I asked.

'Good although a bit disorientating at times. I've caught up with some old friends and it's like I only saw them the week before and I've caught up with others who've been like strangers. It's also strange living back home with my parents – something I never expected to do. They're great, though and it's good for me and the girls to have some quality time with them after living on the other side of the world for so long.'

'How are your girls settling in? They'll have been too young to remember living here before, won't they?'

'They were two and four when we emigrated but they love it here. Lucy's started at the TEC, studying art, and she's already made lots of friends. Erin's studying fine art at Newcastle University. She's settled in really well and even has a boyfriend.'

'So they've both taken after you with the passion for art?'

'Looks like it, much to their mother's disgust. She absolutely hated me doing anything artistic. Always said there was no future in it. Even when my work started taking off, she was adamant it was a waste of time and not a real career. The day the Aus gallery opened, she refused to come. Told me I was making a fool of myself and nobody in their right mind would want to buy my "pathetic little kiddie cartoons" and she wasn't going to hang around while they all laughed at me.'

'Oh my God, Jed. That's awful and so very wrong. Why would she say something like that?'

He released a long, slow sigh. 'Because, unfortunately, that's the type of woman I was married to and I must have had some really thick blinkers on because I never even realised it until then.'

We turned the corner and headed up the hill, our pace slowing slightly.

'Is that when you split up?' I asked.

'No. I probably should have had the guts to end it then but I was the walking cliché of sticking together for the sake of the kids. The three of them were my world.'

'Three? I thought you only had Erin and Lucy.'

Jed sighed. 'I do but, for six years, Ingrid let me believe that her son, Aaron, was mine too.'

I stopped walking and grabbed his arm. 'You're kidding me.'

He shook his head and, under the gentle yellow glow of the street-light, I could see the pain etched across his face. 'I wish. Apparently Ingrid was still in love with her first boyfriend, Declan. They split up when his family emigrated to Aus but I later discovered they'd stayed in touch the whole time Ingrid and I were together. Our move to Aus was nothing to do with her hating the UK weather. It was all about her being with him. He never wanted the marriage and kids thing so she kept that going with muggins here and spent all her spare time with Declan. When she fell pregnant with Aaron, she knew he couldn't be mine because of the dates but decided to pretend rather than risk Declan running a mile from the responsibility.'

My heart broke for him. 'How did you find out?'

'When he was six, Aaron suddenly fell ill. Ingrid was supposedly away with friends which later turned out to mean she was staying over at Declan's. I rushed Aaron to hospital and was told he needed blood so, naturally, I offered mine. They did a test and the doctor said, "Unfortunately you're not a match, but with you not being the biological father, it was a long shot". The bottom fell out my world. I'll never forget the look on the doctor's face. She completely drained of colour, obviously realising her huge faux pas. I begged her to explain but she said she couldn't discuss it any further. It didn't take much Googling of our blood types to discover that, biologically, it was impossible for me to be Aaron's dad.'

So that was the information Joyce had been about to give me when Peter stopped her. How horrendous. I could tell from the tone of Jed's voice that it was still raw and I wanted to hold him tightly and never let go.

'What happened after you found out?' I asked, thrusting my hands into my pockets.

Jed shivered and indicated we should set off walking again. 'My priority was for Aaron to get better. Blood-relation or not, I still loved him. Thankfully, he recovered with no lasting health issues, but Ingrid and I were through. I filed for a divorce on the day Aaron returned to school. Ingrid took the kids and moved in with Declan. Mr "I-don't-want-marriage-and-kids" was suddenly stoked to discover that he was a dad. A week after our divorce came through, they married. He point-blank refused to let me see Aaron and my solicitor told me I didn't have a legal leg to stand on. I begged Declan to let me be part of Aaron's life but he wouldn't budge on access. He said it was too confusing for Aaron and, as long as I was around, it would be impossible for him to bond with his son which, ultimately, was the best thing for Aaron. I could understand his logic and would probably have felt the same way in his position, although I'd like to think I wouldn't have been quite so brutal in severing ties right from the start. It was so unfair on Aaron to completely cut me out of his life just like that.'

'Oh, Jed. That's horrendous.'

'It was. Still is. So, while Declan and Aaron built their relationship, the one Ingrid had with our girls rapidly deteriorated. They said she always put Declan and Aaron ahead of them and that Declan barely acknowledged their existence. They'd always been really close to Aaron but started to resent him for being the clear favourite and they hated being away from me. Ingrid wouldn't let them move in with me, though. It was a fraught couple of years but then she fell pregnant again. Suddenly it was okay for Erin and Lucy to stay at mine more and more often. She gave birth to twin girls and, within a month of their arrival, decided the house was overcrowded so, if the girls wanted to move in with me permanently, that was fine by her. I was heartbroken for them. It felt like a two in, two out policy, but the girls were ecstatic to be living with me so I embraced it. They barely saw Ingrid after that which makes me sad but Ingrid did that to herself by choosing Declan and her new family and being so distant towards our beautiful girls.'

'It never ceases to amaze me how cruel some people can be. You must have been devastated, especially about Aaron.'

'I still think about him every single day. You know I told you that the inspiration for my drawings came from the kids? Well, it was predominantly from Aaron. He used to draw animals all the time and they were usually big and round with huge smiles on their faces. I miss him and it still hurts, but I'll always be glad he came into my life because I found my artistic style thanks to him and, for six amazing years, I had him as my son.'

My heart raced. He'd just played 'the glad game'.

Jed paused and took a few deep breaths. 'I'd forgotten how steep this hill is. Here was me thinking I was fit.'

'It's because you've been talking and because you're full of lager.'

He pointed to a pub a few doors ahead of us. 'I know you're tired so feel free to say no, but do you fancy warming up and having one for the road?'

'I think the cold air has revitalised me so one for the road sounds perfect.'

We took a seat close to the log fire and sipped on spirits.

'Do you ever hear from Aaron?' I asked.

Jed shook his head. 'No, but I never expected to. He was only six when it happened and he probably doesn't even remember me now so I've had to let that one go and do my best to come to terms with it. I feel sorry for the girls, though. They adored their little brother but the two years or so with Ingrid and Declan destroyed that friendship which is so sad.'

'Are the girls in touch with their mum?'

'As Lucy would say, they "exchange unpleasantries" a few times a year and I can even see that petering out now that we've settled here. They've got a good relationship with Ingrid's parents, though. Billy and Pam are good people. They were devastated when it all kicked off and went out of the way to show their support for me and the girls. We've seen quite a bit of them since moving back.'

'The girls weren't bothered about leaving Aus, then?'

'They loved Aus but they were so hurt by what Ingrid did that they'd have been happy to move to England right after the twins were born. I seriously considered it but decided it was better for them to finish school rather than have that disruption too.'

'You must be so proud of them for following in your footsteps.'

He smiled, his eyes twinkling with obvious pride. 'They're amazing kids. I'd have been proud of them whatever they decided to do, but I have to admit that the shared passion for art is a bit of a bonus. They have very different styles to me and to each other, though. Lucy is into big dramatic landscapes and loves using acrylics. Erin loves delicate watercolours and pencils. Very much a match for their personalities.' Jed took a sip of his drink and smiled. 'I think I may have had an attack of the verbals, so it's my turn to shut up and let you talk. Any cheating ex-partners or fake children in your past?'

That plane swooped and looped in my stomach again. I heard Carly's words in my ear once more: *A few minutes of courage might change your life.* He'd just presented me the perfect opportunity and, unless I wanted to dance round it forever and close down whatever it was building between us, I was going to have to just come out with it. 'Hell, yeah. Cheating deviant ex-husband who only married me for his public image, hiding the fact that he and my foster sister hosted orgies in his Surrey mansion every weekend.' I marvelled that I managed to sound so flippant about it.

Jed started to laugh, then stopped and leaned forward, the smile slipping from his face. 'You're not joking, are you?'

My shoulders sagged as I slowly shook my head. 'Gosh, Jed, I wish I was.'

'What happened?'

'Get me another one of these,' I said, picking up my vodka and Coke and necking it, 'and I'll tell you the whole sorry tale.'

\* \* \*

Telling my story for the second time hadn't been quite as emotional as it had been when opening up for the first time to Carly. The pain wasn't quite so raw. The embarrassment wasn't quite so excruciating. And I didn't have that traumatic shock of actually saying it aloud for the first time ever. The alcohol certainly helped and I'd even been able to joke about some of the sights I'd seen in Garth's 'dungeon'.

Huddled over our drinks in front of the fire, we talked about the struggle to come to terms with what had happened to us both and how it still affected us. I told him more about The Best Day Ever and how I missed both sets of parents every day, and he talked about the impact of life without Aaron on him and his daughters.

The more we talked, the closer I felt to him, feeling his pain, understanding it. The scenarios were completely different but the outcome was the same – Jed and I had both been broken. The only difference was that he'd managed to heal. His daughters and his passion for his art had given him strength, courage and purpose every day. Might I have healed sooner if I hadn't tried to be a lone wolf?

It was way past midnight when we stepped outside the pub and made our way slowly up the incline towards town.

'I certainly wasn't expecting to share that with you tonight,' I said. 'Thank you for making it easy to tell you. I've kept it hidden for fourteen and a half years. I only told Carly the full story recently and you've both been amazing.'

'Can I ask why you kept it secret for so long?'

'So many reasons. Shame, embarrassment, feeling stupid for being so naïve. And, of course, if nobody knew, I could pretend it had never happened. Almost.' I shook my head and sighed. 'It seems silly saying that now.'

'It's not silly at all. I completely understand all those reasons because it's exactly how I felt too. Guess how long it took me to tell my parents I'd split up with Ingrid and that Aaron wasn't my son.'

'A few weeks?'

'Try a few months.'

I turned to him, eyes wide. 'Really? You're not just saying that to be nice?'

'Really. I just couldn't bring myself to tell them. They'd Skype every week on a day I had the girls. They kept asking to speak to Aaron too and I'd have an excuse every time as to why he wasn't there. Even got the girls to cover it up. Little did I know they were planning a Christmas visit. Turned up outside the house in a taxi on 23$^{rd}$ December saying "surprise". I had a few surprises of my own in store.'

'Awkward.'

'It was the second most awkward moment of my life after the accidental reveal from the doctor.'

We reached the pedestrianised area at the bottom of town. Five more minutes and we'd be at Castle Street.

'Can I ask you a question, Jed? It's a personal one but I figured that, as we're sharing...'

He laughed. 'Fire away.'

'Has there been anyone since Ingrid?'

'After a year or so, I went on a couple of dates but nothing serious. About three years ago, I had an on-off relationship which lasted a couple of years, although it was more off than on. I liked her and I enjoyed our time together but I always felt like there was something missing. Deep down, I'm afraid I didn't trust her and it wasn't just because of what happened with Ingrid. She travelled a lot with her job and it felt too possible for her to have a fling if she wanted. Turns out I was right to be suspicious. She also had an on-off thing going with a work colleague. She told me she only ever hooked up with him when we were on a break but I realised that, even if she'd been seeing him when she was seeing me, I actually didn't care that much. So I ended it for good and there's been nobody since. Just my girls. Besides, it wouldn't have been fair to start a relationship when we knew we were moving back to the UK. What about you?'

'Nobody at all since Garth.'

'Not even a date?' It wasn't said judgementally.

'Not even a sniff of a date. Just me and Hercules.'

'Hercules?'

'My giant house rabbit.'

'You've got a giant house rabbit? Wait till I tell Lucy. She's obsessed with rabbits, especially giant ones.'

We stopped outside The Chocolate Pot. I took my keys out my pocket but didn't place them in the lock. 'Then you'll have to both come round at some point and meet him,' I said, scarcely able to believe the words coming out of my mouth. I'd only just opened up my home to Carly. Had I really just invited Jed and his daughter to visit?

'Only if you want to,' I hastily added.

He smiled. 'No, I'd like that. *We'd* like that. Thank you.'

We both stood there for a moment, grinning at each other. What happened next? I had no prior experience of this situation. Was I meant to invite him in for coffee? Was he meant to ask me on a proper date? Were we meant to kiss? Shake hands? Say good night and go our separate ways? Had I completely misread the sparks between us? Was it completely one-sided and, as far as he was concerned, we were business neighbours who were simply building a friendship and being empathetic over our disastrous pasts?

'I've got something for you,' Jed said. 'Wait here and I'll get it.' He laughed. 'Not right here on this very spot because it's freezing. You're very welcome to go inside. I'll be a few minutes.'

He ran across the street and let himself into his gallery. I unlocked the door, put the lights on and reached for my yellow mug. I placed it on the coffee machine then hesitated. What sort of signal would making us both drinks send and was that what I wanted? I replaced the mug on the shelf.

Jed reappeared at the door holding a large bubble-wrapped package.

'What's this?' I asked, opening the door to him.

'Open it and you'll find out.'

I rested the package on one of the tables by the window and gently removed the tape from the back. My heart started racing. It felt like a canvas, but surely it couldn't be…?

Peeling off the bubble wrap, I turned it round to face me and gasped. 'It's the lighthouse picture. Jed! I can't believe it! I came across to buy it this morning and it had disappeared. I thought you must have sold it.'

'No. Just put it aside for you.'

My heart raced faster. 'But how did you know? I never even said I liked it.'

'I've worked in this business long enough to notice when one of my paintings speaks to someone and I could tell immediately that something about that one called to you so I put it out the back. I wasn't sure when I was going to give you it but, after seeing you looking at the lighthouse earlier and hearing your connection to it, I knew it had to be tonight. I hope I did the right thing.'

I couldn't speak. Tears filled my eyes and my throat tightened as I stared at the incredible artwork. Taking a few deep breaths to compose myself, I rested the picture against the window and smiled at Jed. 'You did the right thing. This image and these words mean so much to me and now you know why. I can't thank you enough for saving it for me. How much do I owe you?'

He shook his head vigorously. 'You don't.'

'Jed…'

'You wouldn't accept my cheque so you *have* to accept this paint-ing. I'll be seriously offended if you don't.'

I could tell from his stern expression that he meant it. 'Okay. Thank you so much. It's going to have pride of place upstairs. Oh my God, Jed. I absolutely love it.'

'I'll look forward to seeing it when we meet Hercules,' he said, smiling.

Silence.

'So... er... I guess I'd better say goodnight and let you get some sleep.' Jed ran his hand through his hair. 'I enjoyed tonight.'

'So did I. They're a good crowd, aren't they?'

He nodded. 'Yeah. Now that they're not baying for my blood. I have a confession to make.'

'Oh yeah?'

'My favourite part of the night was the walk home and the slight detour, though.' He took a step closer to me.

'Mine too,' I whispered, taking a step towards him.

'Goodnight, then.' Jed closed the gap even more.

'Goodnight.' We were so close we were almost touching and every single nerve ending felt like it was on fire. *Please kiss me!*

And he did. He leaned forward and gave me a gentle kiss on the lips. My heart raced and I felt light-headed as he stepped away.

'Goodnight, Tara,' he said again.

'Goodnight. And thank you. For the painting, for listening, for everything.'

'Same to you. Not for the painting, obviously, because you haven't given me a painting but... I need to quit while I'm ahead. See you real soon.'

I watched him walking down the street in the direction of Castle Park, my fingers touching my lips. When he reached the end, he stopped, turned, and smiled before disappearing round the corner, presumably heading for the taxi rank. *Didn't imagine the sparks, then. Oh my goodness. That was wonderful.*

Picking up my canvas and the packaging, I locked up and made my way upstairs to Hercules.

'I was brave, just like Carly said,' I said, giving him a hug. 'And I think those few minutes of courage might be about to change my life. I have a feeling great things might be about to happen.'

## 34

'Post's late today,' Sheila announced, joining me in the kitchen at the start of her shift on Monday morning and rifling through some envelopes. 'Junk mail and bills by the look of it. And a card for you. Pretty handwriting.'

Putting down the mixing bowl, I reached for the burgundy envelope, my heart thumping at the familiar sight of Kirsten's calligraphy next to the solicitor's redirection sticker.

'Are you okay, my dear?' Sheila asked. 'Is it bad news?'

'It's from my foster parents. They send a card every Christmas and birthday and I've kept them all in a box, unopened. It's been a year of letting people in and Carly thinks it's time to let my foster parents back into my life.'

'I think Carly speaks sense.'

'It's a big thing, though.'

'So start small. Start with the card. If you like what you read, you could open the others. If you don't like what you read, leave it there.'

I smiled at her, grateful for her wise words. 'I'm glad you came to work here, Sheila.'

'Aw, thank you, my love. That's very kind of you. Now why don't you go upstairs and open that card. If it goes crazy down here, we can always buzz you.'

*Be brave.*

I nodded. 'Just make sure you do buzz.'

We swapped places and Sheila picked up the whisk and started mixing. 'Go on. I know it's scary, but you know you need to do it.'

\* \* \*

Sitting on the sofa with Hercules tucked in next to me, I took a deep breath, opened the envelope and removed the contents. I placed the Christmas card on the arm of the sofa and unfolded the cream pages of the letter, written in Kirsten's flowing script rather than typed:

*Dear Tamara*

*It's been 14½ years yet there isn't a day that passes when Tim and I don't think about you and miss you. Every time the phone rings, I hope to hear your voice. Every time the post arrives, I hope to see your writing.*

*I have no idea whether you open my cards and letters. Tim thinks not. He's convinced that, if you'd opened and read them, you'd have got in touch. I'm not so sure. You've been betrayed by the people you love and I can understand the desire to sever the connection.*

*When you left, you asked us not to try and find you and, hard as it is, we've respected that wish because we know how badly Leanne and Garth hurt you. Hurt all of us.*

*You have no idea how often I've typed your name into Google and forced myself not to press 'enter.' Then something appeared on my Facebook news feed recently. I barely ever look at social* media but I found myself drawn to it a couple of weeks ago. I think it was fate because a friend of a friend or something like that had shared and commented on an article about some local business awards in Whitsborough Bay and, as I glanced at the picture, who did I see?

I cannot begin to tell you how proud Tim and I are of the woman you've become and everything you've achieved. I am thrilled that you took your talent and experience and opened your own café. Award-winning café, no less! And your work in the community tells me you have become the person you always wanted to be: someone kind who helps others. Not that we ever doubted that. Our little Pollyanna always was a sensitive and caring individual.

Because you are sensitive and caring, I know that this next part is going to hurt. You may have physically taken yourself out of our lives, but I know that you will still be here emotionally. I was diagnosed with breast cancer earlier this year. It was in one breast, but I made the decision to have a double mastectomy. I won't lie. It was a pretty terrifying time for us. Thankfully, everything's looking good, but it made us re-evaluate our lives. We've sold The Larches and Vanilla Pod, and Tim has taken early retirement. What matters to us now is family and there's a vital part of our family missing. We want you in our lives. We need you in our lives.

As the saying goes, if the mountain won't come to Muhammad, Muhammad must go to the mountain. We have rented a cottage just outside Whitby from Monday 10<sup>th</sup> December until the end of January. My Christmas wish is to have my daughter back. It's been my Christmas wish every year since they drove you away but, this time, I'm determined to make it happen. Life is short and precious. I've been lucky. They caught the cancer in time, but it could have been a different story and I *would have left this world filled with regret that I let you go out of our lives. We never let you go out of our hearts, though.*

*I've put our mobile numbers, the cottage details and the address of the apartment we're renting in London below. Please pick up the phone, text me, email, write. I don't care how you do it but please, I beg of you, make contact.*

*Yours hopefully, with all my love, always*

*Kirsten xxx*


Tears rained down my cheeks as I reached for my mobile and dialled.

'Hello? Kirsten speaking.' I hadn't heard her gentle, soothing voice for so many years, yet it was so familiar to me.

'Mum? It's me.'

And neither of could speak for the next five minutes for crying.

## 35

My phone call with Kirsten was extremely emotional, but the best thing that could ever have happened. After we'd both stopped sobbing enough to speak, she wanted to know all about The Chocolate Pot and the awards I'd received, and I was keen to find out about her breast cancer and the prognosis. We talked about her selling Vanilla Pod and how Tim felt about early retirement.

I paused our conversation after about twenty minutes so I could buzz down to Sheila and ask her to phone Maria and see if she'd cover the rest of my shift in exchange for me working Sunday for her. Sheila laughed and said, 'I've already done that. She's on her way.'

Kirsten and I were on the phone for over two hours. It would have been longer but she had a doctor's appointment so reluctantly had to say goodbye. We agreed not to talk about the past. Not yet. Catching up was amazing. I could picture her eyes sparkling and that warm smile as she spoke. I could hear the love in her voice. I could feel her arms round me when she said she wished she could give me a hug. Everything had changed for us yet, despite so many years apart, nothing had changed at all.

When I hung up, I felt drained from the whirlwind of emotions I'd experienced by reconnecting. Joy and love tinged with sadness and regret.

Moving to the bed for a lie-down, I fell asleep for a couple of hours, waking up with Hercules nudging my arm. I spent the rest of the afternoon and evening working through all the other envelopes, starting with the very first one. It was difficult reliving the experience through Kirsten's eyes – the shock, the disbelief, the guilt that all this had been going on under her nose and she'd had no idea. At that point, she was so disgusted with Garth and Leanne, having forced the truth from them, that she couldn't bear to have contact with either of them.

As the years passed, the letters fell into a similar pattern – wondering where I was and how I was, saying how much they missed and loved me, a little bit of news, and ending with hopes that I'd get in touch. Little was mentioned about Leanne after that first letter until three years later when Kirsten informed me that Leanne was no longer in their lives. A customer caught Leanne sniffing cocaine at work and reported it to the papers. The scandal nearly ruined the chain. Suspending Leanne, Kirsten took over management of Leanne's bistro and discovered roughly £50k defrauded from the business that year alone. Looking into previous years, the figure rose and rose. Then stories of her bullying and harassing the staff emerged, dubious hygiene standards, and Leanne regularly being drunk or high at work. For Kirsten and Tim, it was the final straw. They didn't know or recognise Leanne anymore and tough love was needed. They cut her off financially and emotionally, telling her they would pay for rehab if she was ready to get her life back on track, otherwise she was on her own; after all, she had several hundred thousand pounds she'd defrauded from Vanilla Pod. Kirsten never mentioned Leanne again in her letters and my heart broke for her. She'd lost us both and it had probably just about destroyed her. What if it hadn't left her with the strength to fight the cancer? It didn't bear thinking about.

In the evening, I picked up an email on my phone from Jed asking if I was free that evening for a drink. Completely distracted, I gave the briefest of replies saying I was a bit tied up and suggesting a rain check, then I returned to the letters.

Accompanying every birthday letter was a card. I'd expected them to be birthday cards but, instead, each had a motivational quote on the front about being brave, seeing the best in people, thinking positive thoughts and so on. I regretted never opening them because so many of the quotes would have helped me over the years and may even have prompted me to make contact sooner.

\* \* \*

Pilates on Tuesday evening couldn't have been better timed for emptying my mind and relaxing my body.

'You looked very chilled there,' Karen said as I rolled up my mat afterwards. 'I thought you might start snoring.'

'I very nearly did. It's been a busy few days and I really needed that.'

'Speaking of busy, I was in Jed's gallery on Sunday,' Karen said. 'It was heaving and, oh my God, how amazing are his paintings?'

'They're brilliant.' I smiled, picturing the lighthouse and sheep that had pride of place in my lounge. Then I gasped. How dismissive had I been when he'd emailed the night before? What an idiot. He'd asked me out and I'd said no, without any explanation. What must he have thought? He'd given me a one-off original – I only noticed the 1/1 in the bottom left corner when I mounted it on the wall – which had to be worth a fortune, we'd opened up about our difficult pasts and we'd shared a brief kiss. He'd made the next move by asking me out for a drink and I'd fobbed him off. Damn!

I was still cursing under my breath as I left the leisure centre, no longer feeling relaxed. With a heavy heart, I drove home. Would Jed be in the gallery? I needed to get his attention and explain.

Running up Castle Street ten minutes later, my heart raced when I spotted Jed's first-floor lights on. A doorbell had been fitted so I rang it but couldn't hear any ringing inside. Maybe it wasn't connected yet. I banged on his door and tried shouting through the letterbox, but got no response, and his mobile went straight to voicemail.

Stepping back, I stared up at the first floor, wondering how else I could get his attention. I spotted the gallery phone number on the sign. Shivering, I dialled it and, moments later, heard it ringing inside. Five minutes later, there was still no answer and I was numb with cold. Reluctantly, I disconnected the call and turned away, shoulders drooping.

'Tara?'

I turned round to see Jed standing in his doorway.

'Were you ringing the gallery?' he asked.

'I've been trying to get your attention for the last ten minutes. I wanted to apologise for yesterday. I was completely distracted. A letter came from...' My teeth were chattering so much that I could barely get the words out.

Reaching for my hand, Jed pulled me inside.

'Your hands are like ice,' he cried.

'The whole of me is. Why didn't you answer your phone?'

'I was painting and I had headphones on. I'd just taken them off to make a coffee when I heard the downstairs phone. You're shivering. Come upstairs. We need to get you warm.'

I followed Jed into his studio and sat down on one of the wooden chairs. He grabbed a fleecy sweater from a hook on the wall and pulled it over my head as though I was a small child, before taking one hand at a time between his and rubbing it.

'I think we've saved them,' he said as the blue tinge left my hands and the heat returned. 'Coffee?'

As he clattered about in the kitchenette, I looked round the room. One of the easels was still covered but he'd obviously been working on the other. It was a large canvas with a scene set at night or early in the morning on... *Wait a minute. Is that...?* I stood up and moved closer. Standing on a cobbled street outside a café, a woman was gazing up at the stars.

'It's not finished yet.' Jed appeared by my side.

My heart thumped rapidly as I stared at the picture. 'Is it...? Is it me?' The likeness was astonishing yet I needed him to confirm it in case I was imagining things.

He paused for a moment. 'Yes.'

My heart thumped even faster and butterflies soared in my stomach. 'From the morning of the awards?' I'm not sure how I managed to form the words.

'Yes. I told you I felt compelled to draw you. You're not mad with me that I did it without asking?'

I couldn't take my eyes away from it. 'No. Not mad with you. Dazzled by your talent. How did you do it?'

He shrugged. 'A couple of pencil sketches at first, then—'

'No. Not that. I mean how did you capture me like that? It's like you knew what I was thinking.'

Jed shrugged. 'I just painted what I saw.'

'It's amazing. It really is. What's the other one?'

'It's not finished.'

'Can I have a sneaky peak?'

Jed took a couple of steps towards the other easel, then stopped. 'Actually, better not. It's not ready yet.' He spoke slowly and there was a sadness to his tone.

I could understand the reluctance to show me a work-in-progress. As a crafter, I was all too familiar with how rubbish something could look before suddenly transforming at the final stages. 'Okay. Another time?'

'I don't know. It's not working out how I'd hoped.'

I finally drew my gaze away from the painting and looked at Jed. Bloodshot eyes and dark circles beneath them suggested he was either shattered or worried about something. 'You sound really down and you look exhausted. Are you okay?'

He smiled weakly. 'I couldn't get to sleep last night and I'm shattered.'

Recognising my cue to leave, I said, 'I'd better leave you to it, then.'

In silence, he walked me out and said good night.

'You need this back,' I said, lifting the front of his sweater up.

'Keep it on. I'll get it back from you another time.'

I waved and ran across the street.

It was only when I changed into my snuggly clothes later that I realised that I hadn't told Jed why I'd called for him and he hadn't asked, the painting distracting us both. Standing by the arched window, I gazed across the street, but Jed's building was in darkness. I'd have to try to catch him tomorrow when he closed up for the day. I could have emailed or texted, but I really owed him an apology in person. Again.

I pressed my fingers to my lips and shook my head. That painting. My heart started to thump and those butterflies swarmed again. He'd painted me but it had been so much more than that. He'd captured my thoughts and emotions. He'd seen right into my soul. What did that mean? Was he simply a gifted artist or did it say something about his feelings for me? Remembering the feeling of his lips against mine the other night, a zip of excitement raced through my body.

'What are you doing to me, Jed Ferguson? This wasn't part of the plan.'

## 36

'Are you okay?' Maria asked. It was late afternoon a couple of days later and darkness had fallen. The Christmas lights had just come on, twinkling over Castle Street. Yorkshire's Best was brightly lit but only on the ground floor. The first floor remained in darkness as it had done for the past couple of days.

'Yes. I'm fine. Why?'

'Because you're very quiet and you keep staring across the street. Has something happened between you and Jed?'

Heat raced to my cheeks. 'No. Why?' I could hear the guilt in my voice.

'Oh my God! It has! You wouldn't have said no that quickly if it hadn't.'

I shook my head. 'Honestly, Maria, nothing has happened. Well, something has, but not what you're thinking.'

She stopped stacking the tray of mugs into their cubby holes. 'I'm listening.'

'You know that painting I wanted that had already sold? Turns out it hadn't really sold. He'd clocked that I liked it so he put it aside. He gave me it as a gift and it's an original.'

'Wow! Really? He must think a lot of you.'

'I thought so, but I messed up.'

'How?'

'He emailed me on Monday and asked me out but I was too distracted by getting in touch with Kirsten and suggested a rain check. I went over to apologise and explain on Tuesday night and somehow managed not to do either. I've been watching out for him since then but he hasn't been there. It's been Anastasia each day.'

'So go across and ask her when Jed's back.'

'I *can't* do that.'

'Of course you can. There are plenty of us to hold the fort here. Go on. Shoo!' She practically shoved me out the door.

* * *

'Hi, Tara,' Anastasia said as soon as I pushed the door open. 'How are you?'

'Good, thanks.' I glanced round. There were several customers in the shop. A man was holding a couple of prints while the woman with him rummaged in her bag, probably for her purse. Trust me to pick a busy moment.

'I won't keep you. I wanted a quick word with Jed but I haven't spotted him in here for a couple of days. Do you know when I might catch him?'

She smiled. 'Right now. He's literally just arrived back. I'm sure he won't mind you going upstairs.'

The couple with the prints approached the counter.

'You're sure that's okay?'

'You're friends now, aren't you?'

I nodded, feeling my cheeks flush. Jed must have told her that. *Be brave. This might be your only chance to catch him.* Taking a deep breath, I crept upstairs to the first floor.

'Hello? Jed?'

No answer.

I stepped into his studio but it was empty and the lights were off. He'd obviously been in there as I could hear the kettle bubbling.

The streetlights outside illuminated the dark shapes of the two easels. I could tell that neither were covered but it was too dark for me to make out any detail on the paintings.

Feeling like an intruder, I felt my confidence seeping away and was about to turn and run back down the stairs but curiosity stopped me. *What's on that second painting?* He'd been very cagey about it. Was that because it was another one of me or was that my overactive imagination at work and it really was a case of an unfinished project being unfit for reveal?

The sound of footsteps on the stairs from the top floor rooted me to the spot. The light flicked on and Jed burst into the room, stopping abruptly when he saw me, no doubt looking very guilty in my position halfway between the door and the paintings.

'Tara? What are you doing in here?'

'Sorry for intruding. I wanted to speak to you and Anastasia said you...'

His eyes flicked towards the paintings and I could see what looked like panic in his expression.

'I didn't look at them.' But as I said the words, I automatically turned my head towards them, my heart thumping as I took in the scene on the second painting. *Oh my God!*

'You weren't meant to see that.' He rushed forward, grabbed the dust sheet off the floor and opened it out.

'No! Don't cover it up.'

'But, I...' He lowered the sheet and sighed. 'I guess I'm too late.' There was such defeat in his voice.

'Can I take a closer look?'

Silence.

'Please?'

Jed nodded slowly and I took a few steps forward.

The setting was unmistakable – the covered walkway by The Bay Pavilion. A full moon shone in the starry sky, releasing a silvery ribbon across the sea, leading towards one of the stone arches. A woman wearing a sparkling purple dress was locked in a passionate embrace with a man wearing a tuxedo. My heart raced even faster as I was transported back to the evening of the awards when Jed held me and I'd longed for him to kiss me beneath the stars. Had he felt that way too?

I took a deep breath as I turned to face Jed. 'You have an amazing gift.'

'Thank you.' He cleared his throat and the confidence returned to his voice. 'It's lucky that others agree because I was starting to run out of career choices.'

'You *are* a brilliant artist, but that's not what I meant. Your gift goes far deeper than that, Jed. You see things. *Really* see things. Emotions, thoughts...' I pointed to the other picture. 'I said that you'd captured my thoughts on that painting. It was like you could see into my soul. And, on this one...' *Be brave. You can say it. He painted it so he must have wanted it too.* 'You've done the same. When you held me that night, I didn't want you to let me go. I wanted what you painted. I still do.'

He frowned. 'But I asked you out and you blew me off.'

'I know. I'm so sorry. I didn't mean to do that and I came to apologise on Tuesday but I got side-tracked by the first painting and didn't get a chance to explain...'

His expression softened. 'You don't have to explain. It's my fault. I should have taken things more slowly, especially knowing what you've been through.'

I shook my head. 'My response to your email was nothing to do with that. Something else happened on Monday that was completely unexpected and long overdue and it distracted me from everything else. I spoke to Kirsten.'

His eyes widened. 'Tara! That's amazing. Oh my God! How was it?'

'It was pretty special.' Tears rushed to my eyes and I tried to blink them away but there were too many. 'She had cancer. They caught it but... I could have lost her. I shouldn't have pushed her away like that for so long. She'd done nothing wrong. She'd only ever...' My voice cracked.

'Hey! Come here.' Jed pulled me close and held me again while I sobbed, transporting me back to the arches, being held by a man who had stirred feelings and emotions in me that I'd never expected to experience again.

'I'm sorry.' I stepped back and wiped my wet cheeks with my hands. 'I'm such an emotional wreck at the moment.'

'I'm not surprised. Speaking to your foster mum after all these years... That's huge.'

'I know. It's not just her, though.' *Be brave.* 'It's you as well. It's dreaming about having that—' I nodded towards the second painting '—but being scared of it too.'

Jed looked at me with such tenderness that I felt like I could melt. 'You're not the only one who's scared, but great things come to those who have courage.'

'That's what Carly keeps telling me. I'm trying.'

'Why don't we face our fears together?' He cupped my chin in his hand and gently tilted my head towards his.

'I'd like that.'

I swear my heart skipped a beat as his lips met mine, softly at first, as though worried about pushing things too far. He'd taken that first step and now it was my turn. Stepping a little closer, I slid my arms round his neck and intensified the kiss. Oh my goodness, it was worth it. I'd always thought that my first kiss with Garth was pretty special, but my first proper kiss with Jed completely eclipsed it. So tender yet so passionate.

He brushed my curls back from my face. 'Even better than I imagined when I painted that picture.'

'Even better than I imagined when I was standing in the arches with you.'

I kissed him again, running my hands through his hair and down his back. We both gasped for breath when we parted.

'Sorry,' I said. 'I had to make sure I wasn't dreaming.'

Jed smiled. 'Please never apologise for kissing me like that. And, if it *was* a dream, it was a million times better than any dream I've ever had.'

A flush spread from my cheeks to my toes and I couldn't stop grinning. Unfortunately, work called. 'I hate to say this but I'm going to have to get back to the café.'

'Can I see you tonight? We could go out for a meal or just a drink if there are things you need to do.'

If any sort of relationship with Jed was going to work, the starting point needed to be absolute honesty. I'd told him my story but I needed to show him the real me. Which meant he needed to see my home and meet the other man in my life.

'Can you come over to the café at seven? There's someone I want you to meet. He needs to give you his seal of approval.'

Jed looked confused for a moment, then smiled. 'Ah! Hercules. I can't wait to meet him.'

'I can't wait for him to meet you too. I think the two of you are going to be great friends.'

## 37

I felt ridiculously nervous as I waited in the café shortly before 7 p.m. I'd dressed carefully again, pulling on pale ripped jeans, a plain lemon T-shirt and a thick cable-knit grey cardigan, with my hair tumbling in loose waves over my shoulders.

My heart raced as the door to Yorkshire's Best opened and Jed stepped out onto the cobbles clutching a bottle of wine.

'Very punctual,' I said, opening the door. 'I'm impressed.'

'The traffic was horrendous,' he joked, placing the wine on the countertop. 'It was touch and go as to whether I'd make it on time.'

As soon as I'd locked the door behind him, he took me in his arms and kissed me again, his hands running through my hair. Desire flowed through me and I imagined unbuttoning his shirt and... I reluctantly pulled away. This was meant to be going slowly and my thoughts had been anything but slow.

'Can you still picture how it was before?' I asked as we made our way up the stairs.

'Dark and poky. I remember stud walls everywhere creating all these tiny rooms. It was pretty grim actually. We only ever used it for storage but I used to look up at that amazing arched window and imagine how it could be if it was open plan instead, perhaps with a mezzanine.'

I smiled to myself. He was about to find out.

Taking a deep breath at the top, I opened the door. Hercules was waiting for us, twitching his nose. I scooped him up. 'This is Jed, Hercules. Are you going to say hello?'

'He's gorgeous.' Jed stroked his ears. 'I've never painted a rabbit before. I think he might have to become my first.'

'We'd love that, wouldn't we, Hercules?' As I stroked his back, my fingertips met Jed's and I felt a zip of electricity pass between us. I'd never felt that sort of intensity with Garth. He'd made my heart race, but there was something so much more powerful happening between Jed and me. It excited me yet terrified me at the same time. Could I really do this after shutting myself away from relationships for so long?

'Ready for the big reveal?' I asked, putting Hercules down.

We stepped forward.

'No way!' Jed turned from one side to the other. 'You did exactly what I imagined.'

'Do you like it?'

'I love it.'

Even if he hadn't verbalised how much he loved my flat as we moved round the different sections, I'd have known it from the sparkle in his eyes. I hadn't realised until that moment how much I wanted his approval.

After he'd had the tour, I opened the bottle of wine he'd brought with him and we stood in the lounge, each with a glass in our hands, looking at Jed's painting of the lighthouse which had pride of place on the wall opposite the sofa.

'You know what's weird?' he said. 'I've never actually seen one of my paintings in someone else's home.'

'Really?'

He nodded. 'Customers have sent me photos but I've never seen one in the wild, as it were. Seeing it up on your wall right now, it feels like it was always destined to be here, as though I painted it just for you.'

'I can't help thinking you did, even though you didn't realise it. The lone sheep, the lighthouse at night, the daisies, the inscription. Seriously, Jed, it couldn't be more perfect for me.'

We sat down on the sofa, still gazing at the painting.

'I was so upset when I thought it had been sold. I kicked myself so much for not buying it immediately.'

'What stopped you?' he asked.

'Something really stupid. I thought you might ask me why the picture spoke to me and it was too personal to share.'

'And how do you feel now that I know?'

'Still absolutely terrified but the hardest part is done. You know why I built that wall round me and yet you're still here. My shipping container full of emotional baggage hasn't scared you away.'

Jed reached forward and took my wine from my hand and placed it next to his on the coffee table. He twisted round to face me and took both of my hands in his. 'Nothing you say could scare me away. If anything, it makes me feel closer to you. We've both been badly hurt by the people we loved and should have been able to trust. It *is* hard to take that chance again but I understand that about you and you understand it about me. I think I might have a great big shipping container full of emotional baggage parked right next to yours but I think we can help each other deal with that and come out stronger together. If you want to, that is.'

I picked up our wine glasses again, handed Jed his, and clinked mine against it. 'To dealing with the crap life's thrown at us and making it out the other side.'

'To letting people in,' he said.

'In a year of trying to open up and let people in, I never

expected that one of those people would be you. You were definitely not one of my favourite people at the start of the year and I don't think you were in my fan club either but look at us now. What changed for you?'

Jed smiled. 'I saw you. Really saw you. That day on the cobbles, when you were looking at the sky, something in me completely shifted. Then when I saw you outside the Pavilion, thumping that wall...'

I grimaced. 'No! You saw that?'

'I did, but what I saw was the same sort of pain and anguish I'd been through. I didn't know what had happened to you but I understood and I wanted to be the one to take the hurt away. I wasn't sure whether you'd want me to, though.'

'Is that why you painted the second picture?'

He nodded. 'It was my little fantasy of me being your hero but you being mine too. That's why I couldn't show it to you on Tuesday night.'

'You said it was unfinished.'

'I said it wasn't ready. The painting was complete but I thought it would be too much. After that email, I didn't think you were interested in me and I thought that it would scare you off completely.'

'That's why you were vague about whether you'd ever show me it. You said it wasn't working out as you'd hoped. You meant with me rather than the painting.'

'Busted.'

'What about now? Things working out how you'd hoped?'

'Better than I'd hoped.' He smiled at me tenderly. 'What about you? When did you stop thinking of me as an "arrogant con artist"?'

Cringing, I lowered my head. 'Can you please forget I ever said that? Although that's actually the point when things changed. When I discovered that you didn't know about the extra money or the roof, some of the reasons I'd hated you no longer existed and I started to see you. Then I saw your paintings and I felt like I understood you too.'

Jed kissed me again and that zip of electricity I'd felt earlier made every nerve-ending fizz. We put our drinks down and kissed once more.

'I know you're scared but I promise you we can take things as slowly as you want.' He stroked my hair as I snuggled against this chest. 'I'm not going anywhere.'

And I believed him. Feeling the rise and fall of his chest and listening to the steady thump of his heart, I had never felt so relaxed or safe. I'd never have predicted that when he returned from Australia.

## 38

'Are you absolutely sure you don't want me to come with you?' Jed asked as we stood by my car on Tuesday morning the following week. Kirsten and Tim had arrived at their holiday cottage in a village south of Whitby late last night and I was about to drive up to see them. 'I can ring my mum and ask her to help Anastasia. I've already got her on standby just in case.'

'I really appreciate that but, after so many years apart, it's only fair that I see them on my own. There's so much to talk about.'

'How are you feeling?'

'More nervous than I've felt about anything in my entire life.' I put my hand out to show him how much I was shaking. 'I'm worried about tackling the "big" conversation.' Kirsten and I had spoken several more times on the phone since the first call but had agreed to stick to general chit-chat, saving a discussion about what happened until we met face-to-face so we could support each other through it, knowing how emotional it would be.

Jed pulled me into a reassuring hug. 'I know it will be difficult but it'll also be amazing. The phone calls have already broken the ice and you know they're not mad at you or anything like that. I bet they're nervous too after all this time but you only need to tackle the past this once and then it's out in the open and you can all move forward.'

He gently kissed me, setting off a different type of nervous sensation.

'Let me know when you're back and I can come over if you want some company. I won't be offended if you need some time to yourself, though.'

'Thanks for understanding.' I hugged Jed again. 'I guess I'd better hit the road.'

'You've got this.'

'Thank you.'

I waved goodbye, pulled out of my parking space and drove across town in the direction of Whitby.

My thoughts raced as I drove up the coast road, getting ever closer to our reunion. There was so much to say. Where would we even start? They knew about Leanne and Garth but did they know it all? Did they know about my 'playmates'? Did they know about The Manor? There was no mention of any of it in Kirsten's letters but that didn't mean they weren't aware. And if they knew everything, how must that have affected them? I'd only been ten when they'd taken me in – still a child at primary school. How devastating must it have been to discover that the child they were there to protect had been manipulated and 'educated' in their own home right under their noses by their own daughter and nephew?

Half an hour later, I pulled into a gravel courtyard in front of the stone cottage and stepped out of the car. *Deep breath. Be brave.*

A large wreath on the wooden door transported me back to The Larches at Christmas. Every year, Kirsten and I would make a wreath together from conifer leaves, holly, ivy and bright red poinsettias; another thing Leanne seemed to resent us doing, telling us it was a pointless waste of time when we could easily buy a "far superior" one from a florist.

I was about to knock when the door burst open and there she was, Kirsten Sanderson, the kindest woman I'd ever met. Her long blonde hair was gone, replaced with a short pixie-style crop. She'd gathered a few wrinkles – no doubt caused by stress and worry as well as the passing years – but was otherwise exactly as I remembered her.

She pressed her fingers to her lips, her eyes filling with tears as she looked me up and down as though trying to match the thirty-six-year-old woman before her with the twenty-two-year-old girl she'd last seen. 'It's really you!'

'It's me!' My voice cracked as the tears tumbled. 'I've missed you so much.'

'We've missed you too. Come here.'

We clung to each other, sobbing.

'Do I get one of those?' said a voice.

I pulled away and looked down the hall at my foster father. Thinner, less hair, greyer, but still with that warm smile that crinkled at his eyes.

'I've missed you too.' I hurled myself at Tim and held him tightly.

'It's so good to see you,' he whispered. 'Thank you for coming back to us.'

When the emotions had settled, we made our way into the cosy lounge where a real fire was burning in a grate.

'You're so grown up. And so beautiful.' Kirsten stepped back, holding my hands in hers and looking at me with such intensity that it felt as though she was trying to imprint my image on her brain in case I ever left again.

'I'm so sorry I left you both. I just couldn't stay.'

'We understand. Don't we, Tim?'

'We're the ones who are sorry,' he said.

'No! Don't be. You couldn't have known.'

Kirsten indicated for me to sit with her on the sofa and Tim sat on the armchair beside her.

'How much do you know?' I asked.

Kirsten took my hand. 'Everything. Or at least we think so. I found your letter in my copy of *Pollyanna*. That was clever of you. We confronted Leanne and she pleaded ignorance for days. We were worried sick. It was only when Tim said he was going to the police to report you as a missing person that she started talking.'

'We know about Leanne and Garth's...' Tim paused as though trying to find the right word. '... interests. And we know about the house in Surrey and the secret room.'

Secret room? That was a nice way of putting it. My pulse raced as I pictured 'the dungeon' again – the place that had frequently haunted me over the years.

'It's gone, by the way,' Tim said. 'There was a fire.'

'The Manor burned down? Oh my God! What happened?'

'Arson, but nothing to do with Garth or Leanne,' Kirsten said. 'It must have been a couple of years after you left. Some local kids broke in to have a party and managed to set light to some curtains. They ran off without calling the fire brigade and the fire took hold. With the house being set back from the road and surrounded by woodland, it was only when it was fully ablaze that someone saw the smoke and, by that time, it was too late.'

'The secret room wasn't so secret anymore,' Tim added. 'It was all over the local papers but it made the nationals when they discovered that the Deputy Commissioner of Clubs and Vice was the owner.'

I clapped my hand over my mouth, the irony of his promotion not lost on me. 'No! Bet the news story didn't do his career any good.'

'I think early retirement was the phrase they used,' Kirsten said.

'He loved being in the police.' I shook my head, feeling a tiny sliver of sympathy for him. Losing his job would have destroyed him. Then I thought about the job I'd lost thanks to him. And the home. And the family. The sliver slithered away. 'What did he tell everyone about me leaving?'

'We don't know,' Kirsten said. 'As soon as we learned the truth, we cut him off completely. We only knew about him losing his job because it was in the papers.'

I sat back, taking it all in. 'You know he married me as a cover?'

Kirsten nodded. 'Leanne told us about the rumours at work and how she'd set up dates with her other foster sisters before introducing you to Garth.'

I gasped. 'I didn't know she'd done that.'

She grimaced. 'Sorry to be the one to tell you. Obviously we didn't know about the others and we genuinely believed he loved you or we'd never have—'

I took Kirsten's hand and squeezed it. 'You can't blame yourself. We were together for over three years and I had no idea it was all fake so how could you possibly have known?' I took a deep breath. 'So did Leanne tell you how she got me ready for becoming his girlfriend?'

Kirsten nodded. 'We thought she was being a nice big sister spending all that time shopping with you and doing makeovers. We didn't know she had an ulterior motive.'

Shopping and makeovers? They didn't know. Looking from Kirsten to Tim, I knew I couldn't tell them about my 'playmates'. They knew most of what had happened and the guilt and devastation was obvious in their expressions. If I told them that Leanne's teachings had extended way beyond how to use a pair of GHDs, who could it possibly benefit?

'What about Leanne?' I asked. 'One of your earlier letters said you weren't in touch following a cocaine incident and her stealing from the business. Did that change at all?'

Tim stood up. 'I think it's a good time to make some drinks. Would you like tea, coffee, or a soft drink?'

'Black coffee, please,' I said.

'Tea for me,' Kirsten said.

When Tim closed the lounge door, she shook her head slowly. 'He finds it hard to talk about her.'

My pulse raced. 'She's not dead, is she?'

Kirsten shook her head again. 'It sounds awful to say it but it might be easier on Tim if she was. I don't know, Tamara. We clearly did something very wrong to have raised such a wicked person.'

'No, you didn't. You were brilliant parents. She had everything she could possibly have wanted and a whole lot more but she chose a different path. You didn't teach her to lie and steal and shove coke up her nose. And I'm pretty sure you didn't teach her how to use all that stuff I saw in The Manor.'

'Oh, gosh, no!' Kirsten shuddered. 'I can't bear to think about that. I've no idea how she got into that sort of lifestyle.'

'Which proves my point. *She* got into it. *She* chose it. You raised me too and I didn't choose any of those things.'

She looked at me with such pride. 'No. You chose kindness, like we always knew you would.'

'So what happened to Leanne?' I asked.

'After we cut her off, it was all drugs, alcohol and bad boyfriends, then she turned up and said she wanted to get clean so, as promised, we funded a stint in rehab. She managed a couple of weeks clean, then it was drugs, alcohol, bad boyfriends, rehab, drugs, alcohol... It's been a repetitive cycle for years. We wouldn't hear from her for months and months but, every so often, she'd come back to us with her tail between her legs, promising this was the time she'd *finally* stay clean. We paid for rehab each time, always hoping, but we knew she only reappeared because she was broke again and saw rehab as some sort of luxury retreat. The only way an addict is ever going to change is if they really want to and, sadly, Leanne didn't want it.'

'I'm so sorry. That must have been heart-breaking, especially if you knew she had no intention of ever changing.'

Tim reappeared with a wooden tray containing the drinks and a plate of shortbread biscuits. 'Have you told her about Leanne?'

'Nearly finished. I've told her about rehab.'

'By rehab, you mean her annual holiday?'

It broke my heart to hear Tim sounding so defeated. 'It must be so hard on you both.'

He nodded. 'It has been but it's over now. We're not doing it again. Ever.'

'She turned up a few weeks after my diagnosis, clearly high on goodness knows what, demanding to be taken to the clinic immediately,' Kirsten said. 'Tim told her that she'd need to wait because he was taking me to a hospital appointment. You'd think that the obvious response would be to ask why I was going to hospital but she didn't seem interested. Just continued to place her demands.'

'So I told her Kirsten had cancer,' Tim said. 'And do you know what she did? She laughed. She said it was karma for everything we'd put her through and she hoped it was incurable.'

I clapped my hand across my mouth. Leanne was selfish and manipulative but this was a new low. 'That's... I can't even think of a word for it. Who says something like that?'

Tim sighed and shook his head. 'That was the last straw. She's had far more chances than anyone deserves so I told her we were through. Told her to leave and never to come back.'

'We haven't heard from her since,' Kirsten said. 'We don't know where she is and we sold Vanilla Pod and The Larches afterwards so she has no way of finding us either. The new owners of both know not to pass on any information if she does come looking for us.' She took a sip of her tea. 'Enough about her. Let's talk about you. I can't tell you how much it meant to us both to get your phone call last week. We'd resigned ourselves to losing both our daughters and now we've got you back. Good things come to those who wait.'

'It really is wonderful to see you, Tamara,' Tim said.

'And it's wonderful to see both of you. You probably already noticed it in the article about the awards but I'm not called Tamara anymore...'

Over the next few hours, we talked incessantly, only pausing for some lunch. They wanted to know what had drawn me to Whitsborough Bay and they loved that I'd let fate decide. I told them all about finding the premises and the challenges I'd initially faced in refurbishing the flat. Kirsten wanted to hear about the food I served and Tim was fascinated by my work in the community.

Conscious that I was in danger of dominating the conversation, I made sure they told me more about their major life-decisions around Tim retiring, Kirsten selling Vanilla Pod, and selling their beautiful home. And, of course, I was keen to hear all about Kirsten's health.

I marvelled at how positive they both sounded, despite going through hell, thanks to Leanne and to Kirsten's cancer diagnosis. And me. It could have broken some couples yet they seemed stronger than ever. When I was little, Dad had very clearly been Mum's lighthouse. Much as he'd loved and needed her, he'd been the one with all the light and strength. It wasn't like that for Kirsten and Tim. It was clear that Kirsten was Tim's lighthouse and he was hers. They'd faced many stormy seas and they'd helped each other to safety. It was early days in my relationship with Jed but it scared me that I was already leaning on him too much, just like Mum had leaned on Dad. We'd been out for a meal together on Saturday night and for a bracing walk along the seafront on Sunday after the gallery closed but the conversation had mainly been about me and how I felt about opening up the past with Kirsten and Tim. He'd been there for me while I poured out everything I was feeling – fear, resentment, regret – providing constant reassurance that everything would work out. If there was any chance of us lasting, we had to have a partnership. He couldn't be the strong one all the time.

As the afternoon slipped towards dusk, the inevitable observation came from Kirsten. 'You haven't mentioned any boyfriends or children...?'

I took a deep breath. 'That's because there haven't been any.'

'Because of Garth?'

There was no point lying about it. 'I couldn't bring myself to trust anyone after that so I threw myself into the business and never dated again.'

'Oh, honey, Garth was... Gosh, I don't know what he was but he wasn't representative of most men.'

'I know but the damage was done. I have met someone recently, though. Actually, I met him fourteen and a half years ago and hated him nearly as much as I hated Garth but he's back in my life and things are very different. We're taking things slowly because he has baggage too...'

I told them about how Jed and I first met, what happened when he came back to the UK and how I started to see him in a different light. Colour flooded my cheeks and I couldn't stop smiling as I talked about him giving me the lighthouse picture and kissing me for the first time.

'He sounds like a keeper,' Kirsten said.

'Do you think so? It's been such a long time since I had a man in my life and that one turned out to be a fake. I don't know how to do relationships.'

'I don't think there is a specific way,' Kirsten said, giving me a reassuring smile. 'If you want my advice, I'd say just be yourself and talk to Jed. Tell him when you're feeling anxious and tell him if you think it's going too fast or not quickly enough.'

'I agree,' Tim said. 'Several little things that could be resolved over a couple of uncomfortable but honest conversations can soon fester and grow until all you have is arguments and resentment. We've known too many couples call it quits over the years because they didn't talk about things when they had a chance.'

Kirsten nodded. 'But, equally, don't create problems that don't exist. Jed isn't Garth. From what you've told me, he sounds like a genuine, honest, caring man and I know you already know that because you wouldn't have let him in otherwise.'

I smiled at her insight. 'I think – hope – that he's another of those good things that come to those who wait. If I don't mess it up.'

'You won't mess it up.'

'I hope not. Thank you, both of you.'

Kirsten kept yawning and I could see Tim giving her anxious looks. 'I should probably go and let you get some rest.' I made to stand up but Kirsten grabbed my hand.

'No, I'm fine,' she insisted. 'Maybe a bit sleepy but real fires do that to you.'

'True, but so does recovering from cancer and you need some rest.'

She looked as though she was going to object again but Tim spoke up. 'How about we make arrangements to see Tama... Tara's café? Would Thursday work for you, Tara?'

'Thursday would be great,' I said.

'What about tomorrow?' Kirsten suggested. Behind her, Tim was frantically shaking his head. Clearly Kirsten needed the rest.

'I've got a few things on tomorrow and wouldn't be able to give you much attention. Thursday works really well, though. I can show you round the café and flat and introduce you to Hercules.'

'And Jed?' Kirsten asked, winking at me.

'Yes, and Jed if he's up for it although I'm pretty sure he said there's something on at Lucy's college on Thursday. I'll check with him.' I stood up. 'Before I go, I have something to ask you both. You can say no if you want.'

They both looked at me expectantly, making my pulse race.

'I've asked you to call me Tara but, in exchange, I wondered if I could call you something I've never called you before. Could I call you Mum and Dad?' I'd called Kirsten 'mum' when I first phoned but it had slipped out in a moment of intense emotion. I'd given it a lot of thought since then and, while I would never forget my biological parents, Kirsten and Tim were my parents too and it felt right to acknowledge that. Even though I'd pushed them out of my life, they'd never given up hope of having their daughter back. They were my family.

Tim hadn't cried when I arrived but he broke down now. Hugging me tightly, he whispered 'thank you' over and over again. When he released me, Kirsten took me in her arms and kissed my cheek.

'I'm sorry I didn't say it sooner,' I said.

'You weren't ready. It always had to be your choice but you've made your old mum and dad very, very happy. More good things that come to those who wait.'

\* \* \*

By the time I arrived back at The Chocolate Pot, I felt drained. I loved how they both understood why I'd needed to cut them off and didn't make me feel guilty for doing so. It would have been so easy to talk about the missed years with regret, yet they didn't do that either. They were – and always had been – two very special, loving people.

Standing outside the café with my keys in my hand, I turned

and looked up at Yorkshire's Best. The first-floor lights were on and I could see movement inside. I had planned to send Jed a text to let him know I was back safe, then take a bath and settle down for a quiet evening in front of the TV with Hercules but now I longed to feel Jed's strong arms wrapped round me. I took my phone out of my bag.

'I've been thinking about you all day,' he said as soon as he answered. 'How was it?'

'Exactly how you predicted. Difficult but amazing. Mostly amazing.'

'Where are you?'

'Look outside.'

Seconds later, Jed appeared at the window and waved. 'Do you want me to come over or would you prefer some alone-time? No pressure. Whatever you want.'

I smiled. 'Can you give me ten minutes to freshen up and feed Hercules then come over?'

Being alone had always been my default setting but it didn't need to be anymore. If this thing between us was going to work, I had to keep letting him in and letting him be part of my life.

## 39

Thursday morning dawned mild and bright. The blue skies and sunshine acted like a magnet, drawing hordes of Christmas shoppers into Whitsborough Bay. From about 10 a.m., The Chocolate Pot was packed. I couldn't remember the last time I'd seen a queue before noon on a weekday. Laugher and excitable chatter bounced off the walls and there was the constant aroma of coffee, pastries and chocolate hanging in the air.

Mum had originally suggested driving over to the café for lunch but I persuaded them to come for afternoon tea instead which was just as well because lunchtime was so busy that I'd have barely been able to give them the time of day.

It was still busy as we approached mid-afternoon with only a couple of spare tables, but the lack of queue gave us some breathing space. Leaning against the counter, I absorbed the happy pre-Christmas buzz. This year, I didn't need to dread Christmas. This year things were going to be very different.

At the cottage on Tuesday, Mum had asked if I had plans for Christmas Day. My heart leapt at the thought of a good old-fashioned family Christmas dinner, then sank when I realised I *did* have plans. Months earlier, I'd volunteered to help cook Christmas dinner at The Hope Centre. I certainly wasn't going to let them down now that I had other options. Mum and Dad weren't fazed, saying there were plenty more hours in the day to meet up when I finished volunteering.

Leaning on the counter, thinking about having somewhere to go and people to see when I finished my shift at The Hope Centre made me quite tearful. I was wiping my eyes when Mum and Dad arrived for afternoon tea.

'Tara! What's happened?' Mum asked, a look of panic on her face.

I smiled and shook my head. 'Nothing bad. Just thinking about not being alone on Christmas Day for the first time since I left home and it's made me a bit emotional.'

'Oh, honey. I can't bear to think of you spending all those years on your own. We'll make it really special this year.'

I came round from behind the counter and hugged them both.

'How hungry are you?' I asked.

'Starving,' Dad said. 'We had brunch rather than lunch as we wanted to keep plenty of space for afternoon tea.'

'Food first then and a tour afterwards?' I suggested.

'Sounds lovely,' Mum said. She looked round her. 'I can't wait to explore but first impressions are wonderful. I could not be prouder of you and everything you've achieved.'

'Stop it! You'll set me off again.'

\* \* \*

By the time they finished eating, the café had thinned out and the first floor was closed off and cleaned. I pulled aside the rope so I could show my parents upstairs.

'I love it so much,' Mum said, sitting down at one of the first floor tables. 'It exudes such warmth, don't you think, Tim?'

Dad had wandered over to the windows and was looking up and down the street. 'I completely agree. And this street is just perfect. I love the fairy lights strung between the buildings. Come and have a look, Kirsten.'

'I'll look in a minute.' She was smiling but I suspected that fatigue had taken over again. They'd arrived with several shopping bags so had clearly wandered round town first and it had likely taken its toll.

'Tell you what,' I said. 'Why don't we go up to the flat? It means a couple of flights of stairs but there's an amazing view from up there and then you can relax and maybe even both have a nap while I finish off in the café.'

'Great idea,' Dad said, smiling at me, his eyes conveying his gratitude.

'Two flights of stairs?' Kirsten gave an exaggerated groan. 'I think the only thing that could persuade me to tackle that would be knowing there's a giant house rabbit waiting for me at the top, desperate for cuddles.'

'What a coincidence,' I said, smiling. 'Come on. I'll get you both settled.'

\* \* \*

'Your parents are lovely,' Molly said after I returned downstairs.

'Thank you.'

'Is the rift with your sister all sorted out now?' She grimaced. 'Sorry. Was that too nosy?

I smiled reassuringly. 'No, it wasn't too nosy. It's nice that you remembered. And, no, it's not sorted and never will be. For lots of long, complicated reasons, my foster sister is no longer in their lives which means I can be.'

'That's good. Not for the foster sister, obviously, but it's good for you. It's sad when families lose touch.'

'Still no word from your dad?'

She shook her head. 'I'm actually not bothered about him. He was no help with my brother and he cheated on my mum so it's no great loss. I do miss my grandma, though. He told her she had to choose between him and us. He's her son so what could she do?'

'Aw, Molly. I'm sorry to hear that. Doesn't sound very fair on any of you.'

'It isn't but I can either get upset and mope about it or I can accept it and move on. Now that he's out of our lives, I'm closer than ever to my mum and brother who are great, I've got Nathan...' She smiled dreamily as she said his name. 'And it's twelve more sleeps till Christmas. Happy days.'

A regular appeared to order a takeaway latte so we couldn't continue the conversation. Watching Molly chatting easily to the customer, I found myself smiling at her Pollyanna approach to life. Reconnecting with my parents and starting a relationship with Jed had been giant steps in putting my past behind me. I needed to focus on enjoying the here and now with him and let the future unfold in its own sweet way instead of worrying about the balance in our relationship. It hadn't even been a week and it just happened that I'd had the first scenario requiring support. I might have the second one too but, at some point down the line, Jed would need me and I could be the strong one for him. As Mum said, I should stop creating problems that didn't exist. Or at least try to stop.

* * *

My team had left for the day and I was working my way round the café, switching off the fairy lights, when Jed knocked on the door.

'I wasn't expecting to see you tonight,' I said. 'What happened to the college thing with Lucy?'

'She got a better offer. A friend of hers invited her for a sleep-over so college and I have been ditched. Which meant I was free to come over and do this.'

He bent over and tenderly kissed me. Closing my eyes, I melted against him. Yes, I definitely needed to enjoy the here and now because moments like that with Jed were worth savouring.

'Did your parents like the café?' he asked.

'They're upstairs if you'd like to ask them yourself. Or is that too scary and too soon? I know they're keen to meet you.'

Jed smiled. 'I'd love to meet them and it's not scary at all.'

I asked him to wait outside the door to the flat while I went inside. It was only fair to check whether Mum was asleep as I didn't want to embarrass her if she was. Fortunately she'd had a nap but was now awake and very excited to meet Jed.

It couldn't have gone better. Mum hugged Jed and Dad shook his hand. I didn't feel at all nervous about introducing him and I didn't think it was just because it was spontaneous and I hadn't had time to build the nerves; it was simply because it all felt so right. It was so different to when they'd met Garth. Back then, I'd been anxious about my age, his age and how they'd feel about him being a long-lost family member. Watching them so animated and relaxed in Jed's presence, it was obvious that any warmth shown towards Garth had been about supporting me and my decisions instead of them wholeheartedly advocating the relationship.

At about seven, Dad announced that it was time to head back to the cottage. I was about to protest that they should join us for a takeaway but I could see that Mum was flagging again.

Leaving Jed in the flat, I walked them down the stairs and to the door.

'He's gorgeous,' Mum said, taking both my hands in hers. 'And I don't just mean his looks. I used to worry about you and Garth. I couldn't put my finger on what it was but something wasn't quite right and I used to tell myself it was because you were young and I was being overprotective. Jed couldn't be more different and I know I'll never need to worry about him hurting my little girl.'

'Thanks, Mum.'

I hugged her then Dad.

He picked up an armful of carrier bags. 'If you don't have any plans for Sunday, we'd love it if you could both join us for lunch or dinner. I was going to say so upstairs but I thought we'd better check with you first.'

'Thank you. It's a definite yes from me but I'll have to come back to you on Jed. He's driving up to Newcastle on Saturday to collect Erin from university so they might want some family time on Sunday.'

I waved them off then then made a couple of drinks.

Back in the lounge, I placed the mugs on the coffee table, smiling at Jed who had Hercules sprawled across his knee like a dog. 'I made you a chilli chocolate but don't feel you have to drink it if you need to get home.'

'There's nobody home. Lucy's at that sleepover and Mum and Dad are out for a meal with their friends, Peter and Joyce. I'm all yours if you want me.'

I leaned over and kissed him. 'I do want you.' Colour rushed to my cheeks and I bit my lip. 'Oh, I don't mean... I'm not ready... I'm...'

Jed took my hand and gently pulled me down onto the sofa beside him. 'I won't lie by pretending the thought hadn't crossed my mind but please believe me when I say there's no pressure on you to do anything until you're ready. I'm not going anywhere. We can take things as quickly or as slowly as you want.'

He raised my hand to his lips and lightly kissed it. So tender.

'Thank you for understanding,' I said.

'You don't need to thank me. Just be honest with me. If you feel ready to take things further and then you want to stop, you just have to say. We won't do anything you're not ready to do.'

He put his arm round me I snuggled against his chest. Listening to his heart beating, I felt relaxed, safe and loved. He hadn't said he loved me and I wasn't sure if he'd even admitted it to himself but I certainly felt it from every look, every touch and every word. And, for the first time ever, it wasn't an act. As for how I felt about Jed, I was in danger of falling very hard and very fast.

On Sunday afternoon, I was at my dining table surrounded by needle felted tree decorations. With just over a week remaining until Christmas Day, I'd received a flurry of orders via Etsy so wanted to package them up ready to take to the Post Office in the morning. I was looking forward to an afternoon as The Cobbly Crafter before driving up towards Whitby for dinner with Mum and Dad. Yesterday, Jed had collected Erin from university as planned but had assured me they'd have loads of time to catch up over Christmas and he was keen to accept my parents' invitation.

Jed's number flashed up on my phone.

'Are you busy?' he asked.

'Just sorting out my Etsy orders. Why?'

'I know you weren't meant to be meeting my family until tomorrow night but how do you feel about meeting a couple of them now? The girls have turned up under the guise of Erin wanting to check out the gallery but it appears they're more interested in meeting you and Hercules. I know when I'm not wanted.'

I heard a girl's voice in the background saying, 'Sorry, Dad, but you versus a giant house bunny? The bunny wins every time.'

'Sounds like I'm not really wanted either,' I said, laughing. 'I'm sure Hercules would be delighted by the attention and you know I'm dying to meet your girls.'

'Do you want me to give you ten minutes?'

'Dad!' came a whine.

'You can come straight over if you want. I was going to say warn them I'm crafting and it's a bit of a mess but I'm guessing they won't even notice once they spot Hercules.'

'You could be right there. See you in a minute.'

I stood up and breathed in deeply. This was it. I was about to meet Jed's daughters a day earlier than expected. It was probably a good thing because I wouldn't have all tomorrow to get worked up about it. I'd been invited out for an evening meal with the full family, including Erin's boyfriend, in celebration of Jed's dad's birthday. Meeting his parents didn't faze me but I was apprehensive about meeting Erin and Lucy in case they didn't respond well to their dad having a new girlfriend. Jed had assured me I needn't worry and they were 'stoked' that he'd found someone new, having nagged him for years that it was about time he got his act together.

He'd shown me photos and told me that, personality-wise, they were complete opposites. Erin was the mature, studious, organised, sensible one and Lucy was child-like, scatty, disorganised and prone to speaking before thinking. Lucy had apparently taken the loss of Aaron really badly and Jed admitted that he'd babied her which sometimes meant she acted far younger than her years. Despite their differences, the sisters were exceptionally close and fiercely protective of each other which he suspected was a direct result of being made to feel like unwelcome outsiders when living with their mum and Declan, poor kids.

I'd no sooner reached the bottom of the stairs when there was a knock on the internal door. *Deep breath. Smile. Nothing to be afraid of.*

Jed mouthed 'sorry' to me the moment I opened the door but I gave him a reassuring smile.

'This is Erin and this is Lucy. Girls, this is Tara.'

Erin gave me a warm smile but Lucy launched herself at me, wrapping her arms round my waist. 'I've been dying to meet you.'

I hugged her back, feeling quite choked-up at her reaction. I looked across at Jed who rolled his eyes and I realised this was one of her child-like behaviours but one I was very happy to go along with.

'And I've been dying to meet you both,' I said. 'Do you want to come upstairs to see Hercules?'

They eagerly followed me up to the flat. 'Hercules? Visitors?' He came bounding over to squeals of delight from both girls.

'Oh my gosh!' Lucy cried. 'He's gorgeous. Can I pick him up?'

'Yes, but he's very heavy so I'd suggest you maybe start by sitting on the sofa and getting used to him. He loves company so he'll probably drape himself over you anyway.'

There were more squeals as they followed me into the lounge area with Hercules hot on my heels.

'You're a hit,' Jed said, putting his arm round my waist as we stood by the arched window, watching the girls cooing over Hercules who, as expected, had draped himself across both of them.

'I think *he's* the hit but I liked the hug from Lucy.'

'She's all about the hugs but it usually takes her several meetings before she'd dish one out so I'd say you're definitely the hit.'

'Must be down to you singing my praises then.'

'I might have done, but everything was justified.'

'They're beautiful girls, Jed.' Although both had long blonde hair with sun-kissed highlights, Erin's was shoulder-length and neatly styled with layers framing her face and Lucy's tumbled to her waist in an effortlessly messy style. Lucy had a slender frame, like a ballet dancer, and Erin had a curvier build. Lucy had her dad's green eyes and Erin's were bright blue but there was still no mistaking the family resemblance.

'I'm going to have to get back to the gallery, girls,' Jed said after about fifteen minutes. 'Time to say goodbye.'

'No way!' Lucy cried. 'We've only just got here and look at him. He's loving it.'

'You're welcome to stay a bit longer if that's okay with your dad,' I said.

'Can we, Dad?' Erin asked.

'You're sure they won't be in your way?' he asked me.

'It'll be a great chance to get to know them.'

'Okay,' he said. 'But best behaviour please.'

Ten minutes later, we were seated at the dining table with hot chocolate and brownies.

'I love your flat,' Erin said, gazing round the room. 'It's so big yet so cosy.'

'Thank you. It took a long time to get it how I wanted but Hercules and I are very happy here.'

'My dad's painting looks good,' Erin added.

I glanced round at the lighthouse picture and smiled. 'Your dad is an exceptionally talented artist and that particular painting means so much to me. I'm very lucky to have it.' I turned back to them. 'I hear you're both artists yourselves but different styles.'

Listening to them chatter about their courses, I felt a warm glow inside. They seemed so relaxed in my company and I got no sense of hostility towards me as the new woman in their dad's lives. Maybe them being a bit older helped. The physical and emotional distance from their mum probably helped too.

'We have a confession to make,' Erin said when we'd finished our drinks.

'We didn't really come over to meet Hercules,' Lucy added.

They exchanged solemn looks and nods and my heart sank. Was this the bit where they suddenly turned on me and warned me off their father?

'Oh yes...?' I prompted, trying to sound calm and assured.

'It's about our dad...' Erin said.

'Do you think you know him well?' Lucy asked.

I gulped. 'It's early days but we've talked a lot and I think I've got to know him fairly well.' *Oh no! Definitely about to warn me off.*

'Did he tell you what happened with him and Mum?' Erin asked.

Lucy nodded. 'And do you know about Aaron?'

'Yes to both.'

'Good,' Erin said, 'because we'd welcome your advice on something.'

'Fire away.'

'We never stayed in touch with Aaron after the twins were born and we moved back to Dad's, but he got in touch with me through Instagram a couple of months ago. He said he wanted to say hi and get to know his sisters again so I set up a WhatsApp group for the three of us.'

Lucy stroked Hercules's ears and sighed. 'We used to get on really well but, when Mum and Dad split, it was horrible. By the time we moved back in with Dad, we hated him.'

'Hated is a bit strong,' Erin said.

Lucy rolled her eyes at her sister. 'What would you call it, then? I know it was tough on him but it was tough on us too. We couldn't wait to move out and cut him out of our lives.'

Erin looked at me and shrugged. 'It wasn't a good time.'

'I can well imagine. It can't have been easy on any of you. So how can I help?'

'We didn't tell Dad about Aaron getting in touch,' Lucy said. 'We didn't think there was any point because it quickly fizzled out. Erin set up the WhatsApp group, we exchanged a few short messages about school and stuff, then it went quiet. We assumed he'd lost interest.'

'Until he got in touch on it last week,' Erin continued. 'We've been in touch most days since then and it was all good until I mentioned how excited I was about coming home from uni and seeing Dad's gallery.'

'He lost his shit with us,' Lucy said, scowling when Erin nudged her, presumably for swearing. 'Said he wasn't interested in hearing anything about "that loser". He said that Dad had ruined his life and he hated him.'

I winced. 'That's not good. How did you respond?'

'Lucy had a go at Aaron for dissing Dad but I asked him why he thought Dad had ruined his life. He said it was because Dad didn't want him and we both know that's not true. Dad was desperate to keep Aaron in his life. He got legal advice and he begged Mum and Declan but they wouldn't budge.'

'And you told Aaron that?' I asked.

Lucy cuddled Hercules to her. 'Yes, but he wasn't having it. We haven't replied to any of his messages since Friday. We don't know whether to cut him off and forget about it or tell Dad. What do you think we should do?'

I looked from one pained face to the other and really felt for them. If that was what Aaron really thought and felt about Jed, then Ingrid and Declan had very likely fed the poor kid a pack of lies and poisoned him against Jed. Very unfair to everyone.

'I think you both know the answer, don't you, and you just want a bit of reassurance that you're doing the right thing?'

Erin nodded. 'We need to tell him. Dad will be so upset, though.'

'About what Aaron has said? Yes, he probably will be, especially as it seems Aaron may have some inaccurate information. Who wouldn't be upset at that?' I had to bite my tongue as I really wanted to say something nasty about Ingrid but she was still their mum and I wasn't going to stir. 'But he won't be upset about you being in contact with Aaron, especially when he's your half-brother. I think your dad would encourage that contact, don't you?'

They both nodded. 'You're right,' Erin said. 'We'll tell him on Tuesday after work.'

'Tuesday? Wouldn't you be better telling him tonight?'

Erin shook her head. 'We can't. He's seeing you and your parents tonight and it's Gramps's birthday meal tomorrow night. We don't want to put a dampener on either of those things.'

I bit my lip. Something like this was better out in the open. 'Your dad and I could drive up to Whitby later than planned or I could even go on my own.'

'That's not fair on either of you,' Lucy said. 'I know he's looking forward to it.'

I looked at their earnest expressions. What difference would a couple more days make? 'Promise me you will say something at the earliest opportunity on Tuesday?'

'We promise,' they both said.

'Good, because secrets don't always stay secret for long.'

'At least Aaron's not coming over for Christmas with Mum,' Lucy said.

'Your mum's coming over?' I asked, surprised. Jed hadn't mentioned it.

Erin nodded. 'Tomorrow but we only found out this morning. Grandad – her dad – has started chemo so she's coming alone. The doctors are hopeful he'll make a full recovery but a mass family invasion would be too much for him right now.'

'Your dad does know your mum's coming over?' I asked.

Lucy screwed up her face. 'Yes. That's how we found out. She phoned him first thing today, demanding to see us on Christmas

Day. Barely bothers with us for years and now she expects us to drop everything and fit round her with barely any warning.'

I wasn't sure how to respond but was saved from doing so by Hercules who head-butted Erin as though demanding attention again. Lucy exclaimed that she hadn't shown me photos of Doris either. I had no idea who Doris was but smiled when she thrust her phone in front of me, scrolling through images of a gorgeous Dalmatian. 'Nanna and Gramps reckon she's theirs but Doris says she loves us the most, doesn't she Erin?'

Erin laughed and ruffled her sister's hair. 'I think you'll find it's me she loves the very most, though.'

Roughly twenty laughter-filled minutes later, they headed back to the gallery, taking the rest of the brownies with them and suddenly I felt uneasy. Should I have insisted they tell Jed about Aaron tonight even if that messed up our evening plans? I'd been looking forward to an evening with him and my parents but was that really more important than the conversation Erin and Lucy needed to have with him? I shuddered. There was nothing I could do about it now. We hadn't exchanged phone numbers so I had no way of getting in touch with either of them and it would arouse Jed's suspicion if I asked for their numbers. I shook my head. We'd been together for less than a fortnight and I was already keeping something from him – absolutely not the sort of relationship I wanted.

## 41

Sunday dinner with my parents was lovely but I felt on edge and clearly it didn't go unnoticed. Mum asked me to help her in the kitchen and questioned whether everything was okay. I hated lying to her but she seemed to accept the excuse of always being tired as Christmas approached, especially as she was familiar with that feeling of fatigue from Vanilla Pod.

Jed wasn't so easily assuaged. 'Did something happen with the girls this afternoon?' he asked as we travelled back down the coast towards Whitsborough Bay.

I was relieved to be driving in darkness as he couldn't therefore see my burning cheeks or the guilty expression in my eyes. 'We had a great time together and Hercules has added another couple of groupies to his ever-growing list. Why do you ask?'

'You seem a bit tense and I wondered if one of them – probably Loudmouth Lucy – had said something inappropriate.'

'Nothing like that. I really like them and it was good to meet them before the big meal tomorrow. I haven't got your dad a gift yet. What do you think he might like?'

'He won't be expecting a gift and don't change the subject.'

My hands tensed on the steering wheel.

'Tara!'

I hesitated. Should I tell him the girls had confided a secret in me, which they'd soon be telling him themselves? What if that caused more problems? They wouldn't trust me anymore and that could lead to a conflict. But would Jed trust me if I kept a secret from him? I was stuck between a rock and a hard place and had to hope that Jed wasn't annoyed with me when the girls told him about Aaron.

'Are you worried about Ingrid flying over?' he asked. He'd told me about her phone call on the journey to the cottage, saying how typical it was of Ingrid to be so eleventh hour in letting them know she was coming to Whitsborough Bay for Christmas, especially when she'd have booked her plane ticket ages ago.

'Maybe a little bit.' I hadn't really given her presence a second thought but it was a good way of throwing Jed off the scent.

'I probably won't even see her while she's here. My role will be to pick up the pieces when she lets the girls down again.'

'I'm sorry, Jed. Will it be that bad?'

'Probably.'

'I'll be here for you if you want a rant.'

'Thank you.'

I could feel his eyes on me but he didn't say anything else. Roll on Tuesday when the girls would tell him about Aaron and everything would be out in the open.

\* \* \*

I arranged to meet Jed and his family at the restaurant on Monday night. Le Bistro was a cosy family-run restaurant a few streets back from South Bay and I could easily walk there.

Wearing a khaki wrap-around dress and heeled boots, butterflies flitted in my stomach as I walked through the town. I couldn't decide whether I was nervous about meeting Jed's parents after all, worried about still keeping the secret under wraps, or excited about seeing Jed again. Probably all three. I'd never 'met the parents' before. Garth had severed ties with both of his so this was my first experience. Hopefully they'd like me.

Jed was sitting on one of the metal seats outside the restaurant and my heart soared as soon as I spotted him. 'What are you doing out here? It's freezing.'

'I thought you might feel awkward going in on your own when you haven't met my parents before.'

'That is so considerate. Thank you.'

'I confess to an ulterior motive,' he said, making my stomach lurch. He wasn't going to pump me for information again, was he? Instead, he leaned in and gently kissed me. 'Loitering outside meant I could do that without Lucy whistling or jeering. Are you ready to meet everyone?'

'As ready as I'll ever be.'

As soon as we stepped inside the restaurant and made our way over to the table, the nerves dissipated. Jed's mum, Janice, immediately stood up and hugged me. His dad, Richie, kissed me on each cheek and enthused about how he was more excited about meeting me than he was about celebrating his birthday. I got big smiles from the girls and a fist bump from Erin's boyfriend, Zack, with a compliment that my brownies were 'sick'.

'We've ordered some red and white wine,' Janice said, 'but shout up if you want something different.'

'White wine's perfect, thank you.' I sat down beside Erin while Richie topped up my glass.

'Thanks for not saying anything to Dad,' Erin whispered. 'Tomorrow's the day.'

'Good.'

The food was delicious and the company fabulous. Jed's parents were an absolute delight. His mum was exceptionally warm and bubbly and his dad was full of hilarious anecdotes. Watching them bounce off each other and engage the rest of the family in the conversation, I could imagine they'd been a force to be reckoned with when they ran Ferguson's. Customers must have loved them and they'd no doubt had a thriving business. Richie and Zack had obviously hit it off immediately with banter playing back and forth. It looked to me as though he'd gained a grandson and, from the affectionate looks passing between Erin and Zack, I suspected he'd gained him for life.

They made me feel part of the family and were keen to hear all about their former business.

'We've been past and looked in the window so many times,' Janice said. 'Peter and Joyce have often asked us to join them for afternoon tea but we've always felt like we'd be spying if we came in. Does that sound silly?'

I smiled. 'No. I understand. I'd probably feel the same but you'd be really welcome any time.'

Richie laughed. 'Don't say that, Tara. She'll move in. You'll never be rid of her. She loves a bit of cake.'

By the time the plates were cleared away after the main course, my face and my sides were aching from laughing so much. Gazing round the restaurant at the twinkling fairy lights, the garlands hanging from the wall, and the large tree in one corner, then focusing back on the banter and laughter, I couldn't stop smiling.

'Enjoying yourself?' Jed asked, slipping his hand into mine.

'Loving it. This is the first time I've properly felt Christmassy outside of The Chocolate Pot since leaving London. Thank you.'

He squeezed my hand. 'My family love you.'

'And mine love you too. Bodes well.'

The lights dimmed and a line of waiting staff appeared clapping and singing *Happy Birthday,* the front one holding a large chocolate gateau with a sparkler on the top. We joined in the singing and the girls took photos on their phones as Richie jokingly attempted to blow out the sparkler.

He raised his glass in the air. 'I know it's my birthday so it wouldn't normally be me who proposes the toast but I wanted to thank you for the best birthday gift which I actually got last year – my brilliant son and beautiful, talented granddaughters settling back in Whitsborough Bay. It's the best birthday, Christmas and Father's Day gift I could ever hope for. And we also have two new family members. Welcome to Zack and Tara. We hope you stick around because we already adore you both. To family, old and new!'

'To family, old and new,' we echoed, clinking our glasses together.

'To family? How very sweet and cosy and completely fake.'

I twisted round in my chair to see who'd spoken. A young lad, maybe in his early teens, stood by the table. A long, thick, dark fringe tumbled from under his beanie hat and my stomach did a backflip. There was no way that could be...?

'Aaron!' Erin cried. 'What are you doing here?'

'Aaron?' Jed jumped to his feet; the colour drained from his cheeks. 'Is that really you?'

'Like you care,' Aaron snapped.

'What?'

'Don't act all innocent. I know you ditched me as soon as you found out I wasn't yours. Cheers for that.'

Jed shook his head vigorously. 'That's not true.'

Aaron looked round the table, lip curled up. 'Enjoy your celebrations.'

'Aaron!' Jed cried.

But Aaron had already legged it. Jed looked towards his parents, then me, then muttered an apology and ran after him.

I released the shaky breath I'd been holding and stole a glance round the table. Richie's mouth was open and he was still holding the cake knife in his hand, ready to make the first cut. Janice looked close to tears as she placed her hand on his forearm. Lucy's head was lowered, her hair covering her face, and Erin had her elbows on the table, holding her head in her hands. There were whispers and murmurs from the other diners.

'Sorry about that,' Richie said, voice raised. 'Families, eh? Please don't let our little soap opera keep you from your delicious meals.'

There were a few smiles and even some laughter and soon the volume of chatter increased again leaving only tension at our table.

'Well, that was unexpected,' Richie said.

'It's all my fault,' Erin muttered.

'How's it your fault, sweetheart?' he asked, gently. 'Did you know Aaron was in Whitsborough Bay?'

'No. I thought he was in Aus. Mum's meant to be here alone.'

Lucy pushed her hair out of her eyes and looked up, her cheeks stained with tears. 'She obviously lied. Wouldn't be the first time. Cow.'

'Lucy Ferguson!' Janice said, her voice low but stern. 'I don't ever want to hear you talk about your mother in that way again. Do you understand?'

'Yes, Nanna. Sorry.'

'Why do you think it's your fault, Erin?' Richie persisted.

'Because he connected with Lucy and me on social media. We were chatting to him on WhatsApp last week. He never said anything about coming to the UK but he was obviously planning to surprise us and I gave him the perfect chance by posting on Instagram when we arrived at the restaurant tonight. I'm sorry.'

'I take it your dad didn't know anything about it,' Janice said.

Lucy shook her head. 'We were going to tell him tomorrow. Tara said we should tell him sooner but—'

'You knew?'

My stomach sank to the floor as I slowly turned to face Jed. With my back to the door, I hadn't seen him return. 'The girls told me on Sunday.'

'That's why you were on edge. You said it was nothing.' He looked so hurt and who could blame him? Damn secrets and lies. I *knew* this would come back and bite me.

'I'm sorry. It wasn't—'

'It's not Tara's fault,' Lucy cried. 'We made her swear not to say anything because it had to come from us.'

'Sit down, son,' Richie said. 'I take it you didn't catch him?'

Jed didn't respond. He continued to stare at me, his shoulders rising and falling as he tried to catch his breath from running. What could I say? What was there to say? He didn't look angry with me – just confused and disappointed. So very disappointed.

'Dad!' Erin hissed. 'Tara promised us.'

'You know how much Aaron means to me,' Jed said. 'I was completely blindsided. Promise or not, you could have warned me he was in the country.'

'I didn't know he was.'

'But you knew he was in touch with the girls.'

'That's not—' I stopped. What was the point? How could he think I'd hide something from him as monumental as Aaron being in the country? I thought we trusted each other. I thought we understood each other. I had to get out of there before I said something I regretted.

Taking a deep breath, I placed my serviette on the table and gave a weak smile as I cast my gaze around the table. 'Thanks for a lovely evening, everyone. Happy birthday, Richie.'

I turned to Jed. 'I'd never have hidden something like that from you. Never.'

Then I grabbed my bag and coat off the back of my chair and

ran, just like Aaron had done less than ten minutes earlier. Cries from his family begging me to stay followed me out onto the street. I knew they'd be urging him to do so but I didn't want Jed to follow me. I couldn't face an argument, especially when I was so angry with myself. I should have insisted they tell Jed about Aaron on Sunday evening and gone for dinner with my parents without him if he'd needed time to get his head round it. I could have refused to keep their secret. Yet I hadn't. I'd wanted to play happy families with my parents and with Jed's daughters and, as a result, I might have lost Jed's trust. I might have lost Jed. First opportunity to demonstrate some parenting skills and I'd screwed up.

## 42

By the time I made it back to The Chocolate Pot, my side was burning with a stitch and my feet were throbbing. Running uphill in high-heeled boots after a huge meal and a few glasses of wine was not the way I'd expected the evening to end.

Inside the café, I blew my hair out of my face as I stood with my back against the door, trying to steady my breathing. Was I wrong to run out? Had I made things worse? Would the mature approach have been to stay and plead my innocence? I made my way to the drinks machine, shoulders slumped. This was all unchartered territory for me. Age thirty-six and I had no idea how to behave in a relationship.

Clutching onto my vanilla hot chocolate, I was about to open the internal door at the back of the café when a loud rap on the glass startled me. Heart thumping, I turned slowly. Jed with looking through the window with his hands cupped round his eyes, just like he'd done in January. Back then, I'd been full of hate for the man I thought had deceived me but now all I felt was love.

'Tara!' he called through the letterbox. 'Are you in there?'

Tempting as it was to stay in the shadows and ignore him, I

placed my yellow mug on the nearest table and unlocked the door. I opened the door and stepped back to let him in, keeping my head down. He could be the first to speak.

But he didn't speak. He wrapped his arms round me and gently pulled me to his chest. I didn't resist but I didn't return the hug, standing rigid in his arms. He stroked my hair and tightened his hold. It was only when he whispered. 'Please forgive me,' that I relaxed against him.

Time seemed to stand still as we clung onto each other, hearts thumping, our breathing rapid. I could feel the regret but also the pain with each tightening of his arms. Right now, he needed me and I could act hurt or be angry with him, or I could be his lighthouse.

I pulled away from him and took his hand. 'Let me make you a drink then we'll go upstairs.'

He nodded. 'I'm really—'

'Wait till we're upstairs and we can talk properly.'

\* \* \*

'We can do apologies later,' I said, settling down onto the sofa beside Jed. 'Tell me what happened with Aaron first. Did you find him?'

Jed smiled weakly. 'Thank you. Yes. He'd got lost and must have doubled back on himself because he pretty much ran into me. He stopped, probably shocked to see me there, so I took my chance and asked if we could talk. He was adamant that he didn't want to talk to me but it was obvious from the way that his eyes were darting about that he was scared about being lost. He might have sounded all mature and full of attitude in Le Bistro but the poor kid's only twelve.' He shook his head. 'I said I'd give him some money and point him towards the nearest taxi rank but I wanted him to answer some questions first. He reluctantly agreed and I asked what made him think I hadn't wanted him. I knew what the answer would be, of course, but I wanted to hear it from him.'

'Ingrid and Declan?'

Jed nodded. 'Right from the start, apparently. They told him Ingrid had never tried to deceive anyone and had always believed he was my son, which is absolute crap because Ingrid admitted to me that she'd known from the start that he was Declan's. They also told Aaron that, as soon as I discovered he wasn't mine, I wanted nothing to do with him.'

'What a horrible thing to say to him. He must have felt so rejected.'

'Tell me about it. It was so unnecessary and clearly it's messed him up.'

I lightly squeezed his arm. 'What else did you ask?'

'Whether he'd missed me.'

'Oh, Jed. Of course he did. What did he say?'

'I thought he was going to give me a load of attitude about not giving a toss about me but he looked up and there were tears in his eyes. He mumbled, "maybe before I knew the truth", then he must have been annoyed with himself for a moment of weakness because he shoved his hand out and demanded money and directions. It broke my heart to see him running off again but I couldn't make him stay.' He ran his hands down his face and exhaled loudly. 'What a mess.'

'But not your mess. You didn't do any of that. Ingrid and Declan did. You can't blame yourself for any of it. You didn't walk away from him. You begged them to let you see Aaron and you went down the legal route when they wouldn't let you.'

He looked at me, tears brimming in his eyes. 'I still think of him as my son.'

'I know you do. Hey, come here.' I held him tightly as his body shook with deep sobs. 'I'm here for you. Let it out.'

'Oh, God, I'm sorry,' he said, pulling away from me some time later and wiping his damp cheeks. 'I don't know where all that came from.'

'I'd imagine you've hidden the hurt and grief away and seeing him again tonight has brought it all back.'

'He looked so grown up yet I could see a frightened little boy in there. I'm so angry with them for putting him through that. They could have scarred him for life.'

'What happens next?'

'The girls tell me they're in touch with him and they're going to do their best to smooth things over. I'd like to see him and explain but I don't want to confuse him further. Much as I want him to be, he's not my son and I can't play a part in turning him against his real parents, no matter how much they deserve it.'

'You'll just have to give it time. Let him make his own mind up while he's here or perhaps when he's back in Aus. If you push too hard, it might push him away altogether.'

'I know. It's such a fine line. And speaking of pushing people away, I'm so—'

I placed my finger against his lips. 'There's nothing to be sorry about. You were hurting about Aaron and you thought I'd let you down and you now know the truth.'

'The girls were so shocked to see him. They had no idea he was here.'

'I think your parents were pretty shocked too.'

'And the rest of the diners.' He rolled his eyes at me. 'Not quite the birthday celebration we had planned.'

I stood up and pulled him to his feet. 'I think you need to go home and smooth things over with your family.'

'What about you?'

'I'm fine. Bit gutted I didn't get any birthday cake, but I'm honestly okay with this, Jed. I really do understand. I think your girls need their dad, though, and plenty of reassurances that you're not mad at them for keeping secrets. Plus your poor parents saw their long-lost grandson tonight and, if I'm not mistaken, that's the first time they've ever seen him in person.'

He nodded. 'It was. They've only ever seen him on Skype before.'

'Then they've got to be hurting too.'

'I can't go unless I know I haven't lost you.'

'Do you have a "dungeon" hidden below the gallery and a whole secret life I know nothing about?'

He smiled weakly. 'That would be a resounding no.'

'Then we're all good and you're not going to lose me. Although there's something I do want from you before you leave.' I stepped closer to him and tilted my head.

Jed cupped my face in his hands and his lips lightly touched mine sending a zip of energy racing round my body. I slipped my arms round his neck and pulled him closer, kissing him with more fervour. I'd been worried that I was leaning on Jed but tonight's shock encounter had shown that, early days or not, our relationship really was a partnership. I needed Jed but he also needed me. Now, I could fully let him in.

## 43

The following morning, Jed knocked on the door before Maria arrived and handed me a plastic tub containing a few slices of birthday cake. 'Couldn't have you missing out,' he said. 'Mum and Dad send their love and wanted to make sure you're okay.'

'That's very kind of them. Tell them I'm fine.'

'Can I see you tonight?'

I gave him a gentle smile. 'I think you should spend tonight with your family. Aaron was an important part of everyone's lives for so long and then he was taken from them. You've got so much to discuss about where you go from here.'

He nodded and drew me into a hug. 'Thanks for understanding.'

With the evening free, I went to Pilates then soaked in the bath before having an early night and a much-needed sleep.

On Wednesday, my parents stopped by for lunch in the café then relaxed in the flat with Hercules until I finished work. Jed joined us for a takeaway then stayed back for a couple of hours after they'd gone. He talked about Aaron and all the memories from his childhood that had resurfaced since seeing him again. Ingrid had taken a lot of the photos of Aaron with her but hadn't wanted any with Jed in them so he had quite a collection and had been looking through them, feeling melancholy.

When he kissed me goodbye late that evening, I felt closer to him than I'd ever felt. Aaron's appearance, despite the shockwave at the time, had definitely had positive repercussions. Jed had been holding back and so had I, but that was all gone.

On the Thursday afternoon, Peter and Joyce dropped by for their usual afternoon tea.

'We have company today,' Joyce said, smiling widely. She stepped aside to reveal Janice and Richie.

'You came!' I said, wiping my hands down my apron.

They both hugged me and I reassured then that I was okay and everything was fine between Jed and me.

'Do you have plans for Christmas Eve?' Janice asked. 'After work, I mean?'

'I've been so busy that I haven't thought about it yet. Why?'

'Would you like to come to our house for dinner. Nothing fancy. Just some pasta and salad but all the family will be there and you're family now so it wouldn't be right if you didn't join us.'

With a lump in my throat, I thanked her for her kind invite and said I'd be delighted to accept. Christmas Eve with Jed's parents and Christmas Day with mine? I'd never have predicted that at the start of the year, or even a month ago. So much had changed.

* * *

As soon as Jed opened his parents' front door on Christmas Eve, Doris the Dalmatian bounded down the hall to greet us, dressed as a Christmas elf.

'Strewth! What have they done to you?' Jed cried, scratching her behind the ears. 'Was it Lucy? I bet it was.'

Jed introduced me to Doris and she sat down and offered me her right paw followed by her left then rested her head against my leg. 'That means she loves you,' Jed said. 'And who can blame her?'

He gave me such a tender look that my heart melted. We still hadn't said the 'L' word yet but, with his green eyes fixed on mine, I definitely felt it emanating from him.

I stroked Doris's soft ears. 'Lucy showed me some photos of you and I've been dying to meet you, Doris.'

'A word of warning,' Jed said solemnly. '*Never* volunteer to look through Lucy's Doris albums. Believe me, if you do that, you will *not* escape for hours.'

He took my coat and I sniffed. I could smell garlic but undertones of gingerbread also hung in the air, transporting me back to childhood Christmas Eves.

Richie appeared in the hallway wearing a Santa hat. 'I hope you're both hungry because Janice has made enough pasta to feed a small army.' He gave me a hug. 'Come on through. Let's get you a drink.'

Dinner was wonderfully chaotic. Lucy distributed Christmas-themed hats for everyone to wear, insisting we had to keep them on for the entire meal. With a big smile, she handed me a sparkly angel's halo then giggled as she placed an elf's hat with enormous ears on Jed's head.

A gold and red runner ran the length of the large kitchen table, resting on which were several clear vases containing pinecones, red and gold Christmas baubles, and clusters of battery-operated fairy lights. A silver platter sat in the middle of the table with pine-fragranced candles nestling among a bed of conifer cuttings, shiny green holly, juicy red berries, and more pinecones. I breathed in the fragrance of Christmas and smiled contentedly. I'd missed this so much.

With the pressure of keeping a secret lifted off them, Erin and

Lucy were so much more relaxed. They had the same playful banter I'd seen between Carly and Bethany and among some of my foster siblings before living with the Sandersons. My relationship with Leanne had never been like that. I'd thought we were close but it was blindingly obvious now that she'd been playing a game from day one and there never had been any genuine affection.

It warmed my heart to see Erin and Zack together. The eye contact, shy smiles and tender touches suggested a couple very much in love. Then I became aware that Jed and I were doing exactly the same. Would he put it into words soon?

Over coffee, the conversation turned to Christmas Eves from childhood. Zack's parents had owned a holiday home in Portugal for years where his family always spent Christmas. Unable to bear being apart for the one-month break from university, he'd decided to spend Christmas with Erin's family and then he and Erin were going to fly out to spend New Year with his family. Lucy and Erin talked about being ex-pats in Australia and how they had a very British traditional Christmas dinner on the day itself but enjoyed a more traditional Aussie beach barbeque on Christmas Eve, preceded by surfing dressed in Santa suits.

'What about you, Tara?' Erin asked. 'Any Christmas Eve traditions?'

'Not when I lived with my foster parents because we massively varied what we did. Sometimes we were home, sometimes abroad, and sometimes we were working. But when I was younger, my dad and I were all about the traditions. We'd make gingerbread houses and spend the day doing all sorts of Christmas crafts.' I smiled at the memory. 'I was telling Jed the other day that Dad and I used to wander round the streets when it got dark, judging how pretty the trees were in the windows. The one we liked the most would win a bar of chocolate and a hand-made card from Santa's elves. We never let on that it was us and there was always this buzz of excitement in the neighbourhood surrounding who'd win each year and who the mystery elves were.'

'That is so lovely,' Lucy said.

'And when Dad told us about it, we wanted to play too.' Erin placed a box on the table containing three clipboards with what looked to be score sheets attached to them, some homemade certificates and three large bars of chocolate.

I gasped. 'Oh my God! Really?' Tears pricked my eyes. 'I would *love* to do that again. Thank you.'

'We're in three teams,' Jed said. 'Lucy's joining Mum and Dad, then it'll be Zack and Erin, and you and me.'

'And,' Lucy added. 'Each team has to take a photo of the winner on their street and then the overall winner, chosen by us all from the three finalists, will also get this...'

Zack placed a wicker basket on the table containing all sorts of edible Christmas goodies. 'We thought we could go round some of the streets where money's a bit tighter and this could really make a difference to someone's Christmas.'

'I love that idea.' I smiled at Jed's family. 'Thank you all of you.'

'It was Dad's suggestion,' Lucy said. 'Because he loves you and would do anything to make you happy.' She wrapped her arms round herself and made slurpy kissing noises.

'Lucy!' Erin cried. 'You can't say or do that.'

I glanced at Jed, expecting him to look as embarrassed as me but he was smiling.

'Why can't she?' he said, reaching for my hand under the table. 'After all, it's the truth.'

'Awww,' Lucy gushed. 'You guys are too cute. Can I be a bridesmaid when you get married?'

'Lucy!' Erin clapped her hand over her sister's mouth. 'They've only just started dating.'

Lucy wriggled free. 'And so have you two but I've overheard you talking about getting married as soon as you finish university.'

'Lucy! Shut up!'

'It's true. You—'

Erin covered her sister's mouth again.

Richie stood up. 'Okay, Erin, release your sister and not another peep from you, young Lucy.' He spoke with humour but strength and the girls immediately did as they were told. 'Good. Now let's get wrapped up warm and do our elf bit.'

I smiled at Jed's daughters. The affection they had for each other and for Jed was obvious and I felt so proud that he'd obviously been an amazing dad, bringing up such well-adjusted girls despite what their mum had put them through. I very much looked forward to getting to know them better.

Pulling on coats, hats and scarves in the hall, listening to Lucy squealing as Erin tickled her, I had a sudden sense of belonging. I had my family back and I was now part of Jed's. That cloak of loneliness had floated away.

## 44

Christmas Day arrived and I was up before Hercules again, ready for an early start at The Hope Centre. I loved waking up without the usual sense of dread.

'A very different Christmas for us this year,' I told Hercules as I put some fresh food and water in his bowls. 'No *Friends* binge-athon. No leftovers from the café.' No being alone. No being lonely.

Much as I'd have loved to have spent the full day with my family now that I had one again, I didn't regret volunteering at The Hope Centre for one minute. It was both rewarding and humbling to be part of a team providing warmth and good food to families, the elderly, and the homeless, bringing a little Christmas cheer to what could otherwise have been a difficult day.

Spirits were so high among the volunteers as we laughed, joked and sang along to Christmas tunes that peeling and chopping what seemed to be an endless supply of vegetables didn't even feel like a chore.

By the time we opened the door to the service-users at noon, there was quite a queue. There was chicken broth or vegetable soup for starters, followed by traditional Christmas dinner with turkey and all the trimmings, mushroom and squash wellington, or nut roast. For dessert, there was a choice of Christmas pudding, Eton mess or vegan brownies from The Chocolate Pot.

A few volunteers, including me, stayed in the kitchen cooking more vegetables and mixing extra gravy. The others split their time across serving and clearing.

Through the hatch between the kitchen and main hall, I watched the tables steadily fill. Soon the music couldn't be heard over the bangs from crackers mingled with chatter. It was good to hear laughter ringing out – a moment of lightness in a challenging time.

I found myself watching a slender dark-haired homeless woman, eagerly tucking into a bowl of soup, and a lump formed in my throat. She couldn't have been much younger than I'd been when I arrived in Whitsborough Bay, alone and scared. When I needed to leave home, I had the money, skills and experience to set up a new home and business but I was absolutely in the minority. Most people who needed to leave home had very little and many had nothing.

'You look very thoughtful,' said Jim, placing a stack of dirty plates on the worktop.

'Who's the dark-haired woman over there?'

Jim followed my eyeline. 'That's Zoe.'

'What's her story?'

'I only know the basics. She's been coming here for a few months now. She's seventeen, from Teesside, and ran away when she was fourteen. She hasn't specifically said why but I suspect abuse. She seems like a nice kid. Doesn't do drugs or drink, always polite. Often got her head in a book.'

'Do you sometimes wish you could move them all into your house?'

'Every single day.' Jim shook his head. 'But I sleep at night knowing I'm playing a small part in bringing some comfort.'

I gave him a warm smiled. 'You're playing more than a small part.'

At the end of my shift, I looked round for Zoe but she'd already left.

'I'm going to need to head off,' I told Jim. 'I'm going to be with my family for Christmas for the first time since I ran away nearly fifteen years ago.'

'Sounds like you have a story too.'

'I do, but I was very lucky. Mine was one with a happy ending. Would you do me a favour? If Zoe stops by again in the New Year, would you ask her to come to The Chocolate Pot and ask for me? Any day but Sunday. Tell her there's a hot drink and a meal waiting for her.'

'And what's really waiting for her?'

'I'm not sure yet but the cogs are whirring. It might not come to anything so please don't say there's anything more than a meal in it for her.'

'I won't. Now off you go and join your family. Thank you for today.'

'It's been an absolute pleasure. Happy Christmas, Jim.'

'Happy Christmas, Tara.'

I turned towards the kitchen to retrieve my coat and bag.

'Oh, Tara,' Jim said. 'I don't know what made you run away but I'm glad you did because you've made such a difference to this place. Even if whatever you're scheming for Zoe comes to nothing, you've changed people's lives. Never forget that.'

\* \* \*

Driving back from The Hope Centre to The Chocolate Pot, I felt all warm and fuzzy inside from Jim's kind words, my wonderful day so far, and life in general. Just a quick freshen up and change of clothes and then I'd pick Jed up from his parents' house and drive us both to Whitby for an evening meal with my parents.

Smiling contentedly, I unlocked the door to the café.

'Happy Christmas!'

I squealed as the lights flicked on and I took in the sea of smiling faces in front of me.

'What are you all doing here?'

Jed stepped forward and gave me a gentle peck on the lips. 'You've spent all morning and most of the afternoon doing nice things for other people and we wanted to do something nice for you in return.'

I made my way through the throng, hugging everyone and exchanging season's greetings. Jed's family were there, as were my parents, plus Carly and Liam, Bethany and Joshua, and Maria, Marc and their kids. The tables had been pushed together to make one long banqueting table covered in festive napkins, decorations and crackers. Silver food warmers were spread along the centre, interspersed with wooden bowls overflowing with bread buns, and a giant turkey took pride of place at the head of the table.

'We've made Christmas dinner for those who haven't eaten yet,' Mum said, 'and it's turkey sandwiches for those who've had theirs already. Unless they're feeling extra hungry.'

'I can't believe you've all done this for me. Thank you so much. Do I have time to nip upstairs and get changed?'

'Ten minutes,' Jed said, putting his arm round my waist and kissing my forehead.

* * *

I'd thought that Christmas Eve had been loud but Christmas Day completely eclipsed it. Gazing round the table at my friends and family laughing and drinking, my face actually ached from smiling so much. So this was what it felt like when you fully let people in? It wasn't scary. My protective tower had crumbled but it hadn't left me feeling exposed and vulnerable like I'd expected. It had invited in a feeling of warmth, safety and happiness.

'I'd like to propose a toast,' Jed said, standing up and holding out his glass of bubbly after we'd finished our main course. 'Two toasts actually. Firstly, I'd like to say a massive welcome to Tara's parents, Kirsten and Tim. You raised a wonderful woman and I'm so glad you're back in her life.'

'To Mum and Dad,' I said as everyone else toasted them by their names.

'And secondly a toast to Tara. When we first met, it was right here nearly fifteen years ago and I'm proud to say that I created a lasting impression on her. I'm not so proud to say that it wasn't a positive one.' He paused while everyone laughed. 'They say there's a thin line between love and hate and I'm so glad we crossed that line because I can't remember what life was like without Tara by my side and I never want to be without her again. To Tara!'

'To Tara!'

Had he just told me he loved me? It certainly sounded that way. And I felt exactly the same.

\* \* \*

By 9 p.m. everyone had gone home and the café was clean with the tables put back to normal. Jed said he had to nip over to Yorkshire's Best to get something and would meet me in the flat. I left all the doors off the latch and went upstairs to give Hercules a hug, light the log burner and pour Jed and me a Baileys on ice.

I'd just lifted Hercules onto the sofa beside me when Jed reappeared. 'I know we said we wouldn't do gifts but I've got a gift for you.'

'Jed! No! That's not fair. I *knew* you'd do this and you promised me you wouldn't.' We'd agreed that we'd been together for such a short space of time and, with both working such long hours in the run-up to Christmas, it was going to be a struggle to find time to shop for meaningful gifts so we'd go away together for a weekend in February or March instead.

'I know I did and I will never break any other promises to you but I had to do this and you'll see why when you open them.'

'Them? There's more than one?'

'There are two. Close your eyes first.'

I closed my eyes and listened to his footsteps moving away from me then coming closer again.

'Remember I said I'd never painted a rabbit and I'd love to paint Hercules? I saw an opportunity to make a matching pair with the first painting that spoke to you. Open your eyes.'

I pressed my fingers to my mouth. 'Oh my God!' It was a clifftop scene looking down on the lighthouse but from a different angle and, instead of a sheep, Hercules was perched on the cliff in a field of daisies. The glow from an enormous full moon behind the lighthouse made the colours brighter than on the sheep painting.

'I've captioned it: *When your lighthouse finds you and guides you home.*'

I shook my head in disbelief. 'How do you keep doing it? Every time I think you can't do anything more amazing than the thing you've just done; you go and do something even more amazing.'

He grinned. 'You like it then?'

'I absolutely love it and that caption couldn't be more perfect.'

'What do you think, buddy?' Jed said, nodding towards Hercules. 'I think it's a pretty good likeness.' He propped it up against the wall beneath my original one. They were going to look so amazing mounted together.

'Second gift,' he said, his eyes twinkling with excitement. 'I took a gamble with this one. It's got a connection to your past and, from the positive reaction to the best decorated house competition yesterday, I'm hoping it will make you happy too.'

'Intriguing,' I said, untying the bow and removing the paper. Inside was a plain cardboard box, revealing nothing about its contents. Giving Jed a quizzical look, I opened the lid and gasped.

'You said it got smashed to pay for The Best Day Ever and never got replaced. I thought you might like to keep this with your snow globe.'

'Oh, Jed. I can't believe you found this.' I lifted out the Terramundi money pot and ran my fingers over the money slot. 'It's The Chocolate Pot, just like the one we used to have.'

'Not exactly. Turn it round.'

I carefully twisted the pot round. Painted on the other side was a carousel. 'The Best Day Ever,' I whispered, running my fingers over the picture. 'How did you find such a perfect match?'

'I didn't. I ordered a ceramic pot and I painted it myself from what you described.'

'It's the most beautiful, most meaningful gift that anyone has ever given me. The detail... It's perfect. All of it. I really can't believe you did this for me.' I gently placed the pot on the coffee table.

'I did it for the reason Loudmouth Lucy said yesterday – because I love you and I want to make you happy. I realised earlier that I might have given away how I feel about you in front of our family and friends before saying it to you in person first. I do love you, Tara, so very much.'

'I love you too, Jed. You somehow manage to surprise and astonish me every single day.'

'You do the same to me. And you inspire me too. You've been

through so much yet you've not let life get you down. You've taken a failed business and turned it into the heart of the community, and you've shown so much kindness to others even though you've been hurting inside and needed comfort yourself.'

He lowered his lips to mine and kissed me so softly and tenderly, I felt as though my insides had turned to liquid.

'I think it's going to take a long time for me to see myself the way others seem to see me but thank you for helping me try to do that.'

Jed smiled as he lightly stroked my cheek and kissed me again. 'Back in Aus, when things were falling apart with Ingrid but before I discovered that Aaron wasn't mine, I remember seeing this picture in a shop window. It said, "To see a person – to *really* see them – is to notice all of their magic. To love a person – to *really* love them – is to remind them of their magic when they've forgotten it's there". I stood there, reading those words over and over and wondering what the hell I was doing with Ingrid. She had no magic in her. Never had done. And do you know who popped into my head? You. I remembered that first time I saw you and that overwhelming urge to capture your image on paper. Even when you were at your most defeated, I saw your magic and I intend to remind you every single day that it's there.'

A tear trickled down my cheek. 'That has to be the most beautiful thing anyone has ever said to me.'

'I mean every word. I know you've got stuff to deal with and so have I but I promise you right here and now that I will never hurt you and, aside from the lying about not doing Christmas gifts thing, I'll always be honest with you too.'

I smiled. 'I might forgive you for the Christmas gifts, considering how amazing they were. And I'll always be honest with you too, Jed, and I'll be right by your side, whatever happens with Aaron. I know that he's angry now and is refusing to even speak to the girls but he'll come round. None of us know whether he'll want you back in his life but I'm sure he'll be willing to hear the truth when he calms down. It's just going to take a lot of patience and a lot of courage and I know you've got both.'

As we kissed again, I knew that the ghosts from past had finally been exorcised and the future was mine for the taking. I was glad that I'd met Garth and glad that he'd betrayed me because, without that, I'd never have fled to Whitsborough Bay, I'd never have found my business, my home and my new family, and I'd never have met Jed. I was glad that Leanne had shown me such a lack of respect because I now recognised and valued real, genuine friendships. Glad to have met Garth and Leanne? It really was possible to see the positives in every single situation. And from now on, I was always going to do that. Pollyanna was back and looking forward to the New Year with her friends, the man she loved, and her family.

I was no longer lost and lonely because I'd found my lighthouses. Lots of them. They'd always been there. I just hadn't been willing to let them shine their lights and guide me to safety. Until now. A few minutes of courage really had changed my life and we were both going to face plenty more courageous moments as we dealt with the past and moved our relationship forward but we'd take those steps together as equal partners. We'd be brave.

# ACKNOWLEDGMENTS

*Starry Skies Over The Chocolate Pot Café* started life as *Christmas at The Chocolate Pot Café* and was an independent release two years ago shortly before Christmas. When I secured a publishing deal with Boldwood Books, I was thrilled that they wanted to take on my back catalogue, starting with the Welcome to Whitsborough Bay series and this story. Having not worked with an editor on it, I was excited to see how a fresh pair of eyes would breathe new life into it.

We've had a change of title for several reasons. Firstly, the book has had quite a major edit with several new chapters in the middle and at the end. It's still the same main character, setting and plot as before but there are several new treats along the way. The story finishes later than before too, making the ending even more satisfying. Secondly, the additional chapters in the middle meant that quite a bit more of the story takes place away from Christmas so it didn't feel as appropriate to have 'Christmas' in the title because it's not just a Christmas book. Finally, it's a fresh release so it felt right to give it a fresh cover and new title.

I thank my husband, Mark, and our daughter, Ashleigh, in all of my books and it's only right that I thank them again in this one. I'm really fortunate that Mark is self-employed, like me, so he works erratic hours when the work arises and therefore 'gets' it. He also has a creative passion as a photographer so he never complains about me drifting off into my imaginary world, knowing that he's free to roam with the camera whenever he wants.

Ashleigh is at senior school and her evenings are now full with her usual activities, some after school clubs, and homework. I feel a little less guilty about writing on an evening (fitting it round my day job as an HR Tutor) when she's not available herself!

A fabulous team of beta readers help me by reading my work, spotting typos and providing feedback. Thank you to my mum, Joyce Williams, my good friend and fellow writer, Sharon Booth, and long-term friend, Liz Berry for their work on the original version of this book.

And it's to Liz that I dedicate this book. I try to dedicate my books to someone who has a link to the story in some small way. In *Starry Skies Over The Chocolate Pot Café,* Tara reconnects with her family after reading a letter from her foster-mother and it's through letters that I met Liz. I was 14 and in London for a youth club week-end. The weekend culminated in a rendezvous in one of London's parks during which attendees threw a pompom into the crowd with their name and address attached to it. Liz caught mine, wrote to me really quickly, and I eagerly responded. Over the next decade or two, we wrote to each other regularly and I always experienced a thrill when I got home from school/college/work to find a letter from Liz waiting for me, packed full of news. I lived in Teesside and Liz lived in West Sussex so meeting up wasn't an option but we finally managed it when we were in our late twenties. We've since met on several occasions and it's always so lovely to catch up. Sadly, we don't write to each other anymore as messages on social media have taken over but I am so thankful that Liz caught my pompom that day because she's provided friendship, support and happiness for over 30 years now. Not many pen pals last beyond a few letters but we certainly made it work.

I'd also like to thank my writing friends Jo Bartlett and Lynne Davidson for some valuable insight into the world of fostering. Their guidance on this was really appreciated. If there are any errors in any aspect of how this works it will be down to my misinterpretation.

Another thank you goes to the amazing North Yorkshire-based artist, Lucy Pittaway, who is the inspiration behind Jed's artwork as well as his story as to how he became the artist he is. Lucy creates the most delightful pictures full of warmth and colour, an iconic range being her sheep and highland cows. They feature stunning Yorkshire countryside in all seasons and weathers, with some recognisable landmarks in many of her images. For Jed, I therefore took Lucy's concept but on a Yorkshire Coast setting.

On holiday in the Yorkshire Dales several years ago, my husband and I purchased a limited edition print of Lucy's from a gallery in Richmond. A month before I finished writing the original version of this book, we visited Richmond again to see if we could pick up another of Lucy's prints, knowing she'd since opened her own gallery there. What a surprise I had when I saw where her gallery was: the same premises where I'd set up and run a specialist teddy bear shop in 2003-2005. Running Bear's Pad was a very special time in my life because I started writing while I had the shop, during quiet days, and it was as a result of having my own business that I met my husband. To have started my writing journey in Bear's Pad, to have bought one of Lucy's prints many years later, to have decided on her as the inspiration for the artist in my book, then to discover her gallery was in the same premises where I started my writing journey felt like destiny.

If you'd like to see Lucy's work, please check out: www.lucypittaway.co.uk

There's also a lovely video on You Tube about Lucy's work: https://www.youtube.com/watch?time_continue=6&v=RfaetaCoL7g

I'm enormously grateful to the team at Boldwood Books for being such an amazing and supportive publisher. I'm so proud to be part of Team Boldwood. My editor, Nia Beynon, is a dream to work with, full of fabulous improvements and encouragement. And thanks to Dushi Horti and Sue Lamprell for their copy editing and proofreading talents, as well as the designer Debbie Clement for the gorgeous cover.

Finally, my thanks go to you, my readers and listeners. If you've enjoyed any of my books, it would be amazing if you could tell others by leaving a review online and also recommending my stories to friends and family. Reviews make a massive difference to an author. You'll see some really long reviews but you don't need to write an essay. A positive rating and a short sentence are equally welcome.

Big hugs

Jessica xx

## MORE FROM JESSICA REDLAND

We hope you enjoyed reading *Starry Skies Over The Chocolate Pot Cafe*. If you did, please leave a review.

If you'd like to gift a copy, this book is also available as an ebook, digital audio download and audiobook CD.

Sign up to Jessica Redland's mailing list for news, competitions and updates on future books.

http://bit.ly/JessicaRedlandNewsletter

# ABOUT THE AUTHOR

**Jessica Redland** is the author of nine novels which are all set around the fictional location of Whitsborough Bay. Inspired by her hometown of Scarborough she writes uplifting women's fiction which has garnered many devoted fans.

Visit Jessica's website: https://www.jessicaredland.com/

Follow Jessica on social media:

facebook.com/JessicaRedlandWriter

twitter.com/JessicaRedland

instagram.com/JessicaRedlandWriter

bookbub.com/authors/jessica-redland

# ALSO BY JESSICA REDLAND

*Standalone Novels*

The Secret To Happiness

Christmas at Carly's Cupcakes

Starry Skies Over The Chocolate Pot Café

*Welcome To Whitsborough Bay Series*

Making Wishes At Bay View

New Beginnings at Seaside Blooms

Finding Hope at Lighthouse Cove

Coming Home To Seashell Cottage

*Hedgehog Hollow Series*

Finding Love at Hedgehog Hollow

# ABOUT BOLDWOOD BOOKS

Boldwood Books is a fiction publishing company seeking out the best stories from around the world.

Find out more at www.boldwoodbooks.com

Sign up to the Book and Tonic newsletter for news, offers and competitions from Boldwood Books!

http://www.bit.ly/bookandtonic

We'd love to hear from you, follow us on social media:

facebook.com/BookandTonic

twitter.com/BoldwoodBooks

instagram.com/BookandTonic

Made in the USA
Middletown, DE
02 July 2021